**Hamilton Dodge saw
Starla standing by the
stairs in a demure
wedding gown of ivory silk.**

His emotions were staggering. It wouldn't take much to convince himself that he was in love with this glorious creature who'd consented to become his wife.

They said their vows in the sunny front parlor. Beside him, Starla spoke the necessary words without inflection, then lifted her hand so he could slide the ring his mother had given him to see him safely through four years of war. Let it see him through this marriage with equal indemnity.

But the solemnity of the event didn't strike home until the judge intoned the words pronouncing them man and wife.

Man and wife.

His to have and to hold.

But this was no love match.

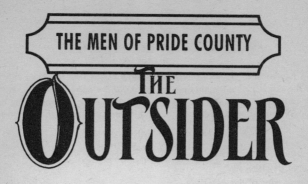

THE MEN OF PRIDE COUNTY

THE OUTSIDER

ROSALYN WEST

AVON BOOKS ◆ NEW YORK

AVON BOOKS, INC.
1350 Avenue of the Americas
New York, New York 10019

Copyright © 1998 by Nancy Gideon
Inside cover author photo by McClain Images
Published by arrangement with the author
Visit our website at http://www.AvonBooks.com
Library of Congress Catalog Card Number: 97-94931
ISBN: 0-380-79580-9

First Avon Books Printing: July 1998

AVON TRADEMARK REG. U.S. PAT. OFF. AND IN OTHER COUNTRIES, MARCA REGISTRADA, HECHO EN U.S.A.

Printed in the U.S.A.

WCD   10 9 8 7 6 5 4 3 2 1

For Lucia—
thanks for your confidence!

Prologue

The chance for escape came only once.

In a train station crowded with uniformed men going to war, no one noticed a furtive couple slipping through the early morning fog toward one of the passenger cars. If they had, they might have remarked upon the striking similarity of brother and sister, and upon the exotic beauty of their refined features: dusky skin, black hair, and startling green eyes. They might have wondered over the young man's hurry or at his sister's frightened demeanor. But wrapped up in their own worries and fears, no one gave them the slightest heed as a single bag was tossed up to one of the porters.

The young gentleman spoke rapidly, with the mild slurring of too much drink mushing syllables already softened by a Creole drawl.

"Are you sure 'bout this? You don't even know this man. How do you know goin' with him will be any better 'n staying here?"

The young woman glanced anxiously toward the train, to where her rescuer waited. Uncertainty tugged at her for only the briefest instant. "Any-

1

thing's better than here," came her tight-throated reply. "I have to go. You know that, don't you?"

Her eyes appeared huge and luminous behind the netting as she gazed up at her brother, begging him to understand. He didn't need to lift the veil to be reminded of the fading bruises on his sister's lovely face. Knowing they were there, and knowing the cause, made him swallow back his argument.

"I know you do, darlin'."

Their embrace was quick and fierce with the desperation of their circumstance.

"Darlin', don't cry. Listen to me. You listen to me, now. This might be your only chance. Guess you gotta take it. You gotta be brave and smart and not get caught should someone come looking for you. You can't let him bring you back, not ever." This last was said with enough vibrating fury to draw several curious looks. He ducked his head in closer to hers, lowering his tone to a hoarse whisper. "Are you sure?"

A slight nod against his shoulder made him relax a notch.

A sudden snort of soot and steam engulfed them as the train prepared for final boarding. They shared a silent moment, then the young man pushed away. His handsome face was no longer taut with urgency, but weary and drained of all emotion.

"Say good-bye now."

The fact of their parting shocked through her, returning the blank of fearful doubt as her arms encircled him.

"Come with me. Come with me."

"I can't, darlin'. You know that."

"I can't leave you here—with him. There's no telling what he might do when he finds me gone."

He pressed a soothing kiss to her temple, glad she couldn't see the starkness of his expression. "Nothing he hasn't done before. It'll be worth it, just knowin' you're safe outta his reach. Go on now, little sister. You get on that train, and don't look back, you hear me? Don't look back and don't come back. Not ever."

She looked up at him then, her forlorn gaze dazzling like precious jewels as his palm cupped the side of her face beneath the veil, his thumb stroking away the trace of her tears.

"Don't you worry none. I'll see to things here for both of us. I'll see the bastard makes good on what he owes us and I'll protect what's ours."

"I don't care about the money, Tyler—"

"But he does. That's all he's ever cared about. And that's why he's not gonna steal our fortune away from us. Trust me, darlin'. Trust me to take care of things. In return, you keep yourself safe and be happy. That's all I ask."

Her small hand fit over his, squeezing tight.

"I'll miss you." Her words quavered.

For a long moment, he couldn't speak. After taking a fractured breath, he forced a smile and said, "I'll miss you, too. You get on that train, now. And you promise you'll look ahead, not back. Promise me."

Instead, she cried, "I love you, Tyler."

He steered her toward the steps, pushing her into the care of the steward waiting to hand her up into the car. She went inside to take a seat at the window, next to the stranger who offered her salvation. Only when her pale face pressed close to the fogged glass for one last parting look did he reply, his voice choked and raw with feeling.

"I love you, too, Star. Enough to never want to see you again."

Chapter 1

Four years later

It took his best friend's wedding to get Hamilton Dodge thinking about whores.

Nothing like seeing someone else so happy to get a man reflecting upon his own sorry state. Not that Dodge begrudged a second of that happiness to Reeve Garrett and his beautiful bride-to-be. He'd never seen a couple so deserving of what lay ahead: pleasures beginning on their wedding night and stretching out for an eternity. Pleasures Dodge had been itching to find for himself for . . . how long?

He looked back, past his brief and rocky residency in Pride County, Kentucky, beyond four years of battlefield hell, to an eager young man anxious to charm the petticoats off his blushing neighbor on the eve of his enlistment. And when Dodge couldn't recall if he'd been successful or not, he knew he was in desperate need of a woman to remind him of what he'd been missing.

It wasn't as if just any woman would do. For all his blustery talk and less-than-proper innuendo, playing the petticoat line had no great appeal. He liked women, sure enough. He liked being with them, talking to them, looking at them, kissing them—hell, just about everything about them from their uniquely delicate scent to the sirenlike quality of their laughter. But a man wasn't raised as the only male in the midst of six older female siblings without one mighty respect for womankind . . . and a healthy dose of awe. Man might strut and snort and brag, but civilization was founded and held by women, and Dodge admired them for that tenacity, for trying to tame the uncouth beast that was man into becoming a useful member of society.

He wished someone would try it with him. He was a man who craved civilizing.

The problem wasn't his willingness to give in after a rousing fight, it was the absence of anyone willing to take on the task. He'd been in Pride for exactly two and a half months and he'd yet to earn a genuine smile from any woman except Reeve Garrett's fiancée. On this, her wedding day, he didn't hold out much hope of Patrice Sinclair confessing to an undying love for him.

The eligible coquettes of the county shied clear of him. It wasn't because he was hard to look at or a bad risk as a husband. It wasn't even the fact that he'd spent the past two months crippled by the bullet lodged in his back. His problem was one of geography; he'd been a lieutenant in the Union Army. Now, as banker in a Confederate supporting town, he held the notes on the properties and lives of a distrustful populace.

To a man of lesser conviction, the obstacles

would have overwhelmed any thoughts of winning the faith of the community and the heart of one of its fair number. But Dodge was nothing if not determined: determined to walk again, determined to have the folks in Pride call him neighbor, determined to claim a bride right here, where he'd sink his roots in fertile Southern soil. He had the patience of a man used to waiting his turn behind the primping of six sisters.

Some things he could wait for, but others were making a more pressing demand. Saving his heart for love didn't mean sacrificing other needs for that same cause. He'd seen little of Pride since coming to town—his name was not exactly on the list of the socially acceptable. He ate his meals at Sadie's, he enjoyed an occasional drink at the Dixie Saloon; but as yet he hadn't stopped in for a visit at Pauline's, where the amount of his coin would offset his politics.

Maybe tonight he'd go get acquainted. Right after he discharged his duties as best man. It was time to see if that paralyzing bullet had allowed feeling to creep back into more than just his legs.

He watched Reeve Garrett pace, his own anxiousness chafing when he thought of what the evening held in store for his friend.

"The way you're fidgeting, you'd never think you'd been sleeping with the woman for better than two months."

Reeve didn't respond to his crude baiting. Instead, he shared a maddeningly smug smile and a prophetic "Tonight will be different."

Dodge contained his groan, considering that difference. Man and wife. An enviable state. One a million miles from where he sat in his wheeled cane-backed chair, with no prospects for romance in sight.

"It'll be a lonely one if I don't get you in front of that judge in about ten minutes."

Reeve fussed with his white bow-tied cravat for the umpteenth time, close to worrying the starch out of it. "I feel like I'm going to a funeral."

"A lot of men in your position would agree."

Reeve glowered at him. "The clothes, I mean." He tugged at the sides of his cutaway jacket, feeling ridiculous as its swallowtails swung over gray striped trousers.

"You could have worn your Yankee uniform and made Patrice a widow before making her a bride."

"Not funny under the circumstances. It's bad enough worrying about Deacon changing his mind at the last minute and refusing to give her away."

"Somehow, I don't think Patrice would let him get in the way. A dozen crazy militants with torches and guns couldn't do it. What makes you think one stodgy brother would have any better luck?"

Reeve sighed. "You're right. Let's go."

Reeve started around to the back of Dodge's chair, prepared to push his friend from the small back room into the hotel parlor where the wedding would take place. That's when Dodge presented him with the gift he'd been saving for this moment. He gripped the arms of the chair that had held him prisoner for the past two months and pushed upward, rising slowly, purposefully to stand on his own two feet.

Reeve gaped at him for a long moment, speechless.

"Well, don't just stand there like a hooked bass," Dodge chided. "Grab those crutches for me before I fall on my face."

Reeve snatched them up, still astounded as Dodge fit them under his arms and took a few precarious swings forward. Then he was grinning as well.

"When did this happen?"

"I've been working on it for a while. Wanted to surprise you. Promised I'd stand up for you, didn't I? Couldn't very well do that while sitting in that chair. Just don't expect me to hold both of us up when it comes time to say your vows."

They were standing by the judge when Patrice Sinclair made her entrance on her brother's arm. In a bell skirt of white silk and Brussels lace, she was a vision to reduce any man to trembling at his good fortune. Reeve was no exception as he watched her sweep down the narrow aisle made by the small gathering of their friends. His gaze fixed upon her in a daze of reverence, while hers settled wide and disbelieving . . . on the best man.

"Dodge!"

With that soft cry, Patrice released Deacon's elbow to race ahead, throwing her arms not about her intended, but around the man beside him, rocking Dodge back with her enthusiastic hugging.

Aware that they'd become the awkward center

of attention, Dodge balanced on the crutches and levered a weeping Patrice away. "You're not supposed to cry before the wedding," he reminded her gently.

Patrice stood back, her wondering gaze taking him in from top to toe with tears and unabashed pleasure. She hit his shoulder with her bouquet of roses and calla lilies.

"How could you keep such a secret from us?"

He grinned. "It wasn't easy."

She smiled and wiped at the flood of fresh wetness glistening on her cheek. "Hamilton Dodge, you've given us the best gift possible."

By not greeting them in the imprisoning chair he'd accepted in order to save her life, he was freeing the two people he cared about more than any others to go on with their future without the burden of guilt over his sacrifice. He knew well the significance of the gift.

"It was no trouble."

She studied him then, her gaze a little too shrewd, too observant, catching the pinch of discomfort mixed with the laughter around his eyes, seeing the faint sheen of effort forming on his brow hinting that the cost of this grand gesture was anything but trifling. And loving him for it. She leaned into him, pressing a light kiss to his cheek as she whispered, "Thank you, Dodge. I owe you the happiness of this day."

"Remember, I'm a banker. I'll see you pay me back with interest."

The judge cleared his throat impatiently. "Miss Sinclair, which of these men are you marrying?"

Patrice looked up with a blush. She reached for Reeve's hand. "This one, your honor."

"Now that we have that decided, shall we get on with the ceremony?"

They fell into their places before the judge, Dodge flanking his best friend, Deacon a stiff pillar of stoic duty as he passed his sister into another's care before stepping back to support their joyfully weeping mother. Everything seemed to be proceeding smoothly until the judge reached the part where he called for anyone who might have objections to the match to speak them or hold them silent forever.

None would have been surprised to hear Deacon Sinclair's somber tones naming some damnable reason, but it was a feminine voice ringing up from the back of the room that declared, "I do."

The gathering turned as one to see a slight woman posed dramatically in the open doorway. Before any of them could react, the intruder claimed, "Patrice Sinclair, how dare you think you could get married without me standing beside you?"

"Starla!"

The bride-to-be raced the length of the room to fall into an embrace with her best friend since childhood.

Dodge didn't need an introduction to know exactly who the woman was. Her features were unmistakable, their delicate Creole beauty marking her as Tyler Fairfax's sister. Fairfax and his group of night-riding bullies were responsible for the bullet in his back, but he didn't extend that grudge to the lovely creature coming toward him. He couldn't. He was lost the moment her vivid green eyes met his in brief curiosity before she cast her arms about Reeve.

All earlier thoughts about looking up a harlot for the night completely disappeared from Dodge's mind.

"Reeve Garrett, I just knew Patrice'd snare you someday," came the husky purr of her voice. "She's had eyes for nobody but you since we were babies."

And from over his shoulder she let her vivacious stare linger thoroughly along the best man.

Here was the smoldering hint of promise he'd been missing, steeped in those bold, assessing eyes. Anticipation tightened in Dodge's chest even as he loosened an appreciative grin.

"And who might your friend be?"

"Starla, this is Hamilton Dodge, our guardian angel. Dodge, Starla Fairfax. The one I was telling you about." This last Patrice said as a significant aside.

"And I can see she's everything you said and more."

There was no missing the way the gorgeous flirt froze up at the sound of Dodge's crisp Northern accent. Her smile didn't fade, but all the warmth was extinguished from her eyes in a blink. Her honey-eyed tone took on a tang of vinegar.

"If my friends speak so highly of you, we shall have to be friends as well."

Hearing the unspoken "when hell freezes over"

in her invitation, Dodge grinned all the wider. "Yes, ma'am. You can count on it."

She snubbed him to look around the room impatiently. "Is Tyler here? I had to rush from the train to get here on time, no thanks to you, Patrice Sinclair."

Patrice's smile thinned, but her words were gentle. "He's not here, Starla. We'll talk about it later."

"Can we get back to this wedding?" the judge requested.

Vows, rings, and a too-long-to-be-proper kiss were exchanged, transforming Patrice into Mrs. Reeve Garrett before the intimate assembly. After private toasts and congratulations, the bridal party went from the small parlor room to a spacious hall where the affluent of the county would soon arrive to offer their best wishes—because of the social weight the Sinclair name carried, not out of any fondness for Reeve Garrett, whom most still considered a traitor for serving on the Union side in a war they wouldn't allow to end.

Dismissed from his obligations, Dodge chose to search out a comfortable chair on the fringe of the gathering where he could succumb to the agony of remaining on his feet. In the three weeks since sensation had begun seeping back through his legs, he'd ignored the doctor's cautionings, pushing his recuperation beyond the edge of endurance to get to this spot, to stand beside the friend to whom he owed his life. That done, he could collapse in happy misery. With a glass of good bourbon in one hand and a cigar smoldering in the other, he amused himself by watching the elite company mill about with practiced insincerity. They were smiling at his best friend through gritted teeth because he was now linked to the mighty Sinclairs of Pride County. And the Sinclairs couldn't be snubbed.

Dodge wasn't one for artifice. His cut-to-the-point bluntness put him at odds with the average silken-tongued Southerner. To Dodge there was a fine line between tact and lying, a line most of those in the room crossed without compunction, though none quite so eloquently as Starla Fairfax.

He never made a conscious decision to stare. The black-haired beauty demanded attention, and who was he to refuse? She was everything he'd ever heard about Confederate women, with their vain need to conquer everything in their path as determinedly as Sherman had on his sweep to the sea. He could imagine a long line of broken hearts, left like smoldering chimneys in Starla's scorching wake. But what man could resist casting himself in the path of purposeful self-destruction? She was the most mesmerizing creature imaginable.

She entranced him.

He watched her flit from gentleman to gentleman, a lunar moth, all dainty gossamer without weight or true substance. She'd light for a moment, fluttering both fan and eyelashes with the seriousness of a fencing foil: *en garde*, parry, thrust, luring each unsuspecting fool into a game he'd already lost. The tease of her smile, the sultry gleam of promise in eyes cold as glittering gems, the musical scale of her laughter playing out in devastating lower registers, the tempting toss of ebony curls—

all were designed to bewitch and intrigue. While Dodge was both those things, he was also wondering why a woman so beautiful, so alluring, could be so good doing something she obviously disliked so much. Because the instant she was certain of her conquest, she ducked away from the besotted swain to home in on another.

The swaying bell of her skirt stilled before Deacon Sinclair, a man so austere and forbidding that most females quaked at his attention. But not Patrice's daring friend. Her performance was flawless; Dodge gave her that. The stroke of her closed fan along the lapel of Deacon's frock coat was meant to stir a flurry of excitement within the breast beneath it. Her luscious pouts puckered her lips into unbearably kissable treasures. But when she leaned near enough to send most men staggering back in a panic of self-denial, Deacon caught her wrists, and with a contemptuous word, pushed her away.

In that moment, Starla turned to catch Dodge's entertained smirk. Instead of blushing at the witness of her failed seduction, she met Dodge's look with one of haughty challenge. Instead of fleeing in embarrassment, she sashayed toward him, her stride purposeful in intent. The edge to her words betrayed her annoyance at his refusal to look ashamed.

"Something amuses you, sir? Share the jest so we both might laugh together. Unless you only find humor at the uninvited expense of others."

He grinned up at her. He didn't have Deacon Sinclair's celibate nature, and the woman had set everything that was male growling to life inside him. She was magnificent this close, her skin ivory perfection against the cloud of raven hair, above the snug dip of her neckline, skin that would feel softer to the touch than anything had a right to.

But a wise man wouldn't give such a woman the power that came with the knowledge that she rattled him to his soul. So he gave away nothing with his reply. "Oh, I have a hell of a sense of humor, ma'am. I was just admiring your boldness in taking on Sinclair. You had to know that was like trying to defeat the Army of the Potomac with a pocket knife."

She almost smiled. Almost.

"How uncharitable of you to liken my attention to that of a siege." The assessment in her gaze grew less flattering. "I suppose you'd be scrambling for cover."

"No, ma'am." He nodded toward his crutches. "I'm not much for running these days. I tend to stand my ground."

She glanced at the crutches. It would have been a simple thing for her to use his infirmity to strip the pride from him. She could have done so with an unkind remark, even with a disdainful glance designed to make him feel less of a man in her esteem. From such a glorious creature, the wound might have been fatal. But no trace of sympathy or intolerable pity softened her mood. Her gaze lost none of its glitter as she said, "Is that so? Then you do more than watch?"

Relieved and revitalized, he snapped to the challenge. "As much as decorum . . . and the lady . . . allow me, ma'am."

"You have no manners, sir." She said it casually, as a comment, not a complaint.

"If someone told you I had, they misled you. We're going to get along famously, you and I."

His confident claim shocked past her air of ennui. He saw the change and wondered over it. Her stare sharpened warily, transforming her from flighty moth to aggressive bird of prey in an instant.

"Why would you think that, sir? You do not know me, nor I you."

"I mean to remedy that, the you-knowing-me part. But I *do* know you. I know you're more like your brother than I first suspected."

Starla frowned, alarmed, agitated by his insight and insinuation. "You and Tyler are friends?"

"Not exactly. We've had—dealings."

"And that makes you think we will, too, is that it, Mr. Dodge?" She trailed the edge of her fan along his jaw to let it pause beneath his chin. Their gazes met and held for a heartbeat, then two. Just when he feared he'd strangle on the thickening sense of expectation, her ripe lips pursed in sultry defiance, daring him to make some foolish claim.

Unable to resist, Dodge grinned wide. "I'd bank on it, ma'am."

Her fan continued up the other side of his face, then delivered a sharp rap to his ear that was neither playful nor coy. It stung like the bite of her pronouncement.

"You'd be wrong."

With that she spun away, leaving him grinning after her, not at all discouraged.

What he did find discouraging was that though she fired his blood into a twenty-one-gun salute, below the waist there was nothing burning . . . not even a spark.

If a woman like Starla Fairfax couldn't bring a man's loins roaring back to life, he was as good as dead. Was that what he had to look forward to? A lifetime of chafing at desires he couldn't satisfy? He couldn't look at a woman like Starla without imagining the touching and all the pleasurable things that would follow that initial contact if he had his way. If looking was all he'd ever be allowed, death seemed preferable.

He quickly hid his misgivings as Patrice Garrett came to kneel beside his chair. She teased him with her knowing smile, coaxing his humor back from the edge of abysmal self-indulgence as only she could.

"Has she broken your heart already?"

Dodge gave her a wry look. "I don't think it was my heart she was trying to rupture."

Used to his blunt ways, Patrice wasn't offended. "That means she's either interested—"

"Or—?"

"She's interested," Patrice concluded.

Dodge wasn't so sure. "In filleting me alive, maybe."

"If you hadn't made an impression, she wouldn't have bothered to give you an honest reaction. She's—how to explain Starla Fairfax?"

"Complicated?"

Patrice nodded at his astute claim. "And you like her! Oh, I'd hoped you would. She and Tyler—"

A sad bitterness broke that happy reminiscence, and Dodge was quick to distract her from her sorrow.

"Now, you hold on there, missy. Don't go ringing wedding bells just yet."

"I won't."

But he could see her eyes measuring him for groom's wear. Surprisingly, he didn't fight her overt matchmaking too hard. What man would object to the thought of sharing a future of days—and nights—with a woman of such beauty and mystery? Until he caught a glimpse of a furtive figure skimming past the doorway to the hall, reminding him of the one detail surrounding Starla Fairfax that could be a problem.

"Take a walk with me."

Though surprised by the suggestion, Patrice supplied his crutches, letting him lever himself up and out of the chair without offering her assistance. She'd never compromised his sense of worth by fussing; it was one of the things that so endeared her to him.

Once the padded supports were wedged under his arms, he started toward the lobby of the hotel, through the throng of well-wishers, pausing often to wait for Patrice to receive hugs of guarded congratulations. She followed without question until they left the noise of her celebration behind. Once in the foyer, she stayed him with a hand upon his arm.

"Dodge—?"

Then she saw what he'd seen, the one missing—and uninvited—guest who would have completed the joyous event in heart, if not in mind.

Tyler Fairfax stood in the shadows of the foyer. He wore clothes that looked slept in, his shirt half untucked, his black hair unruly over eyes red and raw from too much drink. His bleary gaze took in Patrice in her wedding finery, anguish cutting a brief swath through the dull glaze before he pulled his impassive mask together.

"I beg your pardon, *chère*. It was not my intention to sully the evening by showing up unannounced. And unwanted."

Patrice steeled herself behind a chill of bare civility. "Not even you could ruin tonight." She turned to go, but with unexpected agility Tyler caught her wrist. Dodge made no move to intercede. Tyler Fairfax posed no threat except to himself. Dodge recognized the signs of a man suffering from a case of unrequited devotion.

While Patrice stood stiff and still, Tyler lifted her hand with the utmost care to where he could place a brief kiss upon it. His intense stare never left hers, except for a flicker downward to observe the shiny gold ring she wore. A wry smile warped his lips.

"*Bonne chance*, Mrs. Garrett. I wish you well."

Patrice withdrew her hand with a curt, "If that's true, you can stay away from us. And from Starla."

"It's for my sister that I ask a favor."

She glared at him narrowly. "What?"

"When you return to the Glade, take Star with you. It's not safe for her to remain in town unpro— alone."

"Unprotected" was the word Dodge guessed he meant to say. But unprotected against what?

"Patrice, I beg you to do this for her sake, not mine. You've my word I'll stay away. She's just arrived. Her bags are still at the station. She can't come home. Patrice . . . if you ever cared for us at all . . . please."

There was just enough honest agitation in his voice and in the furtive shadowing of his stare to alarm Patrice into nodding.

"All right, Tyler."

Her cool tone offered no opening for further conversation. Still, he hesitated, his stoic facade wavering when he finally said, "Tell Reeve—" But he broke off abruptly and wheeled away, leaving the rest unspoken.

And as Dodge escorted the troubled bride back to her reception, he was disturbed, as well.

What danger was Tyler so afraid would befall his sister upon her return to home and family?

Chapter 2

Home.

The relief of it shivered through Starla
Fairfax as she stood on the cool balcony of Glendower Glade. She'd spent many a social day and
evening at the Glade, enough to feel comfortable
within its sprawling rooms, but it wasn't the house
that embraced her with welcome; it was the sense
of familiarity.

She took in a deep breath redolent of the rich,
fertile scents of Kentucky soil and blue stem
grasses still wet with dew. More subtle aromas
were entwined with those of springy earth, of horse
and fragrant blossoms, of crisp inland air free of
the thick salt tang she'd come to despise. It was
the clean crispness she missed the most in the air,
across the endless pastures and unclouded sky.
Heaven on earth in Pride County, Kentucky. And
no matter what her brother warned, she was home
to stay.

Of course, for now she was just a guest of the
Glade and her best friend since childhood. She
might have felt awkward coming home with the

newlyweds, but the sprawling Glendower horse farm was large enough to afford a Northern Army battalion privacy in one wing and yet house a Southern regiment in the other without one knowing of the other's presence. She hadn't hesitated in accepting Patrice's offer. There was something to say about Providence. She needed the solitude, the benign surroundings, the time to gather her thoughts and the direction of her future about her.

For the last four years she'd made herself forget those she'd loved and left behind. She'd lived someone else's life in a world foreign to her own— until it was more dangerous to remain and pretend than to return and face the demons of her youth. She told herself she was ready to meet them.

All the way up from the Gulf Coast she'd repeated that catechism of bravery. But now, even here, tucked safely within the bosom of the Glade, she felt the tendrils of shadowed recall reach for her, chilling along her flesh like an unhealthy breeze, knotting her stomach in remembered anxiety. The shadows housed at Fair Play. She knew then, as panic tightened, that she'd fooled herself if she thought she was strong enough to greet those memories head-on.

"Good morning."

Starla gave a start at the sound of another's voice, then turned to greet her friend with a smile.

"Why, Mrs. Reeve Garrett, you are the last soul I expected to see before noon."

Patrice wasted no time with false blushes. Her features glowed from a happiness that touched

Starla's spirit with a bittersweet pang. The new bride embraced her warmly.

"I wanted to make sure you didn't feel excluded here."

Starla's laugh held a sliver of its former sharp wit. "Why, Patrice, honey, you're not suggesting something indecent, are you?"

Patrice hugged her hard. "Oh, Lord, I've missed you, Star. Why did you stay away so long?"

Caught up in the same tangle of regret, Starla could think of nothing clever so she stayed silent, soaking up the joy of being with her dearest friend on earth. They'd grown up sharing every secret, every wish. But now Starla could share no more than her gladness. Her motives and her memories were best locked away from even the most sympathetic ears. Patrice would never understand, even if she might forgive.

Starla pushed away, adopting an air of conspiratorial naughtiness. "So, tell me, how you finally managed to snare ol' Reeve Garrett without your sourpuss brother putting a hole in him."

Arm in arm, giggling like schoolgirls, they looked out over the placid pastures of Glendower Glade to tell secrets once more. Starla went teary-eyed at hearing of the deaths of both Reeve's and Patrice's fathers—Avery Sinclair in battle, Byron Glendower to natural causes less than two months ago. She listened pridefully as Patrice told of holding the Sinclair properties until her brother's return and mourned, along with Patrice, the martyred execution of Reeve's half brother, Jonah, at the hands of the Union Army. For a short time Jonah had been Patrice's fiancé. It had taken tragedy and turmoil for her and Reeve to realize they belonged together. Then, finally, Starla asked the dreaded question.

"What about Tyler? Why wasn't he at your wedding? He's all right, isn't he?"

"You haven't seen him yet?"

Starla shook her head. "I came right to the hotel from the station. Nothing's happened, has it?"

If Patrice thought it odd that Starla had gone to a wedding before going to her family's home after a four-year absence—that she'd yet to visit there— she knew her friend too well to mention it. Instead, she addressed her anxiousness.

"Tyler is—fine. When was the last time you heard from him?"

"I haven't, really. Just short messages to say he was well."

"Then you know nothing of what he's been doing since you left." Patrice's expression told her more than any words. She couldn't meet her friend's eyes. "He's changed, Starla."

Knowing her brother, Starla braced to hear the worst. "Tell me."

"Since the war, he's been running with the Dermont brothers."

That said plenty. Starla wrinkled her nose in disgust. "Them! Ugh! Not a brain among the lot of them. Why would Tyler turn to the likes of that trash?"

"Reeve, Mede, Noble—they all left to follow the fighting. Tyler stayed to take care of your father and the distillery. He helped the Dermonts form a local Home Guard. At first they did some good, protecting a few of the small outlying farms from raiding Yankee bands. But when the federals declared martial law in all pockets of Confederate support, like here in Pride, they stirred up trouble, as often with the people they were supposed to protect as not.''

Starla took a deep breath, her heart aching. ''And now?''

''Now they hide behind hoods in the night and frighten those they can into supporting their causes and—''

''And?''

Patrice faced her then, her features toughened to exclude all sympathy. ''And they 'intimidate' those who won't bend.''

''By 'intimidate,' you mean what?''

''Burning barns, killing livestock, sometimes worse.''

Starla's eyes squeezed shut on the images that arose. ''I never should have left him.'' She gazed at her friend in anguish when Patrice gripped her shoulders.

''You cannot blame yourself for Tyler, Star. He made his own choices.''

Her disbelief and pain continued to grow. ''But he wouldn't have done such things if I hadn't gone.''

''He's drinking and he's angry, Starla. He's not thinking about anything the right way anymore. I don't know that your being here would have made any difference. To some men a little power is worse than your daddy's hundred-proof.''

Finally, she had to ask. Her voice thinned with strain. "And my father? He just let Tyler go?"

"No one's seen him, Star. Not for a long time. I guess his illness has gotten worse."

By "illness" Patrice was politely referring to her father's dissipation due to drink. Starla squared her shoulders, drawing on the resolve hidden by her frivolous manner. "Well, I'll just have to keep Tyler in line myself, then. I won't tolerate such boorish behavior." When Patrice didn't react to that claim with any degree of confidence, Starla knew a terrible fear that her brother might already be beyond redemption. She slightly changed the subject. "But 'Trice, you haven't told me why Tyler wasn't at your wedding. He was always so sweet on you, you know. I can't believe he'd not want to be there." Her gaze begged silently not to learn the truth if it was something awful, so Patrice softened the blow as much as possible.

"He had a falling out with Reeve."

"But Reeve was his best friend."

"Reeve took up the Union cause. That made him a traitor in the eyes of most of the county, my brother and yours included. It was rumored that he might have been behind Jonah's death—"

"No! Oh, Patrice, I don't believe it!"

Under Patrice's feminine form, a foundation of rigid steel supported her fierce words. "It was a lie. But it caused a lot of trouble." She glanced away uncomfortably. "For a time, even I considered it might be true."

"But you and Reeve married. You put that behind you and moved on."

"But Tyler hasn't, Starla. And I don't know that he'll ever be welcome here again."

Starla smiled nervously. "Now, 'Trice, you don't mean that. You and me, Tyler and Reeve—we grew up together. We've been friends forever."

But Patrice lost none of her hard edge. "Nothing's forever, Star. I can only hope what's between Tyler and my husband won't come between us."

Starla hesitated, torn by loyalty and love. She hadn't heard her brother's side of things yet, but she knew and trusted Patrice's honesty. And she knew Tyler. The terrible things she'd just learned were fact. And she was to blame through her cowardice.

"I'll make things right, Patrice."

"I don't know that you can." The hint of sadness in her friend's voice both frightened and encouraged her. If there was remorse, there was also regret. That meant all was not lost. Starla cast off her doubts with a bold shrug.

"I will. I'll slap some sense into that brother of mine and have him here apologizing. He's not going to get away with any more nonsense now that I'm home."

Patrice smiled wanly, not unmoved by her neighbor's vow, but not yet convinced she could make miracles happen. "These aren't childish pranks he's involved in, Starla, and the Dermonts are more than teasing bullies. They're backed by some important men. Judge Banning, for one."

"Oh, pooh! Tyler's just a rambunctious puppy. He'll run with a pack if you let him loose, but you keep him at home on a short leash and he's a dar-lin'.''

Patrice said nothing. In her silence an awkward sense of separation settled between the two friends, warning of what might happen to their closeness if they allowed it. Neither was willing to allow it.

''Tell me about you,'' Patrice said suddenly, turning to face Starla curiously. ''Where on earth have you been and what have you been doing these past four years?''

Starla smiled, the gesture chilled with wariness. ''Didn't Tyler tell you?''

''Tyler was very vague.'' A touch of accusation edged in with those words. ''He said you were in Louisville. He also said you were in Chattanooga.''

''He was right. I did a lot of traveling.''

''During a war?''

''Patrice, honey, did you ever know somethin' as trifling as a little ol' war to get in the way of somethin' I wanted to do?''

Patrice had to laugh. ''No.''

''I traveled some. I visited family, but most of all I missed being here. I don't want to talk of where I've been anymore, not when I'm so happy to be back home.'' She turned up her radiant smile to throw Patrice off her line of questioning. Though Patrice knew her friend too well to be misdirected, she chose to let the matter slide.

''I'm glad you're home, too.''

They embraced again like sisters, Starla heaving a deep sigh of relief. Before Patrice could come up with any more uncomfortable topics, Starla linked their arms together.

"Have you got anything to eat down in that big ol' pantry, or were you planning to live on love? I'm starving."

Patrice hugged her arm. "Let's go see."

Once Reeve was lured downstairs by the scent of fresh-brewed chicory coffee, the newlyweds disappeared shortly thereafter, leaving Starla to her own devices once more. A reprieve. She knew it was no more than that. Sooner or later she wouldn't be able to escape the questions. She knew she had to think of what to do. Returning to her family home of Fair Play was out of the question. If she had her way, she'd never set foot in there again. At least, not while her father was alive.

So many decisions, all so weighted by circumstance and heavy with consequence. Her head pounded, denying the clarity she needed to make the right choice.

So instead of spending the day in determined decision making, she used the time to heal her weary spirit, soothing her senses with what went no deeper than the surface. She shook the wrinkles out of her travel wardrobe, clucking over their sad, dated look. Before the war she'd always been dressed in the latest Paris had to offer. Now she was realistic enough to be glad for clothes on her back.

She'd had to look stylish for the role she'd played over the past four years. She'd had to act as if she hadn't a care in the world while inside she was constantly on the brink of emotional collapse. Nothing new—playing dress-up like an an-

imated doll and hiding the truth behind a
painted-on smile. It was a role she was born to.

As exhausted as if she'd waged her own war,
she was eager to accept the terms of truce by coming home again. As long as that compromise didn't
include a return under her family's roof. There
must be a solution; she knew it. But today she
would retrieve her strengths and revel in the sense
of safety.

Even if it was only temporary.

The last thing Starla expected was for the new
couple to be entertaining company on their first day
of married life. The last thing she desired was for
that guest to be the obnoxious Northerner Hamilton
Dodge. He grinned at her dismay without the least
bit of shame. She'd never seen a man who found
so much to smile about—not in foolish gregari-
ousness, but with genuine amusement for the circumstance. She didn't care to be the source of his
entertainment and glared to let him know it. He
grinned wider, a wolfish, faintly predatory gesture
that brought a prickle of threat to play upon her
expression.

''Good evening, Miss Fairfax. You're looking
even lovelier than last night, if that's possible.
Probably because no one can outshine a bride in
full regalia. Not that you look any less stellar this
evening, Patrice. Just more out of reach.''

He bent to accept Patrice's kiss to his rough
cheek, lingering comfortably within the circle of
her arms. The sight unnerved Starla. How quickly
this stranger insinuated himself into the lives of

those she'd known since the days of swaddling clothes.

"Come in, Dodge. Let me rescue you before you trip over your tongue with all those compliments."

"Are you suggesting they're not sincere?"

Patrice laughed and looped her arm through his, mindful of the crutches supporting his weight. "Gracious, no. You haven't enough tact for flattery so I'll just have to believe you. Reeve's already poured you a brandy."

Starla stood at the doorway, watching the two of them head across the cavernous foyer toward Byron Glendower's study, Patrice slowing her step to pace Dodge's awkward use of the crutches. Not used to being ignored, she fumed for a moment, wondering how to upstage the ingratiating Yankee, then growing angrier because she'd have to. These were her friends. This was her homecoming and she was being pushed aside in favor of some hobbling outsider with a grating accent and a pushy manner.

Then Patrice glanced back. "Starla, aren't you going to join us?"

That Northerner looked back, too, one brow arched in mocking question.

She affixed her most dazzling smile. "Just closing the door to keep out the pests, honey." And she glared at Dodge to let him know that in her opinion, she hadn't been entirely successful.

Again his toothy grin flashed in recognition of her testy mood. What an aggravating man. He didn't care that he was being insulted. Nor did he bother to disguise the blatant interest in his stare. She prepared herself for a long defensive evening.

As to Dodge, every moment at the Glade was treasured by this man who'd spent too much time alone. Since coming to Pride, he'd poured his energies into reviving the bank set up by Reeve's half brother, Jonah. The establishment had closed with Jonah's death and Reeve had called him down from Michigan to see what he could do about helping it, and the people of Pride, back on their feet.

The hard part was getting the stubborn community to see him as something other than a forked-tongued devil come to steal their last cent. Like Starla, they winced at the sound of his voice, looking no deeper to discover what kind of man he was. If they bothered, they'd know he was as honorable as he was determined to succeed. He'd learned an important piece of advice from Reeve: the only way to win them over was one at a time. And tonight, the one he wanted to win was Starla Fairfax.

His first assessment of her as a fluffy southern belle had been blown to hell during their first conversation. Now he was possessed by the need to discover just what she was. Intriguing, definitely. Gorgeous, beyond belief. And more than just a bit of a brat.

She was determined to dislike him and now was intent upon pretending he didn't exist as she steered their dinner conversation toward a past he didn't share and people he didn't know. She did it so skillfully, perhaps their hosts didn't see her behavior for the snub it was.

She'd glance at him while speaking, giving the pretense of including him in the conversation but the cold sheen in her stare might well have been a wall denying him access. He didn't mind. He usually did so much talking, it was a relief to sit back over Fairfax Bourbon and simply listen and learn.

And he was learning fast—learning that Starla Fairfax was a complicated piece of work, with as many convolutions as her brother. For all her flashy charm and animated gestures, if one paid attention, he'd see they were all for effect, for keeping others at a distance while she remained safely untouched by the world that moved around her.

Most beautiful women loved to gush on and on about themselves, but that was a subject Starla avoided, deflecting personal questions like the surface of a mirrored pool—making it an irresistible challenge for Dodge to test the waters underneath. Would they be hot and agitated, or cool and murky with mystery?

Only one topic seemed to stir a response in her, and Dodge noted with little enthusiasm that it involved another man.

He'd heard of Noble Banning. He knew Banning had been Reeve's best friend before the war, that his father was a ruthless manipulator in the political arena who owed no allegiance save to himself. And he knew Starla Fairfax lit up like a rocket trail when speaking about him.

"Last I heard," Reeve was saying, "he earned a release from Point Lookout Prison by joining up with the Frontier Brigade."

"Prison." Starla's bright eyes glossed over with

real dismay. "I hope it wasn't terrible for him. One hears such rumors."

Reeve gave her a smile of reassurance. "Noble's a born negotiator. He probably had the prisoners organized and petitioning for starched linens with every meal on his first day there."

Starla rewarded him with a wan smile. "Noble could sweet-talk an old maid out of her garters when he set his mind to it."

Seeing the wistfulness softening her expression, Dodge wondered, with a prick of irritation, if the southern paragon had ever tried charming her out of hers. Or if he'd been successful. Time to wade in, if he had any hopes of ever seeing those garters for himself.

"Offering captured enemy officers a chance to serve in the Western Theater is a fairly common way to control the population since they stopped prisoner exchanges. If your friend was smart, he jumped at the chance right off."

Starla fixed Dodge with a quelling look, incensed that he'd offer comment, outraged by his opinion.

"Noble Banning was a Confederate officer, sir. I doubt he'd jump at the chance to betray the South by joining an enemy army just to escape a little discomfort. Our boys are bred for better fortitude and honor than that."

Dodge didn't back down from her cutting claim. Instead he said, "Funny, how eating biscuits crawling with weevils tends to change a man's thoughts on honor."

Starla set down her tableware with a demonstrative force. "What an unappetizing observation,

Lieutenant Dodge. Apparently you have no consideration for the delicate constitutions of those with whom you dine.''

Dodge blinked. ''Beg your pardon, ma'am, but you don't look all that delicate, and I was just stating a fact to make a point.''

''And your point was what, sir? That our men are spineless cowards who value their personal comforts over the duty they swore to uphold?''

''That's not a conclusion I would ever draw after facing so many of them in battle, ma'am.''

''Or were you merely judging them on the basis of your own lack of fortitude? I am sure that, had you found yourself in such a situation, you'd have been quick to do the smart thing and betray the Cause you professed to follow.''

Patrice looked anxiously between her guests, then to Reeve, who simply leaned back in his chair as if watching a mortar volley. He rebuffed her pointed stare imploring that he do something, offering her a bland smile that forced her to say with false gaiety, ''Would anyone care for pie?''

But Dodge and Starla were locked in a battle of wills across the tabletop. Neither looked ready to concede an inch in philosophy, because the tension tugging taut between them had as much to do with attraction as it did opposing politics—unwise attraction on Dodge's part, unwilling on Starla's.

''I didn't fight for a cause, Miss Fairfax,'' Dodge continued, as if Patrice hadn't spoken. ''I wore a uniform to hold together a country I love against those who would betray its sanctity. I didn't see it as an engagement of ideals or an arena in which to express political differences at the cost of thousands of lives. Honor and ideals are the first things that fall when men go to war. When you're looking down the breeches of a dozen artillery pieces aimed to blow your gizzard to kingdom come, your only duty is to keep yourself and the men you're responsible for alive. That's not cowardice, ma'am, it's survival. And it's nothing a fine lady like you, whose family never lost so much as a night's sleep over the compunctions of duty or honor, could discuss with any degree of insight or opinion.''

Then Dodge reared back as the contents of Starla's glass splashed his face, stinging his eyes. By the time he'd dried off, she'd already left the table.

Patrice was quick with both a towel and an apology.

''Dodge, I'm sorry. I don't know what got into her to behave so impulsively.''

''I'd say it's the lady's way of sharing a high degree of opinion.''

Chapter 3

Starla didn't pause in brushing her hair when she heard light footsteps behind her.

"If you've come to scold me, go ahead. I deserve it for spoiling your dinner party."

Patrice took the brush from her and began to sweep it through the heavy waves of black hair in steady repetitions, a task she'd often undertaken when they were younger to calm her high-strung friend.

"I didn't come to scold you. I suppose putting you two at the same table involved a degree of risk. Something like a keg of powder and a lit match."

"Then why invite the odious man?"

"That 'odious man' saved both our lives, and I happen to be very fond of him."

Starla sniffed. "I don't see why. Arrogant, opinionated, rude—" She broke off when she saw the smile in Patrice's reflection.

"I knew you'd like him."

"Like him?"

"There were enough sparks flying at that table to celebrate the Fourth of July."

"Or burn down the house," Starla grumbled. What was it about the man that put her in such a temper, even discussing him after the fact? She couldn't deny he inspired *something* within her. But she refused to think of it as a spark, and said so. Vehemently. "Like him? You must be tetched."

"Well, I've never seen you put that much energy into building a dislike. That must mean something."

"It means I find him quite reprehensible."

"And handsome."

"Handsome? With that leering grin and bristly face?" And eyes that saw too much. Nice eyes, she remembered—dark, clear, intelligent. With an unapologetic stare that implied integrity. And an unwavering gaze meant to inspire trust. Eyes too intense in their probing, as if he knew she held secrets and was determined to discover them. She shuddered slightly, anxiously. "He's about as handsome as an ol' blue tick hound."

"And just as loyal. You'll never find a better friend."

"Why would I want that ol' Yankee for a friend?"

All teasing left her as Patrice said, "He's a good man, Starla, maybe the best man you'll ever know."

Again the warmth of those dark eyes intruded upon Starla's tightly held disdain, making her resolve falter. Wanting to believe the goodness in any man, let alone a Yankee, was the height of folly: a bitter lesson learned and never to be forgotten

again. Yet something about Hamilton Dodge beck-
oned belief. The fact that she was swayed by it
made her fight all the more to deny it.

"Well, I know all I want to know about your
Lieutenant Dodge. I didn't come home to find myself some fool man to keep me under his thumb.
So if you please, no more trying to push your man-
nerless friend down my throat, thank you. He
would hardly be my choice."

How good had her previous choices been? Starla
refused to consider them.

Patrice simply smiled and continued brushing.

That knowing smile bothered Starla long after
Patrice had gone to be with her new husband.
Imagine, thinking she'd be interested in some dull
Yankee. She paced the perimeters of her room,
restless in the temporary haven. Feeling the press
of her circumstances. Agitated by the persistent image of the banker's smile. God's nightshirt, why
was the man so difficult to push out of her mind?

Reluctant to dress for bed with so much energy
pulling to and fro within her, she stepped out onto
the moon-washed balcony hoping to find solace in
the warm evening air. As she leaned upon the rail,
her wandering gaze caught sight of fleeting movement across the sweep of the lawn where a brick
path led to a secluded gazebo. Her heart leapt.

Someone was down there, and it didn't take her
a second to figure out who.

Starla hurried through the shadows, calling out
as she reached the gazebo.

"Tyler?"

Then he was there in front of her, the moonlight kind to the ravaging of years upon his familiar features. At the first hint of his smile, she catapulted into his arms, hugging to him despite the acrid bite of bourbon clinging to his rumpled clothes and lacing the quick kiss he pressed to her temple. She hadn't planned to cry, but tears wet her face in a torrent, soaking through his shirt and right to his heart.

"Lemme look at you, darlin'," he said at last, easing her away by a tender grip on her shoulders. His fingertips touched her damp cheek. "You look wonderful, Star. Nothin's ever looked better to me."

Through the tears and choking emotion, her own reply was gruff with censure. "And look at you, Tyler Fairfax. I've seen better ruts in the road. What have you been doing? Obviously you've not kept your promise to take care of yourself while I was away. Patrice tells me you've been—"

He halted her words with the press of his forefinger against her mouth and a chiding, "You can't even say hello to me before you start right in a-harpin' on my virtues—or the lack thereof?"

A smile spread beneath his fingertip. She caught his hand and held it to her cheek. "I have missed you so much."

With that candid claim, she brought him to his knees. He blinked at the rush of gladness skewing his vision, smiling with a remembered sweetness to belay whatever else might tarnish his soul. To Starla, this was her brother, and it mattered not what he had or hadn't done in her absence, only that they were once again together. Nothing else was important.

Then she saw a purposeful remoteness mask his expression, dulling his gaze, blanking his features of all animation.

"What are you doing here, Star?"

"Tilly wrote me about Patrice's wedding. You weren't going to tell me, were you, even knowing how much I'd want to be here?"

He never flinched beneath that accusation.

"Tyler, she's my best friend. They're the best friends we've ever had! It was important to me!"

"Keeping you safe is important to me." The flat tone of his voice cut through her anger. "That's why you're going to get on the first train and get the hell outta here in the morning."

"I'm not leaving." Her statement sounded firmer than her courage. She fought not to cringe when Tyler rounded on her with sudden ferocity.

"Yes, you are!"

"Tyler, this is my home. My friends are here. I'm tired of running, hiding, sick of pretending—"

He drew uncomfortably close, fixing her gaze with one of fierce intensity. "And what would you be doing here? You planning to just come on home to Fair Play to be one big happy family again? You ready to start pretending there's nothing wrong, that you got the marks on your face from falling down or that you can close your eyes at night without jumping at every sound? Is that what you want to come back to, Star?"

He stopped when he saw the starkness of her

expression. The hollow terror in her eyes went all the way to her soul. She made a soft, inarticulate sound and he had her in a tight embrace, holding her as if he could crush out the memories, the fears, the damage that had been done with a hurried apology.

"Oh, darlin', don't cry. Don't you cry. I'm not sayin' these things to hurt you. I'm trying to protect you the best I can. An' I can't when you're in that house. I tried, but we both know I can't do a damn thing—"

She pulled back with sudden forcefulness, surprising him with the determination setting her pale features. Surprising him more with her incredible words.

"I came back to protect you."

"Me?" He blinked in bewilderment, then started beneath the stroke of her palm along his cheek.

"Tyler, it's too much for you to take on alone. It's worn you down to nothing. I've spent the last four years, not a day going by without me growing sick with worry over what you were going through up here—with him."

He tried to speak, the effort unsuccessful.

"I can't let you carry it all by yourself anymore. I'm not a scared little girl, Tyler. I can take care of myself. And you need someone to take care of you."

A fractured smile flickered across his lips. "I'm fine, darlin'."

"You're not fine; you look like hell. And what's this I hear about you running with that Dermont trash?"

All the fondness left his expression. His eyes became chips of glittery green glass. "What if I am? I'm taking care of business, Star."

"What business is that?"

"My business and none of yours."

"It is mine when it affects our friends. What happened between you and Reeve? What did you do to turn Patrice against you?"

"I can't change none of that." No hint of remorse, no word of explanation. Then he smiled, a brilliant gesture meant to distract her from her scolding. "Can we put all that aside for a minute? It's been four years, darlin', and I don't want to spend the first four hours of our reunion fighting."

Starla sighed, her pose relaxing. "Neither do I."

For a moment she saw the old Tyler returning to life, the rogue-charmer no one could stay angry with for long. She'd never been able to. His tender concern undid all her suspicions.

"Did they put you up all right at the Glade? I didn't want you to have to stay in a hotel your first night home."

"You did this? You asked them to take me in?"

Darkness skirted his reply. "I didn't want you to stay in town any longer than you had to." Then the heartbreaking smile again. "Are you happy here?"

A shadow of worry made her ask, "Who did you tell about why I left home?"

Tyler scowled, offended. "Not a soul."

"I want it kept that way. No one is to know anything."

"What about New Orleans? Did you tie up all your loose ends there?"

It took her a moment to get control of her features so she could answer with a degree of nonchalance. "It's all behind me now and nothing to lead anyone here."

"There're gonna be questions." His gaze said he had some of his own.

"I'll handle them. I told Patrice I'd been traveling, visiting with relatives. I don't like lying to her. I never liked lying to her." She sighed and glanced back toward the house. "I feel like a little girl again. It's so good to see Patrice. Remember all the times we had?"

Tyler's gaze went soft and bittersweet. "I remember."

"So much is different, yet it's like nothing's changed at all. I keep expecting to see the squire and Jonah."

"They're gone."

She placed a hand on his arm. "But not everything's lost, Tyler."

His smile was small, fragile. "No."

Not sure if that was an agreement or an argument, Starla continued, trying to push her agitation behind her; her worry that he would ask for more details than she was ready to give. So she grabbed for the distraction foremost in her mind.

"The one thing I can do without is that Yankee friend of theirs."

"The banker? Why? Is he bothering you?"

"If you classify being forced to endure his rudeness and sly behavior a bother."

Tyler's stare chilled. "Do I need to teach him manners?"

Recalling the sly grin, and still bothered by the effect it had upon her normal breathing, Starla snorted. "As if anyone could perform that miracle."

"You'd be surprised, baby sister."

The banker and his disquieting effect were forgotten. The quiet menace in Tyler's voice snagged Starla's full attention. This was something new in her brother's character, something she hadn't seen before, and she studied it with the caution one gave to the prodding of something potentially poisonous.

"What exactly do you mean by that, Tyler?"

He allowed a small, tight smile. "I can make things happen here in Pride. I'm not without a certain degree of influence."

Then she understood. "I don't want that kind of assistance." She told herself she didn't speak up so vehemently to protect the likes of that Yankee from the glitter behind her brother's glare.

"Star—"

"I won't have you playing some dangerous game with the Dermonts on my behalf."

"They're not games."

And that upset her all the more. "How did you get so 'influential'?"

"I saw a need and filled it."

"What kind of need?"

"The need of the oppressed to speak out loud and clear against those who would take unfair advantage." He smiled, waiting for a sign of her approval, and was confused when it didn't come.

"And how do you manage that, Tyler? With hoods and torches?"

His expression faded. "By any means I see fit."

Starla just stared at him, her censure and dismay provoking him to take a haughty stand in his own defense.

"I get things done, Starla. Folks respect me—"

"You mean they fear you. You don't earn respect burning barns—"

"Who told you that?"

"Were you hoping I wouldn't find out?"

"I was hoping you'd understand."

She did, all too clearly. And it made her sick inside.

"What's he turned you into? You're becoming just like him!"

That got a reaction. He froze up, a tragic twist of horror working his expression. But it was fleeting, too fleeting for Starla to hope she'd reached him. His eyes narrowed in accusation.

"How could you say that to me?"

"How could you make me think it? Tyler, we've only spent a few minutes together, and already I can see the changes in you. I don't like them; they frighten me."

His smile was thin, even cruel. "I thought you said you didn't scare easy anymore, baby sister."

She didn't waver. "I do when I see the shadow of a monster in the brother I love."

"Then look away, Star. It's too late for me to turn back time. I'm sorry if I've disappointed you. Seems I can't manage to get nothin' right."

"Don't—"

"Don't *what?* Cry over my sorry lot? I won't. I'm paying the price for the choices I've made, and I'm not going to wail over them now. I made mistakes, big mistakes, but I did what I thought I had to—for you, for us. But I won't have you paying for 'em too. I won't let you join me in hell. So you get on that train and you don't look back, you hear? If you can't go back to New Orleans, pick someplace else—anyplace else! 'Cause if everything I've done, I've done for nothin', I don't think I could live with that."

"I'm staying."

The flare of his temper was so sudden and severe, Starla cried out in alarm when he gripped her forearms. "For once in your selfish life, think of someone other than yourself! I didn't throw away my future so you could come waltzing back here on a whim, thinking you can make everything better with a pretty smile. Damn it, Star, you'll do what I tell you, and you'll do it now. I don't have any more of my soul to sell to protect you from your foolishness."

A cold chill came over her, a rigid denial of his battering words and bullying tactics. With an abrupt movement she broke away from his grasp.

"I'm not asking you to," she spat at him. "I don't want any more of your sacrifices thrown up in my face as if they're all my fault. You're not the only one who had to make them. You made your choices, Tyler; now I'm making mine."

She swept out of the gazebo, away from the turmoil of guilt and gratitude he wrung through her. And when he called out her name, she kept walking, ignoring the panicked vulnerability wrenching through his voice, though it was one of the hardest things she'd ever had to do. Because if she was going to stay to reclaim her life, it was obvious to her now that she'd have to do it alone.

He heard a sound in the other room. Night noises wouldn't normally bring him out of bed pistol in hand, except that those noises were coming from the interior of the bank where half the town kept its money.

Dodge shrugged a shirt on over his long underwear and reached for his crutches. A frugal man of few creature comforts, he'd made a home for himself in the back rooms of the bank, saving rent and face before the town—well knowing none would provide him with accommodations. He doubted that movement in the main room meant someone was bent on robbery, but he checked the rounds in his pistol just the same. A constant victim of vandalism since he'd reopened the bank's doors, he had a sense of humor that was growing dangerously thin, especially when it came to pranks in the middle of the night.

As he swung awkwardly through the doorway into the bank proper, two things were immediately apparent: his intruder was seated in his desk chair enjoying one of his cigars, and the man's identity was a mild surprise.

"Mr. Fairfax. Kinda late to be doing your banking. If you'd care to come back during regular hours, I'd be happy to talk business with you."

Tyler sent a perfectly round smoke ring spiraling

toward the ceiling. His manner was relaxed, almost affable. "I ain't here on bank business, Yank."

"Oh?" Dodge tucked his pistol into the rear band of his long johns but didn't surrender his caution. "I can't seem to remember inviting you over for a late night smoke and pleasant conversation."

"The conversation I had in mind won't be pleasant for long if I have to repeat myself again."

Dodge laughed softly. "Forgive me. Sleep must be addling my brain but I can't recall the conversation."

"Stay away from my sister."

He said it easily enough, but the glitter in Tyler Fairfax's direct stare implied anything but goodwill. Yet the subject of discussion brought Dodge to an instant combativeness. He wasn't about to give up on the pursuit of the lovely Starla because of a brother's ire.

"Excuse me? I hardly know your sister."

"And I aim to keep that acquaintance to the minimum. I think I've made my feelings for you very clear."

Dodge grimaced. "I'd say so."

"Now I'm just letting you know, in a neighborly fashion, that my sister don't think much of you, either."

Dodge raised a single brow. That put a different slant on things. A slant that unbalanced his hopes and set his mood awry. "I didn't think I'd made that strong an impression."

"You made an impression, all right. Don't force me to make one in the back of your thick head. Leave Starla alone. She don't need the extra aggravation of having the likes of you pestering her.''

"I'm sorry if she felt being invited to the same dinner table constitutes pestering." He bristled in affront and regret. "You may assure her that whatever worries I gave her that made her feel she had to send her big brother to issue threats were completely unfounded. I'm not such a total boor that a simple "Leave me the hell alone" wouldn't have sufficed. If that's all that's brought you to break illegally into a government institution. . . ."

Tyler smiled, a slow silken gesture of deadly intention. "I jus' wanted to make sure we understood each other."

"Oh, I assure you, Mr. Fairfax, I've had a clear picture of you from the very first. If you'll just lock up behind you when you're finished with that cigar, I'd appreciate it."

Tyler regarded him with a perplexed half smile. "I don't know if you've got balls the size of mortar shells or you're just plain stupid."

His back sore and his expectations strained, Dodge's reply crackled. "I've been accused of both. But I guess you'll have to make up your own mind as to which is the truth. Good night, Mr. Fairfax. And my apologies to your sister if I've in any way offended her."

Dodge maneuvered his way out of the room and shut the door, knowing the gesture of unconcern would knock the other man off guard. He knew Tyler Fairfax wasn't a thief. But he didn't kid himself about what Fairfax was: a very deadly adversary who was as unpredictable as a wet powder charge.

He waited until he heard the outer door quietly close before he returned to the room to check the locks. Scrape marks around the latch plate told how Fairfax had gained entry. Dodge smiled wryly to himself as he settled the crossbar in place so his sleep wouldn't be disturbed a second time.

And as he eased himself down in bed once more, shifting uncomfortably to find a spot where the pain was bearable, he wondered if Starla had sent her brother to warn him away or if the idea was Tyler's own.

He found himself hoping it was the latter.

Chapter 4

It took Starla only a moment to realize the danger of walking the streets of Pride alone.

She'd thought nothing of accepting Reeve's offer of a ride into town so she could do some shopping while he took care of business. The peaceful surroundings at the Glade felt more like a prison after several days spent mostly in her own company. Not that her hosts ignored her, but the air of urgent intimacy sparking whenever the two of them shared the same room excluded Starla and made her chafe with restlessness and reminders of her own failures, of the way a true marriage was meant to be. Her friends would never say they'd prefer to be alone. It wasn't necessary.

Starla kept to herself to give them their privacy, and in her solitude she had ample time to think: about what she'd do, about her argument with her brother, about other fears that had yet to surface beyond uneasy suspicion. Fears that would change everything. The silence and space began to mock her state of indecision, echoing the magnitude of the uncertainties ahead. Finally she knew it was either escape her perpetual brooding or go quite mad.

So a trip to Pride seemed a godsend. Its streets were in an exciting flux of growth, new businesses springing up on the ashes of old. Strangers filled the crowded walks and it was easy to blend within that anonymous bustling stream. So many blue uniforms. Though she was used to seeing them after living in an occupied city, they looked glaringly out of place in Pride, where Southern sympathies had always held sway. She had no fondness for the loud, rude Yankees who pushed past her without so much as a glance of apology, but today she held no malice. Today she was enjoying her independence.

An independence that became an illusion as two burly figures blocked her path.

"Why, Miz Fairfax. I thought that was you!"

She stared up at the two workers from her father's distillery in a moment of abject panic. She recognized them both, not by name but by their reputation as harsh taskmasters eager to do whatever was necessary to earn her father's favor. And right now, she was afraid to find out what that might be.

The larger of the two grinned wide, displaying tobacco-stained teeth. "We heard you was back and was wondering why you didn't come home, instead of staying out there with that turncoat trash. Your daddy was just saying to Benson and me that we should keep an eye out for you, and should we see you, we was to bring you home for a visit."

Terror gathered cold and heavy in the pit of

Starla's belly, but she scrambled to gather her wits. The three of them were standing on a busy walkway; what could happen?

"Why, how nice to see you boys again." Her smile was spun sugar, coating the bitter taste of fear. "You can tell my daddy that I'll be over to see him just as soon as I can. I've got myself an appointment with the dressmaker in just a few minutes, and you know how prickly they get if you make them wait."

The one called Benson returned her smile. It was more sneer than amicable gesture. "She'll just have to wait, missy. Our orders was to bring you direct." And he put one huge hand on her arm, his fingers banding about her elbow like the hoops around a cask of Fairfax's finest.

Starla fought to keep any tremor from her voice. "Take your hand off me, sir. I will not be pawed in public." When he didn't relent, she made her tone icier. "My father will have you horsewhipped."

"Your daddy'll be givin' us a right nice bonus for seeing his little girl home again and that's what me an' Milton mean to do."

The brown-toothed Milton gripped her other arm in a painful clamp. "Don't go makin' no trouble for us, missy. We won't get rough 'lessen you make us."

Trapped between the two behemoths, Starla reeled with panic and indecision. She could either scream for help or be towed back to her father's house like a truculent mule that had slipped its lead and run away. Four years ago, she'd sworn she'd never return there. She thought of what waited in those closed-off rooms that reeked of stale mash and forbidden secrets. Her palms dampened. Her lungs expanded, readying to force a shriek for help from the pinch of her vocal cords. She wouldn't go back, not even if it meant causing an unforgivable scene in the center of town. She'd rather die of shame than suffer under her father's rule again.

Abruptly their path was barred by the cross brace of one of Hamilton Dodge's crutches. Starla's gaze flew to meet the single question in the lieutenant's dark eyes.

Do you want my help?

She could have asked for a more preferable rescuer, but having no choice in the matter, she signaled a frantic *Yes!*

"Excuse me, gents. Don't be hurrying Miss Fairfax off so quick. The lady promised to join me for breakfast, and I hate to drink my coffee alone when I can enjoy it in such lovely company."

Starla flashed him a dazzling smile. "Why, Mr. Dodge, how could I have forgotten you? Please forgive my rudeness." To the men who still retained her arms, she said with frosty clarity, "As I said, gentlemen, we'll make it another time."

But they didn't release her. They paid her no mind at all.

"Stay out of it, Yank," growled Benton. He gave Starla a jerk toward the street to circumvent the barrier of Dodge's crutch.

"I can't do that," came Dodge's quiet reply. For all its lack of volume, his statement carried an unavoidable challenge. The two men paused to reassess him. They smirked between themselves.

Her look of entreaty never left the stocky banker's face. Starla knew she was asking him to take her part against insurmountable odds. Her father's men were brutal creatures, weighted down with more muscle than brain. Next to them, the upstart Yankee appeared small and insignificant, offering about as much opposition as a crippled bug beneath an upraised boot sole. She should have felt guilty about encouraging him to take an inevitable beating while she escaped, but she hadn't called to him to interfere. And he didn't look as though he had the least intention of backing down.

In case they misinterpreted him the first time, Dodge said, again with bulldog tenacity, "Let the lady go."

Milton gave a gruff laugh and shook his head. "And just what the hell are you going to do if we say no?"

He didn't have long to wait for an answer.

Dodge's crutch swung downward in a fierce arc, smashing into the side of Milton's knee with enough force nearly to turn it inside out. The giant staggered back, only his hold on Starla keeping him on his feet. Immediately Dodge jabbed the crutch like a lance into the instep of Benton's foot, causing him to howl in pain and surprise. When Benton took a lumbering swing at the banker, the crutch flashed up into the man's groin. Benton froze, his features purpling as he dropped to his knees.

Freed of Milton's grasp as he bent down to assist his friend, Starla skirted them both with an anxious two-step to slip behind her surprisingly effective rescuer. Dodge could hear her rapid breathing at his back, detailing her fright, and it made him angry enough to think about finishing off the two bastards. But it was more important to get her away from the increasing curiosity of those around them than to exact a justifiable revenge.

He glanced around to where Starla stood in a quiver of delayed shock. His slow smile was meant to calm her.

"They won't be bothering you again for a while, ma'am."

Starla wet her lips. "Thank you, Lieutenant Dodge." Her voice was little more than a whisper.

"I meant what I said about that coffee."

Her stare had all the expression of green bottle glass.

Very gently he placed his palm at the small of her back. He felt tremors racing along her spine in frantic ripples and knew her composure wouldn't last more than another moment or two.

"C'mon, Miss Starla. Sit down with me for a while."

He thought she'd continue to balk when abruptly she gave before the persuasion of his guiding touch and preceded him to his destination of Sadie's boardinghouse. She made no objection when they were shown to a back table in the dining room. There she sat posed for flight on the edge of the chair, her eyes huge and gem-bright in a face pale enough to alarm him. He ordered his usual breakfast without taking his eyes from his strangely inanimate companion, then asked, "Coffee, Miss Fairfax?" No response. "She'll have a cup, too," he concluded with a warm smile for the timid girl who took their order.

Silence settled when they were left alone. Dodge guessed Starla's rigid corset frame was all that kept her upright. She stared straight through him with those expressionless eyes, and he wondered what went on behind them.

The confrontation on the walk had obviously upset her, but instead of becoming vaporish or even angry, she withdrew behind an eerie stillness that had him on edge. He'd seen the look on the faces of men in his unit when they were traumatized beyond their ability to cope. Something had scared the brash Starla Fairfax to the point of blankness, and it was more than just the manhandling of a couple of bullies.

"I wasn't sure you'd welcome my intrusion after you sicced your brother on me."

She blinked slowly. A furrow of confusion marred her brow. It was a response, anyway.

"He paid me a visit the other night and warned me to steer clear. I was afraid my stepping in out there might be interpreted as another nuisance."

"Tyler spoke to you?" Vague puzzlement reached through her daze.

"I understood it was at your request. I hadn't realized I'd made that big an impact on you. Folks don't usually dislike me until after they've met me more than once. If you'd told me yourself to go to hell, I'd have gotten the idea right off. You didn't have to send someone to give me that message."

"Lieutenant, if I wanted you to drop off the edge

of the earth, I'd have said so. I wouldn't send Tyler."

He grinned. "That's the impression I got, ma'am. Just checking. Does that mean you don't want me to fall off the face of the earth?"

A faint curve touched her lips. "I'm reserving judgment, sir."

Dodge relaxed back in his chair, now that he was certain she didn't plan to bolt from the table. She was looking better, the color edging up into her parchment-pale cheeks, the glassiness in her stare becoming a gradual awareness. Her fragile defenselessness had him knotted up with the need both to protect and to comfort her. The first she'd allowed. The second he approached more cautiously. When their coffee arrived, he watched her unsteady hands curl about the cup as if desperate for the heat. An unsettling fierceness threaded about that want to see her safe. A desire to punish those who'd shaken her from her confidence.

"Did those boys hurt you? Maybe you should talk to—"

"Maybe you should mind your own business, Lieutenant Dodge."

The steel in her tone cut rapier sharp. Apparently her recovery was progressing quickly.

"That wasn't the impression you gave me earlier."

His reminder brought a flash of temperament to her gaze. He liked the fire better than the chill.

"I appreciate your help, sir, but don't think my gratitude extends to an obligation to bare my soul."

"Consider my presumptions duly corrected."

She glanced about as if aware of her surroundings for the first time—and of whom she was with. She studied him for a long moment, her look more suspicious than flattering. He could see her asking herself what his motive might be, so he figured it was time to relieve her mind.

"I can't abide bullying. You don't owe me any thanks. Any 'gentleman' would have come to your rescue."

But not any "gentleman" had. Starla frowned slightly. The only one to step in on her behalf was this brash Yankee who now felt entitled to intrude into her life. She couldn't allow that.

"I have to go."

His hand covered hers in a staying gesture. There was no pressure, no clutching fingers, just that firm, warm covering. An unexpected spark of response caused her breath to catch. That spark Patrice had foretold. She didn't pull her hand away.

"You haven't finished your coffee," he pointed out agreeably.

"I really don't—"

"—Have a choice. You don't want to risk bumping into those fellows."

Her features adopted that still mask again, but fear glittered in her eyes. He was right, she realized. She needed to be careful.

"How did you get to town?"

"With Reeve."

"You can keep me company until he's ready to leave—all right?"

She chafed at the lack of options, alarmed by her own willingness to remain as much as by the danger of leaving. Noting her reluctance, he smiled.

"If you can get past my accent, I'm really not such bad company. Some people actually find me amusing."

"I'm afraid I'm not one of them, Lieutenant."

He grinned, not offended. "Damn, at least you're honest. Can't fault you for telling the truth. All right. I'll eat my breakfast and keep my mouth shut. You can sit pretty and pretend you're at a table by yourself. When I'm finished, we'll find Reeve, then I'll fall off the face of the earth and never bother you again."

He seemed sincere enough, even a little peeved, but Starla doubted that Hamilton Dodge would be that easy to get rid of. She'd already seen that hint of bulldog in him. Once he sank his teeth in, she doubted he was quick to let go. Why was that knowledge as welcome as it was worrisome?

But he did keep his word about not burdening her with conversation. His breakfast arrived and he tackled it in silence. And while he ate, she watched him, with displeasure at first, then with begrudging interest.

He wasn't hard on the eyes. His features were cut with a pleasant symmetry, regular rather than dramatic. He wore his dark hair close cropped and paid scant attention to his razor. His dark-stubbled jaw was strong and squared, an indication of that bulldog again, as were the thickness of his upper body and the breadth of his shoulders.

She would have thought him placidly solid and nonthreatening, had she not seen him dispatch those two outside with such lethal speed. The crutches suggested a weakness as false as her first impressions of him. He wasn't helpless nor made up of empty arrogance. His dark eyes warned that there was more to him than just a nice face, a negligent manner, and a clipped, fast, and often profane pattern of speech. His eyes were deep centered, patient, and alarmingly intense. That quality made her uneasy around him more than any other. Patrice called him a good man, a dependable man.

She saw him as a potentially dangerous one.

She started to bring her cup of coffee up for a drink when the smell reached her. Ordinarily, she enjoyed the rich scent of beans and chicory, but this morning something about the odor seemed bitter enough to make her stomach roil in protest. She set it away in a hurry and swallowed hard to keep the creep of acid from coming up the back of her throat.

Before, she'd felt chilled. Now, the room was unbearably warm. Sweat popped out along her brow as the unsettled feeling continued to grow. She blinked hard against the sudden sense of lightness that had everything blurring out of focus. Perhaps she needed to eat.

But one glance at Dodge's plate discouraged that thinking.

Then he tipped back in his chair and lit a cigar.

The instant the first curl of smoke brushed her nose, she went racing for the door.

She was hanging over the edge of the boardwalk, heaving ignominiously into the alley with the hope that it wouldn't take long for her to die, when she heard him lower himself awkwardly to his knees beside her. At the first touch of his hand, she groaned in objection but was too weak to pull away.

"Easy, now." Something in the low croon of his voice conveyed a sense of comfort, as did the wet cloth he pressed to the back of her neck, then to her fevered brow.

Beyond shame, she leaned into him, letting him cool her face and even open the first few buttons to her bodice without protesting. Instead, she heard herself mumbling apologies.

"I'm sorry. I'm sorry. I don't know what—"

"Shhh. It's all right. Don't be embarrassed by something so natural. Five of my six sisters have gone through the same thing."

He was stroking the reviving cloth down her neck, right to the beginning swell of her breasts, without hesitation or modesty. Caught in an agitation of relief and outrage that he should take such liberties so casually, she almost missed his meaning, until he put it plainly.

"How far along are you?"

"How what?"

"When are you expecting the baby?"

She lifted her head, staring at him through the straggle of her hair. *Baby?* Another wave of nausea tore through her belly, leaving her spent and trembling. She'd suspected it. She'd feared to consider it openly, but in the back of her mind, the possibility had been there, a terrible consequence of her sins.

She was pregnant.

And this brash Northerner, who was by his own admission no gentleman, knew it, too.

Starla pushed up from her hands and knees to wobble to her feet. It took Dodge considerably longer to wedge his crutches under his arms and angle his unwilling legs into a position to support him. By then, Starla was breathing in hard, hurried snatches, her stare unnaturally bright with panic.

"I'm no such thing," she denied with a shrill vehemence. "You are mistaken, sir. It's something I ate, is all."

Dodge stared back at her, his gaze knowing and strangely apologetic. She knew he didn't believe her. So she leaned close to him, close enough for him to read the desperate sincerity in her glare.

"If you breathe one word of that slanderous lie, I'll have my brother come calling with six inches of steel that'll see you never spread such vile rumors again."

With that cold promise to seal his mouth shut, she whirled away and ran a zigzag path toward Pride's livery, where she'd have Reeve take her back to the safety of the Glade.

But how safe would she be, now that the past was coming back to haunt her with a merciless vengeance?

Chapter 5

Few things could have surprised and alarmed Starla more than to hear that Hamilton Dodge was waiting to see her.

Patrice relayed the information carefully. And though she hadn't said as much, Starla was certain Reeve had told her friend how rattled she'd been on the drive back from town. Reeve had asked no questions, but it was unlike Patrice not to. Starla sensed her friends were treading cautiously around her. While she was grateful for not having to explain, she had to wonder what conclusions they were drawing on their own.

Now the Yankee banker was here, requesting a moment of her time.

Patrice announced him the way she would a favored courting beau. That in itself was enough to goad Starla into anxious irritation. But knowing what he knew cast a different slant on his purpose. Whom had he told? What would it take to keep him silent? These questions defied the calm manner she tried to project. Patrice claimed the shrewd banker to be a good man. Starla knew only the contradiction of the words "good" and "man."

As she checked her color and the neckline of her gown for modesty, she scowled at her reflection in the glass. He'd seen her at her absolute worst. What was the point in preening? Unless a flirtatious smile could dissuade him from ruining her.

How much more would he demand than that?

True, the Yankee hadn't fallen easy prey to her charms, not like the majority of men she led by their libidos. He seemed singularly immune to her coquetry. That very difference made him dangerous, to her and to her secrets. If he couldn't be manipulated by a few simpering sighs, how could she bend him to her will?

She was searching frantically for that answer when she followed the scent of good cigar out onto the front veranda. In the late afternoon, the smell didn't have the same disastrous effect that it had that morning.

He was seated on one of the inviting wicker chaises cozied up into the shadow of the Glade's cool white brick, feet propped up on a low bench before him. His gaze jumped to her immediately but he made no attempt to rise.

But she felt averse to displaying her manners.

"What do you want?"

He blinked at her bluntness but refused to look put off.

"I came to make sure you were all right."

"How kind. I'm fine. Was there anything else?"

He gave a lopsided grin and an admiring "Damned if you're not the most aggravating female. Come sit with me for a minute. I don't like looking up at the people I'm talking to.''

She didn't move. "I don't want to sit with you, Lieutenant Dodge. I don't want to talk to you. I want to know what you plan to do about this morning."

"It's not me that has to do anything, ma'am. Guess I was kinda curious about your plans.''

His calm hedging undercut her patience. "You don't figure into them, sir. What's it going to cost me to see it stays that way?"

Dodge stared up with a comical blankness for a long minute. She could almost believe he had no idea what she was talking about. She hated that mock innocence almost as much as she hated the fact that she was at his mercy.

"Don't just sit there like a dolt. Tell me what you want to keep your mouth shut.''

If she'd thought him amiable and harmless before, the sudden flash of his eyes gave her warning. The volume of his voice didn't alter, but its tone took on a fierce intensity.

"Sit down.''

She glared. "I don't think—"

"Sit down now.''

That order vibrated with the power of command. She wouldn't have thought him capable of packing such an authoritative punch with simple intonation. She felt intimidated enough to drop down on the bench beside his booted feet but retained the mulish dignity to sit stiff and straight in rebellion.

He drew a slow breath. It fired the spark in his eyes like the pull of the bellows fueled a flame.

Still, he didn't raise his voice, continuing to speak with that level chill.

"I don't know what I might have done to make you think I'd come here to blackmail you, but you're wrong, lady. Dead wrong. You don't know me, so I guess I'll have to forgive you."

"How generous."

"You're damn right it is. You don't know me, so I'll tell you this once. I don't lie, I'm not dishonest, and I don't play games. Now, I'm sorry if that makes me—what did you call me? A dolt? That makes me a dolt in your opinion, but I can live with that a lot better than I can you thinking I'm the kind of man who'd bank on your misfortune. I don't want anything from you, Miss Fairfax. I was trying to be nice because you're a friend of the only friends I have down here. Maybe you just don't understand 'nice.' Forgive me all to hell for having bothered."

He made a grab for his crutches, but they slid away from his grasp to bounce on the stone of the veranda floor. When he twisted to retrieve them, his feet slipped off the bench. The abrupt drop bent his back at a sudden angle, wringing a sharp hiss from him. He continued to flail for the crutches, breathing hard and furiously at the effort until Starla pressed a hand to his shoulder. He glanced up, clearly angry now, only to lose all momentum at her quiet claim of, "I'm sorry."

He jerked back, wincing from the pain of that prideful move. "Don't you dare feel sorry for me."

"I'm not—I don't. I'm sorry I mistook your motives. You're right, I don't understand nice. It makes me uncomfortable when someone does something and expects nothing. That's why I'm sorry.''

"Oh." He settled back, slightly chagrined by his temper.

Rattled by her admission, she demanded, "Well, are you going to accept my apology or not?"

He studied her until she shifted nervously. It shouldn't matter if he did or did not. But he had been kind to her and she repaid him with slanderous suggestion and hurt him in the bargain. She almost wished he had some hidden agenda. At least she'd know how to respond to that.

"Well?"

He smiled at the testiness in her voice. "Apology accepted."

She bent to reposition his crutches within his reach, but he made no move toward them. He watched her instead, his dark eyes brimming with unspoken questions. Inexplicably she found herself needing to answer them, for him and for herself.

"I behaved badly this morning," she began. "I didn't know—I mean, I wasn't sure until you said—"

Restlessly she stood and began to pace under his silent attentiveness, unable to meet his gaze while speaking of the embarrassing particulars.

"He said he wanted to marry me." She laughed softly. "How many foolish females fall prey to that lie, I wonder? I believed him and now I shall pay for that foolishness."

He spoke with practicality, not condemnation.

"If you told him about the baby, wouldn't he change his mind?"

"I doubt it. And even if he did, I wouldn't have him." Her chin lifted with a pride dredged up from shame. "I wouldn't want a man I'd have to trap through my mistake—a mistake my child would have to pay for. Marriage isn't the answer for everything." She canted a look his way to see if he believed her careful fiction only to be surprised by the naked emotion his expression betrayed.

"What kind of man would see his own child as a mistake?" He said that more to himself than to her, but Starla answered with a bitter smile of truth.

"Not a 'nice' man, Lieutenant Dodge. I discovered that a bit too late. If I tell my father, he'd likely insist I marry the man for honor's sake."

"And if you refused?"

"If I refused, he'd most likely commit me."

Dodge had the oddest look on his face, as if he couldn't believe a man would turn against his own daughter. She laughed at his naïveté. "We don't like to live with our mistakes out in the open down here. At least, the women don't. I can hear my father now, ranting about how I've proved him right, that I'm as immoral as my—" She pressed her hand to her lips to stop the words in time. "Forgive me, Lieutenant. I hadn't meant to bore you with quite so many details."

"What will you do?"

His basic question cut to the quick. Her shoulders slumped with the weight of her sigh.

"I don't know. I could go abroad. I could ask around in some of the more unsavory quarters. I'm sure I could find someone who could . . . eliminate the problem altogether.'' Her voice shook at even considering that heinous possibility.

''Don't do that.''

His vehemence surprised her. Then it made her angry to think he'd condemn her. How easy for him, a man, to sit in judgment. ''I haven't that many options, sir.''

''You could marry me.''

Starla turned. She'd misunderstood him.

''What?''

''I said you could marry me.''

A smile quivered on her lips. ''That would be carrying 'nice' a bit far, don't you think?''

''I'm serious.''

He looked it, his dark eyes steady in their hold on hers, his features composed in somber lines. She wasn't sure if the sight relieved or alarmed her. A bitter laugh escaped.

''You said you weren't one for games, sir, yet you play them quite cruelly.''

''It's no game.''

''You'd marry me?''

''Yes.''

For a moment she was too stunned to speak, then the words poured out in a quavering rush. ''Why? Why would you do such a thing? Because you feel sorry for me? Well, I won't tolerate your pity, either.''

''My reasons aren't quite that unselfish.''

She waited to hear them, thinking herself mad for even listening, for even considering. . . .

''I don't know anyone here. I'm going crazy

with just my own company. I didn't know how bad things were until the wedding. Now I know what I want. I want what Reeve and Patrice have.''

''But I don't love you. I don't even know you.''

He shrugged off her protest. ''But you could like me, couldn't you? Or at least put up with me?''

She went rigid by slow increments. Her tone was frosty. ''Just because I made a mistake with one man doesn't mean I'm willing to jump into bed with another.''

He actually blushed and she found that so surprisingly honest, she began to entertain seriously the preposterous notion.

''I'm not asking you to jump into anything, ma'am.'' His face was red but the uncomfortable cant of his eyes said he didn't find the idea totally abhorrent. ''I'm a banker, not a poet. I'm thinking more a business merger than a . . . a—''

''An intimate arrangement?''

He nodded, gratefully. ''Exactly. We're strangers, that's true, but we each want things the other can supply. I'm suggesting a trade-off. I'll save your reputation. I'll give you my name and raise your baby as my own.''

''And what do you get?'' She couldn't help the suspicion edging into that question.

''I get someone waiting for me when I finish at work. I get a meal on the table, someone to ask how my day was, clean clothes. I'm so sick of washing out my own socks.''

''You want me to take care of you?''

A fierce defensiveness gripped his features. ''I'm

not an invalid. I can take care of myself. I don't need a nursemaid.''

''I didn't mean—what I meant was, do you want me to be your servant?''

He relaxed and waved off her flat assumption. ''No. No, that's not what I want. I want—ah, hell, I want someone to keep me from being so lonely I want to scream. I want a family. I want that baby.''

His fervor alarmed her. He was so sure, so enthusiastic, it scared her. But she was thinking about it. Thinking hard and fast, and seeing her susceptibility, Dodge hurried on.

''You need security and I need companionship. Most marriages aren't made on more than that, are they?''

It was starting to sound so good when the whole meaning of the word ''marriage'' sank in. As she'd told him, she knew marriage wasn't the solution to every problem. It sometimes created more problems than it solved. Starla would allow him no illusions.

''I won't sleep with you.''

He was too startled by her candor to respond at first, then he answered gruffly. ''I wouldn't expect you to. I enjoy my privacy, too. Separate beds, separate rooms. I have no problem with that. Once we get to know each other a whole helluva lot better, we can discuss the arrangements again, but for now, you can trust me—like a brother. I've had plenty of practice there.''

Could she? Could she trust him? It all came down to that. Trust was something she guarded as zealously as love. Neither had ever applied to more than a few people. She loved her brother but didn't trust him. She'd trusted the man who'd left her with his illegitimate legacy, but she hadn't loved him. She trusted Patrice, and Patrice said she could trust this man who was offering her a much needed salvation.

Or was she making another huge mistake?

Sensing her lingering hesitation, Dodge made a final petition, his words simple, his tone level, his manner completely open.

"It's like this, Miss Fairfax, I come from a big family. I'm not used to taking a step without falling over someone. I don't want to be alone anymore, especially not here, where I couldn't drag a smile out of someone with a team of horses."

"Then why stay?"

It was a simple question, but he approached it like it held the complexity of the universe.

"I can do good here. What started out as a favor to a friend has become personal. I love a good challenge and I don't accept failure, Miss Fairfax. Not in anything I put my mind to. I'll be a good husband to you and a good father to that baby. I'll respect you, I won't hurt you, and I'll never lie to you. If you can do the same, I think we'll have a pretty good shot. What do you say?"

He put out his hand. She ignored it to ask one more thing.

"Why would you want me for a wife? Because of the challenge?"

He grinned at her brittle tone and summed it up briefly. "You make me feel alive."

He kept his hand suspended, the smile lingering on his face with a confidence she couldn't quite share.

But she couldn't argue with his logic, nor could she deny that what he offered was far better than any of the alternatives.

She took his hand gingerly. His fingers closed about hers in a careful press, but even so, she was quick to pull away.

"I think you should start calling me Starla rather than Miss Fairfax. What do I call you?"

"Call me Dodge. Tomorrow you can call me husband."

"You're what?"

Patrice had none of Reeve's trouble accepting the incredible news. With a squeal of "That's wonderful!" she threw her arms around first Starla then Dodge while beaming in self-congratulation.

"Are you both insane?" Reeve demanded. "You don't even know each other! When did this happen?"

"Just now." Dodge's hand curled protectively over Starla's, containing it for a show of support, and also to hide how his own were shaking.

"Tell me it's going to be a long, long engagement."

To his friend's dismay, Dodge said, "Tomorrow."

Reeve threw up his hands and stalked across the room, muttering, "Are you sure you weren't shot in the head instead of the back?"

Patrice scowled at her husband, then went on to

take full credit for the match. "I knew you two would be right for one another. Didn't I tell you, Dodge? Didn't I tell you she'd be worth holding on for?"

He smiled. "Yes, you did."

Obviously she had no trouble accepting their announcement as fated, but Dodge could see Reeve wasn't going to be as easy to convince. Starla stood at his side, her hand still and cold within his, her face void of expression. No help there in convincing his friend that she'd fallen blindly in love.

"We'd like to do it here," he went on hopefully, "with the two of you as our witnesses."

Reeve narrowed a stare at him. "What's the hurry?"

"She's pregnant."

He heard Starla's gasp and tightened his grip on her hand. Both Reeve and Patrice were looking between them in unabashed shock.

"Who's—" was all Patrice could manage.

"Mine." He spoke the word so firmly and forcefully that to question further would be calling him a liar. Neither challenged him, though both knew he wasn't the father. Starla's fingers squeezed through his as she held up her head and stared at the other couple boldly. It didn't take any more explaining for them to understand what was behind the sudden decision.

"Dodge, have you thought this out?" Reeve asked at last.

"If you don't want us to get married here, just say so," he growled, bristling up with unexpected belligerence.

"That's not what I said."

"Then just what the hell *are* you saying?"

Reeve glanced at Starla in awkward apology. "Excuse us a minute, Starla. The best man needs a word with the groom."

When he gripped Dodge's arm, the banker balked, but when Reeve wouldn't relent, Dodge finally went with him, following him down the hall to Squire Glendower's study, where Reeve poured them both glasses of whiskey. Reeve gulped his down before speaking.

"What the hell are you doing?"

"Getting married."

"To a woman you don't know? Who doesn't even like you?"

Dodge gave a wry smile. "I'll grow on her."

"I'm glad you think this is so damned amusing."

"I don't." He faced his friend with a deadly seriousness. "I know exactly what I'm doing. I'm doing her a favor and she's doing one for me."

"Taking marriage vows isn't the same as trading favors, Dodge."

"Don't you think I know that?"

"I don't think you're thinking at all. Starla Fairfax isn't the kind of woman—"

Dodge glared at him. "Starla isn't what? The kind you marry? Is that what you were going to say?"

Reeve sighed in exasperation. "I've known her all my life. There isn't a man alive she hasn't made eyes at. She's always had a reputation as a tease, and now she shows up pregnant after being gone for four years—do you know whose baby it is?''

''It doesn't matter,'' he gritted out.

Reeve stared at him. ''You're going to toss away the chance of finding the right woman just to give a name to a baby a woman you don't know made with a man she won't name?''

''That's about it.''

''You're crazy.''

Dodge jerked him up by the shirtfront. The movement was fierce and demonstrative, startling Reeve with a sudden hugeness of presence from the smaller man, the same powerful authority that allowed the unpretentious lieutenant to command an army into hell without question. ''What I know is that this may be my only chance to raise a child as my own, and damn it, you're not taking that away from me. You owe me this, Reeve.''

Reeve blinked in sudden understanding as Dodge let him go, acting apologetic but no less obstinate.

''I need something to hold me here,'' Dodge went on in a low, almost angry tone. ''I can't go home. They'd treat me like—'' He broke off to rethink his words, then continued in earnest. ''I want a family to tie me here in Pride. I don't know that I'll ever be able to—that I'll ever have children of my own, and now I've got this chance to help out a friend of yours, a woman who can give me the family I need, and the reason to drag myself up in the morning. Don't you dare tell me I can't make this work. I will. For that baby, if for nothing else. Damn it, if that isn't reason enough—''

Reeve put a hand on his shoulder. ''It's reason enough.''

Dodge expelled his breath noisily, and his hostility with it. He clasped his hand over Reeve's for a brief instant, then Reeve walked back to the sideboard, where he spoke without turning.

"Have you thought about the other two people involved in this grand gesture?"

"You and Patrice?"

"No. You and Starla. I don't want to see either of you get hurt in this."

His friend's sincerity warmed him to his soul. Dodge smiled with grim determination. "It's worth the risk to me. It's a business arrangement, Reeve. I make them all the time and nobody's better at it than I am. Nobody gets cheated. We'll be fine . . . as long as we can keep from killing each other."

"All right. I guess if any one can make Starla behave, you can."

Not exactly confidence-inspiring words to a groom-to-be.

Exactly twenty-four hours later, Hamilton Dodge brought the same judge who'd married Patrice and Reeve to the door of the Glade. He didn't draw a deep breath until he saw Starla there waiting, still of the same mind. He'd worried that perhaps—

Then he saw her standing by the stairs in a demure gown of ivory silk, her glossy black hair swept back beneath a crown of lace and pearls, and his emotions staggered. It wouldn't have taken much for him to convince himself that he was in love with this glorious creature who'd consented to be his wife.

But of course, he wasn't. He was merely

stunned, as any man with eyes would be, by her exotic beauty. On closer examination, he could see how pale she was, how her vivaciousness was tempered to the vaguest of smiles when she saw him. Regrets? Or just wishing there were some other way than having to say vows with a perfect stranger? His mood sobered. This was no love match, so it wasn't smart to consider it as anything but business.

They said their vows in the sunny front parlor, Patrice weeping freely on one side, Reeve grim as a sentinel on the other. Beside him Starla spoke the necessary words without inflection, then lifted her hand so he could slide on the ring his mother had given him to see him safely through four years of war. Let it see him through this marriage with equal indemnity.

As Reeve had predicted, the solemnity of the event didn't strike home until the judge intoned the words pronouncing them man and wife.

Man and wife.

His to have and hold.

An attack of nervous exhilaration took hold of him, rattling him with consequence and conviction. He'd just taken a woman for his wife and had given himself as husband. And that was about as far from a business merger as anything he could imagine.

Panic chilled through his belly. Anticipation slicked his palms. Slowly he turned to his wife of less than a minute as the judge invited him to kiss his bride.

His mouth went desert dry as he bent for his first taste of her kiss. At the last possible moment, she jerked her head to one side, just far enough for his mouth to find her cheek instead of settling upon her lips. It was more than a denial of intimacy on grounds of embarrassed modesty. When he put his other palm to her opposite cheek, he heard her sharp intake of breath and felt her go stiff as stone against him.

He finished the gesture quickly, grazing the soft curve as if it had been the intended target all along, then leaning back to accept Reeve and Patrice's congratulations.

But his smile was forced as he had to wonder if his bride's distaste was directed at him or if it was the manifestation of some deeper loathing.

Had he just made the biggest mistake of his life?

Chapter 6

"I need to tell my brother."

They'd just started along the quiet streets on the outskirts of Pride when Starla made that announcement. Though her voice was carefully modulated, Dodge caught a ragged edge of worry.

"All right. We'll tell him together."

Starla twisted on the buggy seat, her eyes going round and dark. "No!" Seeing she'd startled him with her vehemence, she managed a smile and placed a placating hand on his sleeve. "It would be better coming from just me. If I could drop you off and take the buggy. . . ."

His dark gaze flickered to the hand on his arm, then up to her smiling face. She could see his suspicion and quickly dropped the coquettishness in favor of candor.

"He's not going to like it and if you want to remain my husband for more than these past few hours, you'll stay out of arm's reach of Tyler for a while."

Dodge quirked a smile. "Guess I wouldn't be his ideal brother-in-law at that."

He reined up the buggy in front of a small two-story frame house. The fenced-in front yard and side garden were slightly overrun with weeds, but the clapboards and trim were in good repair. She glanced from its tightly closed curtains to the man beside her.

"Who lives here?"

"We do."

He was watching her face, waiting for a sign of her disapproval or acceptance. She simply nodded, eager to get to the task ahead of her.

"I'll be back soon. Do you need help getting down?"

It was a reasonable question, but his reaction held no logic at all. Like a badger protecting its den, he went into a full aggressive bristle.

"I don't need help."

To prove it, he snatched up the crutches from between them, planted them on the ground, and swung down from the high seat. After a precarious moment, he found his balance and said with more than just a little arrogance, "I told you, I can take care of myself."

More incensed by his harsh tone than impressed by his independence, Starla took up the reins. "So you did. I won't forget again." And with a snap, she left him standing in her dust.

Fair Play.

Starla grimaced at the misnomer. Cole Fairfax had never been honest in any of his dealings that she was aware of. He'd risen from seedy moon-shiner, dumping cane sugar into corn mash, to be-

come one of the finest distillers of bourbon in
Kentucky, and he hadn't done so by making many
friends. He was ruthless in business and even more
so in his personal life. She and Tyler had grown
up in lenient luxury, but that freedom hadn't come
without cost. For the last four years, her brother
had been paying it for her. Now was the time for
her to get out from under the debt altogether.

She knew it wasn't going to be easy stepping
through that front door again. But her anxious im-
aginings didn't contain the gut-level terror that
came over the threshold with her. Or the smack of
fermenting vapors and lingering death that nearly
sent her reeling back in nausea.

''Miss Starla?''

The whisper of disbelief from Matilda, her
mother's onetime maid, was followed by a cushiony embrace and a flood of memories linking her
to the only adult affection she could clearly remember.

''It's me, Tilly.'' Surprisingly, tears burned her
eyes. Matilda had raised her and her brother as best
she could while managing the running of their un-
conventional household. The black woman had
reared them with love, not discipline, but Starla
couldn't fault her, thinking it was the former more
than the latter that two wild children had needed.

''Whatchu' doing here, child? Whatchu' come
back for?'' The scolding tone held affection, but
more strongly it held fear, a reminder of where she
was.

''I need to talk to Tyler.'' She kept her voice
low as her gaze slid anxiously to the closed study

doors. Beyond them was her father's bastion. She'd always thought of those doors as the gates to purgatory. "Is he home, Tilly?"

"You wait right here, child. I'll go get him for you. You wait right here."

She stood in the large foyer, her arms wrapped tight about her as if she could shield away all the awful ghosts still haunting the home of her birth. They rose up all around her, their wailing laments demanding she acknowledge what she'd tried to push away for so long. She closed her eyes, refusing to be drawn back by either memory or circumstance.

"Star? Darlin', what the hell are you doin' here?"

She looked up to see her brother on the stairs, and her heart broke at the evidence of his dissipation. It wasn't even six o'clock and he was already knee-wobbling drunk. His clothing reeked of whiskey and wear, and the only thing more unkempt was his appearance. The females who'd once flocked around her to ooh and ah over her brother's sharp Creole beauty and lethal grace, begging her for an introduction, would have turned away in distaste now. There was nothing attractive about negligent abuse of self and surroundings. Tyler was guilty of both.

"Tyler, I need to talk to you."

He cast a red-rimmed glance at the study doors, then came haltingly down the stairs. His smile unfurled loosely.

"I knew you couldn't stay mad at me."

He'd almost reached the bottom when his knees

buckled and he met the steps with a hard jolt. Instead of trying to lift himself up again, he sprawled back easily, leaning on his elbows as if it had been his intention to recline there all along. Starla bunched her skirts and lowered herself beside him.

"You shouldn't ought to be here, darlin', but it's good to see you." His rheumy gaze roamed her face with a needy fondness, making her task all the harder.

"Tyler, there's something I have to tell you."

He lay back against the slant of the steps, closing his eyes, going bonelessly liquid in body the way only a drunken man can. "What's on your mind, Star? Not here to reform me, are you?"

She hesitated. "Maybe this isn't the best time—"

His unfocused eyes blinked open. "No time like the present, as Daddy's so fond of saying." A bitter curl warped his lips.

"I'm married, Tyler."

The words hit him like a dash of spring water. The shock had him gasping.

"What? When?"

"About an hour ago."

Tyler struggled to catch his breath. "Married? To whom?"

"Lieutenant Dodge."

He shook his head, trying to make sense of her words. "The banker? That Yankee?" His brows lowered then he grinned. "Don't go funning with me, darlin'. You did no such thing." Then he stared at the ring on the hand she extended. Slowly the mirthful expression drained from his face, leaving a blankness that shone dully in the eyes he lifted to meet hers. "You tell me you didn't. You tell me, now."

"Reeve and Patrice were our witnesses."

Tyler drew a strangled breath and pushed off the stairs, stumbling, nearly falling down those remaining, to pace the floor in tight, uncoordinated circles. "You married a Yank. A banker. A stranger! What the hell are you thinkin', girl?" He staggered to a stop, staring at her narrowly. "What did he do? Did he do somethin'—?"

"No. It was my choice."

His features crumpled into a twist of incredulous surprise.

"Why? How could you do such a thing?" Then his gaze flashed like the sudden baring of a stiletto blade he carried. "You'll be a widow again before nightfall."

She surged up to grasp his forearms, only to have him jump back with a vehement flailing of his arms. She pitched her petition low and passionately.

"Tyler, listen to me. Listen! Don't you see? It's the only way I could stay here in Pride and still be free of this house . . . of him." She nodded toward the double doors. "I'm a married woman. He can never make me come back."

Tyler laughed, a hoarse, horrible sound totally without humor. "You crazy? You think he'll care if you got yourself some Yankee husband? The only way you'll be safe is if you put half a country between you and here."

She stood her ground stubbornly. "I won't run

again. I've done nothing wrong. And I'm tired of being punished. This is my home. My friends are here.''

"Friends? How many a those friends you think you're gonna keep when they find out who you picked to marry?''

She set her jaw and glared at him.

"You just made yourself as big an outsider as he is.''

"He's a good man." She repeated Patrice's claim staunchly. Then her confidence ebbed as she added the familiar conclusion. "And he was the only one who asked.''

"Everything's changed now, Star. Everything.'' The snag in his voice clued her to his biggest concern.

She spoke gently, firmly. "Not between us.''

Tyler laughed, his bitterness laced with anguish. "Really? Do you think your Yankee banker husband is gonna invite me to sit down at your dinner table anytime soon? He tell you how he got that bullet in his back?''

"I thought during the war." A terrible insight pierced through her as she whispered, "You shot him?''

Tyler waved impatiently. "No, but I was there and that makes me as responsible as him that did.''

"Starla?''

The faltering cry coming from within the closed study set both brother and sister back in startled alarm. Tyler grabbed Starla's arm, shoving her toward the outer door.

"You get clear of here," he told her tersely.

"Get out, now, and don't you be coming back."

"Tyler—"

"You stay close to that Yank husband and maybe he can protect you."

"Starla!"

Tyler yanked open the front door and pushed her out onto the porch, where the air was fresh with the taste of freedom. "Go on, now. Get."

Impulsively she threw her arms around his neck, hugging hard until he relented long enough to return the embrace. She felt his quick kiss against her hair before he stepped back and closed the door firmly between them.

Tyler leaned back against it for a timeless minute, his eyes closed tight until a clattering from within the study drew his attention. With a fierce expression chiseling his features, he crossed the foyer and opened the double doors.

Cole Fairfax was half out of the chair where he spent his days and nights. He'd knocked over the table next to it to make the racket that had brought Tyler in. He glared up at his son as he struggled to sit back beneath the heavy bundle of quilts. Tyler made no move to assist him.

"Where is she?"

A room away, Tyler regarded him dispassionately. "She's gone. She's outta your reach now."

"I know she's here in town—"

"She's got herself a husband."

"You lie!"

"No. It's the truth. You leave her alone, old man. You leave her alone, or I'll be outta here myself. *Then* what would you do, with no one here to run your precious business?''

Fairfax squinted at his heir, a snide smile on his face. ''You wouldn't give it up. You like the easy life as much as you like the free liquor.''

''Try me, old man. You let Starla alone, and I'll stay here and see to things like I been doing. But you go bothering her, and I'll see this old mausoleum crumbles down on your head, whether you're ready to meet your maker or not.''

From his vantage point on the porch, Dodge watched his new bride angle the buggy up next to the house. He looked for signs of upset in the way she handled the reins, in the way she climbed down and crossed the untended lawn, but outwardly she was as cool as the late-day breeze was warm. Because he considered her dealings with her family personal business, he couldn't ask how things had gone with her brother. So he made himself smile as she stepped up onto the whitewashed boards. He levered up on his crutches and pushed open the front door. ''Home sweet home. After you, Mrs. Dodge.''

She looked startled at the title, then was stoic once more as she swept inside the modest house. She paused to take in the dust-covered furniture in the parlor.

''Have you lived here long?''

''Since I signed the papers this morning. I couldn't very well expect you to live on a cot in the back room of the bank. The folks who owned this place got called back East a month ago and left it to the bank. It's not what you're used to, but it was all I could come up with on such short notice.''

Her quiet ''It's fine'' gave away no clue to her true thoughts.

It was then, as they stood there in the entry hall surrounded by dust sheets and awkwardness, that he realized his mistake. Some welcome this was. He should have had someone come over to open the place up, to shake out the air of emptiness. He should have had flowers waiting. What a dismal greeting—someone else's abandoned home with a stranger for a husband. He should have been thinking of her comfort, but his mind still worked in a bachelor mode, with considerations only for himself and what little he needed to get by. That would have to change.

If she was disappointed, she didn't show it.

''You can do anything you like with the place,'' Dodge told her, hoping to win a little enthusiasm. ''Buy whatever you want so it suits you.'' Then, because maybe she didn't know it, he added, ''I have money. I can afford it.''

''So can I, Lieutenant.''

She moved into the parlor and began stripping off the sheets. The dust cloaked her in a fine aura against the lamplight. His wife. Their house. His palms grew damp against the smooth wood supporting his weight.

Their wedding night.

Starla uncovered a number of fine pieces: chairs, a sofa, occasional tables. She continued through the room, investigating its contents not out of any degree of possessive interest but rather from nervousness.

He blundered on, eager to soothe her worries.

"There are three bedrooms upstairs. You can take any you like. The one in front is attached to a smaller one. I thought that might make a good nursery. But it's up to you. I've got my things in the room down here in back. I'm not quite up to stairs yet."

Apparently, it was something other than the sleeping arrangement bothering her.

"How did you get injured?"

The question caught him off guard. He smiled crookedly. "By not minding my own business."

"Patrice said they owed you their lives. What did she mean by that?"

"She was exaggerating."

"You said you'd always be honest with me."

How could he skate around that blatant trap? He sighed.

"I helped them fend off a bunch of night riders planning to torch the Glade. When Reeve came back, there was a lot of talk that he'd had something to do with his half-brother's death. It got a lot of folks excited and thinking of mischief. I got shot."

He left out the rest: that Reeve had almost been hanged, that Patrice had nearly perished trying to save the Glade's breeding stock from the flaming stables. That he'd been paralyzed and had nearly ended his own life in his despair. But Patrice had kept him hanging on, teasing him with an enticing

image: that of her outrageously beautiful friend.
Starla Fairfax.

And there was one more fact he'd hope not to
have to share, except she already seemed to know
it.

"Why didn't you tell me my brother was involved?" There was no mistaking the edge to that
demand. Dodge responded to it casually.

"I didn't see the need."

"You stand there on those crutches, married to
his sister, and you say you don't see the need?"

"I didn't take it personally. It's not like he came
up behind me on the street and decided to blow my
spine in half."

Starla winced at that, then stated emphatically,
"I love my brother."

"I'm not asking you to change that on my account."

Despite his calming words, she regarded him
suspiciously. Her warning couldn't have been
clearer when she said, "I won't let you come between us."

"As long as you don't figure you need to shoot
me yourself to finish the job, that's fair enough."

He could see she didn't believe him.

"What's between you and me has nothing to do
with your brother, Starla. Men do crazy things
when they're riding in a mob. He's your family,
and there's nothing stronger than family."

He paused, but she had nothing else to say. He
knew of no other way to convince her.

"Why don't you go on up and settle in while I

take care of the horse? We can talk about this to-morrow, if you want to.''

When she continued to study him in silence, he read dismissal in what she didn't say. Philosophically, he turned toward the door, pivoting on the tips of his crutches when he heard the rustle of her skirts behind him.

She stopped at his shoulder, her palm touching one side of his face as she stretched up to brush a brief kiss upon the other.

''Thank you, Dodge,'' she whispered as softly as that kiss, then she was gone before he could react.

He stood in the hall, his mind spinning, his heart careening madly, his fingertips against the damp impression she'd left behind. After a moment, he drew a rattly breath and exhaled it noisily.

Reeve was right. He was crazy. What had he been thinking, to believe he could keep house with a woman like Starla Fairfax—Starla Dodge—and not get wound up in false hopes and heartache?

Things just might work out all right.

Starla curled up on the surprisingly comfortable bed and let her eyes close, locking out the sense of desperation that had nagged her thoughts night and day.

Hamilton Dodge. What a strange man. Practical and proper in one regard, yet surprisingly unpredictable the next. He'd promised she had nothing to fear from him, and she wanted to believe him. Several times she'd caught the too familiar flare of desire simmering in his dark stare. She'd been gar-

nering those looks since she was nine years old.
But instead of acting on those feelings, he kept
them checked behind his nonthreatening smile.
Trying to lull her suspicions, or genuinely trying to
make her feel at ease?

He'd given her his name, this house, the run of
his accounts, almost as if she were his wife in truth
instead of just on paper. So far he'd demanded
nothing in return. Maybe he wouldn't, maybe he
would, but she couldn't afford to let down her
guard.

Marriage wasn't always a sanctuary. It could be
its own kind of trap. The law of man bound her to
the Northern stranger, but what law would bind
him to his promises?

She heard the door open and shut downstairs and
the halting shuffle of movement as her new husband neared the steps. Despite his promises, she
held her breath suspended, listening, alerted to the
first hint of sound that said he was attempting the
stairs. Her heart began a mad beating. Their wedding night. She squeezed her eyes shut against
memories of discomfort and degradation. Of harsh
breath scorching her face and shame abrading her
body.

Please keep your promises.

Then she heard him move on, the sound growing
muffled as the distance increased. She sagged upon
the mattress in trembly relief.

I want to trust you, Lieutenant Dodge.

She closed her eyes again, picturing his pleasant
face, his dark, intelligent stare. Remembering the
firm pressure of his hand engulfing hers as they'd

confronted Patrice and Reeve with their intention of marrying. And the uneasy yearning that had come with the feel of his ring circling her finger.

I need to trust someone.

Chapter 7

"Now, *this* is a sight I never guessed I'd see."

Starla turned, using a flour-dusted hand to push a lock of wayward hair from her eyes. She had no smile of greeting for her best friend. She was too hot, too frustrated.

"Laugh all you like, Patrice Sin—Garrett. I never thought anyone would ever want to marry me for my domestic skills."

Patrice came through the back door into the small, sweltering kitchen. "I didn't know you had any."

"I don't," Starla grumbled, smashing the dough she'd been mercilessly kneading down on the floured board. She scowled as the powder puffed up and settled like locomotive ash all over the floor. "I'd be a gracious hostess and offer you a libation, but I don't believe I have anything here."

Patrice seemed unconcerned. "Where's Dodge?"

"At the bank, I gather. He was gone when I woke up."

"And he left you with instructions to bake bread?"

"No, not exactly. But he did say he wanted someone to keep his house and wash his shirts." Starla shuddered expressively. "Laundry. 'Trice, I've never touched a soiled garment in my entire life except to drop it on the floor for someone else to take care of."

Patrice smiled, not with the hoped for sympathy, but with a sad understanding. "Times have changed for us, haven't they? How naive we once were, dreaming of having the whole county at our feet."

"You do, Patrice. You have it all. The Glade, the man you love, a future." Starla broke off and went back to the vicious manipulation of her dough. "I suppose you think that's strange talk coming from a new bride and mother-to-be."

Patrice slipped her hands over her friend's, stilling their frantic motion. Starla didn't look up right away, and when she did, her eyes were swimming with unshed tears. Her jaw was gripped against any further self-pitying words.

"I fought against a whole way of life to get what I have now," Patrice began. "I made choices that broke my heart and betrayed those I loved. But I don't regret any of it. And I no longer cry over what used to be. I make do with what I have."

Starla withdrew her hands and wiped them on her skirt, leaving great white splotches. "You think I'm silly and spoiled." A statement, not an accusation.

"No. I know you too well ever to think that. But

I *will* think badly of you if you don't take a good look at what you have now and appreciate how lucky you are.''

She meant Dodge, of course. Starla wondered a bit jealously how the brash lieutenant had managed to win over her friend so quickly and completely. Probably the same way he'd gotten her to disregard her better judgment in taking him at his word. Because there was something innately honest about her banker husband, making her want to believe. A weakness that rubbed against her grain of sensibility. ''Would I be trying to make bread if I didn't appreciate him?''

''Appreciate him, or poison him?'' Patrice examined the dry lump of dough and chuckled. ''I fear this would be better suited as a fire brick.''

Starla threw up her floury hands, frustration cresting on a wave of inadequacy. ''I have no talent for this charade. I've never cooked or cleaned or cared for another. I fear your friend has made a terrible bargain in taking me as a wife.''

Patrice embraced her anguished companion. ''Oh, I don't think so.''

''He'll be so disappointed . . . not that I care, mind you.'' Her tone toughened in her defense. ''I didn't promise him that he'd have an angel in the kitchen.''

''Dodge is a smart man. I'm sure he knew what he was getting.''

Starla made a doubtful noise and stepped back. She picked up the disastrous effort at baking and tossed it out. ''If he was so smart, he'd have never given me another glance. He doesn't know anything about me.''

''He'll learn.''

Starla grew suddenly somber. ''What if he doesn't like what he discovers?''

''Don't underestimate him, Starla. I have a feeling your husband can handle just about anything.''

Except the truth. Starla turned away to hide her apprehension.

''You can trust him, Starla.''

Again, that unfaltering confidence. Starla wished she could share it. But then, Patrice didn't know everything there was to know, either. If she did, she wouldn't make such a claim.

If she did, she might not have even come to see her.

She gave a slight start when Patrice touched her elbow to offer a piece of advice.

''Give it time, and give him a chance. I know you'll both be good for each other.''

Starla said nothing. What good could she be to him? A woman carrying another man's child. A woman filled with secrets too awful to expose. A woman with no skills beyond the ability to be a selfish, cunning survivor. *Just like your mother.* Her lips trembled, then firmed.

If those were her skills, then she would draw upon them. She would make this a home for herself and her child and for the man who'd provided it for them. She would do whatever was necessary to secure her place in this house, because in doing so, she would be safe. And because she wouldn't make the same mistakes again, she would do it with her eyes wide open. She wouldn't be blinded by trust.

She shook the flour from her skirt and smiled ruefully at her misguided efforts. She wasn't making the most of the skills she had. She was a hostess, not a housemaid, and she wouldn't confuse the two again.

"You must excuse me, Patrice. I have to clean up this mess and get my house in order. I refuse to give my husband a reason to be disappointed in his choice."

"He won't be, Star. And you won't be, either."

Starla took a determined breath. "He and I will become friends. I just have to get used to that abrasive voice."

"Friends is a good start, but Starla, he's going to want more than that eventually."

She looked at her friend through eyes opaque as rough gems and said with a flat chill, "That's all I can give him."

Dodge looked up from his paperwork and stared, momentarily stunned speechless by the sight of his new bride standing at the doorway of the bank.

Though he hadn't seen her before he'd left for work, she'd never been out of his thoughts. Which was why he was going over his misfigured accounts one more time. Just the memory of her flitting through a corner of his mind had a way of distracting the whole of it into daydreams. Images of how she must look stretched out on the bed in the upstairs of their house. Of her all tousled and rumpled from sleep.

The fact that those musings tightened a knot in

his belly, but not below, created another, more so-
bering distraction.

But none of those fancies acted as strongly on
his system as the reality of her at his door, carrying
a large hamper that smelled suspiciously like lunch.

"Good morning."

She smiled at his warm welcome and came inside. "Good afternoon," she corrected. "I lost
track of time myself while baking bread. I thought
I'd bring you some lunch."

He stared at her, trying to equate this cool picture
of elegance with that of a woman standing at a hot
stove, not quite managing that miracle. He pushed
back his chair.

"I'm ready to take a break." He moved aside
all the tasks he hadn't been able to concentrate on
and focused on what preoccupied him.

She approached him with a confident poise that
was too studied to be true. She was nervous around
him. He could understand that, and it made her
gesture all the more significant. Under his bemused
gaze, she spread his dinner out before him as if
setting the table for an honored guest. Touched and
amazed, he murmured, "Did you do all this yourself?"

"You left so early this morning, I thought you'd
be hungry." She poured him lemonade, dished out
a piping hot stew over fresh bread, then stood back,
waiting for his reaction, the picture of a docile wife
eager and able to serve.

With one taste, he knew the truth.

Only one place he knew of had gravy so rich
and smooth. The meal hadn't come from his home

kitchen; it had been made at Sadie's. He'd taken three meals a day there for several months, often enough to recognize the fare. He glanced up at Starla, who hovered anxiously at his elbow.

"How is everything?"

He swallowed and gave her a neutral smile. "It's good."

She beamed with self-congratulation, as if the effort had been hers alone. But in fairness, she'd never said she had cooked the food, only that she was responsible for bringing it to him. He took another bite and chewed thoughtfully. Should whose kitchen it had been matter more than the gesture itself?

"I appreciate you thinking of me," he said, without looking up. "I wasn't expecting this."

"Then I surprised you. Good. I've heard a good marriage is made on surprises."

He studied her features, unmoved by her flirtatious manner. "A good marriage is made on lots of things. Any in particular you'd care to discuss?"

She blushed prettily, but beneath that coquettish shock was a deeper alarm. She forced a smile. "I've no great experience in marriages, good or bad. You'll have to enlighten me. I'm sure you're a font of knowledge."

Her tone prickled with impertinence, but it was a way to divert him from her original statement. He was already beginning to recognize her tactics. What kind of family had she grown up in? He didn't know anything about them, other than that Starla didn't want to visit her home, and her brother was a dangerous piece of business. Time to do a little reconnoitering. He was a fair tactician himself.

"I know your father owns the distillery, but I've never heard anything about your mother."

Starla fidgeted with the papers on his desk, compulsively straightening them into a flawlessly even stack. "I wouldn't know what to tell you. She's been gone since I was five and Tyler was nine."

That surprised him. "I'm sorry. I didn't know your mother had died."

She looked up, meeting his regretful stare without a blink. "I don't know if she has or hasn't. When I said gone, I meant left. I have no idea what happened to her or where she is."

He never expected to hear anything like that. He didn't know what to say to her, but he at least retained the presence of mind to shut his sagging jaw. Five years old. A baby. How could a woman—a mother!—abandon her children at such a tender age? He didn't ask, but she must have seen the question in his expression. He wasn't very good at hiding his thoughts.

Starla went on with a casual shrug. "My daddy was too busy building his business to pay us much mind, and we were pretty much left to our own devices with our maid, Tilly, to keep us from running wild. So you see, Lieutenant, what I know of family, I learned peeking through other folks' doors."

The want to express his shock and outrage nearly blocked out reason, but somehow he kept from doing the unforgivable and embarrassing her further. Instead, he waved a negligent hand. "I have enough family for both of us. I believe I mentioned my six older sisters, all but one married, supplying me with a crop of nieces and nephews. When we get together, you can't take a step without tripping over someone.''

He might have imagined her delicate shudder.

''Is your father a banker, too?'' She almost sounded interested. That was a start.

''No. He builds furniture. He was disappointed that I didn't choose to carry on the family business, and they'd about given up hope of me ever carrying on the family name.''

His words came out with a tang of bitterness as unplanned as it was unwise. He scrambled to recover from the blunder of pressing her to provide.

''They'll be thrilled to learn a new Dodge is on the way.''

Starla went alarmingly still. The hand that wore his ring pressed unbidden to her still flat middle. She spoke in a colorless monotone. ''But my child won't be a Dodge except in name.''

It was his turn to react with a defensive agitation. ''Well, that may be the best they're ever going to get.''

Starla wasn't sure how to interpret his sudden flash of temper. Was he angry because they were trying to foist an illegitimate baby off as his own? That hurt. She winced for both herself and her unborn child.

Then she considered his words more carefully, and the extent of his annoyance. He attacked his meal with the fierceness of one devouring an enemy.

She knew little of his injury beyond the fact that it had lamed him. Was the damage more severe than she'd been told? Did he fear or did he know for sure that he couldn't father any offspring of his own?

Was he too ashamed to admit to what most would consider a tragedy, but which to her would be seen as a blessed relief?

Was that why he'd been so eager to wed her by making such bold promises? *Like a brother* . . . was that all he could be?

She had no idea how to ask, and then no opportunity as a care-worn woman peered into the bank. Dodge immediately became all charming and businesslike.

"Afternoon, ma'am. Can I help you with something?"

The woman looked behind her furtively, then stepped inside. "My name is Wheeler."

Dodge cleared his desk of his remaining dinner, making no complaint about not finishing. "Mrs. Cameron Wheeler? You own that plot out by the river."

Encouraged that he knew who she was, Ella Wheeler came closer. Her anxiety rolled off her in palpable waves. "My Cam, he don't know I come here. But I gots to talk to you, Mr.—?"

"Dodge. Pleased to meet you, Mrs. Wheeler. This is my wife, Starla—"

"Fairfax?" Ella's eyes widened. But her troubles were obviously too great to take second place to speculation. "Mr. Dodge, I gots five little 'uns at home and the bank's about to take everything we own. I don't know what else we can do.''

A handkerchief was passed from banker to weeping woman.

''Mrs. Wheeler, please sit down.'' Dodge glanced at the file on his desk, then up at Starla. ''Mrs. Wheeler and I need to have a talk. Would you mind leaving us alone for a minute?''

Starla felt an instant of rebuff, then swooped down to gather the remnants of the meal she'd provided. Dodge continued as if she'd already gone.

''Mrs. Wheeler, you grow vegetables, am I right? Well, ma'am, I'm not much of a vegetable fancier. They're all right in stews and such, but I don't know what I'd do with acres of them. I'd have to pay someone to pick and sell them or take the time to plow the crops under and turn them to something I'd use. Ma'am, I just don't have time for such things right now. You'd be doing me a big favor by keeping your farm and working it so I don't have to deal with it.''

Ella Wheeler blinked swollen eyes at him, the first vestiges of hope beginning to glow there. ''But we can't pay the note and the taxes are coming due—''

Dodge smiled, the gesture radiating enough warmth to nurture the Wheelers' crops and the wan woman's dreams. ''What if the bank was to extend your note and cover the taxes for now, just for now, until you can sell your produce and take care of your family's needs?''

Ella drew a shaky breath, but her optimism dampened. ''My Cam, he be a proud man. He won't take no charity. Not from no Yan—'' She broke off, flushing slightly.

''Good. Then I know he'll work hard to pay me back. How old are your children, Mrs. Wheeler?''

Taken off guard by his interest, Ella brightened. ''They run seven to seven months, Mr. Dodge.''

''Quite a spread. I've got a passel of nieces and nephews that age. Hell to keep up with, begging your pardon for being blunt, ma'am.''

But Ella beamed. And Starla marveled at the connection her husband had made so smoothly to the worried farm wife. He'd managed to anchor the poor woman's spinning world with a tether of trust. He looked up, catching her puzzled scrutiny.

''Starla, is there any lemonade left?''

At his gentle prompting, she slipped into the role of gracious hostess. ''Why, I do believe so. Mrs. Wheeler, might you like a glass on this positively steamy day before you get down to dry ol' business talk with my husband?''

The woman looked startled by the offer of hospitality from someone of Starla Fairfax's status, then pleased.

''Why, yes, thank you, Mrs. Dodge.''

Starla poured, aware of her husband's gaze lingering on her face with a distracting intensity. When she spared him a quick glance, he winked, causing her to come close to spilling the drink on his customer.

''Here you go, Mrs. Wheeler. I'll let you two get on with your business. Perhaps we can chat later, Ella.''

Starla's use of her first name flustered the weary

farm wife to speechlessness. Her charm seemed to have a similar effect on Dodge, at least until Starla left the room.

"Your wife is very kind, Mr. Dodge," Starla heard the woman say. Then came his soft, gratifying claim.

"Yes, ma'am, that she is. I am a fortunate man."

Starla found herself frowning, wondering what else Hamilton Dodge was . . . the soul of sincerity, or a clever businessman bending emotion to his advantage?

Chapter 8

Though she thought it would be easy to be unaffected by her new husband, Starla found herself reluctantly intrigued by Dodge. Quite a feat for a woman used to being charmed by the most wealthy planters in the land. Annoying to a woman set on keeping her distance from the man she'd married.

As the days passed, Dodge and Starla fell into a comfortable routine, living under the same roof more like brother and sister than husband and wife. Dodge was gone by the time she awoke, leaving her to the private indignities of morning sickness. By noon, when she could finally move about without groaning, Starla would stop at Sadie's, then deliver the meal to the bank, where Dodge, always appreciative, never let on that he knew where the food had come from.

She learned about him by watching him work. She admired his directness and his intelligence. But what truly amazed her was the kindness that seemed to motivate him to help the people of Pride, especially those families like the Wheelers from whom he had nothing to gain. She didn't understand, and her curiosity drew her closer. Was it to be believed?

Banker and Yankee—two of the most hated words in her father's lexicon. Put together, they should have spelled out a notorious evil, but she saw nothing but goodness in Hamilton Dodge. His wasn't the ingratiating charity meant to earn a greater reward at a later date. There were no strings on his generosity. Having known only the ruthless side of business, she was at a loss watching her husband struggle to win over the citizens of Pride.

Another mystery was his patience with her and her secrets. Though scrupulously open about his own family, he asked no questions about hers. Nor did he pry into that part of her past that sent her home in disgrace, unwed and with child. She wondered over the man she'd married. Was it consideration or disinterest on his part?

He kept his word about not pressuring her into the intimacy he was entitled to by virtue of their marriage. She continued to be wary, but he gave her no reason. Since his attempt to kiss her before the judge, he hadn't touched her. Because of his restraint of will, or due to the difficulties of his recovery?

Of all the things he was candid about, his injury wasn't one of them. How badly had he been hurt? How badly was he hurting still? He refused help, no matter how much more difficult it made his tasks. No limitations stopped him, even if it meant a discomfort he never disclosed. She couldn't feel sorry for someone so determined to be independent, not that he would accept her sympathy any better than he would welcome her aid.

Helplessness and ignorance nettled him. She couldn't make him angry by scorching his shirts or shying away from his proximity, but his inability to do something or to make another understand his intentions provoked him into dark humors better left undisturbed. As Patrice had said, he was a good man but not a saint.

Her husband. A title as empty as it was uninvolving. After two weeks, Starla was chomping with boredom. Patrice was wrapped up in her new role as wife, and the still recovering economy of the town allowed for no frivolous entertainments. True to his word, Tyler stayed away, refusing her his company.

As her brother had warned, it wasn't long before Starla noticed a shift in her social standing, now that she was the wife of the town's Northern banker. Neighbors who'd always shown her an exaggerated deference before the war now snubbed her on the street. Refusing to look ashamed or to be ignored, she made a point of strolling with the same nose-in-the-air pride, speaking to those she encountered in a loud voice until they acknowledged her. Having to push herself in the face of their rudeness wounded, then angered her.

Time to change things.

She was up early, for once untroubled by the nagging nausea. The thought of spending the morning cooped up in the little house provoked her as she listened to Dodge readying to go to work, abandoning her to the monotony of her days. What did he do when he was not maintaining the charade of married life with her? Impulsively she dressed and raced down the stairs, slowing as he turned from the front door to regard her in surprise.

"Well, good morning. Come to see me off?"

His pleasant expression rubbed her the wrong way, making her tone clipped. "I thought I'd go in and have breakfast, if you don't mind the company."

"Fine by me."

An overwhelming lack of enthusiasm.

Most men would have been reduced to humble gratitude just by the granting of her presence. But Dodge wasn't most men. How that rankled her on this particular morning.

Unperturbed by her peevishness, he held the door open wide, letting her sweep through it ahead of him. Just as she did into Sadie's, when they arrived there. Only to be jerked up to a stop at the sound of Delyce Dermont's voice.

"Good morning, Mr. Dodge. Your table is ready for you. Did you want your usual?"

Starla turned in surprise. Although Delyce was the sister of the terrorizing Dermont brothers, she was a girl who wouldn't normally say boo to a ghost. But for Starla's husband she had a sweet smile and rosy cheeks. And Starla was beside herself with a flutter of foreign emotion as Dodge grinned back, all sunny, warm, and teasing.

"Thank you, Delyce. You spoil me shamelessly. My mouth's been watering for a taste of your biscuits. Set an extra place this morning. My wife is joining me."

Delyce shot a startled look at Starla, and her meek manner returned. "I'm sorry, Miz Fairfax— Mrs. Dodge. I didn't see you there."

No wonder, Starla thought crossly. The twit was too busy fawning over a married man. *Her* man, in name, if not by any other claim. Starla bared her teeth in a smile no woman could fail to mistake as territorial.

"Why, that's all right, Delyce. It's just good to know that my husband's been in such solicitous hands. I'll have a cup of tea and some biscuits, lightly buttered."

"Yes, ma'am," the young woman muttered, before scurrying off to the kitchen.

Starla glared at a clueless Dodge, then swept to the delegated table. She didn't see her husband's bemused smile, for he was quite sober of expression when he joined her. She met his innocent stare with one sharp enough to cleave stone.

"My mouth's been watering for a taste of your biscuits," she mocked with a fairly good imitation of his clipped Northern syllables. "Think you ought to slather on a little more butter, there, honey? One might get the idea that you're eager for more than a taste."

Unwisely, Dodge grinned at her. "Why, darlin'," he drawled in a thick Kentucky accent, "are you accusin' me o' somethin'? If you are, speak it plain."

Starla's glare shot sparks. "Why are you being so *nice* to her?"

"I'm *nice* to everyone."

"You're not that *nice* to me," she huffed.

Regarding her with a discomforting intensity, Dodge leaned back to remark dryly, "I wasn't aware you wanted me to be *nice* to you."

She wasn't aware until that moment of what she did want. She wanted her husband to smile and flirt with her instead of regarding her with a smug tolerance. She didn't want to be merely tolerated. She wanted to be adored. Even if it was just for appearances. But Dodge refused to be charmed out of his cynical indulgence, nor could he be cajoled into putting on a show.

"Besides," he commented, "with the whole county at your feet, I didn't think you'd miss one less to trip over."

"I don't find that amusing, sir. Nor do I enjoy your making eyes at that woman right in front of me."

"If that's what you think, the problem's with your eyes, not mine."

No apology. She scowled at that, skewering Delyce with another slashing stare when the girl returned with their cups. The timid server ducked away as quickly as possible.

"There's no need for you to be rude to Delyce."

Starla's gaze shot up to fix on his. "Excuse me, sir. I don't need you to correct my behavior."

"You do when it's as unpleasant as it was just now. I won't have you ruining all the inroads I've made with these people."

Her eyes squinted dangerously. "And just what inroads have you been making with Delyce Dermont?"

"Keep your voice down."

"I will not. You haven't answered my question."

"I'm not planning to."

"Because I guessed the truth?"

"No, because you're being foolish. Starla—" He slipped his hand over hers. She jerked away so abruptly that she spilled her tea all over the tablecloth. Seeing the mess she'd made gave her pause, and Dodge suggested with a frigid politeness, "Maybe you should go home."

Delyce came bustling over with a stack of rags to blot up the spill. Chagrined, Starla helped her, murmuring apologies as she did so. Finally, when Delyce went to fetch her another cup of tea, Starla gave Dodge a look that managed to be both prickly and remorseful.

"I'm sorry. I don't know what got into me to act so—foolishly."

After a long gauging beat, Dodge smiled in easy forgiveness. "It's the baby." When Starla glanced around nervously, he said, "We've been married almost three weeks, enough time to have accomplished such a thing without creating scandal."

"I-I guess you're right."

"I was going over to see Doc Anderson after I close up tonight. I want you to go with me . . . just to make sure everything's all right."

She nodded, still feeling silly and embarrassed enough to be docile. And soothed by the idea of his concern until she realized his worries were for the child she carried, not for her.

Dodge didn't tease her, nor did he note her sudden quiet. He was too unsettled by the unexpected evidence of her jealousy. Was it because another woman had dared to tamper with something that belonged to her . . . or because she was beginning to care for him, maybe just a little? He absorbed the sight of the lovely woman seated at his table, his wife, his in the sight of God and the law, but as much a stranger to him now as when they'd said "I do." Was it too soon to hope her mood was starting to thaw, that they could have a marriage in truth, with all the benefits he longed to explore?

He was so distracted by the idea that he failed to see the Dermont brothers reel into the dining room after an ugly all-night drunk in the bar.

But they saw him and his new bride.

"Well, lookee here. Ain't this a sight? Starla Fairfax, fraternizing with that Yankee scum. You best get up from there, 'fore your daddy gets wind of things and drags you on home to give you what for."

Hearing the grating sneer, Dodge was about to turn to confront Ray Dermont when he caught a glimpse of Starla's face. She'd gone alarmingly pale, her green eyes huge and glittering. It had to be more than a run-in with the town bullies to send her into such a state of apprehension.

"Ain'tcha heard, Ray," Poteet Dermont, the middle brother drawled, "they's married. One of our own, taking up with lyin', stealin' vermin. A crime, it is, wouldn't you say so, boys?"

"Nothin' we can't take care of," Ray continued, bumping against Dodge's back as the trio swaggered past them. "You'd look mighty fine in widow's weeds, Starla darlin'."

"Guess I'll have to work on my aim some, eh, fellas?"

Up until that moment, Dodge had never known who'd left the chunk of lead nestled up against his spine. Poteet Dermont's boastful claim settled it for him with a chilling certainty. Dodge looked up slowly, his stare fixing on the grinning drunkard.

"Don't get me riled, Dermont, or I just might forget we're in a public place."

The razor edge of that soft-spoken warning gave the brothers momentary pause, but they were quick to laugh it off.

"Whatcha gonna do, Yank?" Ray sneered. "Beat up on us with your crutches? C'mon, boys, let's get us somethin' to eat. All this funnin' gives me an appetite."

They moved on, but not before Poteet gave Dodge's crutches a kick, sending them skidding across the floor and well out of his reach. Their ridiculing laughter followed Starla as she left her chair and scrambled to collect them.

Dodge gripped her arm.

"I don't need your help."

His harsh tone froze her.

But as Dodge twisted in his chair and leaned over to retrieve them, he lost his balance, falling hard to his hands and knees, much to the amusement of the Dermonts. His ears ringing with their howling taunts, Dodge resisted Starla's help.

"Let me alone! I can take care of it myself." And he did, grabbing the tip of a crutch and using its padded crossbar to snag the other and pull it close enough for him to reach. He levered himself

up to his feet, awkward, angry, oblivious to the
wounding effect his words had had on his wife. She
followed silently as he wound his way through the
tables filled with gawkers, some not polite enough
to hide their smirks at his expense.

Once deep gulps of fresh air had vented the humiliation from his brain, Dodge readied to apologize for his hurtful attack, but one look at Starla
told him it was too late. She stared through him,
her features set in a lovely mask, her eyes snapping
with jewel-like fire. She wasn't interested in hearing that he was sorry for shaming her in front of a
roomful of neighbors. Instead, she leveled her own
derisive claim.

"Poteet Dermont rubs your face in the fact that
he shot you and you just sit there."

Wincing at the vicious thrust of words, Dodge
replied, "What did you expect me to do? Hit him
with my crutch?"

"Go to the law if you can't take care of him
yourself." The fact that she didn't think he could
was clear in her condescending tone.

"There is no law in Pride except the military,
and I'm not in uniform anymore. And there's no
proof, other than his bragging. I didn't see who
pulled the trigger. I doubt that his brothers—or
yours—would come forward with the facts."

His mention of her brother brought a deep flush
to Starla's face, but her tone remained crisp and
cold. "So you're just going to let it go?" You're
going to let them laugh at you in front of the whole
town?"

His gaze narrowed. "You can laugh with them, if you like."

"I don't think it's funny."

"You think I'm a coward for doing nothing."

Her silence was his answer.

"Your belief in me is truly touching." With that wry observation, he started down the walk toward the bank, planting his crutches and swinging through them in aggressive arcs. He didn't think anything could darken his mood until he saw the front of the bank.

The shutters had been torn from the windows. He didn't need to look closer to know all the glass was gone. Cursing under his breath, he pulled the keys from his vest pocket and unlocked the heavy door. He crossed into a sea of red.

The scent was unmistakable: thick, metallic, carrying him back to the battlefield, to the drone of flies and the screams of the dying.

"Oh, my God," Starla gasped from behind him. "What is that?"

"Animal blood. Someone's idea of a joke."

Starla pushed past him, lifting her skirts so they wouldn't drag through the pools of crimson staining the floorboards and splattering the walls amid shards of glass. While Dodge surveyed the damage, she went out the back, returning with a bucket of water, rags, and a broom. Seeing her intention, Dodge's jaw tightened.

"You don't have to—"

She cut him off bluntly.

"If I don't, who will? You can hardly open for business with the place looking like a slaughterhouse. It's not exactly confidence inspiring.'' She waited for his reply, but he just stared at her, his eyes a glaze of uncertain emotion. ''Well, don't just stand there. Go about your regular business while I tend with this mess,'' she said.

For the next few hours she soaked and scrubbed the stains and swept up the broken glass, all with a somber determination that humbled and rankled her husband. Dodge watched her work, seeing her frustration with him in the fierce way in which she tackled the job. His pride prickled at allowing her to clean up after him, but he was warned to say nothing by the furious way she punished the floor-boards into yielding up all but the faintest tint of red. He tried to concentrate on his daily accounts, but the figures before him weren't nearly as entic-ing as the one that bent over to create a hypnotic sway of skirt and hips.

What a fool he was for treating her so badly. It wasn't her fault, any of it, yet he'd hammered her with the full force of his anger. And she'd taken the abuse without complaint. What a strong woman he'd wed, strong and stubborn, and so gorgeous, even on her knees, rubbing her knuckles raw; it hurt him to draw a decent breath.

''Starla, that's enough.''

She continued to circle the cloth with a single-minded vengeance.

''It's not going to come clean.''

She looked up then, her features flushed from exertion and taut with unvoiced concerns as she considered his statement, then answered flatly, ''It never does.''

With that she stood, pressing her palm into the small of her back as she surveyed the extent of the vandalism. The floor held a pinkish tinge, but the walls looked good.

"I'm going home," she announced with a weary finality.

"You'll meet me at Doc Anderson's?"

She nodded.

His apology should have come then, or at least his thanks, but when he said nothing, Starla left without a backward glance.

"You keep pushing so hard, and you're going to end up paralyzed or dead."

Dodge took a long draw on his cigar, refusing to give credence to the words as he waited for the same doctor who gave him that prognosis to finish his examination of Starla.

It wasn't as though he didn't know the risks. With the bullet still lodged so close to his spine, the slightest shift could accomplish what Poteet Dermont had failed to do on that dark night at the Glade. It wasn't as though the grinding pain didn't remind him quick enough when it was time to ease off.

It wasn't his inability to walk that was foremost among his worries. It was his inability to do other things.

Could anything be worse than having to spell everything out to the inquisitive and suddenly dense-as-a-brick doctor?

"The spinal cord's a funny thing. As I said, most wouldn't have survived what you did; the rest would never have stood, let alone thought of walking. You suffered a traumatic injury. Things are going to recover at their own pace—if they do at all. Pushing as hard as you are and worrying about it on top of the rest isn't going to help matters.''

''What is?''

''Letting time do its work, letting nature take its course. For now, just be glad to be breathing.''

''Thanks for the advice.''

Dr. Anderson had grinned at his growly claim. ''You're welcome. Rest. Let the lovely lady wait on you awhile. Give her a chance to get your full attention—if you know what I mean.'' He winked.

Dodge knew. It wasn't that he had no patience with the wait; he just had no tolerance for the uncertainty.

His strength was coming back, but not fast enough. Not when he had a job to do and a wife to take care of. Not when men like the Dermonts could shame him in front of her with impunity.

Not when his desire to have a real marriage increased with every restless night spent alone while his bride slept in a separate bed on the floor above him.

Dodge levered up on his crutches when Starla emerged from the doctor's back room. She didn't look at him. Alarmed, he cast a questioning stare toward the physician, who eased his worries with a smile.

''Congratulations. You'll have a healthy new mouth to feed come spring.''

Dodge shook the man's hand as if he'd accomplished the act himself. Of course, Anderson knew that wasn't the case, but Dodge didn't fear the doctor would spill the truth. He was the type who favored his oath over opinion and gossip.

"Anything special we need to do?" Dodge asked, giving consideration to Starla's wan features.

"You, rest. For her, plenty of fresh air and exercise. Take care of each other. This is a special time. Enjoy it."

But as Dodge watched his wife climb the stairs of their too quiet home without a word to him, a bittersweet sorrow spread through him. A child in the spring . . . that knowledge quickened all sorts of eager anticipation. But Starla's lack of excitement dampened the joy of the occasion.

Did she still love him, that fool who filled her with his child, then refused to wed her? Did she wish to share these special moments with him, rather than with a surrogate husband and father? Dodge hadn't considered how those questions would chafe at heart and mind when he'd taken on the care of woman and child. He hadn't realized how fixed he would become on the life his wife had led in the four years she was gone from Pride, how he couldn't stop the comparisons between himself and the baby's father and Starla's relationship with both of them. She saw him as her rescuer and the source of her future security. He'd told Reeve that would be enough.

Now he was fighting to convince himself of it.

And it wasn't a fight he was winning.

Chapter 9

S ound shattered through him, its impact almost physical. His eyes sprang open only to squeeze quickly shut against a glare of dazzling light. In a heartbeat he recognized the danger.

They were under fire.

Mortar shells lit up the night sky as they screamed toward their encampment like banshees. Dodge scrambled out of his tent into the chaos of men dying. He tried to call out orders to organize the panicked soldiers, to ready them to return fire, but his words couldn't compete with the deafening roar of the artillery barrage cutting them to pieces. Within moments he was the only one standing among a litter of corpses.

Brightness continued to light the sky in eerie flickers as Dodge knelt beside the first body lying facedown in the mud. He gripped the man's shoulder and rolled him over, rocking back in horror at the sight of his friend Reeve Garrett's face twisted in a grimace of death. Dodge stumbled back, bumping against another of the fallen. His breath coming in hoarse, anguished bursts, he flipped that man over, revealing the face of another friend. And so it went as he crawled through the mud and gore among the dead, turning over man after man, staring down into the still faces of not only those he'd commanded, but friends from childhood, faces of family, until the sobs of grief and guilt choked him.

A tremendous punch of agony tore through his back, propelling him facedown into the sea of mud. He wallowed helplessly until he managed to tip his face up to the flashing heavens. He tried to lift himself out of the mire.

But he couldn't move. His body was as useless as a length of cordwood, the muscles deadened, unresponsive.

''No.''

That's when the smell reached him. Above the scorch of gunpowder, over the stink of the mud.

The scent of death.

It rose all around him, the mud and rain becoming a fast-rising tide. He struggled to get his elbows under him, to find enough leverage to lift his head out of the ever-deepening pool. But his body wouldn't obey the frantic commands of his mind.

It rose up to his ears.

''No.''

He lifted his chin, fighting to keep his mouth and nose clear, but the level surged up too fast, closing off his light, his air.

As he drowned in the blood of those who'd fallen.

''Dodge?''

It had taken all her courage for Starla to enter

the darkened room, to sit on the edge of the bed beside the thrashing man.

His stark cries had awakened her—horrible, harsh sounds of dread and pain and fear that scared a rash of gooseflesh along her arms and had her trembling. Horrible memories of her own made her cower in the dark while shocks of lightning heightened the nightmarish quality of her recall: memories of another man's voice, wild and rambling in the throes of narcotic delusion, of irrational temper and sometimes violence when she dared to interfere. Those reminders held her helpless for a long moment until she recalled that this wasn't that man; this was Dodge. And he'd promised never to hurt her.

But what if in response to his pain, Dodge relied on the same opiates that she'd watched destroy another?

Don't go to him! No man is as good as his word! He'll make you regret it if you intrude. Didn't he say he didn't need or want you?

But her conscience betrayed her, goading her into snatching her robe and creeping down the stairs, hugging close to the rail as the low, anguished sounds led her toward the back bedroom.

She could see him tossing in a tangle of sheets, eyes closed, his features taut beneath a sheen of sweat as he struggled against whatever haunted his dreams. Asleep, not insensible. Relief left her weak. She should have withdrawn then and left him to his subconscious battle, but something about those tortured pulls of breath played harmony upon her own remembrances of what it was to feel helpless and alone. She crossed over to him, all the while chiding herself for becoming involved in his nightmares. She'd had enough of her own. She didn't need to fight his as well.

At the first light touch of her hand upon his shoulder, he came awake. His eyes flashed open, his gaze darting wild and disoriented about him until it fixed on her face with a desperate fear. She jumped in alarm as his fingers clamped over the top of hers, squeezing convulsively into an inescapable grip.

"Reeve? Is Reeve alive?"

Though his question seemed ludicrous, his fractured tone had Starla answering with a gentle assurance.

"Reeve is fine. You were dreaming."

"Dreaming," he repeated both in doubt and tremendous relief.

Starla tried to twist her hand free, but his hold on her tightened until her panic began to grow.

"Dodge, let me go."

Her increasingly urgent pulling had no effect.

"Let me go!"

The fright in her voice finally reached him. His hand opened, allowing her the freedom to surge back, to scramble warily to her feet, rubbing her wrist.

"I'm sorry," he muttered, scrubbing shaking hands over his face to dry the sheets of cold terror clinging to his skin. "I didn't mean to scare you. I have dreams sometimes. I'm fine now."

But a sudden crack of thunder had him cringing back, his fists balling over his eyes to shut out the light that accompanied the sound. His breath escaped him in a jagged rush.

"It's just a storm."

He nodded, understanding her explanation, yet still responding to the next flash and rumble with irrational panic, crossing his arms over his head as if to protect himself against some sort of expected fallout.

"Dodge?"

"I'm sorry I woke you. I'm—I'm all right. These things never used to bother me—*oh, God*—" He braced against the next rattle of sound, tensing until it was over, then letting go in a shuddering relief. He was breathing hard—distraught, still caught in the fearful throes of his nightmares.

Cautiously Starla sat beside him, clasping her hands together to restrain herself from the want to touch him, to soothe his fears, imagined or not. Abruptly he rolled onto his side, tucking up against the wall, rocking himself in short, hard thrusts as the foundation of the house vibrated from the fury of the storm.

"I can't make it stop. I can't make it stop."

The torment in his wrenching claim broke Starla's reserve. She touched his shoulder, feeling shivers of reaction as she slowly rubbed the taut muscles of his arm. Another sharp crack and sizzle made him clutch at her, dragging her down across him. The threat of that sudden closeness eased with the evidence of his distress.

"I can see their faces." He moaned in despair.

Carefully Starla fitted herself to his strong contours, encircling him with her embrace as she had her brother, when they were younger and he was troubled by fitful dreams.

"Close your eyes."

He rolled toward her then and she held his dark head to her breast, blocking out the lightning dance with the wrap of her arms. His jerking breaths blew hot and uneven against the curve of her bosom, heating through thin silk, warming deeper with their erratic pattern of anguish. She pressed her cheek to the soft bristle of his hair and murmured, "It's all right. Just close your eyes. It'll all go away."

She held him while the storm raged, absorbing the fierce shocks racking him with each loud percussion. Finally the roars ebbed to a gentle timpani, and his breathing slowed and deepened into restful slumber.

She should have returned to her room, but while giving him comfort, she'd begun to receive it in exchange. As her fingertips stroked from her husband's brow to his stubbled jaw and back, she took a quiet pleasure in the repetitions. The cadence of his breathing, the steady throb of his pulse, calmed her spirit. The act of easing his demons helped quiet her own.

She thought of what he'd said, that their marriage was a partnership, like brother and sister, where each could depend on the other. For the next few hours, while rain tapped on the glass and Dodge slept in her arms, Starla let herself relax and enjoy the simple act of closeness without fear.

Which perhaps was why, when she woke to the pastels of dawn with the feel of his kiss on her lips, she responded with a quiver of curiosity.

In all her flirtations, in all her coy encouragements, never had she allowed the familiarity of a kiss. Just the thought of that grinding pressure mashing tender lips against her teeth, the slobbering aggression of a tongue thrusting down her throat, startled feelings of helplessness and invasion. It was a gesture of greedy domination that sickened her more than all but the most personal of exchanges, one she swore would always have to be taken from her, never given.

So why was she giving back to Hamilton Dodge as they lay side by side in the warm haven of his bed, when it was threat, not capitulation, that should have controlled her reactions?

He'd awakened to the unfamiliar delight of not being alone.

The realization that it was Starla sharing his sheets shocked him to his soul, until, with an embarrassing flush of memory, he recalled what had drawn her into his room. He hadn't had that particular nightmare for a long while. It must have been the stale scent of blood in the bank, the frustration of his own helplessness, that had lured it back to taunt him.

Starla had come to comfort him and had stayed to console him.

Looking into her face scant inches away on his pillow, he was neither comforted nor consoled. A strange, shivery panic flooded through his chest and closed fistlike around his heart. A more primal heat scorched along his veins, trailing fire and longing, then stopped just short of full-blown passion. What stirred his emotions into a frenzy of need left his loins frustratingly unaffected.

Right now, it was for the best. He would never have dared touch the soft spill of her hair if not in complete control of his more basic responses. It wasn't his intention to claim his bride with ungovernable lusts. He needed to win her with restrain and respect . . . and trust.

But wisdom couldn't quite win out over the desperate desire to taste the soft mouth denied him before the judge . . . a quick taste to satisfy all that massed in complex yearning as her warm breath caressed the part of his lips.

Sweet. She tasted sweet as his every urgent dream, as tender as the uncertain sentiment unfurling in his heart as he lingered just a bit too long to savor the sensation.

Dodge felt her intake of breath and knew she was awake. Refusing to react with a guilty withdrawal, as if he'd intended to steal something he knew would not be given freely, he made one more soft sweep of her lips before starting to pull away. And that was when her hand slipped to the back of his neck, halting the movement, holding him there as her eyes opened to gaze into his with a wonder her wariness couldn't conquer.

''Kiss me like that again,'' came her breathless whisper.

So he did, softly, slowly, searching out a response from her guarded heart, seeking an answering pressure with his unhurried exploration of each tempting swell and tender indentation. Her hand never moved on the base of his neck, her fingers lax but the support never lessening as gradually she kissed him back.

Dodge had kissed his share of women, but never had he been as moved as he was now by the innocent response of this woman he'd wed. A woman pregnant with another man's child who parted her lips as if she'd never done so with any other.

How could that be?

Either she was a splendid actress . . . or she'd never given herself willingly to the father of her baby.

He pulled back, agitated by his thoughts and by the feelings threading through him in strands of fire and fierce possession. If he didn't encourage some distance between them, he feared he'd push past the limits of her willingness as well.

"You should go now," he advised. The husky urgency in his tone must have convinced her of that wisdom. She slipped across him and was out the door before he could draw another breath to thank her for her compassion.

Starla brushed her hair until the trembling in her hands made continuing impossible. Clutching the brush as if to still the frantic pounding of her heartbeat, she regarded her reflection in her bedroom mirror, shocked by the sight of her wide, green crystal eyes and the pale parchment skin now tracked with tears. She wasn't ever one to cry silly tears over something so trivial as a kiss.

Or was the cause of her distress the fact that the kiss wasn't trivial?

She'd believed herself safe beneath this roof, with this man. She'd taken his assurances as truth. She let herself begin to trust the man she'd married because he posed no physical threat, believing that without having to endure his touch or his intimate possession, there was no danger in letting him get close.

What a fool she was to have underestimated him so—and herself as well.

The danger Hamilton Dodge posed wasn't to her body; it was to her heart.

It was time for Dodge to say hello to his new in-laws.

The visit wasn't one he looked forward to, but he couldn't escape its necessity if he was ever to understand his bride. So much mystery was kept locked inside her, and he'd have to find the answers himself if he wanted to know the whole truth.

It shouldn't have been difficult to learn about a family as prominent as the Fairfaxes. Everyone in Pride was usually free with an opinion, whether it was close to the truth or not. But mention the Fairfax family and no one had a thing to say. What caused the fear and unhappiness his wife had tried to hide with her fiercely contrived flirtations? It had something to do with the neglected mansion on the far side of Pride, where her father, the reclusive Cole Fairfax, stayed behind closed doors, locking the gossips of Pride out and the secrets of the Fairfaxes in.

A harried-looking black woman answered his

knock at the front door with suspicion instead of welcome.

"Whatchu' want here?"

Dodge ignored her wariness and affected his most winning smile. "You must be Tilly. I'm Hamilton Dodge. I'm Starla's husband."

"Miss Starla wouldn't go an' marry a Yankee. Get your lying self outta here."

He was quick to brace his hand against the door. "I'd like to see Cole Fairfax."

"Mista Fairfax don't see nobody."

"I'll speak to Tyler, then. Please."

The old woman's features scrunched up warily, but she said, "I tell him you's here." Then she slammed the door firmly, leaving Dodge on the porch. He smiled wryly at the greeting he'd received and decided if Tyler Fairfax was going to come down and blow him to his maker, he'd might as well wait in comfort. He angled himself into one of the big wrought-iron chairs sitting dusty with disuse on the deeply shaded veranda. He was just positioning his crutches within easy reach when he heard Tyler's low chuckle.

"Well, I'll be damned. If it ain't my favorite Yankee, come calling bold as brass."

Smiling with deceiving good nature, Tyler strolled out onto the porch. Nothing even faintly affable shone in the cold glitter of eyes bruised from lack of sleep and hard drinking. He leaned against a pillar with a sloppy grace, waiting for his uninvited visitor to speak his piece.

" 'Morning, Mr. Fairfax. Forgive me if I don't get up, but I just got down."

Tyler waved a negligent hand. "No need to be polite on my account. I seem to recall telling you there'd be little politeness involved in our next conversation."

"The situation is different now."

"Not to my thinking."

"Starla and I are married."

Breath hissed between Tyler's clenched teeth as he bared them in a fierce smile. "Did you come here for congratulations? When hell freezes over, Yank."

"I came to see if we could bury the hatchet without any bloodshed for Starla's sake. She'd like it if we could at least tolerate each other."

Tyler's grin twisted into a sneer. "I don't think that's gonna happen."

"I thought you cared about your sister, Fairfax. Doesn't her happiness mean anything to you?"

Tyler's expression went taut, becoming all angles and hollows. "I've thought of nothin' else my entire life. Don't you lecture me on what Starla wants or needs to be happy. It ain't you, Yank. You ain't man enough to give my sister what she needs."

Dodge went dangerously still. "I don't think that's something I care to have you speculating about."

Tyler gave a harsh laugh when he took Dodge's meaning. "My sister'd never let the likes of you touch her. That ain't what I'm talking about. You can't protect her, Yank. So you're no good to her at all."

With his thoughts now derailed from a challenge

to his manhood, Dodge blinked in bewilderment. "Protect her? Protect her from what?"

"The past, Mr. Dodge."

"What kind of danger is she in? How can I help her if I don't know?"

Tyler smiled again, that slow, thin smirk of contempt. "My point exactly. What good are you? Good day, Yank. Watch your back."

Chapter 10

When Starla didn't appear with his noontime meal, Dodge had too much time to consider the consequences of what had replayed in his mind all morning. In the quiet interior of the bank, with the mournful tick of his clock tolling the monotony of minutes, he wondered how much damage he'd done with that kiss.

His back hurt, his head pounded, and his eyes felt gritty from lack of restful sleep. Conspiring to sour his mood was Reeve's nagging prophecy that he'd want more from his marriage than a convenient bargain.

He hated to be proved wrong.

He'd been wrong to think companionship would be enough. Wrong to believe he could easily win over his bride. Wrong again to suppose this marriage could turn into the close family unit he longed for. He couldn't fault Starla for any of his misconceptions. She'd been honest from the first. She'd told him she didn't love him, that she wouldn't sleep with him. Reeve had hinted that he was inheriting a whole host of troubles, but he'd chosen to ignore the warning.

The kiss was what had awakened him to the sham he clung to.

He'd married a woman weighted down with secrets, who feared his touch almost as much as she despised his background. He'd confidently assumed the role of her protector without knowing what challenges he'd face, or whether he'd be able to meet them. Tyler Fairfax vowed he'd fail. His own wife was doubtful enough to keep her worries to herself, unconvinced that he could solve them. He himself didn't know where to turn to find the answers he needed to piece together the riddle of his wife's past. Getting Starla to trust him hadn't been the snap he'd vainly thought it would be. She was wary, and more than that, she was afraid. How could he protect her if he didn't understand the danger?

How could he assure her of her safety when he was dependent on two sticks of wood to support his weight, when bullies like the Dermonts felt free to insult him, and the people of Pride were afraid to come to him for aid?

He rubbed his palms along the tops of his thighs. Just the feel of contact would have thrilled him a month ago, but now all he felt was the weakness, the debilitating numbness that lingered, laced with pain, reminding him of how far he had to go before he could guarantee the promises he'd made.

He'd have to push harder. He'd have to show Starla she could depend on him for strength as well as sympathy. He'd have to prove he was worthy of the fragile trust she'd extended with that soultwistingly sweet kiss before he could ask her to give him more.

He wanted more. He wanted more with an ache that sank to the bone, with a desperation clawing up from a well of loneliness so deep the echo went on forever. He wanted his bride to turn to him in passion and pride with the certainty that he wouldn't fail her.

He couldn't give those certainties now, not when he couldn't stand alone. Not when the root of his passions remained frustratingly lacking.

The sight of his crutches leaning next to his desk symbolized all he struggled against. He'd fashioned them himself, with almost loving attention. He'd been so proud to take his first steps dependent upon their support. But now they were a barrier rather than a bolster. With a low, angry curse, he slapped them away, satisfied by the clatter they made as they hit the floor. Then, with a sigh, he recognized how infantile his behavior was, and that it would serve him right if he had to crawl after them.

He was in the process of fishing for the crossbar of the closer crutch when he heard the front door open. Relief and anticipation collided as he hauled himself upright, eager to greet his wife. Then he sat, blinking, in a moment of confusion.

"No hello?"

"Oh, my God," was all he could mutter, as an eager young woman filled his outstretched arms.

Starla paused in the doorway, lunch basket hanging from the bend in her elbow as she stared in an odd clutch of dismay at the sight of another woman in her husband's embrace. The obvious joy in their faces sparked in her feelings of envy, hurt, and anger, as surprising as they were unexpected. As unexpected as her desire to tear the two of them apart.

She must have made some sound, for both teardampened faces turned her way. And Dodge had the temerity to grin.

"Starla, I want you to meet my sister, Alice."

A sudden blow to the midsection couldn't have left her more winded. While she stood in a slackjawed daze, Alice climbed off her brother's lap and approached with hand extended.

"So you're the woman who managed the miracle of snaring my brother."

The tang of accusation held in that claim was something only another woman would hear. Starla bristled and affected her brightest smile.

"He was most eager to be caught, as I recall."

The two women shook hands. Alice's grip was firm, almost mannish, her manner aggressively Northern. Starla was used to her husband's bold assertiveness, but in another female, the brashness was less flattering. Obviously older than her brother, Alice shared his pleasant looks and stocky build, as well as the shrewdly direct stare. That stare dissected Starla into tiny pieces after finding the whole unacceptable.

"You didn't travel all this way by yourself, did you, Allie? Is Frank with you?"

Alice reluctantly turned from her critical appraisal and smiled. "Frank is helping your father put together an order. You know them, nothing's as important as work. I brought the children with me, and your mother. They're at the station, waiting for our bags. I came ahead. I couldn't resist the surprise.''

''Yes, the surprise,'' Starla drawled sweetly. ''I had no idea we were having visitors.'' Her gaze skewered Dodge's. He met it with a blameless lift of his brows.

''When we got the letter from your friend Mrs. Garrett saying you'd gotten married, we just couldn't stay away. She assured us you had room to put us up for a short stay . . . unless you'd prefer we went to a hotel, you being newlyweds and all.''

''Of course you can stay with us. It's no bother.''

Two things struck Starla: Dodge hadn't told his family of their marriage, and she didn't have a voice in the arrangements now being made. Both added to the stiffness of her stance and to her sense of being pushed outside the warm circle of this reunion, a situation intensified with the arrival of Marian Dodge and Alice's two children.

Being surrounded by the Dodges was like nothing Starla had ever experienced. Her own family was nonexistent, and glimpses into her friend Patrice's family displayed the strict and proper decorum of a Southern home.

The Dodges, on the other hand, were boisterous, loud, and gushing with affection. They all talked at once, punctuating sentiments with hugs and fond touches. Her husband sat in the middle of the melee, a niece on one knee, a nephew on the other, grinning from ear to ear. Glad to be overlooked, Starla edged quietly on the outskirts of the conversation, providing tea and milk with the sobriety of a well-trained servant . . . until Marian Dodge spotted her. Then the topic of talk turned uncomfortable.

"We were surprised to learn of your marriage from someone other than family."

Dodge tried evading with a smile. "I didn't know you corresponded with Patrice."

"She and I began writing after your—accident." Mrs. Dodge's bespectacled eyes touched anxiously on the crutches, then darted away. "I had to have news from some source, since you were so stingy with yours."

"I'm not much for letter writing."

"Even wedding announcements?"

There was no eluding the pointed truth.

"I'm sorry, Mother. We planned to write you, now that we have even better news to share."

"And what is that?"

"Starla's expecting. We just found out yesterday." He caught Starla's hand, drawing her into the suddenly too quiet circle, where Marian looked alarmed and Alice stricken. "I was hoping Father had come with you so I could tell him face to face, seeing how rabid he's always been about continuing the family tradition."

"That would be rather difficult, in view of the fact that you've already chosen to break with it."

"Alice," Marian warned curtly, then turned a frigid smile upon her new daughter-in-law. "This is all so sudden—a new daughter, and now a new grandchild. I don't know what to say."

"Say you're happy for us."

She gave her son a lengthy stare, then said, "I hope you will be."

Noting that she'd volunteered no opinion other than that vague wish, Dodge felt his smile fade. He drew Starla's hand up to press a light kiss on her knuckles, the gesture one of possessive claim. "Starla, why don't you take our guests home and see they're settled in? I'll close up early and be there directly."

Wanting to be alone with the narrowed-eyed women about as much as she desired being shut in a room with two angry wildcats, Starla forced a malleable manner.

"I'm sure they're tired after their long trip." She withdrew her hand and leveled a commanding glare at him. "Don't be long."

Marian Dodge obligingly disappeared into the upper rooms with the children, but Alice lingered below, bent on dragging out all the details about Starla's relationship with her brother. She began with a loaded observation.

"Expecting in what, two weeks' time? My goodness, when Frank and I decided to start a family, it took us over four months to conceive."

Starla gave a clenched-teeth smile. "We both wanted children right away."

"I'd have thought you'd want to wait, what with my brother still recovering from his injuries."

"He manages very well. You know how determined he is when he sets his mind to something."

"And was he determined to marry you? Is that

why he chose to wed someone we've never heard of?''

Starla paused in the act of sugaring their second cup of tea. The entire contents of the bowl wouldn't sweeten Alice's innuendos. It was obvious what the woman was implying.

"It was a sudden decision but certainly not a rash one. Hamilton—''

"Hamilton? He lets you call him that? He loathes the name. Our mother is the only one he allows to use it, and then when she's very angry with him.''

Starla hesitated. She could hardly admit that she called her husband by his impersonal surname. So instead, she manipulated a rosy blush and cooed, "We do have names we use for one another, but they are—private.''

Alice narrowed a look at her as if displeased by the idea of her brother sharing intimate pet names with a Southern stranger. She didn't look the type to be swept away by anything cloyingly personal. Nor would she be put off with anything less than the whole truth.

"Tell me, how did you and Tony meet?''

Tony. Starla took a moment to equate the name to Dodge in her mind before replying. "At my best friend's wedding. A romantic beginning, don't you agree?''

"It must have been some wedding to shake him from his usually practical senses. I've never known Tony to be careless in his involvement with women.''

Enough, Starla decided. "Wouldn't you like to

make sure your children are settled in? Children sometimes get frightened in a strange place.''

''Yes,'' Alice agreed. ''This is a strange place, for all of us. One I don't think any of us will get used to.''

After the woman went upstairs, Starla chewed on those words. Were they supposed to apply to Dodge as well? Dear Tony who must have been out of his mind to have shown any interest in her at all? She was still stewing when the object of her ire arrived. She met him at the door with a glare as cold as a February freeze.

''Your family is all settled in upstairs.''

He wasn't a stupid man. ''This wasn't my idea, Starla. I wouldn't have invited them without discussing it with you.''

She waved toward the stairs. ''But here they are.''

''Was I supposed to put them up in the hotel?''

When she didn't answer, his attitude chilled. ''I trust you'll do everything possible to make them feel at home.''

''Oh, they already feel at home. It seems *I'm* the one who's the outsider here.''

''If you feel that way, I'm sure it's not because of anything they've done.''

''You're sure.'' She repeated the words the way she'd pull back the hammers on a double-barrel scattergun. ''Silly ol' me. Why would I feel excluded just because you invited a passel of strangers under my roof who make no bones about poking their noses into our business, then treat me like a lying Rebel slut who stole away their precious little Tony?''

He took in her fury, his impassive expression betraying nothing for a long moment. Just when she began to fear she'd provoked him into one of his rare rages, a totally inappropriate smile spread across his face. She let both hammers drop.

"This is not amusing! I will not be insulted and sneered at in my own home."

She couldn't know it had been the way she'd referred to the house as her home that had circumvented any irritation he might have felt at being wedged into the middle of an awkward situation between two factions of his family, old and new. Before she had an inkling of what he meant to do, he clasped his crutches under his arms, freeing him to reach out to her, snagging her into an engulfing embrace. She went immediately rigid, her heart pounding against the broad wall of his chest in a fast and frantic rhythm. But because she didn't pull away, he was encouraged enough to brush a light kiss against her temple.

"This is my house, too, Starla," he told her firmly. "I'll tolerate no bad manners, not from you—" His arms hitched up tighter when she drew a protesting breath, stopping her interruption as he added, "And not from anyone else. If they're rude to you again, I'll carry their bags to the hotel myself."

She went still against him, apparently surprised by that vow. Her voice was small and uncertain.

"You'd do that for me?"

"Yes."

For a moment she relaxed, her body melting gratefully along his, a maddening contrast of soft bosom and cutting corset stays. Intoxicated by her unexpected yielding, Dodge spread his hands wide, pressing her closer.

Starla's response was instinctive. Her palms flattened against the satin of his vest, pushing fiercely to find leverage as she ordered breathlessly, "Don't. Let me go. Don't!"

She stumbled back from him the instant his grasp loosened, but before he could speak an apology, a rustle of skirts warned them they weren't alone.

Startled, yet wisely deciding to remain silent, Marian Dodge looked at the two of them, then said, "Alice was wondering if there were any extra blankets for the children."

"I'll get them." Starla tore her glassy gaze from her husband's and turned to hurry up the stairs, brushing past his mother without a glance.

Damn. His life had just gotten more complicated.

Dodge moved into the parlor, propping himself up in front of the sideboard to pour himself a stiff drink. His mother didn't have to say a word for him to feel her censure.

"I don't remember you imbibing so early in the day. Is your back bothering you . . . or is it something else?"

He gulped down the bracing liquor and waited for the burn to subside before facing his mother's too-knowing study.

"I'm fine, Mother."

"If you and your bride are having problems—"

"We're not having any problems. She's pregnant, she upsets easily."

"Does our being here upset her? Maybe we should go to the hotel—"

He sighed heavily, seeing no way to win this particular argument. "Stay. Please. Get to know each other."

"You've hardly had time to do that, have you?"

"What I know, I like, or I wouldn't have married her. Is there anything else you want to get out in the open? You're hardly the soul of diplomacy."

"Why did you marry this woman?"

"I love her."

Dodge was almost as surprised by that statement as she was, not because he'd told her a lie, but because it was the honest truth. A truth that staggered him.

To turn their talk from unstable ground, Dodge asked, "Why didn't Father come down with you?"

"He couldn't get away."

The pain of that was like a long-festering splinter. Couldn't, or wouldn't? Dodge pretended it didn't matter by keeping his tone casual.

"Allie told me he and Frank were busy with some big order. Is Frank working out all right?"

Marian was blunt. "He'd rather be working with you." Then she threw up her hands. "I know, I know. That was settled long ago. But you have to realize how hurt he was by your decision not to go into business with him. It was your great-grandfather's dream—"

"It was the right decision for me. Just like coming here and marrying Starla was right for me."

She spoke her mind without reservation, a family trait. "I don't understand you, Hamilton. Are you purposefully doing everything you can think of to break our hearts?"

"That's not fair." He wasn't immune to the sharp barb of guilt she intended him to feel.

"Your father wants you home; we all do. Haven't you carried this little show of temper far enough?"

"You don't understand, do you?" He shook his head sadly. "I didn't just walk out on the family on a whim. I tried to explain that to you. This is what I want to do with my life."

"What? Throw all our traditions away on behalf of slaveholding Southerners who thank you by putting a bullet in your back?" Her words caught in a sob. She put a fisted hand to her mouth until she was in control again. Still her voice trembled. Though a strong woman, she was also a mother fearing for her youngest child. "Don't do this. Come home where you belong, where we can care for you properly. It's no sin to admit to weakness. Or to making the wrong decisions out of stubbornness and pride."

He was trying to frame his answer in a manner that might make an impression on her when he saw Starla standing in the doorway. From her unnatural pallor and the pinch of her lips, he guessed she'd heard enough of their conversation to be alarmed.

However, her tone was carefully modulated as she said, "The children are all settled in. I planned on frying chicken for supper, if that meets with your approval, Mrs. Dodge."

Marian looked from her son's stoic features to the startlingly lovely creature he'd married. She made herself smile. "That sounds so formal, dear. Call me Mother. Or Marian, if you prefer."

"Would chicken be all right for supper . . . Marian?"

"That would be fine, dear. Just fine. Don't go to any trouble for us."

No trouble. No trouble at all.

Starla whipped the cooked potatoes, milk, and butter with a vengeance until her arm ached with the effort and the potatoes were smooth as custard.

Trouble. That described the Dodges in a word. A plague of trouble descending upon her house with their questions and their prying and their ploys of affection to lure her husband away. A deep, cold panic lay behind her irritation. What if they succeeded? Where would that leave her and her unborn child? Where would she go if Dodge turned away? As often as she vowed not to give him any power over her emotions, she'd unwittingly placed her future in his hands with the claim "I do."

A whiff of smoke reminded her to check the stove, where dark warning curls escaped around the edge of the oven door. With a gasp she wrenched it open, rearing back as a scorched cloud billowed out. Fumbling through the burn of anxious tears, she grabbed the pan of biscuits and began to pull it out before the sear of hot metal shocked her into dropping it onto the kitchen floor with a clatter.

"Starla?"

She turned toward Dodge, shaking with irrepressible sobs. With surprising agility, he crossed the room.

"What's wrong? Star, what's the matter?"

She extended her hand. Words tumbled from her trembling lips. "I burned my fingers."

His expression dissolved with tenderness. He took her hand and dipped it into the water basin, holding it there until the searing pain began to lessen. Then, as she gazed up at him through eyes like molten emeralds, he lifted those reddened fingertips to his mouth. His kiss miraculously made the sting disappear.

"Is that better?" His words were gruff with emotion.

Yes, it was better. Somehow, all it took was the warm link of their hands, the unpressuring gesture of concern. She found herself fanning her fingers along the rough burr of his cheek and jaw, running her thumb over the curve of his mouth. The sudden flare of responsive heat in his dark gaze satisfied rather than intimidated.

And that startled her into an anxious retreat.

He didn't try to prolong the connection, nor did he pursue it. Instead, he told her softly, "Don't be afraid of me. I won't hurt you."

He didn't understand. She wasn't afraid of him at that moment.

She was afraid of losing him.

Chapter 11

❧⟳⟳❧

Dinner went surprisingly well, with no one commenting on the well-done chicken or overly crisp biscuits. Starla played gracious hostess beneath mother- and sister-in-law's scrutiny and remained quiet to observe the workings of the Dodge family. Their spontaneity bemused her, for while the children displayed proper table manners, they were allowed to speak up, oftentimes interrupting the flow of conversation without fear of reprisal. And the adults listened.

Amazing.

She'd never seen anything like it. It put her heart in a tender twist. Was this what Dodge would be like with the child she carried? Was this how he'd act if he'd married a more responsive woman? She was seeing a spontaneity in him that had been missing in all the weeks they'd been married. Around her he treaded lightly. With his family, he did what he liked without caution. A twinge of envy squeezed at her even as her reserve kept her carefully aloof from the free-flowing affection.

And when the meal was over and the boy and

girl had been excused, no one complained about sticky fingers or greasy kisses as they embraced mother, grandmother, and uncle. They regarded Starla with uncertainty and shy smiles, waiting for an invitation to approach. Such beautiful children. She could feel Dodge watching her as she swallowed her anguished longing. Shy with them herself, she merely returned their small smiles and kept them at a distance. Letting them get too close would open up too much dangerous emotion.

And it was with still greater shyness that she stood in the doorway to her husband's bedroom as the members of the house settled in for sleep. Preparing for bed, Dodge had stripped out of his shirt and shoes and regarded her questioningly, wearing only his long johns and trousers. For a moment she stood paralyzed with anxiety.

"Was there something you wanted?" he prompted at last.

Starla swallowed hard.

"I wanted to know if I should share your room. Your family will expect it and think it odd if I stay upstairs."

He stared at her unblinkingly. "Oh. Yes, they probably will." No invitation followed and she began to fidget.

"Then may I come in?"

His gaze settled on the white-knuckled tension of the fingers holding together her robe. "Are you sure you want to?"

"I'm not afraid of you."

Bold words belied by the brilliance of her glass-green stare. She was clearly terrified.

"Come in, then."

She edged cautiously into the room with all the enthusiasm of a woman stepping into a pit of snakes. She looked everywhere but at the big unmade bed where they'd spent the previous night so comfortably. The memory of his quiet breathing, the warmth of his sleeping form against hers, stirred a tremor of unsettling sensation not altogether unpleasant.

She wasn't the only one nervous with the situation. Dodge moved around the room with an uncommon awkwardness, his self-consciousness making him clumsy. Minutes ticked by as he wasted time with trivial matters, carefully selecting his next day's attire and laying it out in neat folds, shuffling through the papers he'd brought home with him with a fixed intent. Starla seized upon his distraction gratefully.

"If you have work you need to do—"

"Just some reading to familiarize myself with the files. I usually do it in bed."

"Don't let me disturb you. The light won't bother me."

"Are you sure?"

"Quite sure."

Neither of them moved toward that beckoning expanse of tousled sheets.

Finally, Starla took a breath and turned her back long enough to shed her silky robe. She slipped under the covers, bundling them up under her chin as if suffering a chill, her back braced stiffly toward the shared middle of the mattress, her eyes determinedly closed.

Seeing her unnatural posture, Dodge smiled ruefully. It was going to be like sharing his covers with a cigar store Indian.

Resigned to a sleepless night, he sat on the edge of the bed to prop his crutches against the nightstand and to wriggle out of his trousers. He heard Starla's pattern of breathing race in the silence of the room. After making a bolster of pillows to support himself, he eased back, teeth gritted while he lifted his legs up onto the bed as if they were twin sticks of wood. Then he waited with a taut patience for the clutching spasms working along his spine to twitch down the muscles of his thighs.

Starla watched him.

Hating that she should witness signs of his weakness, he forced himself to relax and pretend he wasn't on the edge of a scream. His hands shook too fiercely from the strain for him to pick up the papers from the night table. Instead, he fisted them in the covers until the sensations of discomfort became manageable once again.

Starla said nothing. He was relieved when she turned her head away, pretending to seek slumber. Her form was too tense for that miracle.

He tried to read. Nothing he scanned with restless inattention stayed with him. Nothing held his interest quite so completely as the contour of his covers dipping from shoulder to waist and up the rounded hip of the figure lying next to him.

He wouldn't think about his earlier admission to his mother. Love wasn't something he could logically condone with this woman of secrets who feared his touch and kept so fervently her own council.

Finally admitting defeat, he set the papers aside and turned down the lamp. Darkness made the circumstance sit no more easily. The impenetrable shadows implied a certain degree of intimacy between those taking shallow breaths in hurried tandem. Until Starla's quiet voice slipped through the silence.

"Are you going with them?"

"With who, where?"

"With your family up North?"

Dodge turned toward her but could only make out the vague silhouette of her figure with its back to him.

"Why would you ask that?"

"I heard you and your mother talking."

"Oh." A long pause. "Is that what had you all upset in the kitchen?"

"I wasn't upset."

"No."

"I was not."

"I meant, no, I'm not going with them."

The gust of her relief was faint but no less apparent.

He chided gently, "Did you think I wouldn't consider your feelings?"

Her silence said she hadn't thought he'd considered her at all.

"Starla, look at me. Look at me."

Her head turned slowly. It was too dark for him to see her features.

"I married you. You are my wife; your child will

carry my name. Doesn't that mean anything to you?"

In a voice so small and frail it knocked a hole in his heart, she said, "I don't know what it means. I told you, I don't know anything about how a family's supposed to be."

He wanted to hold her so badly his arms ached from their emptiness, but he didn't dare. "It means I won't leave you. It means you can trust me to take care of you and the baby. Do you believe me? I don't want to have to keep telling you over and over again."

"I believe you." Her words quivered, but he couldn't tell if it was from uncertainty or emotion.

"All right, then. It's the three of us, together— right?"

"Right." Stronger this time. Dodge smiled.

"Good. Good night, then."

He could feel her studying him in the darkness and waited for her to say what was on her mind.

"Do you hate your father?"

"What? No. No, of course not. My father's a good man and I love him. Why?"

"Why are you so angry with him?"

"I'm not."

Her silence chastened him for that lie.

"I am, I guess. He wanted me to be certain things I didn't want to be."

"So you ran away."

"No; running away doesn't solve anything. I told him his future wasn't my future."

"And he understood?"

"He was hurt. I still don't think he's gotten over it."

She rolled toward him, coming up on the prop of her elbow. "But you did it anyway."

"I had to."

"Why?"

He chuckled uneasily. "You don't ask any simple questions, do you?"

"Just questions. You don't have to answer them if they're too personal."

"I just don't want to bore you with the details."

"I'm not bored. Tell me about your family. I want to understand."

"All right. I promise to stop when you start snoring."

She pushed at his arm playfully, and somehow her hand seemed to linger there, resting lightly at his elbow. Quivers of awareness tingled from fingertips to collarbone.

"I love my family," he began, as if to qualify things he might say to suggest otherwise. "And they love me. I've never doubted that. Not ever."

"You're very lucky." The weight of earnest in that claim surprised and moved him.

"Yes, I know. I guess I'm going to sound spoiled and ungrateful when I say their love was smothering me to death."

"Are you? Ungrateful?"

He shook his head. "It was the hardest thing I've ever done, walking away. I grew up the youngest of seven, the only son. I never lifted a finger for anything, I never wanted for anything, so I guess— yes, I *was* spoiled, spoiled by the love of my family, by the certainty of it. I grew up with the comfort of knowing exactly what was in store for me. I'd work with my father and his father to learn wood shaping and furniture making, and someday I'd teach those skills to my own sons. I was safe, secure and soft, never having to make a decision for myself.''

''What happened?''

''Reality. The knowledge that everyone wasn't decent and honest and caring, like my father. He got swindled by one of his customers and nearly lost everything; the business he'd inherited, the house he'd built with his own hands—everything. I saw fear in my father's eyes and that shook me out of my complacency. It made me realize that I couldn't go through life with blinders on, taking what I had for granted.''

She inched closer to him, intrigued by his story, unaware of the way her nearness catapulted his heart into his throat.

''Did he lose everything?''

''Almost. We went to a banker, our neighbor. He sat in my father's office while my mother and sisters cried in the other room, night after night, working on ways to save what we had. He worked numbers like he was doing magic, pulling loans and collateral out of a hat in ways that amazed us. But what struck me, really struck me, was the way he took away the fear, the way he gave my family back their sense of security.''

Her hand rubbed along his arm in an absent caress. ''And that's what you wanted to do for others.'' The admiration in that statement warmed all the way to the soul.

"Yes. I couldn't think of anything more worthwhile than working those same kinds of miracles. I got a job in the bank the very next day."

"And your family disapproved? Why? Couldn't they see what you were trying to do?"

"They saw what I was leaving behind, and they thought that included them. I was turning my back on family tradition. I was taking a risk with my future. My father yelled. My mother cried. My sisters were furious with me for refusing to see reason, for not doing the right thing."

"But you were. You were doing what was right for you."

"And doing a damned good job of it, too. I'd become a partner in the bank when the war started up. Then that became another right thing to do that they couldn't understand. They haven't forgiven me—for enlisting, for endangering the family line for four long years, for coming home just long enough to make them angry and hurt all over again when I got a telegram from Reeve asking me to come to Kentucky to save his neighbors' security, for getting shot, then for not coming back home to let them fuss over me. That's what they don't understand, why I'd chosen to make things hard for myself."

Her fingers pressed the swell of his forearm. "I do. You needed to feel free."

It was that simple, and that complicated.

"I can't go back with them, not as a failure."

"You're not a failure." Her indignation

squeezed his chest the way her hand did his arm, with a fierce, reaffirming pride. "You've done good things here for the people of Pride. You've given them the chance to keep what they have, whether they know it or not. Another man might have taken over the bank and stripped them of everything right down to their dignity. Someday they'll realize that and thank you."

"Well, that someday isn't tomorrow or the day after. And I'm nowhere near on my feet, either businesswise or personally."

"Am I supposed to feel sorry for you, then? Are they?"

Those were just the right words to summon his determination as he growled, "No. I won't tolerate anyone's pity."

"Then what about your wife's help?"

His silence was steeped in wariness and reluctant pride. Starla rushed on before her courage failed her.

"I can't cook or clean house, but I know my numbers. I could help at the bank—"

"No."

"I could help with the filing and the accounting while you talk to the people to let them get to know you. We could have parties and invite those who wouldn't dare spurn a Fairfax—"

"No."

"Why not? I could help you get back the strength in your legs with exercises, and—"

"*No!*" That escaped him fiercely in a strangling of fear and stubbornness—at the thought of her subjecting herself to the daily dangers associated

with the bank and its enemies, of her exposing herself to the frailty of his body and its failings.
"No."

"But I can help you. Together, isn't that what you said?"

"I'm saying no, now. I don't want—"

"You don't want my help. I see."

She obviously didn't see, but he couldn't explain without stripping himself bare to the insecurities of self. To the lingering fear that he'd lose her if she knew just how helpless he really was. That she'd lose respect for him as a husband, as a man, if she knew he couldn't respond to her as one. So he let her roll away from him, balling up in a knot of unwarranted hurt and dismissal, letting her believe that he didn't value her offer, when in fact it worked upon his heart as nothing had before.

But he couldn't soothe away the pain without admitting the whole truth: he was afraid and he was in love with her. And by hiding both things for the wrong reasons, he was unknowingly destroying what he'd hoped to preserve: their marriage.

Waking beside her husband, Starla had never felt such tearing loneliness, because everything around her was an illusion. She had no marriage, not the kind she dreamed of. That was her fault, her failing. That would have been all right if she'd had a partnership, the kind Dodge had promised. But he'd taken *that* hope from her, too. He wanted nothing from her but a child to promote his family's lineage. And even that was a lie. There was nothing else he would take, nothing she could give. Not comfort, not companionship, not cooperation. They were strangers and he seemed to prefer it that way.

Wasn't it better that he didn't truly know her?

She'd met members of his family. If these good and decent people couldn't understand their own son's decisions about his life, how would they ever come close to accepting the choices she'd had to make? And Dodge, having been raised surrounded by security and love—how could he ever see justification in what she'd done in her past? In her acceptance of what had been done to her? He might give lip service to tolerance, but if the truth were told, he'd pull back in blank horror just as his godfearing family would.

She was living a lie. And the longer she stayed, the more she wanted to remain, to believe the pretense that he would care for her; that the child she carried would be his in name, if not in fact; that she would be safe to explore emotions long bottled up inside for her own self-preservation; and perhaps that they could build a relationship strong enough to weather the truth so she could relieve her arms and heart of the emptiness that grew more intolerable each day.

Seeing him with his sister's children had filled her with both anguish and hope.

In the pale silvery light of morning, she gazed at her husband's face. He might not be gloriously handsome, but she liked the even symmetry of his broad brow, squared jaw, and lean cheeks. Such an honest face: strong, firm, appealing. She stopped her hand just shy of touching that rough cheek, fearing she'd wake him.

How different things would be if the child she carried was shared between them. Then perhaps he'd view the two of them as a blessing rather than a bargain.

Deep inside, she knew from experience that that wasn't necessarily true.

If she were different, she could wrap her arms about him and lay her head upon his chest and be the affectionate wife he deserved. She was cheating him, out of a real wife, out of a true heir. And because she couldn't give him those things, she couldn't share the benefits of wedlock with him, the cherished benefits of love and belonging.

Or could she?

Cautiously she placed her palm on his slow-rising chest, and when he didn't stir, she was emboldened to rest her head there as well. With a quiet mutter, he moved his arm, opening a hollow in which she nestled with a disturbing ease—disturbing because it felt so right.

She closed her eyes to absorb the confusion of contentment and conflicting alarm as his elbow bent and his hand fell big and warm upon the cap of her shoulder, securing her against him. The movement of his lips along her brow put the edge back in her demeanor, forcing her to back away, but only until he snared her with the intensity of his gaze.

He didn't say anything, but his eyes conveyed a multitude of messages from blatant desire to hopeful communion. She started when his hand fit to the back of her head, but her resistance was only a token one as he guided her back down to him.

Her breath blew fast and faint against his mouth, halting at the first light brush of his kisses, once softly, again briefly, a third time with a lingering determination that finally loosened the tight seal of her lips. Though her fists remained clenched against his shoulders and her breaths continued in jerky gasps, her mouth yielded sweetly, parting for his ever-deepening claim. When her tongue touched shyly to his, flares of urgency streaked through his blood, pounding in his temples, blotting out thought and cautious reasoning with the roar of passion.

She met the thrust of his tongue with an uncertain moan and a slight stiffening, but she allowed it and even encouraged it by taking his face between her hands, rubbing his stubbled jaw restlessly. Desire burned hotter, brighter, more fiercely than Dodge could control with any degree of moderation. He wanted her madly, with a mindlessness that overrode restraint, with a wild tangle of love and longing that drove him toward one goal: to move within her as deeply as she'd managed to burrow inside him. It was a goal he had thought impossible until the fire racing through his veins had begun to build and curl in his loins, beginning to push for a response that had him trembling.

Anxiously he gripped the curve of her rib cage, hands spreading wide, thumbs cutting in beneath the plump of her unfettered breasts. He heard her sharp inhalation but was too far gone with the feel of her cushiony bosom as he filled his palms.

When she moved against him, his body read encouragement even as his mind refused to interpret the frantic sounds he devoured with his kiss as ones of panic or protest.

Abruptly he saw stars.

Her sudden punch clacked his teeth together with enough force to rattle his skull. She hit him not with a maidenly slap but with a clenched fist and a hard ridge of knuckle that knocked every trace of desire from his head while she shoved off him, scrambling to a safe distance.

Slowly, gingerly, Dodge worked his jaw back and forth. He blinked to refocus his eyes and glanced down to where Starla huddled at the foot of his bed, sucking at her bruised knuckles.

"Lord above, you pack one helluva wallop."

Tears wobbled on the inky fringe of her lashes as she stared back at him, scared and angry and defiant, and ready to flee at the first aggressive movement. But flat on his back, Dodge was helpless as a turtle.

"You're not going to hit me again, are you?"

She showed him her knuckles. "I hurt my hand."

Gently, carefully, he curled her fingers into his palm, where she let them remain while they regarded one another with a wary mix of emotions.

"Do you trust me, Star?"

"Yes." An answer incongruous with the way she sat stiff and trembling.

"Then tell me, did he rape you?"

A horrible blankness smothered the alarm brightening her stare. She pulled at her hand, but he wouldn't release her.

"It won't change how I feel," he promised, trying to reassure her. "But it'll help me to understand."

A flash of fury tightened her features as she hissed, "You don't understand anything about me. How could you? Let me go." She jerked harder. "Dodge, let me go. Please."

That last was a fierce plea, so prideful and shaky it wound his emotions in knots. He let go and she darted from the room in a flutter of pale silk.

Muttering a curse, Dodge closed his eyes and exhaled heavily. Though she hadn't answered him, he was sure he'd hit upon the truth. The bastard who'd gotten her with child had done so by force, shattering his innocent and once trusting wife with undeserved guilt and fear. Instead of bemoaning the broken pieces he'd inherited, Dodge would do his damnedest to put them back together. He would court his wife with tenderness and care, lavishing her with all the time and gentleness that had been denied her. If it took months, or even years, he'd heal the scars left cruelly upon her, earning her trust and then her love.

He'd have her in his bed each night as long as their company remained, and he vowed she'd feel safe there with him, starting tonight, with his apology. He'd be patient and have all the time he needed to win her over.

He was wrong.

Chapter 12

Starla dropped the bombshell over dinner.

How clever she was to have planned the whole thing to give him absolutely no choice but to go along with her announcement. He wasn't too worried when his mother and sister, children in tow, arrived to take him to lunch. They told him Starla wasn't feeling well and he assumed she wanted some breathing room away from his family, so he generously gave it. When he arrived home that late afternoon, it was to find the table set formally, with extra services at one end: for Patrice and Reeve, Starla told him with a smile. After all, they'd been instrumental in bringing the whole family together. He'd disregarded a quiver of uneasiness to accept the situation at face value . . . only to be hit between the eyes right in the middle of the second course.

That's when she told him, along with everyone else, that she was leaving.

From the first Patrice and the Dodges had hit it off famously. Marian greeted her with a warm embrace that froze Starla clear through as the woman thanked her for taking care of her only son. They chatted companionably while Dodge and Reeve shared a drink and Starla served up a meal she'd had delivered from Sadie's. Starla watched as the Garretts and the Dodges conversed easily, and she couldn't help think that mother- and sister-in-law would have preferred Dodge had married someone sensible and well grounded like Patrice Sinclair, rather than the flashy Starla Fairfax. Perhaps then her Southern allegiance could have been forgiven. She tried to smile and join in the comfortable laughter, but a lump was wedged in her throat.

On her way to and from the table to deliver the main course, she paused behind her husband's chair, giving in to the impulse to let her hand trail lightly along his shoulder. He stopped in mid-sentence to glance up in question, his dark eyes crinkled, a smile lingering on his lips from a joke Reeve had been telling. He waited, his smile growing slightly crooked, his brows knitted in question as she considered saying nothing and forgetting the whole thing.

But it was too late for that.

Instead, she bent to sketch a kiss across his cheekbone, straightening as he sucked a breath of surprise, turning away from his look of confusion—and worse, delight. She resumed her seat and started up before her courage faltered, before the taste of his warm, rough skin and the look in his unsuspecting eyes distracted her from her purpose.

''Guess this is as good a time as any to tell you all good-bye. I've got some family matters I've been neglecting terribly, and Dod—Tony and I thought this would be a good time for me to go, what with his mama and sister here to keep him company while I'm away.''

Patrice glanced at Dodge. He looked gut shot. Then she turned to her friend. ''Where are you going?''

''Louisville. To my daddy's sister's. I won't be gone long. You probably won't even have a chance to miss me.'' A dazzling smile spread to cover the tug at her voice. ''I've been having such fun tonight the time has simply gotten away from me. If you all would excuse me, my train's leaving in less than an hour and I don't want to miss it. Auntie June would be so distressed if I didn't arrive as planned.''

Alice was aghast. ''Tony, you're going to let her travel in her condition, alone and at night?''

''Oh, Alice, Tony knows I'm no shrinking Southern violet. I can take care of myself, the same way your daddy trusted you to come all this way without him. Besides, he can't run off and leave bankin' business. This town depends on him so.''

Again her voice threatened to fail her. Escaping with dignity was harder than she'd thought. She wished she'd given in to her craven want to sneak out leaving a note for all concerned.

But she couldn't put Dodge in the awkward position of explaining her absence.

He wasn't as well versed in lies as she was.

''I'd better be going.''

Dodge overcame his stupor, pushing himself to his feet as she rose and readied to run.

''I'll take you to the station.'' His calm statement betrayed none of the turmoil of the gaze locked into hers.

"There's no need for that, sugar. Patrice can ride with me and bring the buggy back. My things are already packed. Stay here and entertain your company. Besides," and her tone lowered with what sounded like tender concern, "you look so tired."

If she was so damned worried about him, why had she waited until he was wedged like a steer in the slaughter chutes with nowhere to turn, no way to escape, before she delivered the killing blow? It certainly wasn't for kindness' sake. She wanted to flee him with as few complications as possible. That's why she'd packed and loaded her things while he was treating his relatives to a pleasant lunch. That's why she'd made her announcement before an audience—so he'd have no way to argue her decision without causing them all embarrassment.

He'd wed a very clever woman, but he wasn't about to congratulate himself now.

He was too afraid he was about to lose her.

"Patrice," he said, with a calm that belied the frantic pace of his heartbeat, "I'd be grateful if you'd see my wife to the station for me and make sure she gets off safely."

"Of course I will." Patrice rose, flashing him a knowing expression filled with sympathy and reassurance.

Then, to Starla, he said, "I trust you'll at least allow me to see you to the door."

He fought with his crutches, clumsy in his apprehensive rush. Starla reached out to take hold of them, twisting them the right way, steadying them until he could plant them under his arms. Her expression was carefully neutral. He followed her into the foyer, where they paused at the front door. Seeing that they were alone, Dodge pressed his case.

"Don't go."

Starla looked nervously over his shoulder and called, "Patrice, are you ready?" Then she gave a start as his fingertips grazed her cheek.

"I'm sorry. I didn't mean to scare you. Just don't run away."

She caught his hand in one of hers to still its caressing motion and pressed her other one to his lips to still words that would break her heart.

"You don't have anything to apologize for."

His fingers seized up around hers. "Tell me what I did wrong."

"You didn't do anything wrong. It's not you." Her eyes began to burn as painfully as the back of her throat. "Patrice!"

"Don't leave me." That low, rough statement, made more as a command than a plea, nearly undid her. Then Patrice, her rescuer, appeared in the hallway, making it easier for her to smile flirtatiously and tap his cheek.

"Don't be silly. It'll only be a few days . . . a week at most."

He said nothing. The intensity of his stare pierced her to her troubled soul. At the last moment, she put her arms around him, tunneling her face against the crisply starched folds of his shirt-front while her fingers threaded through the short hair at his nape. His hands settled judiciously just below her shoulder blades, resting firmly but without pressure until she chose to step back. She couldn't look up at him before whirling toward the open door and whisking past Patrice into the night.

She was crying by the time she reached the buggy and dry-eyed again before Patrice joined her on the seat. Neither spoke until they'd pulled away from the tidy little house to whir through the streets of Pride. Then Patrice stopped holding her tongue.

"If you're thinking of leaving him, so help me, I'll strangle you right here and now."

"I'm not."

"Then why did you spring your little trip on him like a bear trap right in the middle of the pecan chicken?"

"You wouldn't understand."

Patrice wasn't taking any of her haughty airs. "You're right about that. I don't understand how you could tear the heart out of that man right in front of everyone and carry it off like a trophy that doesn't mean a damned thing to you."

"Patrice, I declare! Your language."

"Never mind my language. How could you hurt and humiliate him like that?"

"And how could you take his side without hearing mine?"

"Because I know both of you. And I know Dodge is an honest, decent man who would lay down his life to keep a promise."

"What does that make me?"

"I don't know what to make of you, Starla; I never did. You play games with people's emotions as if you had none of your own. And I won't let

you do that with Dodge. I care too much for him
as a friend.''

''I thought *I* was your friend.''

Refusing to yield to Starla's fragile tone, Patrice
said, ''He never lies to me. There's no train going
anywhere near Louisville tonight or tomorrow, or
even the day after that.''

Starla said nothing. Her hands clenched the reins
in shaking fists until Patrice put hers over them.

''Go back to him. Don't run away. You can
make things work out between you.''

''I'm not running away from him, Patrice—honestly. I do have something I have to take care of.''

''What? If you can't tell him, at least tell me.''

''I can't tell anyone. Not ever. *Not ever!*''

She dropped the reins to hide her face in her
hands, and as the well-trained animal slowed and
finally halted at the edge of the road, Patrice took
her weeping friend into a comforting embrace.

''I'm sorry, Star. I didn't mean to make you
cry.''

Starla sniffed and rubbed at her eyes. ''Everything makes me cry these days. Dodge says it's the
baby.'' She said his name with such tenderness that
Patrice was as confused as she was frustrated.

''Let him take care of you both, Starla. He's got
so much to give.''

But Starla straightened and picked up the reins.
''There are some things he can't take care of. I
have to myself.'' Dragging the horse's head up and
snapping it into a brisk pace, she let the breeze
finish drying her cheeks as she looked determinedly
ahead.

Knowing Starla as she did, Patrice saw that the conversation was over. She was no closer to understanding what haunted her friend.

All night the southbound train clattered toward the Gulf Coast. Starla gave up on sleep. Each time she closed her eyes the image of Dodge's stricken face was there to torment her. She hadn't meant to hurt him; she'd had no choice. She couldn't move ahead toward a life with Dodge with so much still pulling her back into the past. The stress of living on lies took a savage toll, pushing her out onto the thin wire of truth, where it became harder and harder to find a point of balance. She wanted Dodge to be that balance. She wanted him to be her future.

But first she had things to settle.

Her hand clutched at the crumpled letter delivered to her only that morning. The contents had rocked her world and sent her into a panicked scramble to recover what she could while concealing her motives from those who cared about her.

It tore at her heart not to tell them why she had to leave. But how could she, without revealing all?

Finally, exhaustion, coupled with the constant rocking of the rails, lulled her into a restless slumber from which she awoke to the thick scent of saltwater. New Orleans. Rumpled and sore, she claimed her scant baggage and found a rented hack to take her to the exotic French Quarter, to the Creole-style house set beneath shading live oak trees bearded in Spanish moss where she'd lived the last four years as Mrs. Stephen Fortun.

Walking in was like taking on another person's

life. The smells of chicory coffee and frying beignets were as familiar as the patois of hurried French coming from behind the servants' stairs. As familiar as the sudden clomp of tiny feet on the hardwood landing overhead and the sweet voice crying out, ''Mama!''

Chapter 13

Starla bent down to receive the hurtling impact of a three-year-old's unconditional love. For a moment, with eyes squeezed tightly shut and heart opened wide, she felt all the loneliness she'd known in her lifetime wash away.

And just as quickly, the taint of guilt and unforgivable sin resurfaced to stain the purity of a mother's emotions. She released the child and straightened.

''I declare, you've grown a foot since I last saw you. Stand back and let me have a good look.''

She gazed long and hungrily at the delicate child, who, with his huge green eyes and lanky black hair, and even with the softness of youth to hide the beautiful structure of his face, was so much like her brother it brought unexpected tears to her eyes. And she redoubled her determination that this innocent child grow up in the embrace of a normal family—feeling loved, special, and protected from evils no child should have to experience, let alone try to understand.

The way her little boy was trying to understand

why his mama found it so difficult to hold him.

"Have you come to stay, Mama?"

She brushed lovingly at the rumpled shoulders and sleeves of his coat, forcing words through the tender thickening in her throat. "Not for very long, I'm afraid. I have to go back soon."

"Will you take me with you this time?"

She shuddered with the fracturing of her heart as she said, "We'll see," knowing he was too young to read the lie in those words or to recognize the pain in her eyes. Soon he would learn to see through her placating falsehoods and be cynical enough to doubt the seeming truths she told. That's when he would truly begin to look like Tyler, when the happy trust in his uplifted gaze grew jaded with wariness—when he learned to hide his disappointment and tears behind an insincere smile.

These were the things she would teach her son, unless she decided soon what she would do.

"Christien, go find *Grandmère* and tell her I've come for a visit."

Though reluctant to leave her, the child did as told. She watched him scramble up the stairs with a toddler's energy that was more enthusiasm than coordination. A sad smile shaped her lips as the image blurred before her eyes.

"I love you, baby," she whispered hoarsely.

Her welcome back into the Fortun household was as nonexistent as it had been when she'd arrived at its doorstep four years prior, on the arm of Stephen Fortun, a wealthy rice planter's only son who'd announced her to his startled parents as his

new bride. As quickly as he'd ensconced her in his
family home, he was off to join his Louisiana regiment, not to return for three long years—leaving
his mysterious young bride in the care of strangers,
alone, and soon, they discovered, pregnant.

Stephen's father, Robert Fortun, was thrilled to
learn his legacy would continue. He treated Starla
with a courtly politeness that couldn't quite offset
his wife's chill hostility. For those three years
Starla shared their home, but never their affection
or acceptance. As Starla Fortun, she'd lived as a
prosperous member of New Orleans society. Giving birth in the absence of her husband, she appeared a sad and intriguing figure, becoming one
of the most sought-after belles of the city. But the
enigmatic younger Mrs. Fortun entertained no company and kept to herself in the elegant house on
Chartres Street. It was a quiet, contented life watching her son grow up—or at least, that's how it appeared.

But her luck wasn't to hold. Called home at the
death of his father, Stephen Fortun returned from
the battlegrounds a changed man. From that time
until his self-destruction eight months later, Starla
lived on the edge of a nightmare, one that truly
began the day Stephen was buried and his inheritance passed to his son.

Starla didn't care about the money; she hadn't
married Stephen for it, and, contrary to whispered
rumors, she hadn't hurried her husband to his death
to claim it. What she did care about was their son,
Christien. But what her widowed mother-in-law,
Sally Fortun, cared about were the family name and

the family fortune, and she was quick to strike to maintain both by fighting for custody of Christien against a woman she claimed was unfit to raise him.

Starla had never seen the battle coming and was unprepared for the clever woman's vicious slanders. A member of high society, Sally Fortun could not let it be known that her only son had died at the hands of his own weakness for opium. Instead, she created a grand fiction that his wife's continued infidelities had led the poor man, a war hero, to take his life in a fit of tragic despair. And such an unfaithful woman could not be allowed to raise her only surviving kin.

Help came to Starla in the guise of one of Stephen's friends, Beau LeBlanc, an ambitious young lawyer she'd met at a soiree. His offer to aid her in the fight for Christien seemed too good to be true. She gave him her trust, her every confidence— and she'd been cruelly betrayed. The Fortun money had bought off LeBlanc's honor and Starla had been forced to flee the city. That was when she'd discovered that LeBlanc's treachery had not only stripped her of her child's love but had filled her with another.

It was those two vipers, her mother-in-law and her lawyer, that she faced that day in the elegant parlor.

"It was wise of you to respond so quickly to my message," LeBlanc began with a benign smile. Why had she never seen his shallow charm for what it was, a mask over raw and ruthless ambition?

"What do you want?" she asked without a trace of civility. She had no desire to pretend with these people. They meant to tear her child from her, and she refused to be polite about it.

"Why, what's best for Christien, of course," Sally cooed with false sincerity. "That's all we've ever wanted. That's why I've asked Monsieur LeBlanc to draw up papers that will resolve the matter of his future without any . . . shall we say, ugliness."

"Let me see them."

Starla's heart went cold as she read the document, which, in professional jargon, stripped her of parental rights to her own son, giving custody of him, and thus control of his accompanying fortune, to his grandmother. With her signature attached, it would cover over all the unpleasant truths, all the nasty trickery, all the potential threats. All she had to do was sign, and four years of her life would disappear forever.

But Christien would be lost to her.

"We are not totally unsympathetic," LeBlanc continued. "Mrs. Fortun has agreed to be quite generous. She'll give you a thousand dollars for your inconvenience."

Starla stared at them aghast and outraged. Her voice was a strained whisper. "Inconvenience? Is that what you call it?"

"Call it whatever you like," Sally snapped. "Just take the money and get out."

"Do you expect me to sell my child so cheaply?"

That surprised them. They sat back and exchanged glances.

"Give her two thousand," Sally said at last. "Just get her to sign."

"And what if I don't want your money?" she countered.

LeBlanc smiled in the face of Starla's challenge, proving he felt it was empty. "Take it, my dear, and count yourself lucky. The matter goes to court in thirty days. You can't win; you know that. But you have everything to lose." He let that linger, an undefined threat. Starla didn't need him to spell it out for her. She knew what he was willing to do and say to win Christien from her. She carried proof of it.

"I need time to think."

Sally's patience ended. "You have until morning. Then the offer is rescinded."

"Don't force us to make trouble for you." LeBlanc stated it plainly. "Take the money and have done with it. You're a beautiful woman, Starla. It shouldn't be hard for you to start over. What man could refuse you anything you wanted? And what other choice do you have?"

She shivered at the evidence of lust thickening his words. And she recoiled from the truth he spoke with such confidence.

What choice *did* she have?

As she looked down at her sleeping child, hating herself for not being able to embrace him without feeling the possible taint of his conception, she struggled for the right thing to do for Christien.

If he were to remain, she would have to sever

all ties and claim to him. That was the only way to be sure LeBlanc wouldn't attempt to exact revenge upon her. He was a vain creature who felt himself humiliated at her hands, and that made him dangerous and not above stooping to despicable means.

She knew that for a fact, and she was afraid.

But after knowing the abandonment of a mother's love, how could she wish the same unhappiness upon her own child? Even within the opulent home Sally Fortun would provide for him, he would always recall that his mother had not cared enough or had not been strong enough to keep him at her side.

After nearly fifteen years, she still found herself wondering if it was somehow her fault that her own mother had run away, while alternately blaming the woman she could scarcely remember for leaving her to face a nightmare on her own. She didn't want to spend the rest of her life knowing her son resented her.

She touched the boy's head, threading her fingers through hair fine as silk. How could she leave him to his heartless grandmother? Yet how equally difficult it was to take him with her to Kentucky. How could she win the right to Christien without revealing a truth that would forever damn him? Dodge would know the truth. In knowing it, would he take her back? Would he accept Christien?

The image of her husband's smiling tolerance as his sister's children climbed all over him warmed her heart with an ember of hope. Perhaps he had enough love to bestow upon this blameless boy.

But how, then, would he treat her, knowing that she was guilty of a huge lie of omission when she said her vows without telling him everything?

Everything. . . .

She withdrew her hand and scrubbed her palm against her skirts.

Was there enough love in anyone's heart for a mother and child of their circumstances? How could she expect Dodge to forgive her when she couldn't forgive herself?

The alternative was to take Christien and begin anew where no one knew them or would ever have reason to suspect their past. To leave her home, her family, her friends . . . her husband.

To escape the constant fear of someone finding out her secret and suffering for their disappointment.

A whore, just like your mother. Nothing but a lying whore. . . .

She surged to her feet and paced the darkened room, the soft, sonorous sounds of her son's breathing failing to comfort her. She had to get away from that voice, from feelings of being unclean and unworthy. And therein lay the conflict of heart and mind, the heart saying, "Go to your husband and confess your sins; trust him to forgive you and ask him to help," and the quick, clever, self-preserving mind whispering, "Go to your husband's accounts and take all you can to see you safely out of everyone's reach. Only then can you and the boy be free and safe from the censure of those you love; then no one can hurt you."

What am I going to do? she cried softly to the

unresponsive night. But, deep in her heart, she knew the answer.

There was only one time when Dodge could remember ever feeling worse. That was when the shock of taking a bullet dulled enough for him to realize he couldn't move his legs. That slashing panic and the certainty that nothing in his life would ever be the same was how he felt now. Only then, he'd hoped he would die, and now, he knew he was going to live.

The first day Starla was gone, Dodge's mother and sister were cautious, biding their time, guarding their tongues. He'd moved through the hours in a daze, too tired to feel, too afraid to think. After another sleepless night, his mood fluctuated wildly, from moody despair to irritable shortness. He was caught between the sentimental wish to immerse himself in anything that would remind him of Starla and the practical side that pushed him to go to the bank to lose himself in the dependability of his accounts.

But nothing added up the way it was supposed to: not his figuring, not his future. And he was damned if he knew what he was going to do about it. How could he win over a wife who'd run away?

''Is she worth it?''

Dodge glanced up from the lines he was drawing through the gravy and potatoes on his plate to find his mother's empathic gaze upon him.

''What? Who?''

"This woman who runs away and leaves you helpless."

"I'm hardly helpless, Mother."

"Don't get testy with me, young man. You know what I mean."

"I'm afraid I don't. Would you clarify it for me?"

Marian sighed, seeing the combative angle of Dodge's jaw, so like her husband's. "You say this is what you want, but I've yet to see you look happy about it. Your job at the bank makes you miserable and the woman you married breaks your heart."

"That's not true."

"I have eyes, Hamilton. A good thing, since you don't see fit to share anything with me."

Though Alice wanted to hear more of the conversation, she pushed away from the table, announcing, "Come, children. It's time to see to your studies."

After the expected grumbles, they dutifully marched upstairs on the heels of their mother, leaving the table a place for adult conversation.

"What is it you want to know, Mother? What do you think I'm keeping from you?"

"Is the child she's carrying yours?"

Dodge rocked back in his chair, stunned to silence by her unexpected candor. Finally he said, "Why would you think to ask such a thing?"

Marian noted that he didn't deny it. "Your wife is somewhat . . . cold."

"Cold? To you?"

"To you. To everyone."

"She's very reserved."

"I think it's more than that."

Feeling pressed to defend Starla and their relationship, he said, "Not everyone comes from a family as demonstrative as ours. She lost her mother when she was very young. Showing affection is something that doesn't come easily to her, especially before an audience."

"And in private?"

"That's private."

"Is the child yours?"

He looked everywhere but into her direct stare. She read the truth in the way he hedged around it with irritation and a bristling defense.

"I'm not going to dignify that with an answer, Mother. You come into my home—uninvited; you make unpleasant and unfounded insinuations about my wife, the woman I love—"

"Does she love you?"

Again he struggled for a response, but before he could give it, she held up her hand.

"Don't bother to make up some fairy tale. I can see the truth."

He stared at his plate. For a moment the barriers came down.

"Why did she marry you, if not for love? Because of the child?"

He glanced up, his expression complex. "Wouldn't that be reason enough?"

"*Is* it?"

He didn't reply, and after a minute, she knew he wasn't going to.

"No man wants to admit a mistake to his

mother, but that's what you made when you came down here, when you took this woman in. Don't be so stubborn that you'd rather ruin the rest of your life than realize your father was right.''

''Is that what you think I'm doing?''

''What would you call it? You've put all your money and efforts into a bank that people won't use. You marry a woman who may or may not be having your child, who doesn't love you. You refuse help from those who do care and totally refuse to accept the facts.''

''And what facts are those, Mother?''

She should have been alerted by the softness of his voice, by the sudden stillness of his expression.

''That you may never walk again. Your doctor tells me you push yourself, that you *torture* yourself daily, most likely for no reason. That this banking venture is going to fail and if you continue, someone will probably succeed in killing you the next time. That this woman who has bewitched you will never make you a good wife and will never make you happy.''

''And I can save myself from all that by going home with you.''

''Yes.''

''By leaving these people, some of whom depend on me for their very lives. By confining myself to a wheelchair, where I should be grateful for a life in which I have no freedom. By leaving a woman I've pledged myself to, to whom I've promised my love and loyalty for as long as I live. To break my vow that I'd take care of her and her child so they'd never have to fear anything or be alone. Why didn't I see how simple it all was before? Is that why my father didn't come? Because he knew I'd fold and come whimpering back with you the minute you pointed out those basic truths?"

"No. Your father didn't come because he knew you wouldn't change your mind. He knew that no matter how bad things were for you here, you wouldn't abandon them because you'd made a commitment. He knew you'd drag yourself on hands and knees if you had to in order to make things work. And that you'd succeed, because you're his son, and no matter how it breaks his heart, he's too proud of you to beg the way I just did. Now, if you'll excuse me, I think your sister and I should begin packing to go home."

She paused, giving him the chance to stop her, but when he didn't, she rose with a quiet dignity and left the room . . . leaving Dodge to chafe at her words, and to wonder at their truth.

They left the next morning, and he didn't try to convince them to stay. There was no comfort in their presence when he knew they thought he was wrong in what he was doing, when he knew they were waiting for him to fail.

It was always hard to say good-bye to the children. They hugged him in genuine regret, not understanding any of the darker undercurrents between their elders. That was the beauty of children: their simplistic vision.

"Good-bye, Uncle Tony."

"Will you come see us soon, Uncle Tony?"

"I'll try. Maybe when I have a new little cousin for you to meet. How would you like that?"

"A baby? When?"

"In the spring."

"Will you bring Aunt Starla, too? She's pretty."

Dodge smiled. "Yes, of course I will." But when his gaze lifted, he saw the doubt in both his mother's and his sister's eyes. "She's my wife." He said that to clarify everything else.

His sister embraced him tightly, wetting his cheek with her unexpected tears to make him feel churlish in his behavior.

"Give my best to Frank."

"We love you, Tony. Don't forget that."

"I won't."

"Be happy," was all his mother would say as they held one another.

If only he knew how to effect that miracle.

"I'm sorry it wasn't a better visit and that Starla couldn't be here to see you off."

His mother had no comment, for which he was grateful. Instead, she said, "Do come and visit us. Everyone loves an excuse to fuss over a new baby—a new Dodge."

Suddenly close to tears himself, he managed a gruff, "I promise," as they stepped up onto the train. He waited on the platform until the sight of them waving was obscured by swirls of soot, then distance. A sense of loneliness surrounded him like that hazy steam swallowing up the familiar.

He went to work, not that there was much to do except sort through files concerning people who'd never seen fit to step inside the bank. With each folder he set aside as inactive, the tide of futility increased, until he was dangerously close to going under. He wasn't providing a needed service with the Pride County Bank. He was holding onto an institution that had died with its founder. Reeve had been wrong to bring him down to save something that didn't want saving. Was he equally wrong in trying to make a place for himself among this foreign and hostile population?

Deciding no harm would be done if he closed up early, he was securing the front door lock when a quiet step behind him alerted him that he wasn't alone. He turned to face a hulking figure he remembered as one of the men who'd accosted Starla on the sidewalk. There was no fondness in the man's blunt greeting.

"Mr. Fairfax wants to see you."

"Tyler knows where to find me."

"Not Tyler; Mr. Fairfax. Up at the house. You're to come with me."

An invitation or a command? Dodge didn't worry over semantics. A face-to-face with Cole Fairfax suited him just fine.

How else could he get to the truth?

Chapter 14

⌒~⊙⊙⌒

The room smelled like death.

Stepping inside the men's parlor at Fair Play took Dodge back to the horrible memory of coming upon a battlefield where a change in weather and desperate circumstances had prevented the burial of the dead. That putrid odor of what had once been life returning to the ground in a state of decay was something one never forgot.

Cole Fairfax was dying—not a pleasant death, but one of slow decline by degrees. Like most powerful men used to having command over everything shy of nature itself, he didn't like losing. It made him short tempered, and, Dodge guessed, dangerous, without the threat of consequence to hold him in check. Once a man knew he was dying, what reason did he have for restraint?

"Mr. Fairfax? I'm Hamilton Dodge."

The old man gave him a narrow study that concluded with a wry smirk. "You're Lieutenant Dodge? After the thrashing you gave my men, I was expecting someone more . . . formidable."

Dodge shrugged.

"Come in and close the door."

Shutting himself in a stagnant tomb held no appeal, but Dodge did as requested and moved further into the shadows stretching across the interior. With all the draperies drawn to seal out the light, it took a moment for his eyes to adjust to the dimness. Dodge could make out the slumped figure of a man settled into a huge thronelike chair. Slowly the sickness-ravaged features came into focus. Dodge held tight to his reaction. The man was little more than an animated cadaver, with fever-bright eyes set in the midst of sunken flesh and prominent bone, but those eyes burned with shrewd intelligence . . . and with smoldering hostility.

"I understand you married my daughter."

"Yes, sir."

"A Northern boy. What are you, some sort of banker?"

"Yes, sir."

"You get around pretty good for a man who should be dead."

That comment tore away the mask of ignorance. Cole Fairfax knew everything about him.

"Some folks are harder to kill than others. You should appreciate that, Mr. Fairfax."

The old man gave a rusty-sounding laugh. "Yes. Some of us don't have the God-given sense to let go." His features hardened. "How is it that you have set up housekeeping with my Starla and now is the first time we've met each other face to face? Don't you Yankees have any respect for family?"

"My highest priority, sir. It was my understanding that you were a recluse and not given to accommodating audiences. I came to pay my respects before but wasn't allowed inside.''

"Well, you're here now. You'd best be givin' me a reason why I should be handing the future of my little girl over to a stranger's hands.''

"I think it's a bit late to justify what's already taken place. Starla and I are man and wife.''

"Don't you think I could change that state of affairs, boy? You don't know who you're dealin' with, do you?''

"On the contrary. I think I know you quite well.''

"Then you know I don't like folks who take what's mine.''

"I didn't take her from you, Mr. Fairfax. She's still your daughter. And now she's my wife as well.''

"Your wife.'' Something dark and ugly moved through those glittering eyes. "How can you make such a claim when she belongs here, in this house, with me? You know nothing about her.''

"I know that she said yes and we are married.''

"The girl's incapable of making those kinds of decisions for herself. She's of a delicate nature and fragile mind, like her mother before her. What she wants one week won't do the next. She isn't the type to commit to any one thing or any one man. It's a flaw, a fatal flaw. So you can see why I'll do whatever needs be done to keep her here, safe at home, where she can be cared for properly and guided away from such ill-advised fancies.''

"I hardly think our marriage can be considered an ill-advised fancy.''

Fairfax smiled, an expression so filled with smug certainty that Dodge knew a shiver of alarm. "So she's been faithful to you. A good and dutiful wife in every way."

"Yes. In every way."

Fairfax stared at him, anger congealing to make fiery blotches in his sunken face. "You are a liar, sir. What you have is no consummated marriage, but a sham, a deception, to steal a daughter from her father's arms. Is it our money you want? The influence of our name? You'll not have them, not while I live." He must have seen Dodge's expression flicker, for his smile turned grim as he vowed, "And I do plan to live longer than you. Long enough to bring Starla back where she belongs."

"Starla belongs with me, by her choice and the laws of Kentucky. What you want, Mr. Fairfax, doesn't matter. I had hoped we might get along, but I can see now that isn't going to happen. So let *me* tell *you* how it's going to be. Starla is my wife, and that's a fact you can't change, whether you like it or not. Your relationship with your daughter is between the two of you, but I won't let you distress her, especially not now, while she's carrying my child."

That struck the old man like a hard blow to the gut. He wheezed, choking on his shock and outrage. "My little girl will raise no bastard pup of yours. Do you think because you've bedded her you've won her away from me? Think again. *Think again!*"

Spittle flew from the old man's lips as they curled back in a snarl. Then an unnatural calm claimed him, settling him back in his chair with a frightening surety.

"You've won nothing, Lieutenant. Starla will be back here where she belongs, with her family. She tried to run away before, but this is her home and she'll never leave it. If you try to stand in the way, I'll see you buried. Have I made myself clear?"

"As glass, sir."

"I don't think so. I don't think we have an understanding quite yet. But we will. Soon."

Dodge angled around on his crutches, moving with all the fierce dignity he could manage in his refusal to show intimidation. Leaving the stale room behind, he drew a deep breath of fresh air in the hall, then heard a low chuckle.

"So how did you an' my daddy get along?"

"He's a crazy son of a bitch. Who the hell does he think he is?"

Tyler's smile never faltered. "He thinks he's God, Yank, and here in Pride, you'd be a fool to doubt him."

God. Dodge slammed his desk drawer shut, still seething over the interview of the day before. Cole Fairfax was a devil if ever he'd seen one—a dark demon used to getting his way through whatever evil proved necessary.

Dodge wasn't afraid of him, but he was understandably cautious.

He understood small town hierarchies. Even the craziest bastard could rule with impunity, provided he had enough money. And the Fairfaxes had plenty. Was he being careless to believe himself beyond the old man's reach? Was he being blindly arrogant to think he could keep Starla safe, even after her own brother claimed no one could protect her?

And from what?

He brooded over that question, wondering if the smartest thing to do would be to grab up his wife the minute she returned, and to move the both of them up north, where he'd have a guaranteed job. If she came back.

But that would be running away, admitting that he'd let a dying old man's threats scare him off what he wanted.

Knowing he couldn't keep Starla from danger kindled a slow-burning fear in his belly, one fueled by righteous anger.

Where was she?

Missing her warred with the logic saying she was safer staying away. At least until he was stronger, until he could cast off the crutches and stand as a man to command the respect owed a man. He flexed his knees, gritting his teeth. Just when was that going to be?

The front door of the bank opened, announcing a customer. Determinedly Dodge set aside his personal turmoils to adopt a professional face.

" 'Afternoon, ma'am. How can I help you?''

He didn't know her name, but he could guess her occupation. She was probably much younger than she looked, having been aged by long hours and a hard life. Unnaturally blond hair topped a garishly made-up face and a gown too vulgar for daylight. She gave him an uncertain smile.

"Mr. Dodge?"

"Yes, ma'am."

"I'm Irma Sue Fielding. You hold my daddy's note."

"Charles Fielding? Yes, ma'am—that is, the bank does."

"My daddy's in a terrible state, what with that note overdue and him with no way of seeing it paid."

"Have your daddy come in to talk with me. I'm sure we can work out some terms."

She responded to his reassuring smile with one of sly suggestion. "I come to see if I could make the terms for him."

Only a saint wouldn't have caught on to what she had in mind by way of collateral. Gently, firmly, Dodge said, "I think it'd be better if I dealt with your father."

She sashayed closer, bringing the smell of old beer and cheap cologne with her, along with the stale scent of illicit sex. "Don't you like me?"

"I'm sure you're a very nice young lady, but I'm married, and I'm not looking for—"

Someday gravity would work cruelly against Irma Sue Fielding, but for the moment it was more than kind as she spilled a tremendous bounty from the bodice of her dress with a healthy bounce. Dodge blinked, his mind completely blanked by the spectacle as Irma Sue wiggled down so her impressive breasts sat inches from his face and her palms moved boldly along the tops of his thighs.

"My friend told me how you got yourself hurt and how certain things might not be working the way they should be. I ain't no doctor, Mr. Dodge, but I bet I can cure what ails you, if you'd be inclined to overlook my daddy's note for another month.''

"Miss Fielding, I—"

The rest of what he had to say was smothered in her pillowy breasts as she pulled him toward her, hugging his head to her bosom with one hand as her other began a skillful manipulation in his lap. Too stunned to react at once, Dodge struggled to draw a breath and some saving sanity, all the while Irma Sue's deft touch created enough chaos to make him wonder rather wildly if she wasn't the answer to his plaguing doubts.

Maybe he'd been listening to the wrong experts.

But even Irma Sue's expertise couldn't crowd out the sudden image of Starla's face or prevent the shock of clear thinking that made him ask, "What friend sent you to me?"

It wasn't Irma Sue who answered.

"Don't tell me this is another sister."

The sense of standing at the edge of an abyss with stones trickling over the rim had him hauling back out of the grip of Irma Sue's considerable charms only to plunge straight to hell at the sight of Starla staring at both of them with a skeptical glower.

He couldn't breathe.

"Am I interrupting something?"

Without looking around, Irma Sue drawled, "We're right in the middle of some delicate negotiations here, so wait your turn, honey."

Dodge grabbed the front of Irma Sue's gown and

yanked it up, earning an indignant squeal. He never glanced away from Starla's steady stare.

"We're finished, Miss Fielding. In fact, we were finished before we started. As I said, send your daddy to talk to me."

"Well, what got you changin' your tune in such a damned hurry?" Irma Sue huffed, as she got to her feet.

"His wife," Starla said, with the lethal clang of a drawn blade.

The muddled harlot looked between the two of them and decided, wisely, to make for the door before all hell broke loose . . . leaving Dodge to do the impossible.

"I can explain."

"I bet you can." Starla walked past his desk, her step brisk with annoyance.

"It wasn't what it looked like."

"I see. And now you think I'm blind as well as a fool."

"No, of course not. I—aw, hell." How could he expect her to believe him when he couldn't convince himself? "She was trying to get her father's note postponed."

"A convincing argument. Was she successful?"

Alerted by her continued calm, Dodge dragged himself to his feet. His mind scrambled in a dozen different directions; numbed by Irma Sue's touch, spinning from the effect of Starla's return, reeling with the fear of losing her, of hurting her. . . .

She had her back to him, her gloved fingertips trailing along the edge of the teller's cage in a gesture that made his skin quiver in response. How could he be so stunned by her beauty after only a few days' separation? Eagerness and apprehension twined through him as he followed her behind the teller's window.

"I didn't know you'd returned."

"Obviously. Otherwise you wouldn't have invited Irma Sue to begin negotiations."

"Do you know her?"

"She's a slatternly acquaintance of my—of the Dermonts."

Dodge paused. Tyler had sent Irma Sue. Why? To discover if he was aiming his pistol without the proper wadding? Or because he'd seen Starla's arrival and sought to alienate them? Had he in fact succeeded?

"Is she the kind of woman who appeals to you, then?"

She turned toward him, her question seemingly sincere. It took him aback.

"I'm not interested in any woman except you."

"I see. So you would rather it had been *me* smothering you in my bosom."

"Yes. I mean, no. I mean—hell, anything I say is going to dig me in deeper. Nothing was going on between me and that woman, I swear to God."

"Nothing? Would you say no to a woman who offers everything in favor of one who refuses you anything?"

"Starla, you're the only woman I want. And I've wanted you since I first saw you."

"So," she said softly, with an absence of inflection, "you would have a wife who acts the whore for you."

"No."

"Then you wouldn't like for me to bare my breasts for you, to put my hands upon you, like so."

Her palms flattened against the front of his snug silk vest, exciting a sudden lunging gallop of pulse beats. His gaze fell to the soft curve of her bodice as his imagination went momentarily wild.

"You would say, 'No, stop,' to me if I were to continue with what she was doing?"

"I—" He couldn't assemble the words as blood pounded into his head with the first stroke of her fingertips along the front of his trousers. The fact that it was Starla, his *wife*, touching him flushed all memory of other women from his mind. His hands tightened on the grips of his crutches as he swayed in the thrall of temptation. His eyelids flickered, then focused on Starla, who stared unblinkingly into his face.

This was wrong. He knew it even as she said, "Now I know what's expected of me if I'm to stay with you."

"Starla—"

She knelt at his feet in a pool of lilac-colored satin. He was reaching down for her elbows, planning to pull her up, when the door to the bank opened again.

"Mr. Dodge? Oh, there you are."

"Mrs. Bishop." Did she notice how ragged his voice sounded? From where she was standing, she could only see him from the chest up on the other side of the teller's window. Starla was completely out of sight . . . and beginning a devastating massage through the wool of his trousers. He forced his breathing to remain even.

"Mr. Dodge, I was wondering if we could discuss that loan for the expansion of my dressmaking shop."

"Now?"

Starla had untucked his shirt. His abdomen quivered as her lips brushed beneath his navel.

"Yes, unless you're busy. I've talked over the monthly payments with my husband, and we thought if we hired on another girl, we'd have no problem keeping up with the—Mr. Dodge, are you all right?"

He was swaying slightly for balance on his crutches, finally forced to grip the edge of the counter as Starla worked his trouser flap open. Her cool fingertips touched him.

"Yes . . . yes. I—I'm fine. You were saying, about the loan. . . ." He breathed harder. The tightening vortex of heat was spiraling where Starla was purposefully raising havoc.

Raising, swelling, growing hard, harder.

He couldn't focus his attention on the elderly customer chatting away as the shock of Starla's silken kiss stroked over him. His knees buckled. His hands curled around the bars.

"Mrs. . . . Mrs. Bishop . . . could we go over this tomorrow? I was—I was getting ready to close up. My wife just returned from a short trip, and I . . . want to be home to welcome her back."

Myrna Bishop suddenly went all soft with sentimental smiles. "Why, of course. Why didn't you say so? Tomorrow it is. All the best to your wife."

"All the best . . ." he moaned, as the door closed behind the oblivious woman. He rested his cheek against the cool wood of the counter, his eyes closing, his breath altering into short, harsh bursts as his fingers clutched and spasmed around the bars. Starla's mouth was on him, her tongue swirling, teeth scraping gently, beginning a rhythmic pull that seemed to draw from the soles of his feet to the roots of his hair to the very core of his being.

He gasped hoarsely, at first surprised, then lost to shuddering shocks of pleasure that racked him until he was but a drained shell. He couldn't lift his head from the counter top. His eyes felt too weighted to open. Only his desperate grip on the bars kept him from pouring like liquid to the floor.

Oh, God, never before . . . never in his life . . . the rest drifted away on a heavy sated cloud.

The sound of a crutch clattering to the floor roused him from near slumber. He didn't want to move. He didn't want to stir from this blissful sense of rediscovery.

He certainly wasn't impotent!

He'd flushed enough through his system to seed a desert.

He was grinning with an almost drunken foolishness when he finally made his eyes flutter open at the sound of the front door closing.

Dodge locked up the bank in record time, rushing home in a fever of anticipation that didn't permit him a clear thought until he stepped into the foyer and saw Starla there. Only then did wild elation give way to reality. She met his look with eyes cold as emerald chips.

He didn't know what to say to her. He settled for the obvious: "I'm glad you're home."

She said nothing.

"How was your trip?"

"Long. I'm very tired."

And she was angry with him. Angry, and somehow different—as if he'd suddenly taken a tremendous plunge in her estimation.

"Where are your mother and sister?"

"In Michigan by now, I'd imagine. I've sent them home."

"Oh." The word conveyed a wealth of feelings. Surprise. Relief. Curiosity. Gratitude. But she had voiced none of those things. She stared at him, waiting.

For what? God, he wished he knew something, anything, about her. That he had some way to reach through the silences and secrets.

Finally he just reached for her.

She stiffened as his arms circled her, but she allowed him to bring her to him, to hold her against the hurried thunder of his heart, riding out his massive sigh of relief.

She'd come back; nothing else mattered.

The words "I love you" tasted bittersweet on his tongue but he held them back because there was so much she held back from him. Like why she'd brought him to such a point of exquisite paradise only to abandon him.

Like where she'd learned to do such a thing with a man.

It didn't matter, he told himself; it shouldn't. He loved her and she had come back to him. They were on the brink of intimacy and he no longer feared failure in that area.

Why, then, when she stepped back from him, did she look at him as though she loathed him?

Chapter 15

The house was quiet without the invasive Dodge family there. Silence accentuated the fact that it was just the two of them, alone. Starla stood in the doorway to her husband's bedroom, observing him before he was aware of her presence.

She'd been eager to get back to him. That irony provoked an awful ache. Because the sense of hurt was too difficult to bear, because she felt herself close to tears over what she'd walked in on at the bank, she made herself focus on his failure, not hers. Her good and decent husband, the man she'd let herself trust, was no different from any of them—deceitful, led by their lusts, easily controlled by a tug on the trouser band. She shouldn't have been surprised, but she was. She'd wanted to believe his pretty words about honor. She'd needed to think of him as a safe, dependable haven.

Then came the unbidden whisper. If she *was* more a wife to him, he wouldn't seek out others. *A man can wait only so long before taking what he wants. . . .* She understood that and she'd made the most of it: in surviving her upbringing, and in latching onto an escape from Fair Play. She knew the game of manipulation and how to make it work to her advantage. A game of detachment and calculated response. She'd been a fool not to play it from the first. But she'd hoped . . . she'd hoped Dodge would be the first to give without first taking.

She held tight to her disappointment. If she wanted a happy ending to her life, she had to write it herself. And it began here, with this man. She could escape, either with him or through him. But it was up to him.

He saw her then and stopped what he was doing. A hint of caution colored his gaze, reminding her to play her role carefully. She forced a smile and moved toward him, making no attempt to hold the front of her silky robe closed. She watched heat darken his stare as he took in what that gap revealed: her body, outlined in wisps of lace. He wet his lips and spoke with an odd huskiness.

"Did you come to say good night, or was there something else you wanted? I can apologize only so many times."

As if words would be enough to heal the fracture of her faith. She let none of her emotions show in her face.

"Perhaps I came to see if there was anything else *you* wanted."

What he wanted was no mystery. It blazed in his eyes, it thundered through his throat beneath her knuckles. He wanted *her*. She made herself stand before him, a gift partially unwrapped, hinting of delights inside, should he decide to take them. She froze as he lifted his hand, but it was only to capture her own, to enfold it within the curl of his fingers, to hold it pressed over his rapidly beating heart.

"I'm fine," he said. "I have everything I want right here."

She'd come to him for one reason: to gain control through confusion. She was afraid that when he stopped feeling guilty, he'd start asking questions: about her trip, about its purpose—questions she didn't want to answer. But a man couldn't think with his head when his lust ran rampant. That's what she'd counted upon. Then why did she feel as though it was *she* who was confused—by his simple yet elegant words, by the yearning steeped in his dark eyes?

She smiled, canting her gaze downward with a flutter of her lashes. It was a practiced seduction, one that startled most men into excited thoughts of conquest.

But why was Dodge beginning to frown?

What was she doing wrong?

He levered back on his crutches. The wanting was still there, a hot coal of desire, but banking it was a containing suspicion: she was moving too fast.

"You missed me."

"Yes."

"Enough to grant me a favor?" She glanced up at him, tempering her coy manner with just enough directness to put him at ease.

"I would do anything for you."

She hated the way he said that because it created

a false warmth inside her, a sense of believing what she knew to be untrue.

"I'd like to work in the bank with you. I know you said you didn't need my help when I asked before, but—"

"Yes."

"What?"

"Yes. If you want to work there, that's fine with me."

"Oh." She smiled. "Good. It's settled, then."

"When would you want to start?"

"Tomorrow?"

"All right."

Now she was suspicious—of his quick agreement, of the reasons behind it. Why had he changed his mind, after being so adamant about not wanting her interfering in his business, both personal and professional? Was he afraid she'd try to run from him again?

That wasn't good. If he was wary, he'd be watchful. She had to lull his caution. She could do this, she told herself. She could earn his trust.

She began with a grateful smile. "Thank you, Dodge. I want to be useful . . . to you, and to the people of Pride."

She felt the slightest wince of guilt with his approval. Then it was his turn to knock her back on her heels in surprise.

"I met your father yesterday."

She wasn't in time to catch the initial jerk of reaction or the shudder that followed. But her tone was carefully modulated when she replied, "Really? And what did he have to say?"

"He wanted to congratulate us on our marriage."

She stared at him dead on and drawled, "I doubt that very much." She started to pace around the room in agitation and anger. "Did he tell you that you'd made an unfortunate choice?"

"Something like that."

"Did he tell you I'm mentally unstable? That I was dangerous to myself and others, and prone to fits of delusion and melancholia?"

A pause, then a soft, "No. He didn't."

Starla halted her travels and her ramblings, having committed a serious faux pas by revealing more than necessary. "Well, it's not true."

He didn't respond. Instead, he crossed to the unmade bed and eased himself down, setting aside the crutches and positioning his legs on the mattress so he was sitting upright, braced by the headboard. His expression gave nothing away—not doubt, not curiosity, not dismay.

"He said you belonged at home with him, that I'd be asking for trouble if I got in the way of that."

Starla hugged herself against the sudden pervasive chill. "My father is a very possessive man. He drove my mother away with his need to own her. He sees me as a substitute."

"You don't need to be afraid of him."

"You don't know him."

"I think he and I got a pretty good look at each other's hands. But I didn't show him all my cards."

She faced him then, her features taut and pale. "This isn't a game, Dodge. Not to him."

"Not to me, either. I never gamble with what I can't afford to lose. And I won't lose you, Starla."

There was such strength in that claim. It drew her, unbidden, across the room and into his open arms. There was such surety in his embrace, it made it easy for her to cling, to get lost in the tight wrap of his care so that it didn't matter if he wanted her only for sex, or for the child she carried. It didn't matter because he was going to keep her safe, and that was worth any sacrifice.

"Don't be afraid."

She felt his quiet command clear to her soul. It shook loose all the fears long since relegated to dark corners where they crouched ready to spring and ruin any chance at happiness. They prowled now, those awful truths, those past sins, reminding her in ugly whispers that she wasn't worth the care this man was showing her. If he knew her—really knew her—he'd cast her away in disgust.

Maybe he wouldn't.

That fierce thought intruded upon the other cutting miseries, pushing them aside to let a glimmer of hope flicker through. Perhaps Hamilton Dodge could handle her sordid past, if they were presented to him in small doses. If he was given enough time to adjust.

Better than to risk the danger of him learning all in one unforgivable jolt.

"It was after my mother ran away."

"What was?"

"I was very young and I didn't understand. I couldn't believe she'd abandon me."

Dodge's arms drew her closer, making a safe haven for her confession.

"My father . . . was so angry, and Tyler was so stunned. I couldn't stop crying, and finally the doctor was called in to sedate me. Between them, they decided it might be best for me to be taken from the site of my loss."

"They institutionalized you." He said it softly, without condemnation, but a sliver of steely fury lanced through his words.

"For a month. I don't remember much of it, except for the terrible loneliness. It was Tyler who finally made my father bring me home. I don't know what he did or how he did it, but he saved my sanity."

She lifted her head to look at him, her features pale and drawn, her expression earnest.

"I'm not unstable, Dodge. But I will go crazy if I have to go back to Fair Play."

Without hesitation, he replied, "You'll never have to."

A sudden flurry of emotions crowded through her, pressing upon her heart, confusing her mind. And then came the movement of his hand upon her head, a feather-light caress, like his quiet whisper as he pulled her back into the lea of his shoulder.

"I love you, Starla."

She wasn't prepared for his show of tenderness. Squeezing her eyes tightly shut, she pretended it didn't affect her. It was a lie: he couldn't love her; he didn't know her. If he did, he'd never say those words and mean them.

She didn't want him to love her. She wanted him

to want her, to need her, to desire her beyond reason or restraint. She understood those things and their rewards. Love was something else, altogether foreign, something that scared her. Something that made her hate herself for doing what she had to do to provide for the child she carried and the child she refused to lose.

Using Dodge's passions against him was one thing. Abusing his heart was another.

I love you.

Just words. They didn't mean anything.

She blinked away her tears.

Having Starla in the bank did nothing to relieve Dodge's workload, because he simply couldn't concentrate upon anything but her. She graced his front counter in a gown of lavender broadcloth, its tiers of satin-banded flounces and lacy bodice inset too dressy for common daytime wear. But there could be nothing common about his wife, even if she'd been clad in homespun.

She hadn't misled him about her gift for numbers. In the hour since they'd arrived, she'd worked her way down half the length of his weekly ledger, correcting mistakes and making proper tallies in a neat feminine script. With her head bent over his books, her teeth worrying the corner of her ripe lower lip while she concentrated, Dodge felt sure he was either the luckiest man alive, or the most cursed.

She took his breath away; unfortunately, with it went his power of reason. Yesterday they'd thrown out nearly all the rules of their nuptial arrangement, but today they were like strangers again. He never should have said the words. She'd been nervous as a hummingbird around him ever since. She'd said nothing about it, and he'd have doubted she'd heard him except for the pointed way she'd avoided eye contact. Hell, she'd had no problem making contact a lot more intimate than that. Shockingly so.

Where had she learned tricks that would make the boldest harlot blush?

She glanced up then and caught him scowling. Immediately he altered his expression to one of amicable welcome and her eyes darted away in alarm, and, he thought, in irritation.

What had he done? What had so changed their relationship? Her trip was the reason for her change in behavior since her return, for her almost desperate need to please him. It was pretense. He'd seen her genuine emotion shine through enough to know the difference—when she was watching his sister's children, when she gazed up at him after their first kiss, when she spoke about her brother. That was the real woman he'd wed, the one he loved. How was he to reach her when she was determined to play the role of another?

Usually he enjoyed a challenge, but this one was getting too damned frustrating. The only mysteries he wanted in his marriage were those he uncovered in the dark.

"Good morning, Mr. Dodge."

He stood awkwardly to greet Myrna Bishop, noting the way her gaze cut between him and Starla with a knowing pleasure.

"I cannot apologize enough for delaying your homecoming celebration with your wife. I trust it went well."

"Yes, thank you. Very well."

"And you, dear," she cooed to Starla. "So lucky you are to have such an attentive husband. Did he surprise you with his greeting?"

"Oh, yes. I was quite surprised." She neatly evaded his look. "Mr. Dodge tells me you're expanding your shop. How exciting. I'll make sure all my friends are aware of it. Heaven knows, none of us can get enough of the latest fashions after that beastly war."

Practically salivating at the thought of the elegant Starla Fairfax Dodge's patronage, Myrna collapsed in the chair before Dodge's desk and urged him to begin drawing up the papers. While he was finishing and Myrna gushed over Starla's gown and offered free alterations, Starla had no opportunity to wonder how the news of her condition had spread so quickly. Charles Fielding stood hat in hand, his head hanging.

"My Irma Sue tol' me some a what happened yesterday, and I come to tell you both how sorry I am for the way she behaved. I hope she didn't cause neither of you fine folks any embarrassment. It weren't my idea for her to barter her—well, you know—"

"No need to worry, Mr. Fielding. I am glad you came in, though. I've been considering your note and thinking up ways we might make payment easier for you. Have a seat."

Overwhelmed with gratitude, the scruffy farmer

took the proffered seat, his attitude toward Pride's banker totally reversed.

Starla glanced up from her accounts to watch Dodge work with the people of Pride. He was firm and fair, and after they got over their initial distrust of his accent and his occupation, his customers were quick to warm to him and his creative approach to their finances and their futures. When they left, it was with feelings of relief and hope, and their glances in her direction made one clear statement: *You've found yourself a good man.*

Part of her silly self still wanted to believe it.

Part of her was afraid it was true, and that she was using him disgracefully.

"Well, I declare, I'd never have believed it if I hadn't seen it with my own eyes. A Fairfax working for a common wage."

Her annoyance was tempered as she recognized the voice behind the drawling criticism.

"What would you know about the word 'work,' Tyler Fairfax? You've never done a lick of it in your life."

Tyler leaned across the counter, his grin sassy, his eyes full of hell. Starla was so glad to see him like his old self that she reached out to drag him up against the teller bars to press a wet kiss on his cheek.

"Hey, kin I have one, too?"

She scowled at Virg Dermont, the mildest of the brothers. "I save them for family."

"I'm practically family, ain't I, Ty?"

"Leave her alone. Besides, she's stingy with them kisses, now that she's got herself a husband.

Hey there, Yank . . . nobody put another hole in you yet?''

''Not yet,'' Dodge replied with a smile of tolerance, because he enjoyed seeing Starla so genuinely happy.

''He been treating you all right, Star? Give me the word an' I'll put one in him right now.''

Starla grabbed both her brother's hands, just in case he wasn't fooling. ''He's treating me fine.''

Tyler snorted. ''Makin' you work like a shop girl? You call that fine?''

''It was my idea. I was going plumb crazy sitting around the house.''

He grinned wider. ''Nothing domestic about you, darlin'. You're pure extravagance. An' worth every penny.''

Bubbling over his flattery and the fact that he appeared for the most part sober, she laughed and prodded, ''What do you want, coming in here with all that silky talk?''

His smile faded and his green eyes grew opaque. ''I heard you was expectin' and come to hear if it was true.''

''It is,'' she replied carefully.

''Are you happy about it?''

''Why wouldn't I be?''

He glanced in Dodge's direction, his look far from friendly. ''Jus' makin' sure.'' Then he was all smiles again as he slipped her grasp. ''I gotta go, little sister. You take care an' try not to get no blisters on them lily-white hands.''

''What do you know about blisters, you ne'er-do-well?''

Tyler and Virg sauntered by Dodge's desk, both of them adopting vaguely menacing smiles. Tyler leaned closer to say, "Can't hide behind her skirts forever, Yank."

Dodge was still bristling long after he and his companion had strutted out.

So they thought he had Starla working in the bank as insurance against their threats. Insulting, irritating, and totally untrue. But let them think that, let her think that rather than the truth.

The truth was, he feared leaving her alone or out of his sight for long, lest Cole Fairfax make good on his claim to snatch her back home again.

Better she stick where he could see her. And that was a pleasure he'd never get tired of.

But tired was the word for the rest of him when at last it was time to shut down for the day. He'd had a steady run of customers, all of whom had asked about his pregnant wife. It was no difficult stretch, connecting one to the other. The people of Pride were doing business with him so he could provide for his growing family.

That's what a small town family did for its members.

Were they beginning to accept him as one?

Cautious yet optimistic about the state of his business and his marriage, he worked his way over to the teller's cage where Starla was counting out the day's deposits. A tidy stack.

"A good day's work," she commented, the pride in her tone soothing him like a caress.

"Must be they like seeing your pretty face there better than mine."

She smiled at him and his heart was gone.

"We'd better put that in the vault. Wouldn't do for mice to eat up our profits."

While Starla banded the currency, she noted the way he was rubbing at the small of his back as lines of tension creased his brow.

"I'll put it away for you," she offered.

He heard nothing beyond her kindness. He saw nothing beyond her want to help. And he gave her the combination without a second thought.

As she dialed the lock on the great steel vault and slipped the deposits inside, her gaze did a quick inventory and her mind carefully filed away the sequence of numbers in the combination.

Should she ever need it.

Chapter 16

An invitation to dinner at the Sinclair Manor was a welcome break. Eager to dress up and go calling, Starla raced about like a summer storm, all hurricane force and drama. Dodge watched in amused tolerance as she discarded a fourth gown with a petulant kick.

"It's just Reeve and Patrice, her stuffy brother, and her mother," he reminded her.

She had no patience with his practicality. "I want to look nice. Where's the harm in that?"

"You always look spectacular, Star. Wear the bright pink. It makes you dazzle."

She held up the magenta silk with its overlays of sheer pink lace before her image in the mirror. The neckline was a trifle daring for a less than formal dinner, but he was right about the color. Its vivid hue rouged her skin and made her eyes spark like emerald chips. And the snug-fitting bodice with its plunging waistline would make the most of her trim figure, while she still had it.

She disappeared for a moment beneath a brilliant pink waterfall, emerging flushed and mussed as she turned her back to Dodge.

A bit flustered by the domestic intimacy of her request, Dodge leaned on his crutches, freeing his hands to work up the small fastenings at the back of her dress. The hooks and buttons were devilishly tiny, but harder than making them behave was keeping his thoughts in line as the warmth of her skin heated his knuckles.

"All done." He hoped she didn't notice how oddly breathless he sounded.

Starla tugged at the bodice, fluffed the off-the-shoulder lace, then glanced into the mirror only to be startled by the sight of them together.

Dodge stood behind her, his clean-shaven face pleasantly handsome, his broad-shouldered build framing her own petite form with support. He smiled when their gazes met in the glass and wondered why she'd thought him only average looking. There was an attractive aura of power about her husband—of confidence steeped in his dark eyes, of compassion softening the curve of his lips. She saw a depth to him that went beyond the surface prettiness of many of the men she'd known and admired. And that strength of will and determined purpose stirred a sudden and quite unexpected flurry of response within her, making her press her palm to her middle to still the quivering.

Noting the movement, Dodge wrapped his arms about her, one big hand covering hers, the other resting warm and easy against the curve of her waist. His expression arrested her with its tender anticipation.

"Is it the baby?"

"No, it's too early for that. Just nerves, I think."

She didn't move or push away his hand; she was feeling a surrounding sense of contentment edged with a shiver of longing.

I love you, Starla.

If only that were true. If only she could believe those sentiments would never change. She'd hungered for the taste of love all her life yet feared if she sampled what her husband offered, the result would be too bittersweet.

He bent his head until she felt his breath blow soft and hot against the bare slope of her shoulder. A tremor raced along her limbs. She kept her focus on their reflection, watching the top of his head as she experienced the first galvanizing brush of his lips. Her trembling grew wild, quaking through her, seeming to tighten low in her belly into a strange knotting ache that had nothing to do with distress. She lifted her free hand, placing it lightly atop his head, letting her fingers thread through the dark gloss of his hair until they clenched tight when his mouth rested on the sensitive juncture of her throat.

Alarm and awareness radiated from that tender spot down to the tips of her barely covered breasts as they shivered with her hurried breathing. A blind, mad urge to turn her head, to catch his mouth with her own in hopes of relieving the tension between them, was nearly impossible to overcome. Her willingness frightened her more than the thought of his kisses. Confused by that panicked desire, and feeling herself at a point of impending danger, she still hadn't the strength to pull away.

Instead, in a shaky voice she murmured, "We're going to be late."

He straightened slowly, letting his freshly scraped cheek linger against the soft curve of hers as his gaze probed their reflection, searching for an honest reaction in her wild and clouded stare. After a moment he said, "You're a vision."

She touched her fingertips to the cool image of his lips on the glass and replied, "You're a dream."

He grinned, releasing the friction like steam from a kettle. "That's better than when you considered me a nightmare."

"I never did," she said, pouting prettily.

"How soon she forgets."

As her expression grew somber, he wished fervently that it could be in his power to make her forget everything that had come before their marriage. That it would be possible to erase the lines of apprehension, the pinch of painful memory that too often marred her perfect features.

He lifted the back of her hand to his lips. Perhaps someday he could work that miracle.

"We'd better go," she said, this time stepping away from him with a twitch of restless energy.

And he'd never wanted anything so much in his entire life as the love of this woman he'd made his wife.

The manor was a tribute to Old South elegance where Starla had run wild and free, more like Patrice's sister than her best friend. Looking forward to an evening when she and Dodge could relax and let down the barriers they held firm within the home they shared, Starla knew a stab of disappointment when Patrice greeted them at the door with a "tell me everything" look. The fond embrace she had for Starla was given with equal enthusiasm to her husband.

"Oh, it's good to see the two of you. Dodge, be warned, Deacon means to drag you off for business, but then that will give Starla and me time to chat."

Time for Patrice to try and drag out every detail of her married life, Starla thought. So much for a relaxed evening. With her hopes of claiming a sympathetic ear fading, Starla realized she'd find no neutrality from the friend who plainly adored Dodge. There'd be no dropping her pretended role with the woman who wanted so much to hear only how well things were going. Adopting her false smile and taking her husband's elbow, Starla entered the manor as if stepping among strangers instead of friends.

The meal was strained, with most of the conversation carried by Patrice and her mother, Hannah Sinclair. Reeve and Deacon seemed to be waiting to pounce on an oddly withdrawn Dodge, Reeve out of curiosity, Deacon in impatience. Starla made light small talk and puzzled over her husband's mood. He was drinking way too much, for one thing, and was too quiet, for another. Hoping she'd have a chance to ask him what was wrong once they were dismissed from the table, she was disappointed when Deacon hustled him away behind the closed doors of the study. Catching his wife's signal, Reeve escorted Hannah into the parlor, leaving the two childhood friends alone.

"When did you get back?" Patrice demanded.

"Day before yesterday."

"I hope you got your wanderlust out of your system and will be content to settle down."

"Like a good wife, you mean."

Patrice arched an eyebrow. "Exactly."

"I'm doing my best, Patrice." But the shortness of her words betrayed her.

"I can't believe Dodge is making it difficult for you."

No, not her perfect paragon, Hamilton Dodge. Starla gritted her teeth and murmured, "No, of course not. As you said, he's a good man."

Knowing her too well, Patrice was immediately suspicious. "He wasn't harsh with you because you left, was he?"

"Dodge?" Her surprise was genuine, much to Patrice's relief. "Gracious, no. He's . . . very tolerant."

"Then what's wrong?"

"Nothing."

"Starla, tell me."

"Nothing's wrong. Why should anything be wrong?"

"Because you leave town at a moment's notice. Because you're married to a wonderful man and you're about to start crying."

"Oh, Patrice," Starla sniffed miserably. "Things should be wonderful."

Patrice hauled her over to a low chaise, then hurried to close the doors to give them privacy. "So what's wrong?'' she demanded, as she dropped down and seized Starla's cold hands.

''He—he told me he loves me. What does that mean?''

Patrice laughed in delight, then grew somber in the face of her friend's obvious distress. ''It means you're very lucky.''

''But what does it *mean*? That he wants to sleep with me? That he wants my child to have his name?''

''It means he cares about you, Starla, for yourself.''

Ebony curls swung wildly as she shook her head. Patrice gripped her hands harder.

''Why is that so difficult for you to believe? You're smart, as sassy as blackstrap molasses, and so beautiful there were times I wanted to just slap you for blinding every boy to my appeal. You could have had any man in Pride County.''

She made a wry face. ''They only wanted to get into my petticoats and show me off on their arms. They didn't want *me*.''

''And is that all you think Dodge wants?''

''I don't know. I thought I did, but all the rules have changed.''

''You do know. That's why you're so afraid. If he only wanted a petticoat and a pretty face, you wouldn't be scared to death of him. You'd lead him around by the nose the way you have every other man you've ever met.''

''He wants more than I can give him, Patrice. He deserves more. He wants a big, happy family like the one he has up north. He wants a wife to

meet him at the door with kisses. He wants someone who'll never lie to him, and I've told him nothing else since the day we met.''

''And you're crazy about him, aren't you?''

''No!'' She took a sobbing breath, then admitted,
''I don't know. I'm all mixed up, half the time
wanting to hate him, half the time wanting him to
hold me.''

''You're in love with him,'' was Patrice's sage
decree.

''But I don't want to be! It hurts too much to
care. When you love someone and they let you
down, it's worse than dying.''

''There are things worse than love, Starla, things
like loneliness. He's not going to leave you. He's
not that kind of man.''

''But if he knew some of the things I've done—''

''Tell him.''

''I can't.''

''Then how important is it for him to know?
Live from today onward. It's the only way you can
be happy.''

Patrice waited for Starla to respond. When she
didn't, all her friend could do was sigh and hope
she'd made some impression on the wall around
her heart.

Because although Starla couldn't drive Dodge
away with the truth, Patrice knew she could well
lose him through neglect.

''Have you made any progress in breaking that
son of a bitch's hold on my property?''

Dodge eased back on the sofa and watched an agitated Deacon Sinclair attack the length of the room in long angry strides. "The papers you signed are legally binding."

"Are you saying that little weasel can throw my mother and me out of our home and there's not a damn thing I can do about it?"

"Sure," he wanted to say to the arrogant aristocrat, "there was something you could have done about it by not being so blinded by greed and pride that you'd sign away your family's future to the likes of Tyler Fairfax. There was something you could have done about it if you'd bent that damned Southern snobbery to come see me when I still could have made a difference."

But Dodge didn't say those things and was rather surprised at himself for thinking them so strongly that they must have shown on his face, for Deacon stopped and gave him a narrow look.

"Out with it. 'I told you so,' right?"

"No one can tell you anything, Deacon. Far be it from me to be the first to try."

Patrice's brother glared for a moment, then had the good sense to look chagrined. In a more contrite tone, he asked, "What can we do?"

Dodge took another long swallow from his whiskey, sucking air into the burn as it went down. He'd hoped the liquor would dull the ache that had been massing in his back all day, but all it did was slow his mind.

"I can advance you the money to buy your mortgage back."

"The bastard won't sell it to me. Not even for

more than what I originally borrowed.''

''Have you tried appealing to his better nature?''

Deacon scowled. ''Does he have one?''

''Not that I've ever seen. So what does he really want?''

''To make me squirm.'' And how that grated on a man like Deacon Sinclair.

''There must be something he cares about, some leverage we can use.''

''He doesn't care about money or honor or anything a gentleman holds dear. Reeve was once his friend and he was ready to let him hang.''

''He cares about Patrice,'' Dodge remembered.

Deacon bristled like a wolf protecting its cubs. ''I don't want my sister involved with him. This doesn't concern her. She's made her own life. She doesn't need me complicating it with my problems.''

Dodge could sympathize there. Tyler Fairfax was no one to mess with. He finished off his drink and nodded for Deacon to pour him another. It was hell to remain seated with the constant pins and needles stabbing him from the small of his back to the soles of his feet. He shifted but could find no relief. Then Deacon distracted him from his discomfort.

''There is one other person he might listen to.'' He fixed a long stare on Dodge.

Dodge laughed. ''Oh, he'd rather shoot me than listen to a word I said.''

''I meant your wife.''

''Starla?''

"If she was to talk to him, maybe he'd see reason."

"You can ask her."

Deacon pursed his lips. "She's never cared much for me. It would be better if you asked her." His gaze slid to Dodge on that silky suggestion.

On the surface, it didn't sound too unreasonable a thing to ask. Then the connotations sank deeper through the haze of alcohol to kindle a slow-burning ire.

"No."

Confused, Deacon was ready to argue when Dodge came off the sofa, his teeth gritted against the pain and the insult.

"I will not use my wife and her family to further my business or your ambitions. Tyler Fairfax may be scum on your little pond, but he's Starla's brother and I have to respect her feelings for him. I don't have a problem with you pleading your case to her, but I'm not going to place her between me and Tyler. There are certain things I value more than my business, Sinclair. If you felt the same way, you wouldn't be in this mess."

Dodge didn't wait for Deacon to rage at him. He angled out of the study and into the hall, bellowing, "Starla, we're leaving."

She and Patrice came running, alarmed by his display of temper.

"What's wrong?" Starla asked in a low aside.

"It's time to go. Patrice, thank your mother for her hospitality and say good night to Reeve for me." He was out the door before Starla, racing after him, had time to question him further.

Their carriage was halfway down the drive before she dared put a staying hand on his arm.

"Dodge, what happened?"

Tension spasmed through his jaw, but he said nothing. He whipped the horse up to a greater speed, the ride growing bumpy and precarious.

"Dodge, what's wrong? Tony, talk to me!"

He glanced at her then, surprised by her use of his abbreviated name. "It shouldn't involve you."

"Oh. I see." But the coldness in her tone said she didn't.

"It's business, Starla, and should stay business."

"Of course." She looked straight ahead, her fine profile a chiseled perfection of hauteur.

Dodge cursed fiercely to himself. "It has to do with your brother and Deacon Sinclair. Sinclair wanted me to stick you in the middle of it and I refused. It didn't make him very happy with me."

"What's Tyler done?"

"Starla, I don't want to drag you into this."

She gave him a stern look.

"Deacon was desperate for money and borrowed it from your brother, using the mortgage to his properties as collateral. Now Tyler's threatening to sell and he won't let Deacon buy the mortgage back."

"So *that's* what he's been up to. Why would he want to steal their home from them?"

Dodge shrugged. "I don't know. All that was going on before I got here."

"Why didn't Deacon just borrow the money from you and the bank to begin with?"

"You know Deacon. . . ."

"He's arrogant, prideful, and sometimes so stupid you wouldn't think he had a brilliant mind. To gamble his home, his history." She shook her head, mystified. Then her expression sharpened. "And Deacon wanted me to go to Tyler to get him to do the right thing."

"That's about it."

"Why didn't you ask me?"

"Because he's your brother, Star. And I'm your husband. And this is business, not a personal matter. I didn't want to put you in the position of having to choose between us. You told me you wouldn't let me, and I won't."

She stared at him, stunned to think he'd protect her feelings over his profits. And she told him quietly, "Sometimes I like the chance to do the right thing. I've no fondness for Deacon Sinclair, but his family practically raised me at that house and I don't want Tyler to tear it from them on some petty whim. I'll talk to him."

"Only if that's what *you* want to do, Starla."

"It is." She touched his arm again. "And thank you for not pushing your choice on me." She wondered if he realized how much the gesture meant to her. It gave her a sense of value she'd never known before, raising her above his business, his earnings, and his customers in a way her father would never have done for his family. He amazed her by taking that stand.

And she loved him for doing it.

The carriage wheels struck a deep rut in the road, sending them off the seat to land with spine-shattering impact. Dodge's hoarse cry had Starla turning toward him just as he pressed the reins upon her.

"Take these," he groaned, sliding off the seat to his knees in the carriage's boot.

"Dodge?" She wrestled for control of the horse, guiding the animal to a standstill and looping the reins about the whip post so she could give full attention to her husband.

He was in pain. Why hadn't she seen that at dinner? Why hadn't she guessed that he was using the Sinclairs' fine liquor to quench not a thirst, but the fires of agony?

"What can I do?" She touched his shoulders, feeling frightened and helpless.

"Nothing," he said through gritted teeth. "It comes and goes. *Ahhh . . . God!*" He glanced at her, seeing her alarm, and managed a strained smile. "I'm sorry. Don't be scared. It just gets to be a little more than I can handle at times."

"Let me get you to the doctor." She started reaching for the reins.

"No. There's nothing he can do." He leaned against her knees and she was quick to support him with the wrap of her arms. "Just have to work through it."

"You need to lie down."

"No. If I don't keep moving, everything stiffens up. I can't bend . . . *God* . . . I'm sorry."

She held him while his hands clenched in the bright silk and lace of her skirt. Holding him steady within the curl of one arm, she picked up the reins with the other.

"Hang on for just a minute longer. I've got an idea."

He half-lay across her lap, nearly swooning in and out of consciousness. He was dimly aware that they'd left the main road but was not sure of their destination until she asked, "Do you think you can stand?"

He looked around through the veil of pain, surprised to see she'd brought them to a pond. "Why are we here?"

"I thought the water might make it easier for you by supporting your weight and taking the strain off your back."

Simple yet brilliant. Why had he never thought of it?

She hopped down from the buggy, then extended her hands to him, coaxing, "Come on. I'm not that delicate."

With plenty of effort they managed to wrestle him down from the buggy and over to the wrought-iron table and chairs by the water's edge.

"We used to come here as children. Tyler taught Patrice and me how to swim under the moonlight after we sneaked out of our rooms. It was Reeve and Jonah's favorite fishing hole, too. It doesn't look very big, but it's deep. Can you swim?"

"Usually." It was his way of saying he wasn't sure if he could manage it in his present state.

"I'll go in with you, then."

She presented him with the back of her gown, and when he'd worked his way down that row of maddening hooks, she released the tape on her hoops so they'd collapse on the ground, then let the weight of the voluminous skirt carry the gown after it.

Starla Fairfax Dodge, bathed in moonlight and clad in only her chemise and drawers, was all the anesthesia he required.

With her tiny feet bare and her slight form wearing little more than the wrap of his arm about her shoulders, Starla stepped into the tranquil water, gasping at its sudden chill. Just as she'd said, the bottom dropped away rapidly, and soon they were immersed to their armpits.

"Now, just float and let yourself relax. I'll hold onto you."

He placed himself in her hands, letting his body become buoyant, supported by the prop of her palms beneath his shoulders. He let his head rest on the cushion of her bosom and his legs ride the gentle current, closing his eyes, consciously disconnecting himself from the knot of pain in his back. And gradually it eased, allowing him to move his feet in slow kicks.

"Better?"

He opened his eyes to see Starla's face outlined by the heavens, her beauty outshining them. The pain of his injury became nothing compared to the pain of her indifference.

But if she was indifferent, would she be shoulder-deep in water, tending him with tender ministrations? She'd shaken the walls of those glorious heavens with her silken touch and her sensuous kisses. Again he felt the sharp stab of jealousy for whomever had taught her to wring such pleasure from a man. But he wondered now, as he'd wondered then, if any man had shown her a reciprocal paradise.

He didn't think so.

And on this deep-starred night, beneath the heaviness of a harvest moon, he vowed not another day would pass without her knowing exactly what it meant to be loved.

Chapter 17

There was tremendous satisfaction in feeling her husband's discomfort ebb away. Gradually the tension drained from his shoulders and the creases smoothed around his closed eyes. His breathing altered from harsh snatches to deep sighs of relief as he began to tread water on his own. She continued to support him, not because he needed it, but because she was rewarded by the connection.

No man had ever depended upon her before.

No man had ever said he loved her before, either, no one except her mother, just before she'd disappeared. She'd had but a fleeting time to experience that love, and now she was afraid to when the chance came again.

She didn't want to love the man she'd married. She didn't want to be drawn into caring about him, into feeling his pain, into sharing his dreams, because if she lost him, she'd die. It was that simple.

"I want you to go back to the doctor in the morning."

Dodge didn't open his eyes. "I already told you there's nothing he can do. If it were up to him, I'd be in a wheelchair or under his knife. But dead either way, to my thinking.''

''Then we'll go to another doctor. Pride's a small town.''

''Reeve already had two of the country's best specialists come down. They said the same thing. To take the bullet out would probably leave me dead or totally paralyzed. But leaving it in's like carrying around an unexploded bomb. They said it was my life and up to me how I wanted to spend it, sitting safely in a chair, or pushing the limits as far as I can stand it. Some days I can stand it better than others.''

''You could die.''

Starla realized the impact of the words for the first time. She'd never given much thought to his injury, thinking of him as working his way through a slow recovery. But never had she considered the danger he was in with that bullet nudged up against his spine.

She spun away from him. Without her support, water closed over his head in a rush. He came up sputtering, splashing after the figure of his wife.

''Starla. Starla.'' He caught her arm, but she refused to be turned toward him.

''You didn't tell me you could die. You never told me that.'' Her voice was thin with shock and shaking with anger and accusation. ''Let me go. Let me go!'' That last sobbed from her, and with it went her resistance.

He swung her around, getting only a glimpse of her tear-streaked face before crushing her to his chest. ''You don't have to worry, Starla. I've already made sure you and the baby will be taken care of, should anything happen to me.''

That knowledge should have taken the fear away, but somehow it didn't come close. Her palms slapped against his shoulders, levering for distance as she cried, ''Do you think that's what I care about? What'll happen to me if you're gone?''

He stared at her blankly, not understanding why she was so wildly upset. Until she took his face between her hands and kissed him hard enough to drown him in a sea of unexpected sensation by the time she jumped back.

They regarded each other in breathless surprise.

''You should have told me,'' Starla said at last, the edge of accusation back in her voice.

''I never thought to; I'm sorry. I guess I just accepted the risks and didn't give them a second thought.'' His gaze searched her face, seeking the meaning behind that fierce, unplanned kiss.

''Well, maybe I wouldn't have been so ready to accept them. I've lost everyone I've ever cared for. If I'd known, I wouldn't have—''

''Married me?'' Dodge supplied tersely.

''Wouldn't have let myself care about you,'' she concluded. ''You lied to me.''

Which meant she *did* care. It was more of an admission than he'd expected her to make. Which left him in the delicate position of talking his way out of the fact that he'd hurt her.

''You can stop caring about me now if you want to. I guess I'd deserve that.'' And the hint of a smile he gave her made her temper soar, as if he

were daring her to try to shut him out of her heart
at this late date.

"I should hate you," she complained.

"That would solve everything, wouldn't it?"

She scowled and pouted, refusing to look at him
until his fingertips skimmed under her jaw to tilt
her head up, coaxing eye contact.

"I'm not planning to die anytime soon, Starla.
Unless it's from pneumonia standing out here in
this damn freezing water."

A smile teased about her lips. "It's not that
cold."

"Then you do care about me?"

"Maybe a little," was her grudging claim. "Although you're a damn Yankee and a banker to
boot."

It was all the reassurance Dodge needed. He
leaned toward her. Initially, she angled her face
away, but when he paused, making no attempt to
push himself on her, Starla turned back and lifted
up for the reacquainting warmth of his kiss.

The marvelous thing about water was the way it
held Dodge up, making it possible for him to stand
on his own, to put both arms about his wife and
pull her tight against him to feel the perfection of
fit from lips to toes. Chilled nipples made inden-
tations upon his chest, but the water wasn't cold
enough to extinguish his ardor. There was no way
for her not to feel it growing, with only the wet
hug of his drawers and her filmy underthings to
disguise the hard rise of his interest. She didn't pull
back, but he could feel the way her breathing
changed into quick little panicked snatches.

Slow. Don't scare her. It was hell to remind himself of that as her body bowed in lithe surrender
upon the unyielding contours of his own.

But this wasn't about him. It was about her and
what she wanted, what she needed. And for him to
gift her with that, he'd need a little more clothing
between them.

"Let's go home," he whispered against her lips.

She tucked her head against his shoulder and
nodded without saying a word.

By the time they entered the dark house, it
wasn't the pain Dodge suffered from, it was the
chill. He'd given Starla his frock coat to wrap about
her bare shoulders, and his own fine shirt had
quickly soaked through. It was hard to think about
romantic kisses when his lips were blue and his
teeth chattering.

"I'll put on some hot water while you get out
of those wet things." Starla was once again all cool
efficiency and didn't even smile when he snapped
a salute and replied, "Yes, ma'am."

She took her time. When she returned bearing
two steeping cups of tea, Dodge was wrapped up
in a woolen robe, his feet were bundled in thick
socks, and he half-reclined on the bedroom chaise.
His eyes were closed and he didn't respond to her
presence. Sleeping, she thought. Grateful for the
respite so she could get out of her own cloying
garments, she set aside the tea and his damp coat
and hurriedly shed all her clothing to the pucker of
her skin.

"That tea smells good."

With a gasp of surprise, Starla yanked the heavy quilt from the foot of the bed to swaddle it about her nakedness before turning to meet Dodge's steady gaze. She gave him a narrow glare for not announcing that he was awake before she undressed, but he refused to appear shamed. He looked tired and cold and somehow vulnerable because of those things, and she was lured into dropping her guard. She carried the steaming cups to him. He took his then patted the edge of the chaise.

"Sit here, with me."

She perched cautiously, but when he remained slumped against the cushions, contentedly sipping his tea, again she relaxed, snuggling into the cocoon of covers and sampling the warmth of the tea. She gave a slight jump when his hand settled upon the curve of her hip, providing a bolster for her back. When she shot him a look, he was leaning back with his eyes closed, seemingly harmless. The moment she was lulled by that image, his hand shifted, beginning a slow, firm massage, first with just his thumb, then the heel of his palm, and when she arched her back with a sigh of hedonistic pleasure, he applied both hands to the task, kneading her shoulders, rubbing the slope of her back through the bulky quilt. His hands were strong, able to apply a blissful pressure even through the batting.

"That's nice," she purred.

"You'll be wanting a lot of these as the baby gets closer."

"I'll hold you to that."

"My pleasure."

His arms circled around her, his hands spreading wide-fingered atop her abdomen and revolving slowly.

"I can't wait to feel the baby moving."

"A few more months," she predicted.

"We should think of names."

Starla went quiet, then murmured, "I'll let you do that." Distracted by her melancholy, she allowed him to hug her closer. He didn't want her to be thinking about the child's unfortunate conception, but rather of them, as a family.

"I'm going to spoil this baby shamelessly," Dodge warned happily, then nuzzled her neck. "Just like I'd spoil his mother, if she'd let me."

"I'm already so spoiled it's a wonder you can stand me."

His low chuckle brushed warm against her neck. When had they gotten so close? she wondered in alarm. She was lying back against his chest, within the curl of his arms, her head intimately pillowed on his shoulder. What surprised her more was her disinclination to move.

"Spoiled with possessions, maybe, but not with the things that really matter."

"Like what?" Her tone sharpened. She wiggled and tried to sit up, but he held her tight.

"Like letting yourself be held all wrapped up in a warm blanket. Like it?"

She nodded tentatively, staying where she was.

"Like being pampered and not having to worry about what you have to give back in return."

Now she was alert more than alarmed, attuned

to the seducing caress of his voice, to all he was suggesting, to all he was doing.

While one arm continued to lie easily about her middle, his other palm roamed freely, fondly, over the fabric of the quilt, stroking up her arm, along her torso, sweeping over her breasts without pausing long enough to earn an objection . . . taming her to the weight of his hand and the feel of his touch, familiarizing her with his closeness. All very unhurried and unthreatening, and purposefully arousing.

Starla wasn't aware of that danger, though. She concentrated on the delicious feeling of being surrounded by luxurious warmth, by the liquid sensation of peace and protection. She was sprawled across him so that her glossy black hair spilled over his shoulder and invited him to bury his face in its damp curls, to whisper kisses against the side of her neck. She stopped thinking and just let herself feel.

"Warm enough now?" he asked, words stroking against her throat to elicit a slight shiver.

"Mmm, yes. Are you feeling better?"

"More than you can imagine."

The soothing cadence of his voice took the suggestive threat from his words, so Starla let them pass without reacting with worry or suspicion. She didn't want to risk ruining the quiet moment between them. She'd known so little peace. She let herself drift in the comfort of his embrace, her spirit gentled by the continued movement of his hand, over her hair, along her shoulder, down the curves of her torso and hip, suddenly against her skin. Before she had time to gasp, he'd moved safely outside the covers again, but moments later, his warm palm found its way once more within the bundle of the quilt to rub warmly over the bend in her knee.

He continued that sensory play, slipping in and out of the covers, his touch always moving, never lingering long enough for her to voice a protest, until she began to anticipate the brush of heat over bare skin . . . skimming lightly up the curve of her calf, circling the rounding of one hip, flirting up the quiver of her belly, tickling along her sides, buffing the full underside of her breast. She was no longer pleasantly warm. His fingertips traced a hot glow along her skin, kindling restless fires within the sudden heaviness of her breasts, and then low, near the juncture of her thighs. Part of her wanted to put those fires out now, while they were under control, but another urged her to let them rage, to let them burn wild with the slow passion Dodge ignited.

With an abrupt, unplanned movement, her tossing opened the flaps of the quilt, giving him access to the clean line of her nakedness. The air felt deliciously cool against her too-warm skin, but his touch felt better.

''Dodge,'' she moaned in confusion.

''I liked it when you called me Tony before.''

''Tony, what are you doing?''

''Spoiling you a little. Is that all right?''

His knuckles grazed her rib cage and she found herself arching, encouraging him to move higher.

Her body's freedom to ask for what she didn't dare nudged a recessed panic.

"I don't know," she admitted with a whisper.

"I want it to be all right with you. You're going to have to tell me that it is."

He made slow revolutions over her stomach, creating aching tension above, yearning pressure below. She stretched up one arm, curving it around so she had the back of his head cupped in her palm. He lowered to nibble the sensitive union of bowed neck and graceful jawline until her fingers fisted in his hair.

"Tony . . ."

Tremors raced along her body, shaking loose the last of her resolve, making it impossible for her to deny that she didn't desperately want what he was offering.

"It's all right with me."

With that concession of trust, his touch grew bolder.

Her breathing fluttered wildly as his attention centered on her breasts, kneading their fullness, exciting soft little moans of wonder from her as he aroused their sensitive tips into hot points of need. She'd never known her body was capable of such exquisite feeling, of such unfettered responsiveness to this man's touch. Sensation prickled along her skin, waking shivers of surprise and delight. His touch was something she never wanted, something she'd feared, but now, as he woke her to pleasures undreamed of, she craved nothing quite so much.

While he continued to tease and tempt her breast with one hand, the other began a slow downward stroke, and the lower it traveled, the higher Starla's anxiety grew. The freedom to enjoy what he was doing was gradually replaced by uneasiness and a mounting sense of shame. Her knees lifted, pressing tightly together, locking him away from more intimate exploration and herself from further discovery. His palm moved gently along her thigh and hip, but her tension defied him.

"Starla, I'm not going to hurt you. You know that, don't you?"

Her head nodded jerkily upon his shoulder as her breath rushed fast and frantic, and beneath his hand, her heart pounded like that of a trapped animal's.

His lips brushed warmly and seductively along the slope of her throat, tasting her fear, trying to coax her trust. Her hand moved restlessly through his hair, mirroring her uncertainty but not willing to let go.

"I want to show you something," he crooned, as his fingertips glided up the outside of her thigh, then down the sealed inner seam between the clench of her legs. She trembled.

"Will I like it as much as the rest?"

She felt his smile. "I promise."

Because of that smile, because of the husky arrogance of his tone and the simple fact that he waited for her to decide, she relaxed her muscles, letting her feet slide down along his legs, letting her knees part timidly.

He worked up her passions with a maddening leisure, beginning again at her breasts, stroking, plucking, tantalizing until she arched and cried out for more. He palmed her flat belly, the curve of her hip, and then the tender down of her womanhood, making her quiver and ache with a foreign expectation. Her senses were knife sharp, not with anxiousness, not with fear, but rather with a desperate need to know what her body seemed already to understand with its sudden embarrassing wetness, what it invited with the slight lift of her hips.

She gasped as he saw to his promise, with revolving pressure from the heel of his hand, with deeper intimacy that involved his fingers and a touch so glorious she couldn't seem to catch her breath. He found her body's rhythm and moved with it, intensifying it, using it to exact sudden wild shudders so violently out of her control that they tore his name from her throat and stripped her of all but the volcano of sensation exploding inside her, through her. When it was over, tears of wondrous emotion quivered in her eyes.

She was scarcely aware of Dodge wrapping the quilt up around her. Her warmth was from within, a deep, heated pleasure born of trust and unexpected triumph. Her body limp with relief, her spirit sated, Starla curled up against her husband's side, her eyes closed, her lips smiling softly as she felt his kiss brush her brow.

No one could ever take this moment from her, the moment she first realized what it meant to be cherished.

Chapter 18

❦

Starla woke gradually, shifting languorously, the sheets creating a delicious friction upon bare skin.

Bare skin. . . .

She sat up with a gasp, the covers clutched to her bosom as she surveyed the room for possible threat. Dodge's room. Where her drying clothes were draped over the back of the chaise where last night he'd awakened her body to unbelievable splendors.

Coloring hotly at the memory, at the way even now it stirred an answering restlessness within her, Starla glanced about, confused to find herself alone. It was early. Surely Dodge hadn't already left for the bank. Not without waking her.

A rattle of china in the hallway and a low, vivid curse announced her husband's approach. Smiling, Starla sank back down in the covers and waited for him.

He was carrying a tray laden with tea and toast in one hand, balancing it precariously. But what surprised her was that he'd exchanged his crutches for a cane.

Cups clattered. Liquid splashed.

"Damn it!" He grinned at her apologetically. "I'm not very good at this yet."

Seeing disaster in the tipping of the tray, Starla slipped out of bed, forgetting modesty, to relieve him of the burden.

"I've got it."

And he had her.

No sooner had she'd rescued the tray than Dodge wrapped his free arm snugly about her waist, drawing her naked figure up against him. She gasped at the abrupt mashing of her breasts to his satin waistcoat and quickly set the tray aside, lest she drop it. She didn't know which to react to first, her situation or his.

"What are you doing?" she stammered.

"Trying to keep from falling down. And a very nice crutch you make, too." His hand moved familiarly over her backside, making her squirm against him, which itself was a reward.

Clasping his waist to steady him, she scolded, "Should you be trying this so soon?"

He grinned wider, deliberately misunderstanding her. "It's nothing you didn't let me get away with last night."

Blushing fiercely, she said, "I meant walking with a cane."

"Oh. Well, I wouldn't know unless I tried. I doubt I'm up to running up and down stairs, but I can manage the length of the hallway all right."

"With a tray of tea? You're going to hurt yourself."

He frowned slightly, annoyed by her lack of

praise at his accomplishment. He'd wanted her to be surprised and pleased, not haranguing.

"I have a bullet in my back. How much more hurt could I be?"

"You know what I mean. You're pushing too hard." Anxiousness colored her words with the memory of what she'd learned the night before. The last thing he wanted while clutching her close was for her to view him as fragile.

"I'm not pushing hard enough. I'm going to be walking on my own by the time the baby is born." He said it as if there wasn't the slightest chance that it wouldn't be true. Starla sighed in exasperation.

"If you insist on this foolishness and end up flat on your face, I'm not going to pick you up."

He grinned, relieved by her warning because it showed such a lack of pity. "Fair enough."

His gaze lowered to chart the ample contours of her bosom where it flattened against his chest, the sight distracting him from all else. His hand slid up the curve of her spine, disappearing into the cloak of her hair.

"I was going to surprise you with tea and toast in bed. I didn't expect to get such a nice surprise in return."

"The tea is getting cold."

"I can reheat it." His fingers turned, looping her tangled hair in them, tugging slightly to raise her face to his. His gaze was devouring. "My God, you're beautiful. If they modeled those monument angels after you, they'd never be able to keep the dead men down."

She scowled at his questionable compliment, then stiffened because she was obviously having the same effect upon him.

"Tony, please. . . ."

"I plan to."

He bent slowly, giving her plenty of time to turn away if she wanted. She stared into his eyes, her gaze uncertain and wavering, but she didn't move. She met the covering warmth of his mouth with her own slightly parted lips.

His kiss was light at first, a playful nibble meant to quiet her fears and relax her tension. The instant he'd accomplished that, his purpose intensified with slanting persuasion. He could feel her fingers clutching at his vest as a long shiver shook through her. Then came the shy touch of her tongue sliding along his lower lip, beginning an unbearably sensuous flirtation with his. She was soft and pliant, and the effect her willingness had upon him was devastating. He wanted to delve into her mouth in search of answering passions, but it was too soon, her trust in him too new to jeopardize all they'd accomplished so far.

So he turned his face to one side, breathing hard into the force of his raging desire, while her nude form languished against him.

Nobility exacted a terrible price sometimes.

"You'd better go get dressed before I decide to close the bank for the day."

Not missing the rough edge of warning in his voice, Starla slipped his embrace and darted from the room. Dodge looked over his shoulder to appreciate the vision of bare flanks and luscious legs as she disappeared up the stairs. He let out a ragged breath and shook off the gut-twisting effort of restraint. After taking a few wobbling steps forward, he was further distracted by the spears of discomfort pricking at his spine. He ignored them, just as he ignored his doctor's advice and his wife's worries.

He was going to walk again, and soon.

He had a wife and child to protect, and he'd do so on his own legs, as no man's inferior. Or die trying.

They were on their way to breakfast, Dodge depending more than he cared to upon his cane and his wife's surprisingly strong grip. His steps were slow, but they were his own, and each was a savagely won victory. Starla clung proudly to his arm, her head held high. As always, her fashionable appearance did him credit, giving them a look of comfortable and confident affluence, an important impression to make when doing business with other people's money. They drew considerable attention, a combination of Starla's astonishing beauty and Dodge's graduation from crutches to cane, and whether its citizens liked to admit it or not, they were a familiar sight on the streets of Pride.

And that recognition brought a smugly pleased Hamilton Dodge that much closer to his goal.

They were about to cross a wide side street when a carriage came careening to a stop in front of them, and in a swirl of petticoats, Patrice Garrett swung down without waiting for her white-knuckled husband's assistance.

"God above, 'Trice, you're gonna get us killed with the way you handle the reins," Reeve grumbled, but Patrice paid him no mind. She was busy embracing his friend.

"Look at you!" Patrice held Dodge back by the shoulders, endangering his balance but delighting him nonetheless. "This is wonderful. I can't believe you're almost walking."

"I *was* walking until you almost ran us over." He grinned through his complaint. "We were on our way to breakfast. Would you care to join us?"

Without asking her husband's opinion, Patrice took hold of Dodge's other arm. "We'd love to. Reeve, don't scowl at me. You can do your stuffy ol' business better on a full stomach. Besides, I was dying to find out what sent the two of you off in such a rush last night."

Dodge stiffened, his jaw gripping tight, but it was Starla who answered for them.

"Just some business differences. Patrice, no one needs to tell you what an old pooh your brother can be."

What no one needed to tell Patrice was that there had been a major shift in her best friend's relationship with her husband. She could see it in Starla's quick defensiveness, in the solicitous way she guided Dodge's steps down from the porch and studied his face for indications of distress. The signs of a woman in love. Patrice shot her husband a knowing look.

"Since we didn't have a chance to do much socializing, why don't you come out to the Glade again tonight?" So she could set Reeve on Dodge to pump him for information while she cornered Starla for the same.

"Sounds good," Dodge began.

Then Starla brushed against him to say, "Maybe for a little while. I like to retire early these days."

Dodge gave her a startled glance. Was she suggesting they had other plans for the evening hours?

Then she destroyed that raw lusting with an upward look at him, through eyes so meltingly shy and insecure, he'd have cut out his own heart before disillusioning her. He smiled, reassuring her that her first attempt at genuine seduction hadn't fallen short of the mark.

"Just for a little while. Starla needs a lot of spoiling."

As flickers of fragile passion danced in her emerald gaze, it was all Dodge could do not to swoop down to her soft lips for a soul-ravaging kiss. But he was also aware of Patrice's intuiting stare and Reeve's smirk of amusement, so he refrained. Instead, he offered his lovely bride a covert wink that had her moistening her lips in response.

They could forgo breakfast and lock themselves up in the bank. The cot in the back wasn't the most comfortable, but it would do in a pinch. . . .

Reeve's sudden sharp inhalation knocked his amorous thoughts off track. Dodge looked about, alert to danger.

He saw only a Union officer on horseback wearing cavalry insignia from a frontier battalion. It wasn't anyone he recognized, but from his reaction, Reeve apparently did.

Reeve strode out into the street, grabbing the officer by the arm to drag him out of the saddle and into an engulfing hug.

"My God," Patrice murmured. "It's Noble."

Noble. Noble Banning.

Starla's Noble.

She'd gone still as stone beside him, not even breathing as her stare fixed on the handsome cavalry officer. The minute he and Reeve separated, she flew out into the street with a squeal of joy to fling herself into his arms, kissing his scruffy face madly.

The sight hit Dodge like a heart attack.

"Oh, Noble! Noble! I never thought I'd see you again."

"Stand down, Starla darlin' and let me get a look at you. My God, you're a sight for sore eyes."

Dodge felt sick.

Turning his wife for inspection was the rival from his worst nightmares: tall, toned, handsome as sin, and Southern to boot. How the hell could he hope to compete with that?

Dodge was vaguely aware of the support of Patrice's arm about his middle. Without it, his suddenly strengthless legs would have failed him. Of all the times to be tottering and off balance—when Starla finally remembered him and hauled her old beau over to exclaim, rather breathlessly, "Noble, this is Hamilton Dodge. My husband."

Surprise widened Noble Banning's ice-blue eyes, but his smile and the offer of his hand were genuine. "Husband? I've got to shake the hand of the man smart enough to catch Starla Fairfax."

Dodge's return smile felt stiff. The other man's grip was firm and strong.

"I've heard a lot about you."

Noble blinked at the clip of his accent. "But I guess not enough about you."

"Dodge and I served together," Reeve explained easily, looping an arm about the tall Southerner's shoulders. "We took turns saving each other's hides. I brought him here to take over Jonah's bank, though most of Pride would rather have their hides torn off than take his help. Bunch of fools."

Noble still smiled, but Dodge, being an outsider, caught an edge that Reeve, as his old friend, wouldn't. Dodge wondered if Noble Banning was going to prove himself to be one of the fools.

"Patrice Sinclair, you look gorgeous as ever."

Patrice opened her arms wide, nearly letting Dodge fall. He managed to catch himself as she stretched up to hug Noble, saying, "It's Patrice Garrett now."

"Why, a man goes away for a while and his whole world gets turned upside down."

He said it with a grin, but Dodge had to wonder what part of the man's world his own marriage to Starla had upended.

Patrice continued to hug to Noble's arm. "We were just talking about getting together over dinner. Please say you'll join us out at the Glade."

"You remember the way out there, don't you?" Reeve teased.

"Blindfolded," Noble assured him. "Nothing would make me happier. But first I've got to go home to see my folks. And to get out of this uniform. Four years is long enough.''

''It's good to have you home,'' Reeve pronounced, pumping his friend's hand.

Dodge would have preferred to have Noble Banning anywhere else.

Talk of him dominated breakfast: Reeve's best friend, Starla's lost love, the paragon of Pride County. Dodge could hardly swallow.

After he'd opened the bank and started to work, he'd catch Starla leaning on her elbows at the teller window, her eyes dreamy and far away—dreaming about whom, he wondered irritably. Not about a short, lame husband with an abrasive accent whom she begot of a bartered marriage, he was damn sure.

He shuffled through his papers, wishing he could get rid of the awful queasiness making knots in his gut. He heard a whisper of silk and looked up to see Starla standing next to him. He blinked quickly to hide the feelings in his eyes.

''Do you mind if I leave a little early? Myrna Bishop has a new dress ready for me and I'd like to have it for tonight.''

He didn't mention that she had a whole closet full of goddamn dresses that were good enough.

''Go ahead.'' She hadn't been much use for anything all day, anyway, what with her eyes filled with stars—and the dashing image of Noble Banning. He looked back at his papers and was surprised by the quick kiss Starla dusted against his temple. When she was gone, he let his head drop into his hands and groaned miserably.

He wasn't sick; he was going to die. It was going to kill him to lose her to another man.

It was the dress that nearly killed him.

Red.

Deep red velvet, as sensuous to the touch as it was sinful to the eyes. The plunging vee of the neckline was mirrored in a row of chevrons down its sweeping pleated skirt with satin rosette bows over loops of ribbon, dazzling with a small agrafe of diamonds in each center. Against the rich hue, her amply displayed bosom was pale, its shadowed valley inviting a man's gaze to lose itself in the looking.

When she saw him staring, Starla pirouetted with a childlike excitement.

"Do you like it?"

"I'd like to take it off you." And bury it deep in the back of her wardrobe, where Noble Banning would never set his eyes upon it. But Starla blushed prettily, interpreting his words differently.

"Shame on you, Lieutenant Dodge. Behave yourself."

Behave himself. With his wife's glorious chest exposed for her former lover's appreciation. She should be hoping he didn't commit murder before the night was over.

She stood before the mirror, strangely self-conscious for a woman of her stunning looks as she fussed with the heavy weight of her hair. She pursed her lips.

"Are you sure? It's not too . . . cheap?"

"Cheap? You could pay off the mortgages on

half the farms in Pride with what it must have cost you.''

She frowned at him, hurt by his grumbling assessment. ''I meant 'cheap' as in 'vulgar.' I wouldn't want to look less than a . . . lady.''

The vulnerable tug in her tone shamed him for his ill temper. He put his hands on her bare shoulders, gratified when she didn't flinch at the contact. He touched a kiss to that soft skin.

''No one could ever mistake you for less than a lady, Star. You honor me, as always.''

Unexpected tears sparkled like the diamond-center rosettes, but she quickly blinked them away. ''You're too kind.''

No, he was too truthful.

It was an evening in hell.

Dodge didn't mind the focus centering on a long-lost friend returned to the fold. He didn't mind that Noble and Reeve shared a friendship that excluded him. He didn't really care that the ladies were all aflutter when Noble smiled, or that the topics of conversation predated his own arrival in Pride. He was as fascinated as the rest of them by Noble's tales of Indians and western adventures.

What he minded was the change in Starla.

She was a rose in bloom: delicate, blushing, beautiful.

Alive.

He'd never seen her without the cautious coloring of suspicion and wariness. But tonight, he was seeing the young woman she once was, bubbling with animation, an endearing mix of shyness and flirtation that took a man's breath away. All for Noble Banning.

It scared the hell out of him.

The woman was his wife. His. But only because a piece of paper said so. Not because of any consummation. Not because of any claim from her lips.

"Awful quiet tonight."

Dodge smiled faintly as Reeve joined him out on the front porch, where he stood wreathed in cigar smoke and melancholy.

"Not much to say that can match massacres on the frontier."

Reeve gave him a long look. "That bothering you? It shouldn't, you know."

"I know, and it doesn't. He's a colorful character."

"He's a helluva friend. We go back a long way. All of us do."

Dodge nodded, saying nothing.

Still marveling over the fact that he could stand at all, Reeve gestured to the cane. "Oughtn't you to give it a rest for a while?"

"Don't fuss. You're as bad as Starla. If I wanted to be mothered, I'd go home."

"I thought you were home."

Again Dodge answered with silence. Then, after a beat, he said, "I foreclosed on my first farm today."

"Who?"

"The Emmericks. Know 'em?"

"Everyone knows everyone around here."

"Five kids, all of 'em crying, the husband cussing, the wife spitting on me. Helluva day."

"You couldn't do anything for them?"

He shrugged. "I can't save them all, Reeve. Maybe if they'd talked to me a couple of months ago, before they got in so deep to the rest of their creditors. Then Emmerick took to drinking and gambled away what little they did have, instead of working to build it up. Gave them to the end of the week. I hate being the villain."

"You didn't make their trouble for them, Dodge."

"I didn't make it any easier for them, either. You can rescue a dozen, but it's the one you let go that everyone's going to remember."

"Unless you're one of the dozen."

Dodge sighed. "I guess."

"What else?"

"What else, what?"

"What else has got you dragging so low? Something a little closer to home?"

He took a long draw on his cigar and blew a series of irregular smoke rings toward the moon.

"I warned you, didn't I? You've got the look of a man chewing on his heart. Believe me, I know the look. And it's damn near always fatal."

"Thanks for the encouragement. You're a true friend in need." Then he spoke it plain, hating the fact that he spoke at all. "Were they lovers?"

"No. She chased 'em all but wouldn't let any of 'em catch her. Too afraid of what her daddy would do. She might have slowed down for Noble, if he'd been willing to chase her back, but he never did—not seriously, anyway."

"Was he blind?"

"Blinded by the law. That's all that's ever held his interest. Starla wasn't exactly his ideal of a lawyer's wife."

Dodge's gaze narrowed slightly. "Why's that?"

"Too fond of trouble, between her and Tyler. Noble was looking for a deep pool, and she was the rapids, all shallow turmoil, fast moves, and sharp rocks. Don't squint at me like that. I know what I'm talking about."

"But you don't know Starla."

"It's true she's been gone for years, but I know enough to know you've got your hands full. Are you worrying that she's still in love with Noble? Don't be. I don't think she understands the concept. You worrying she's still thinking of chasing after him, maybe you got a right to be. What are you going to do about it?"

The tip of his cigar flared bright and hot. Dodge sent a stream of smoke jetting through clenched teeth.

"I'm going to trust her."

"Think that's smart?"

"Think it's about time someone did."

Laughter heralded the approach of Noble Banning with an attractive married woman on either arm. Patrice slipped to Reeve's side, but Starla remained firmly where she was. Her stare fixed upon his, but Dodge couldn't read what flickered through its mysterious depths. He thought he recognized regret—regret that she was free to remain where she was, with the man she preferred?

They made a dramatic couple—Banning all tall, dark sophistication and Starla a dazzling flash of femininity. The way the Southerner was perusing her attributes gave no indication that he'd be opposed to a good chase. Dodge forced a smile.

"It's getting late and I've got some work waiting. It was nice to meet you, Banning."

Noble took his hand. "Likewise. You've got yourself quite a woman here."

"I know."

Starla's protest came as no great surprise. "Can't your work wait until morning? The night's still young—"

"Why don't you stay? Mr. Banning can bring you home, if he doesn't mind."

Dodge waited for Starla to decline, but with a tip of her chin and a tighter cinch on Noble's arm, she glared straight at him and said, "I'm sure Noble won't mind."

So much for his wife's eagerness to retire early.

And as he drove back to Pride alone, Dodge learned a lot about the nature of trust.

Mostly that it made for bad company.

Chapter 19

He woke from a panicked dream of drowning in the blood of those he'd led into battle.

Shaky and breathing hard, Dodge glanced at his watch. It was just after midnight; he'd been home for over two hours. And he was still alone.

Unable to close his eyes again for fear of seeing the familiar death-ravaged features from his nightmare, he dressed, and using his crutches for support, went into the darkened front room. There his restlessness couldn't be contained. What would Starla think, arriving home to find him up, pacing the house? That he was waiting up for her? That he didn't trust her?

Within minutes he was unlocking the door of the bank, seeking to lose himself in the challenge of business. He lit only the lamp at his desk, where he found Deacon Sinclair's predicament awaiting his solution. The problem was, he couldn't seem to find one.

Plagued by images of driving the frail Hannah Sinclair from her family home while Patrice spat on him, he went over the papers again, making notes to himself on a separate sheet until he'd exhausted every possibility, and himself in the process. Knowing he was missing something, but no closer to an actual solution, he rubbed his eyes and consulted his watch. Almost two. Surely Starla would be home by now.

Yawning, he gathered his work in a pile and dropped it into his desk drawer, locking it securely. Deacon's problems would have to wait until morning. Tyler Fairfax left him no easy course of action, except maybe to go right to the source.

He never expected that source to come to him quite so soon.

He bent to fit the key into the outside doorlock. A sudden smothering darkness enveloped him from behind as a sack was pulled over his head, muffling his curse and blinding him to the identity of his attackers. The door was wrenched open and he was thrown down onto the floor. He heard the sound of at least five pairs of footsteps coming inside after him—and felt the impact of five different boots meeting his ribs and face.

Sucking air through the coarse weave of the sack and the thickness of his own blood, he was dragged up to his feet to greet the fists of his faceless tormentors, cowards all. Finally, when he hung by his pinned elbows, close to insensible, he heard a fierce voice he recognized from the curses hurled at him that afternoon.

"Try to steal my life away, will you? Well, there's my note paid in full." Papers were shoved down Dodge's torn shirtfront. Gritty laughter mixed with the ringing in his ears. "Now, I'm giving *you* until the end of the week to move the hell out of town, you sonofabitch, or we'll be back for more.''

The moment his arms were released, he crumpled to the floor, his awareness waxing and waning. He felt the vibration of heavy bootsteps leaving the bank until the last man knelt down to whisper, ''How can you expect to protect her when you can't protect yourself?''

And with Tyler Fairfax's question swirling through his mind, Dodge lost consciousness.

For Starla, the evening put an end to a fairy tale: Noble Banning, her handsome ideal, smiling, laughing, unchanged by the years except for a certain tightness about his mouth, a hint of sadness around his eyes. She'd been so wildly in love with him, she'd have stood on her head naked on the front lawn to get his attention.

But she could never quite win it. How that had broken her young girl's heart so many years ago. Though she'd understood why she wasn't good enough to deserve him, she'd hoped she was worthy of one fine thing in her life, and Noble was all she'd dreamed of. Noble, in his Confederate gray, coming back from the war to sweep her away from her abysmal life.

But of course, that had all changed. Circumstances were different now.

The evening could have been a dream, adrift upon sweet memories and golden moments, stirring tender sentiments and wistful sighs of what had been, what almost was . . . could have been but wasn't, because the focus of those dreams was no longer Noble Banning.

She wore the red dress for her husband. Her excitement, her anticipation, her enjoyment of the evening wasn't due to the return of an old friend and an unrequited fancy; it was due to a very real opportunity to grab onto what Patrice had called the best thing ever to happen to her. It was her chance to move on to the kind of life, the kind of love, she'd also dreamed might exist, if only she were worthy.

A life with Dodge.

Though his earlier tender passion had given her every reason to hope, perhaps she was still dreaming. For Dodge's odd behavior had put a halt to her anticipation.

She thought at first it was jealousy, and that prospect delighted her. What woman didn't want her husband to bristle around other attractive men?

But when she'd come upon him and Reeve on the Glade's wide porch and his dark eyes had made that erroneous assumption in connecting her to the man serving as her escort, she'd seen the truth. Jealousy didn't imply caring, it smacked of possession. Dodge wasn't agitated because Noble was an attractive man, he was anxious because he feared he had cause for worry. He feared she would betray him.

Because he didn't believe for a minute what she'd been trying to show him all evening long. That he, not some long past ideal, was the man she wanted with all her heart and soul.

She'd been nothing more than a pretty possession her entire life. Here, she thought, for the first time, she was more to the man she'd married. She could let down the pretense, she could risk being herself. She could embrace the idea of happiness after a lifetime of wondering if it was something not meant for her.

She was wrong: his idea of the future and hers were two very different things.

As Noble drove her home beneath the moonlight and the stars, everything might have been perfect. But only had they been two different people.

"You look well," he told her.

Starla smiled. "I am."

"Marriage seems to suit you. You're even more beautiful than I remember."

There'd been a time when she'd have killed to hear those words, but now she merely smiled again and heard herself say, "I'm going to have a baby."

At first he appeared shocked by the idea, then he nodded. "Good for you."

And Starla saw for the first time that it could be. She'd viewed her pregnancy, when forced to think about it at all, as a curse, a punishment for her failure to live a proper life. She felt no attachment to the child, no excitement about her baby and its eventual arrival. But sitting there on the buggy seat with a man she'd once loved with her whole heart, she placed her palms over the smooth hug of her gown where life would soon begin its altering contours, and she felt a stirring of contentment. This child had brought her to a new beginning, and she was just starting to realize what a fortuitous event that was.

If only she could hold onto it.

"How'd you end up marrying a Yankee?"

She shot him an arch look. "How'd you end up wearing the uniform of one?"

He laughed but didn't answer her question. "He seems like a good man."

"He is. The best."

Noble's smile grew bittersweet. "He's a lucky man."

Starla laughed softly. "No, *I'm* the lucky one." How funny to figure out, finally, how true that was. In spite of his behavior, in spite of her concerns, she wanted nothing less than a lifetime with her banker husband.

Their carriage spun by the lane leading down to the pond where Dodge had kissed her and awakened her to the dawning of passion. Funny, how the direction of life changed, even when one was not aware of it.

"And you?" she asked the man beside her. "There's been no woman lucky enough to capture your heart?"

A month before, even a week or a day before, she might not have noticed the melancholy in his smile.

"Not yet."

There was someone. Someone who'd broken the heart of Pride County's most eligible heartbreaker. Hers melted, thinking of his unhappiness. Hugging his arm and leaning against him, she vowed, "Don't give up on love so soon. It'll find you when you least expect it."

She was proof of that, wasn't she?

*   *   *

"Dodge?" She looked around the bedroom, finding it as empty as the rest of the house. "Tony?"

His evening clothes were neatly hung away. The covers were in a terrible twist, the pillows on the floor. His cane was at the bedside, but his crutches were gone.

It was one o'clock in the morning. Where could he be?

Sighing, she realized he'd probably gone to the bank.

There were things she wanted to discuss with him, things she'd put off too long. Things like what they were going to name their baby. Things more important than the way he'd wounded her with his actions this evening.

She was the one who'd steadfastly denied him everything. Why should she be surprised that he'd be hard to convince of her sudden change of heart?

She had to convince him, and soon. She had less than thirty days to get her life in Pride in order, to establish a family foundation strong enough to support her past mistakes.

Thinking he'd be home soon, she curled up on the chaise in the parlor to wait, tucking up the voluminous skirts that he'd wanted to take off her. When she opened her eyes, it was daylight . . . and she was still alone.

Anxious, annoyed, and even a bit alarmed, she threw a light cloak on over her evening gown and started for the bank.

From the sleepy early morning sidewalks of

Pride, nothing looked amiss inside the bank. A single light burned on Dodge's desk, but he wasn't at it. Starla tried the door and found it unlocked.

"Tony?"

His crutches were on the floor. She paused to pick up a flour sack lying next to them. Something dark and now dried stained its weave. She stared at that stain, certain it was meaningful, but the significance escaped her.

Perhaps he'd gone into the back and fallen asleep on the cot. But without his crutches?

Sure enough, he was stretched out on the poorly slung frame, his face turned toward the wall.

"I declare, can't you get enough of this place during the day that you have to sleep here at night, as well?" She made her tone light to disguise her hurt that he hadn't come home. "You've just enough time to change and wash up and get back here before business hours." She knelt down and took his shoulder, tipping him onto his back. His head lolled. She got her first good look at him. "Oh, my God. Tony!"

His features were mottled with an array of bruises and smears of blood.

Pausing only long enough to make sure he was breathing, Starla raced to gather cold water and clean cloths. As she dabbed at the nasty split discoloring the corner of one eye, he groaned and began to come around. She caught his hands as they flailed wildly.

"It's all right, Tony. It's me."

He blinked his eyes open, struggling for focus. Unwisely, he tried to sit up, falling back, clutching at his ribs with a low moan. Starla continued to clean him up, holding her breath as the true damage became clear. He had a bad gash by his eye, a split in his lip, puffy swellings on both cheek and jaw.

"Who did this to you?"

He closed his eyes, his attention drifting. Suddenly it was very important to Starla to learn who'd beaten her husband. She wrung the wet cloth out over his face, the sprinkling of water rousing him once more.

"Tony, who did this?"

He pushed the cloth away, still ignoring her question. This time, she knew he'd understood her. And she knew the answer.

Her brother.

"Tyler did this?" she cried in outrage, shocked, then furious. Dodge still wasn't talking. He attempted to rise again, and again dropped back, hugging his middle. "Let me take a look. Did they break anything?" She assumed it was a "they," not believing Tyler alone could have inflicted so much damage. Not believing he'd have acted alone to do such a thing.

He fended her off, muttering, "I'm fine. Don't. Let me alone. Don't need your help."

"Whether you need it or not, you're going to lie there and take it. Now stop being so foolish and let me see."

She jerked up his shirt a bit roughly, earning his sharp gasp, the sight of his chest making her echo it in dismay. She pressed one of the vivid bruises, causing him to wince.

"I'm going for the doctor."

"No. Just get me home."

"You're not going to move until Doc Anderson tells me none of your ribs is broken. So don't you move, you hear me?"

"Yes, ma'am," he murmured, too hurt, too weak to do much else.

Reluctant to leave him, she touched his sore face, her emotions twisting. Then, bending quick to kiss his brow, she hurried for the doctor's home, knowing it was too early to find him in his office.

And after she sent him grumbling in the wrap of his night robe and slippers to get dressed, Starla knew of another stop she'd have to make before going back to her husband's side.

Everything hurt. Breathing hurt, moving hurt, even thinking hurt.

After Doc Anderson poked and prodded and pried, then pronounced no serious damage had been done, Dodge had gotten his battered ribs taped and had two small stitches taken at the corner of his eye. He'd obediently swallowed down some powders for the pain and was waiting impatiently for them to begin to work as he dragged himself across the bank on his crutches in complete defiance of the doctor's orders to stay abed. Being beaten insensible wasn't something to take lying down.

There on his desk was the note on Emmerick's farm and enough cash to see it paid in full. Both were blotched with his blood. Falling into his chair with a groaning curse, he pulled out his ledger and registered the payment dutifully, angrily. He didn't have to wonder how Emmerick had gotten the money. Tyler Fairfax and his Home Guard friends had gotten to him, paying his loan in exchange for recruiting his favors. He wondered if Emmerick realized which would be the more costly in the long run. In ignorance, he'd join Fairfax's band of night riders to terrorize other small farm families like his own, bullying them and scaring them from using the resources at the bank, from trusting the lawful avenues proscribed by the new federal government. Making Fairfax and those like Banning's father who silently supported his efforts more powerful. And more dangerous with each success.

Dodge could see what was coming: those brave few who'd begun to trust him would shy away, once news of the beating was circulated. They'd be watching, waiting, to see how their town's banker dealt with the brutality leveled upon him. Would he bow before the intimidation and sneak away? Or would he stay on in foolhardy disregard for his safety?

His safety wasn't his concern. It was Starla he worried about.

How can you protect her when you can't even protect yourself?

How, indeed?

A show of strength and retaliation was all men like Emmerick and the Dermonts understood. Dodge knew he'd have to do something quick, or risk losing the confidence he'd begun to inspire in the meek and helpless of Pride. But to strike back meant going up against the one man he'd hoped to avoid in confrontation. He'd have to go after Tyler

Fairfax, and in doing so, he'd break Starla's heart. He might also lose her.

If he hadn't already. . . .

When she'd bent over to kiss him on his bed of pain, he'd seen she still wore the red dress from the night before. Which meant she hadn't been home to change. And with her closeness, she'd brought an unmistakable scent, the spicy fragrance of Noble Banning's cologne.

Where the hell had his wife been all night while he was getting his ribs kicked in by her brother?

He lowered his head into his hands, not wanting to think about it just yet, not while he was so distracted by the hurts of both body and soul. He'd vowed he'd trust her, and though that vow was strained to frail threads, it was enough to hold until he had a chance to speak to her, to ask her for the truth.

Yet when had she ever told him that?

The door to the bank opened and he gazed up wearily, hoping to see Starla there. He couldn't imagine where she'd gone after fetching Anderson, unless it was home for some fresh clothing and some needed rest. It wounded him to think she wouldn't at least check in to see how he was doing, to see if he was in danger of spitting up his lungs, thanks to Tyler's tender touch. But she hadn't come, and she wasn't here now.

It was Delyce Dermont in the doorway. Her usually pale features were stark white with shock and distress.

"Delyce, what is it?" A terrible fear gripped his insides.

"Mr. Dodge, you'd better hurry. Something awful's happened to your wife. The doc's with her now."

Oh, God. . . .

"Where is she?"

"At Fair Play."

He didn't wait to hear more.

Chapter 20

The Dermont brothers lounged on the front steps of Fair Play like a pack of dirty hunting hounds. Empty bottles scattered about their feet testified to what the nose claimed on closer inspection: they were all drunk. Their clothing bore stains of all-night revelry and spatters of her husband's blood.

Starla approached in a glaze of fury that overwhelmed any fear she'd had of coming home.

Ray Dermont sat up, his sloppy smile little more than a leer as he beheld her red dress.

"Well, g'morning, missy. Up early or out late?"

"Where's my brother?"

"I do believe he went to round us up some more refreshments. Care to tip a few with us, Starla honey?"

"You've had more than enough, of our liquor and my tolerance. You'd better crawl on outta here. Be gone by the time I'm finished talking to Tyler, or I'll take a buggy whip to you."

He laughed off her threat, a nasty gleam of speculation flickering in his eyes. "Hear that, boys?

She's gonna teach us some manners."

Poteet chuckled. Virg let out a loud snore.

Ray continued. "Tried to learn 'em once, but they didn't take. 'Course, we didn't have a teacher purty as you. Bet you're mighty good at them lessons." He licked his lips as she climbed past him on the cement stairs. His hand caught her skirt. "Mighty fancy get-up. Steppin' out on your Yankee already?" She jerked away from him.

"Get out of my way, varmint. And don't think for a minute that you're going to get away with what you did last night."

"Since when is drinkin' and whorin' a crime?" Poteet challenged lazily.

"Is *that* how you got blood on your shirt?"

Poteet shrugged. "Some gals like it when you rough 'em up first. Bet you like it that way, too, learning at your daddy's knees like you did."

Her slap cut his vile laughter short. Before she could draw back, he'd snagged her wrist in a painful grip.

"You pig. Let me go! Tyler won't stand for you manhandling me. He'll cut your gizzard out and feed it to you."

"Have to go whining to Ty, wouldn't you, 'cause your Yank banker ain't good for nothin'. Why, hell, our little sister Delyce could knock the stuff outta him. He ain't no man."

Poteet gave her a push, knocking her back into Ray, who'd managed to gain his feet. His arms banded her waist to keep her from going at his brother.

"I suppose you consider yourself a man," she

sneered, ''hidin' under pillowcases with whiskey for courage. Some man you are, Poteet Dermont. You're not fit for my husband to walk on.''

''That right? Well, your husband don't do much walkin', now, does he? I took care of that.''

Starla threw herself against the restraining circle of Ray's arms, spitting curses equal to any they could think of while Ray laughed.

''Whoa there, sweet thing. Got lots of spunk, don't you, gal? Looks like you need to work a little of it off. Got nobody t'home to see to that, do you? My guess is he ain't good for anythin' a'tall. Damn shame, fine woman like you with no real man to give you what for.''

His hands shifted high and low for some crude groping as she fought him. His whiskey-soaked breath burned against her cheek.

''I'm a real man, honey, and I'd be more than happy to give you whatever you need.''

With a shriek of outrage, Starla freed one hand, using her nails to score four furrows from ear to chin along Dermont's thick neck. He gave a howl of surprise, catching her hand in a crushing hold, swinging her away from him with a violent force.

''You bitch!''

For a moment, Starla teetered on the top step. Then, with a slow-motion certainty, she felt the slick bottoms of her evening slippers slide on the smooth stone. She stretched out her hands, trying to catch her balance, missing the railing, fingertips grazing Ray's sleeve as he took a purposeful step back out of her reach. She fell. The edge of the second step banged her hip, the next one bit into

her side. Her head cracked against the brick walk
to send the world spinning. From someplace far off,
she heard her brother's voice.

"What the hell's going on?"

"Weren't my fault, Ty," Ray was whining.
"She just come at me like a crazy woman."

"Starla? Star? You all right, darlin'?"

She almost thought she'd be until Tyler tried to
lift her. Pain ripped through her middle. With the
faint cry of her husband's name, she slumped in
Tyler's arms as a hot blackness engulfed her with
streaks of fire.

Tyler Fairfax sat on the front steps of his family
home balled up into a space a ten-year-old could
have occupied, his arms wrapped around his legs,
his face buried in his knees.

"Where's Starla?"

His dark head lifted slowly. Unfocused eyes
stared up at Dodge without the slightest recognition. Grabbing a handful of his shirt, Dodge jerked
him off the steps to wobble on his feet.

"Where's Starla?"

Tyler blinked in confusion, muttering, "She's
inside."

Dodge let him drop back into the boneless crum-
ple. As he started up the steps with the solid plant
of his crutches, Tyler added, "The doc's with her.
He won't let you in."

Breathing hard into his fear and agitation, Dodge
looked down upon his wife's dazed brother. "What
the hell happened?"

It took a long moment for Tyler to find the words

within the bourbon-laced muddle of his mind. "She fell. Here on the steps."

"Were you two arguing?"

Tyler shook his head. "I was inside. I didn't know she was here until—until after. Ray said—"

"Ray Dermont?"

"Ray said she came at him like a madwoman, that she lost her balance when he put up his arm. He couldn't catch her in time."

"Did Dermont have his hands on her?"

The low, throbbing fierceness of Dodge's voice cut through Tyler's stupor. He shook his head.

"No. Ray'd never touch her. I'd kill him if he tried."

Something didn't fit right, but until he heard it from Starla herself, Dodge was forced to let it go.

"Did the doctor say anything about her condition?"

One glimpse of Tyler's welling eyes said more than he wanted to know, more than he could believe.

"No," he argued. "She's going to be all right. She's going to be just fine."

Tyler stared at him blankly, as if the reassurances were beyond his comprehension, then he looked down the drive. His tone was curiously soft and completely lost.

"I don't know what I'll do if she dies. She's all I have."

Gritting his teeth, Dodge lowered himself to the step beside his grieving brother-in-law. He couldn't quite bring himself to offer a display or any further words of comfort. They sat side by side in silence, waiting for words they were afraid they wouldn't want to hear concerning a woman they both loved beyond the limits of their own lives.

When they finally heard footsteps, Tyler crossed his arms over his head as if expecting a terrible blow. Dodge turned. Then, seeing the grim-faced doctor who'd so recently stitched him back together, he struggled to stand, using a firm grip on Tyler's shoulder to bolster him.

"How is she?"

"I wish my news was better."

Dodge swayed slightly, unable to absorb the impact. "How bad is it?"

"She has a concussion that's kept her from regaining consciousness. That's not good. She broke a rib and there's a lot of internal bleeding. I haven't been able to stop it."

"But you will."

Anderson looked away from his commanding stare. "My chances would be better if . . . if she wasn't with child."

Dodge squeezed his eyes shut. After a moment, he said, "But she is."

"She's young and strong. I'll do everything I can to prevent complications."

"But you can't guarantee there'll be none?"

"No. I understand a man's desire to have an heir, but you'd better prepare yourself for the worst."

"She can have other children. . . ."

The doctor pressed his shoulder. "I wish I could tell you the odds were in your favor, but with this kind of injury, and the severity and internal trauma of it—I'd be lying to you. Most likely she won't be able to conceive again.''

The news buffeted him with chilling consequence.

No children. No family. Where was the fairness? The justice?

''Do whatever you have to do to save her, Doc . . . to save them both, if you can.''

The next two hours were the longest Dodge could remember. He wished for some of Tyler's oblivion as each thought, each fractured dream, wrought fresh slashes of anguish and guilt. What kind of future would he and Starla share, a future barren of promise because of his stubborn stand against a town that didn't want his help? He challenged and second-guessed his every move, from asking Starla to marry him to the words they'd exchanged before she'd gone to fetch the doctor, knowing he was somehow responsible for her lying upstairs in her family home, about to lose the only child she might ever have.

The only child she could ever give him.

The only thing that hurt quite as much as that knowledge was the thought of losing Starla. . . .

''Mr. Dodge, Mr. Fairfax.''

They turned.

Doc Anderson looked at them for a long moment, then said, ''I've done all I can do. It's up to God and Starla now.''

Dodge forced himself to ask: ''And the baby?''

The doctor shook his head sadly.

He choked down the shock, then said, "I want to see her."

Anderson halted Dodge's struggle to stand. "Not now. She needs total quiet and time to heal. Matilda has instructions to come for me if—when—she wakes. Until then, no disturbances of any kind. Mr. Dodge, I suggest you go home and to bed if you're going to be any good at all for her when she really needs you. Mr. Fairfax . . . sober up. Good morning, gentlemen."

After the weary doctor left, Dodge looked longingly at the house. Surprisingly, he found an ally in the man who'd only hours ago tried to beat the hell out of him.

"I'll send Tilly to let you know when there's a change."

Dodge stared at Tyler for a minute, then simply said, "Thank you." He fought his way up, fitting his crutches under him, and was about to start for the buggy when Tyler gripped his wrist.

"Don't blame yourself," Tyler told him, sounding suddenly sober and possessed of a somber truth.

Dodge couldn't find the voice to reply.

He couldn't go back to the home they shared, to the house where they'd discussed which room to use as a nursery. Instead, Dodge found himself at the bank, sitting behind his desk, wondering with an odd calm if it was proper to close the doors, citing a death in the family.

He never heard the door to the bank open but suddenly found himself engulfed in Patrice Garrett's embrace as she wept. "Oh, Dodge, I'm so terribly, terribly sorry. We just heard. She'll be all right. I know she will."

Numbly, he marveled at the speed at which bad news traveled in a small town as he leaned his forehead against her perfumed shoulder. Eventually, he noticed Reeve standing behind his wife, looking awkward in his sympathy as he offered, "Is there anything we can do?"

Yes. Give me back the last twelve hours! He settled for saying a quiet, "No. Not just now."

Patrice rocked back, then gasped at the sight of his face. "What happened to you?" He winced as her fingertips brushed his swollen cheek.

"Had some company last night. That's what got Starla worked up enough to go to Fair Play. It's my fault—"

Patrice hushed the rest with the press of her hand over his mouth. "Don't say that; don't think it. It's not true, Dodge."

But he did, and it was. He regarded her impassively, knowing better than to argue. Instead, he said, "I need some coffee."

Flanked by his best friends, Dodge worked his way down to Sadie's, where the dining room was just beginning to fill up with those eager for an early lunch. He looked purposefully away from Delyce's teary gaze as he headed for his usual table.

It was then that he heard the sneering drawl from a group of diners he passed.

"Well, boys, thanks to me there's one less Yank bastard to worry about."

Dodge stopped, not quite believing what he'd

heard from Ray Dermont. Patrice gripped his elbow, urging him onward.

"Let it go, Dodge," she cautioned.

He turned slowly to confront the Dermonts.

"What did you say?"

"You heard me, Yank, or are you deaf as well as lame and just plain dumb?"

A sudden blanking coldness seeped through Dodge's mind as he said, "Are you telling me you're responsible for what happened to my wife?" His attention riveted to the gouges scratched into Ray's beefy neck. Rage quivered through him, quickening a dangerous tension. "Did you put your hands on her?"

"Hell, Yank, who hasn't put their hands on her?"

"That's a lie."

Dermont laughed, missing the deadly edge in Dodge's soft-spoken words. "Joke's on you. Didn't you know she was a whore, just like her mama?"

Ray Dermont had time to blink once. Dodge gripped a handful of his hair and drove his face into the tabletop, pulping his nose before throwing him over backward, chair and all. Reeve stepped in, setting his pistol down on the table, a warning to the other two brothers that it would be best for them just to sit back in their chairs and relax.

His features unrecognizable through the twist of controlling fury, Dodge sat astride Ray Dermont, determined to pound his head through the floorboards. He might have succeeded had Dermont not pulled a knife from his boot. Spotting the movement out of the corner of his eye, Dodge deflected the jab meant to take him under the ribs and wrested the blade away. He swung it up over his head and was beginning the downward arc toward Dermont's black heart.

"No, please!"

Delyce's frantic cry made Dodge pause long enough for some degree of sanity to return. Leaning close enough for his seething breaths to scorch the other's face, Dodge whipped the knife edge up against Ray's throat, raising a line of red beading.

"If anything happens to my wife, nothing this side of hell's going to keep me from finishing this."

"Told you not to mess with him," Reeve said to the other two Dermonts. "He's a tough little bastard when he gets riled." He bent to grip Dodge by the elbows. "C'mon. I don't think you need any coffee."

As Reeve hauled Dodge to his feet, Poteet Dermont made a foolish grab for Reeve's gun. With a move so fast that none actually saw it, Dodge stabbed the knife blade through the back of his hand, pinning it to the table. As Poteet howled, Dodge told him with a cold ferocity, "Next time my aim will be better."

With Reeve steering him toward the door, Dodge headed for it under his own power, his steps uneven but managing to support him. Only when he entered the foyer did his knees buckle. He depended on Reeve to hold him up until Patrice levered the crutches under his arms.

"I want to go see my wife."

"I can't imagine anyone getting in your way," his friend mused.

But Reeve was wrong. When Dodge arrived at Fair Play, he found his entrance barred by the two burly men he'd vanquished in Pride. They were backed by four others of equally impressive bulk.

"I want to see my wife."

"Mr. Fairfax wants to see you in his study."

"Tell Tyler—"

"Mr. Cole, not Mr. Tyler."

His patience frayed, his resources draining, Dodge allowed them to escort him into a different room. Now the wizened old man sat behind an expensive teakwood desk. In a creased if ill-fitting suit, his eyes clear and fixed upon his guest, Cole Fairfax was more imposing than he was pitiful. Dodge knew a prickle of alarm.

"What can I do for you, Mr. Dodge?"

"I've come to see Starla."

"I'm afraid I can't allow that. You see, her health is very fragile, and it's obvious you aren't capable of caring for her."

"I want my wife."

"But she doesn't want you, sir."

Few things could have struck him as badly just then. His tolerance gave.

"I'm taking her home."

"She *is* home. You heard the doctor, Mr. Dodge: my daughter can't be moved, and I will not allow you to further endanger her life now that she's where she belongs. Do you honestly think she'll want to see you? Her child died because of your stubbornness. There's nothing left to tie you to my family. My lawyers will see this sham of a marriage ended, and if you come here again, I'll have you shot as a trespasser.''

Dodge stared at him, too stunned to object.

''Gentlemen, see Mr. Dodge out, and see that he doesn't find his way back here again.''

Chapter 21

Twilight slanted across the pale features of the woman in bed, the deepening shadows making her stillness seem more sinister to the man clutching her hand so tightly.

To Tyler Fairfax, the whole world narrowed to the soft whisper of his sister's breathing. He'd sat for hours watching that gentle rhythm, considering each repetition a further sign of forgiveness for his sins. It had been a long time since he'd requested any favors from above. In truth, he'd almost forgotten how to pray, but seeing Starla lying there, hovering between here and beyond, reminded him of a lot of things he'd forgotten. The words, the vows, the bargaining were all sincere when he'd spoken, and he hoped God wasn't as big a cynic as he was so that He'd actually believe Tyler would come through on those promises if He'd only let his sister live.

He hadn't slept in days. Weariness threatened his vigil and it became a battle every time he blinked to force his eyelids to rise again. Maybe he needed a little respite, just to rest the ache in his eyes and the terrible gnawing at his soul for a few minutes.

From the chair he'd angled next to the bed, he slumped on the edge of the mattress, pillowing his cheek on his sister's upturned palm. In seconds the edges of awareness began to blur and ebb, which was why he doubted the reality of her fingers moving against his damp face. Until she spoke.

"Tony. . . ."

"Star? Starla, darlin'?"

He sat up to the incredible reward of watching his sister's eyes fluttering open. It didn't matter that there was no recognition in her foggy gaze, only that she'd defeated the greatest obstacle. She'd decided to come back to him.

"It's all right, darlin'. I'm here."

"Tony?"

"It's Tyler, darlin'. An' I'm gonna take good care of you, so you jus' rest, y'hear?"

She seemed comforted by the words, by the stroke of his hand on her hair. Her eyes flickered shut, and on the quiet sound of her sigh, Tyler forgot most of the vows he'd made. Except one.

To keep his sister safe.

"How is she?"

Tyler stiffened at the sound of his father's voice behind him. An uneasy prickling stirred against the back of his neck, but he didn't turn. He hadn't known the old man was strong enough to climb the stairs.

"She's gonna be all right, I think."

Cole Fairfax said nothing more for a long moment. When he did, his words struck terror into Tyler's jaded soul.

"My little girl's back home again, just the way it should be, the three us. Like it was before. Our darlin's come back. An' that's the way it's gonna stay—right, boy?"

Tyler squeezed his eyes closed against the nightmare images his mind created. His reply was little more than a whisper.

"Jus' like before."

Dodge had drifted off into a restless slumber on the parlor chaise when a soft knock at the door startled him into all manner of panicked thoughts. The hour was late. Visits close to midnight rarely had good consequence.

He stared at the Fairfaxes' maid, Matilda, with a paralyzing dread twisting through his middle. He couldn't make himself ask it.

Is she dead?

"Mister Tyler sent me to tell you Miss Starla has waked up."

Dodge's knees went watery. Only the support of his crutches held him up. For a moment, he could only breathe slow and deep into his relief.

"Did she ask for me?" he said at last.

"He didn't say nothin' about that, sir, only that I was to tell you what I told you."

"Thank you. And thank him for me."

With a nod the old woman slipped away.

After the weakening sense of relief had passed, Dodge returned to the front room, to his solitary thoughts. With Starla out of danger, he had some serious consequences to consider. The baby was no longer there to hold them in an unconsummated marriage.

Cole Fairfax's threats could become reality.

Would Starla want to come back to him? Was there anything left to keep them together? The baby was gone. Noble Banning had returned. He found himself helpless to retrieve his own wife from her father's home. What could he do? There was no law in Pride—except that privilege made power, and might gave right to those who could claim it. He had the military expertise and the simple daring to plan an assault upon Fair Play to retake his bride. A fierce possessiveness growled through him, pushing him to make that commitment to a cause, the same commitment that had made him a good, even great, commander on the battlefield. But he wouldn't commit without that cause. And he had to know if Starla wanted to be claimed. She'd had enough bullying men in her life, pulling her in all directions without a care to her feelings.

He had to know the state of her heart before he could act upon the forces driving his.

It was early. Dawn had just begun to sketch pastels along the horizon and the town of Pride slumbered lazily in the dog days of summer.

Dodge had finally fallen deeply asleep, so the sound of another visitor at his door dragged him up out of a healing oblivion. He tried to stand and found he couldn't. The effects of his beating several nights before—though now it seemed like weeks—had congealed into a solid protesting ache, making movement next to impossible. Until his guest gave a yell.

"Hey, Yank. You in there?"

Tyler Fairfax?

Dodge pulled himself up onto his crutches and moved painfully to the door to open it. It was Fairfax, all right, standing on his porch with a bundle in his arms.

"Got something for you, Yank. Where do you want her?"

Dodge stepped back, stunned past coherent thought as Tyler carried Starla inside. One look at her still, wan face snapped his stupor.

"In the back."

Tyler followed and carefully laid his sister out on the bed she shared with her husband in all ways but those of a wife. After solicitously tucking her in, he turned to Dodge.

"She belongs here with you, not in that house with him. You take care of her, Yank, or I'll know about it."

"I don't—"

"I know you don't." Tyler grinned at him wryly. "So don't try. I heard tell about your run-in with the Dermonts. Figured you'd done my job for me there, so I'd do you this favor in return. Guess I was wrong about you not being able to hold your own. Jus' don't go turning your back so easily."

"I won't."

They exchanged measuring looks, each reassessing what he'd originally seen in the other. Tyler nodded toward his sister.

"He ain't gonna like it that she's here. You be careful now, y'hear?"

"What about you? He's going to know it was your doing."

Tyler smiled again. "What can he do to me?"

But the haunted shadows in the back of his eyes had Dodge wondering. He put out his hand. Tyler gave it a look, then laughed.

"Let's not get sentimental 'bout this. I still don't like you, but she does, an' that's all that matters, I guess."

He never did take Dodge's hand or stay to hear his thanks. And Dodge found himself hoping that Tyler Fairfax's act of uncommon decency wouldn't land on him with brutal consequence.

The doctor paid a visit mid-morning. He had nothing to say about Starla's change of residence but examined her and pronounced her safely on the mend. He did have a word of warning for Dodge, though, cautioning him not to let her fall too deeply into melancholy over the loss of the child. Dodge agreed while not knowing how to lift himself out of his own.

He sat with her steadfastly, heartened by her improving color and by her longer bouts of awareness. She recognized him, finally, but had yet to understand what had happened to her. He despaired over how to tell her.

It was the next morning, when she met him with a lucid gaze and a furrowed brow, that he knew the time he dreaded had come.

It was something terrible. That truth came to

Starla slowly as her strength began to gather, and with it, the knowledge of her own discomfort. She waited until Dodge bent to brush his knuckles across her brow to ask him to explain.

"What is it, Tony? What's happened?"

His dark gaze canted away from her in an uneasy evasion, quickening her anxiety. "What do you remember?" he asked.

"Going to Fair Play to see Tyler. The Dermonts were there. I remember falling on the steps, and pain in my head and in my—" Her hand pressed to her side, and Dodge's stare following the movement then darted away as she drew her own conclusions. "Tony?" The rest came out in a fragile tremor. Her voice fractured. "The baby?" she whispered.

She watched him draw a deep, composing breath, heard the rattle of his inhalation. But his tone was steady, almost too calm, when he relayed what the doctor had told him, finishing with, "I'm sorry, Starla."

When the numbing shock wore off, Starla experienced a strange sense of sorrow over the little life she'd secretly resented, the child she'd feared she wouldn't be able to mother. It was Dodge's excitement over the birth that had finally awakened a similar enthusiasm within her. It was through him that she'd begun to believe she could learn to love what had been created in terror and violence. And now the opportunity was no more. It left her empty inside, and unsure of how to grieve.

Just as she was suddenly unsure of Dodge.

If only he'd look at her, or tell her how he was feeling. . . .

Was he blaming her?

If he did, he never expressed it. For the next weeks, he was tender and solicitous about seeing to her every need. When she was capable of moving around on her own, he went back to work at the bank, then spent the early evening hours telling her about his day. All very nice, like they were the best of companions. But never did the subject of the child come up. And never did she see a spark of anything beyond compassion in his dark eyes.

During the long, sweltering days that capped the end of summer, she had her share of visitors: Patrice and Reeve, her brother, even Noble Banning. All were careful to tiptoe around the topic of her loss in their determined cheerfulness.

They must have all held her to blame. She didn't care what they thought; only Dodge mattered.

And she was losing him.

She could feel it, day by day, the gulf between them widening. He was polite, and he smiled, but when she caught him unawares, she could see such sadness in his eyes that it broke her heart with guilt and shame. He was thinking about the children they'd never have, that she could never give him. And he was thinking about the only chance at a family they'd had. It was only a matter of time before that sorrow steeped into resentment and he grew to hate her for trapping him in a marriage that couldn't give him the one thing he wanted most—a family.

Her hope of a future, her blanket of security, was beginning to unravel.

She owed him everything and now could give

him nothing . . . nothing but the guilt of having destroyed their future, nothing but the shame of what she hid in her past. He deserved better. He deserved happiness.

A package arrived that morning from Michigan. Dodge had already left for the bank and Starla sat staring at it, debating whether or not to look inside. It was addressed to Mr. *and* Mrs. Hamilton Dodge. Curiosity finally won out.

A card lay on top of a tissue-wrapped bundle from Alice.

''For the next addition to the Dodge family.''

A clogging tightness burned in the back of her throat as she opened the tissue to find a neat stack of infant garments. She lifted one out, fingering its tiny sleeve and delicate ruffles. She blinked against the tears that wouldn't come.

These were the clothes Alice's children had worn, all painstakingly kept to hand down to the next generation of Dodges. Clothes perhaps that her husband, himself, had worn. Heirlooms. Treasures. Meant to be used.

But not by her children.

Very carefully she refolded the miniature gown, placed it with the others, then carried the box upstairs to the room that would have served as a nursery. There she tucked the box away where someday Dodge would find it. And someday make use of its contents.

She'd just returned downstairs when a soft tap at the door drew her away from melancholy thoughts. Upon answering it, she found a distressing visitor.

"Hello, Starla. I had a hell of a time finding you. You didn't tell me you'd married again so soon. May I come in?"

She stared at Beau LeBlanc as he stood there smiling on her front porch. A terrible weakness quaked through her legs, but she forced them to hold her. She wouldn't show weakness before a man like LeBlanc. She opened the door wider.

"Come in."

He glanced around the house with a casual assessment. "Not quite up to what you've been used to. I thought you'd have chosen better."

"What do you want?" Anxiety raced through her mind. What if Dodge were to come home early? How would she explain her visitor? What if someone had seen the lawyer arrive and mentioned it to him? A sickening fear tightened about her heart.

"You left New Orleans so suddenly, we didn't get the chance to conclude our business. But it did give me some time to check up on you and what you've been doing. A Yankee banker? You'd settle for that after casting me away?"

Not wanting to discuss Dodge with him, she snapped, "Why are you here?"

"To give you one more chance. After all we've been to each other, I felt I owed you that much." He reached out a hand, but Starla shrank back. Beneath her fear, and growing stronger, was a fierce rage that he would come here, that he would play upon her vulnerabilities, as he'd tried once before.

"Don't you *dare* put a hand on me. Speak your mind and get the hell out of my house."

LeBlanc let his hand drop to his side. His smile warped with amusement. "If that's the way you want it. The hearing's a week away. When you ran out, Mrs. Fortun felt it implied a disinterest on your part to make any trouble. I told her she was wrong, that she didn't know you the way I did. Was I right, or were you planning to let things proceed quietly?"

"You're not getting my son."

LeBlanc laughed. "I told her you had more spunk than you let on. So I figured I'd take a little trip up here so we could have a chat. You, me, and your husband." He pounced upon her sudden pallor. "You have told him about Christien and your troubles down in New Orleans, haven't you?" At her silence, he grew bolder. "You're a smart girl, Starla—a survivor—or you wouldn't have put up with Stephen for so long. You've started a new life here, with a new man, a man in the community's eye. Have you considered how that man's business is going to suffer from the scandal you're going to bring him?"

She hadn't . . . not until this moment.

LeBlanc pressed folded papers into her cold hand. "I'm staying at the hotel in town until my train leaves late tomorrow. Bring me those papers, signed, and you can get back to your banker. If not, I guess I'm just going to have to ruin you."

Starla sat in the darkening parlor, the unsigned papers crumpled in her shaking hands. Behind her placid expression, her mind was spinning frantically.

What could she do?

At one time, Dodge had been her answer. She'd felt sure she could count on him to protect her. But that was when she was pregnant, when she had more to offer him than just trouble and ruination. How badly did he want to keep her as his wife? Enough to suffer what LeBlanc had in mind?

She had to do something about Christien. Now. She had to prepare for whatever LeBlanc was planning. She knew him too well not to figure he would strike at her through Dodge. Whether his weapons were ones of violence or ones of truth, either would wound beyond reparation. How could she wish either upon the man who'd done so much for her? She paced the house in restless circles, her heart pounding, her mind frantic.

Escape: it was the one solution she kept coming back to. At first she dismissed it in dismay. Leave her husband? Leave her home? But the more frightened she became, the more it began to look like rescue instead of running away. Rescuing Christien from his scheming grandmother. Rescuing Dodge from her father's wrath and LeBlanc's attempt to ruin them. Rescuing herself from an endless well of grief and guilt. If there was an alternative, she couldn't find it.

One thing was certain: she wouldn't give up her child. She had one chance to atone for the sins of her past—by providing her son with all the love and security she'd never known. By letting him grow up unscarred by doubt and guilt. Nothing mattered but that. Not her own happiness. Not the cold calculation of what she planned.

Only Christien mattered. And if she was smart, and quick, and clever, she would be in New Orleans before LeBlanc knew she was gone. And she'd snatch Christien from that house of opulent emptiness so they could begin their lives together. Just the two of them.

Chapter 22

Once Starla had decided upon a course of action, time flew quickly. That made it easier for her. She could pretend, as she filled a bag with her most valuable possessions, that she wasn't going to be leaving the rest behind forever. She could hide the truth from herself so she wouldn't see each move as taking a step away from everything she'd come to care for. It was the only way to get through what she had to do. She'd treat it all as a game, not as a very permanent and far-reaching action.

She sat down to write a quick note to Tyler so he wouldn't worry. She'd have it delivered from the station. She didn't think about Dodge; that was something she couldn't do, not until miles and miles separated them. Only when she was out of reach of her weakness for him would she write to explain. She'd worry about how she could possibly make sense of her situation later. It wouldn't matter what she said, anyway. He'd never understand.

Dodge. . . .

Don't think; *don't feel,* she reminded herself savagely. That was how she survived. That was how she'd go on surviving.

She saw the buggy coming and forced her knees to steady and her mouth to smile. Inside, she deadened anything that might interfere with her plans. She watched him step down from the carriage, suppressing her pride in the fact that his stance was so solid. He used only a cane now. Then he turned and she steeled her heart not to soften to the sight of the weariness and troubles lining his brow. Instead she'd be thankful for his usual preoccupation with his work.

"Don't unhitch the horse."

He paused, glancing down at the bag she carried. "Going somewhere?"

She smiled. "Only to the dressmaker's." She hoisted the bag. "That blue gown she just finished for me, the fit's all wrong. She said she could repin it after closing." She waited, but he didn't respond. "Is that all right?"

"As long as you're sure you're up to it. The doctor said you were supposed to rest."

She smiled and relaxed a bit. "I'll be fine. Patrice asked me to stop there for supper afterward, 'cause Reeve's got some business out of town, so don't worry if I'm late. You know how we are when we get to talking. Time just flies."

A pause, then, "Tell her hello for me."

He was making it all so easy. Why, then, was anxiousness crowding up around her heart so hard she could barely breathe?

He stood by the buggy, waiting to help her up into it. She'd known this would be the most difficult moment, when she had to stand near him, smiling as if nothing was amiss.

"You drive carefully, now," he told her, his tone gentling with concern. "And don't be too late. There are some things I want to discuss with you when you get home."

She would never know what those things were.

She smiled with a carefree wave. "All right. I'll watch the clock."

He took her bag and placed it in the boot. They were close enough for her to smell one of his good cigars on him. She'd grown fond of that scent and breathed it in as if to make it last. He put his hands on either side of her waist and she reached up for the seat. But instead of boosting her, Dodge held her a moment longer, his hands dangerously familiar in the way they fit her. When she glanced at him in question, she saw a glimmer of odd intensity in his eyes. Fearing that if he looked much longer she'd give herself away, she leaned forward to kiss his cheek, meaning the gesture to be a quick good-bye. She hadn't counted on how hard it would be to pull away. Her lips grazed the rough burr of his skin. Her fingers tangled in the hair at his nape. Oh, how she wanted to cling forever to everything she had. But knowing she wouldn't have him for much longer, even if she stayed, made it easier for her to let go.

"I left supper for you on the stove. Don't work too hard." She choked out the words. She had to turn away, stretching up for the seat. He lifted her and she quickly slid across the cushion, tucking her skirts around her. She found the reins and cracked them on the horse's rump, startling it into a trot because she needed to get away before the tears burning behind her eyes began to fall.

She didn't look back. She didn't have to. The image was carved upon her heart.

Using her key, she unlocked the door to the bank. The room was dim, but she could still see well enough for all the memories to come crowding back. She meant to go straight to the vault, but she hesitated as her gaze touched upon the faintly pink floorboards she'd scrubbed with such vigor, the glass windmill that had been Jonah's still sitting on the corner of her husband's tidy desk. The bars of the teller's cage made slanting shadows on the wall, crisscrossing her own as if she were in a prison of her own making. She closed her eyes as ghosts filled the room: Tyler, leaning on the counter to tease her with his grin, and then leading an endless parade of Pride citizens mouthing their gratitude to the one man in the county who could save them—the man she'd married.

With a fierce oath, she shook off those images and strode purposefully toward the vault. She knelt before it, calling the combination up with a remote clarity of mind. Tumblers clicked into place and the heavy door opened. Then she was scooping the contents into her bag, enough to see to her ticket and to a new start for herself and Christien. She didn't look around but kept her focus ahead, on what she was doing and where she was going, not on what she was leaving behind.

She stood, aware of how much heavier her bag

had became—not because of what it weighed, but because of what it carried.

It carried the hopes of the people of Pride. It carried the seed of her husband's ambitions, just as she'd once carried the seed of his dreams.

No matter how many times she told herself that the money would be repaid, she couldn't block off the picture of Dodge discovering it was gone. Nor could she shut out the thought of his humiliation as he tried to explain who had taken it. He didn't deserve to be so horribly disillusioned.

She clutched the satchel to her hammering heart. There was no time to return the money, no time for last-minute pangs of conscience. She couldn't go back.

But how could she go on?

The selfishness of a lifetime failed her.

How could she leave the man she loved to face the sins of what she was doing? Could it be worse than asking him to share the shame of what she'd done?

In minutes she could be miles away.

But could she outrun her sense of shame?

She reached for the heavy safe door, needing it to support her failing strength while she tried to shore up her flagging courage.

That was when she understood. What she was doing took no courage. She could hear Dodge's voice claiming, *Running away never solves anything*. She was running because she lacked the courage to stay, the courage it would take to trust in her husband's claim of love.

She had no time to cry out as her wrist was

gripped firmly, spinning her around. To face her fears in the form of an accusing Hamilton Dodge.

She gave a soft moan, her knees giving out, but his hold on her arm was too tight to allow her to fall all the way to the floor. The bag dropped from nerveless fingers, the impact sending up a fountain of greenbacks.

"The Glade is the other direction, Starla. Did you think Patrice was going to charge you for the meal?"

She hung from his imprisoning hand, cringing beneath the harshness of his tone.

"Tony, I can explain."

He glanced down at the contents spilling out of her bag, the angles of his face grating together. "Put it back."

Without a word, she bent, using her free hand to shovel the money back inside the safe, where it fluttered about until he slammed the door shut. Giving the dial a spin, he said, "Remind me to change the combination in the morning."

All she could think to sputter was, "How did you know?"

"Patrice came to see me."

"Patrice?"

"She told me she and Reeve were dining with the Bannings. A going-away party for Noble. Imagine my surprise when you said she'd asked you out to the Glade. In fact, imagine my surprise when you stopped off to pick up a little traveling money."

He'd known. And he'd followed her.

"Wha-what are you going to do?"

"I'm going to listen to that explanation, then I'm going to buy you a ticket to wherever it is you were planning to go."

Starla fought not to cower. She'd never before had reason to fear Dodge, but this cold-eyed man was a stranger to her. A stranger who'd been hurt and lied to beyond the limits of his endurance. She didn't know what he was capable of. His hands were white-knuckled, as if he were trying to keep himself from striking her. He toed her nearly emptied bag.

"Pick that up. We're going home."

With that fierce claim, he hauled her out to the buggy. She scrambled up, not waiting for his aid as she fought to contain her weeping, certain it would earn her no sympathy.

Dodge angled the buggy up next to the modest house. Starla leapt down and dashed inside, seeking refuge in a huddle on the parlor sofa. She buried her face in a velvet pillow and sobbed until she heard her husband enter the house with a slam of the door. Then she sat up, dashing a rebellious hand across her eyes to greet him boldly. That bravery faltered in the face of his deadly calm as she waited for him to speak. She expected recriminations decrying how she'd betrayed his trust, but that wasn't how he began as he stalked the room with a fierce tap of his cane tip.

"Are you in love with him?"

"With whom?" she squeaked in confusion.

"Banning. Who the hell else would I be asking about?"

"No."

"No, you're not in love with him, but you were sneaking off with him!" He raised his hand to brush it back through his bristled hair. She cringed at the movement, and that made him angrier. "Damn it, I'm not going to hit you."

But the way he gripped the head of his cane gave her no tremendous confidence.

"I wasn't running away with Noble."

"Just thought he might like the company, is that it? If you were so damned sick of mine, why didn't you just say so, instead of lying to me and robbing my bank?"

He began to pace again, not trusting himself to stand near her. How could he tell her how it made him feel, to learn of her unhappiness in such a brutal fashion? How could he explain how it hurt to have her lie to his face without a betraying blink? Or how it tore the soul from him to watch her use the trust he'd given her to cheat not only him, but the townspeople who'd placed their funds in his care? He couldn't explain and he couldn't begin to understand. And he couldn't bear to look at her now to see the huge tears welling in her eyes, eyes that even in the face of her duplicity shone with such innocence.

"I would have had the money from the bank replaced out of my trust fund." She sounded insulted by the suggestion that it was stealing.

"And that makes it all right, is that what you think?"

"No. Of course not." Her gaze lowered to the hands twisted together in her lap. She looked like a repentant schoolgirl, guilty by deed rather than intention. Dodge knew that wasn't true. He knew it, yet his mood still softened. But pain and pride kept his tone crisp and curt.

"Did I give you some reason to be afraid to come to me? If you needed money, I'd have given it to you. If you wanted to leave me . . . I'd have let you go." Though he wouldn't have wanted to. He saw her shoulders shake slightly. He sighed fiercely. "Why didn't you just tell me you wanted out of our arrangement?"

Arrangement. That sounded so much more impersonal than marriage, implying no emotional involvement, no intimate commitment. If only he could have kept it that way, he wouldn't be crawling over hot coals now. Could he blame her for not feeling the same way about him? Was that why he felt so angry, so betrayed? Because all the emotional ties were on his side alone?

She didn't look up. Her voice was small, but still strong with conviction. "I thought it would be easier this way."

"On whom?"

"Both of us. I thought this way it would be easier for you to get on with your life, to find someone else who could give you the children you wanted."

"You thought—" He couldn't continue. He turned away, but not before she saw the quicksilver brilliance in his eyes. "You thought I'd cast you off because you lost the baby? Why would you think that, Starla?"

"You said you wanted to marry me because of the baby, because you wanted a family. I couldn't give you those things anymore, and I know you were too kind to tell me I was no longer of any use—''

''Starla, I told you I loved you. Didn't that mean anything at all?'' He looked back at her to find her gaze upon him, somber and sad.

''People say they love you all the time, then turn right around and leave you. My mother said she loved me, too. I didn't think the one thing had anything to do with the other. Why else have you kept your distance from me all this time if not because you regretted our bargain?''

''Because I—because of that damned dress!''

''What dress?''

''The red one. The one you wore so Noble Banning couldn't keep his eyes off you. How long did it take for him to charm you out of your garters while your brother and his friends were kicking my face in? Is that when you two decided to run off together?''

She sat staring up at him, her features perfectly immobile. Finally, she rose with an icy dignity, took one step toward him, and slapped him hard enough to shake his eyeballs.

''If you weren't such a stupid man, you'd know I wore that dress for you, because—oh, what difference does it make? You saw what you wanted to see, what you expected to see.''

She whirled away, ready to flee the room, but Dodge caught her wrist, holding her in place.

''What else was I supposed to think? You were out all night and came home smelling like him—''

''So I must have slept with him, based on that

evidence. Like the evidence I had with you and Irma Sue?''

''I never—''

''Neither did I!''

He took a ragged breath, struggling for control, for a calmer reasoning. ''Damn it, Starla, if you're lying to me—''

''Have you always been so honest with me? Were you forthcoming with the truth about your injury? Did you tell me your life—our lives—were in danger because of your work at the bank? How was I to know you didn't blame me for the baby when you wouldn't say anything to me at all? Tell me, how was I supposed to build a future on all that honesty?''

He couldn't answer right away, because she was right in all she said. She was right to be angry with him. He'd told himself he was telling those lies to protect her, but they were lies nonetheless. He took another breath, this one shaky with dread.

''Do you still want a future with me?''

The shimmering in her eyes totally belied her whispered words. ''Let me go, Tony.''

''No. Not unless you tell me you don't want me.''

Brightness continued to well, and with a blink, dissolved into a wash of tears. ''I don't—I don't want to hurt you.''

''Then why are you leaving me?''

''Because—because I love you too much to stay.''

He forced a jerky swallow, then another, grabbing for air as if every particle had been sucked from the room—then finally just grabbing for her. The reality of her hugging to him with an equal fervor sent all logic careening. "My God . . . I've been waiting forever to hear you say that!"

She was sobbing. "You have to let me go. You don't understand what could happen."

His grip on her tightened. "Then you're going to tell me. Right now. You're going to tell me everything."

"I met him at a party at the manor when Patrice's father was going off to war. His name was Stephen Fortun, and he was in Pride on business, buying horses from Squire Glendower. He was drunk and he proposed to me. I—I was having a bad time of it at home, so I said yes."

They sat side by side on the parlor sofa, letting the natural darkness shade the room as Starla's narrative shadowed the atmosphere.

"I didn't tell anyone what I was doing or where I was going. I was afraid my father would try to come after me. We stopped in Chattanooga long enough to get married. He took me to his home in New Orleans, then went off to join the fighting. We—I have a son, Tony. He's three years old. His name is Christien."

Starla felt his surprise and the intensity of his gaze upon her, but she couldn't look up at him, not until she'd told him everything: about Stephen's return and his dependence upon opium, which turned him into a violent and irrational stranger. About his mother's refusal to accept her only son's weakness, and how her greed for the family's money made her blame her son's death upon his widow so she could have sole guardianship of Christien and the fortune he'd inherit. Of how she'd allowed herself to be intimidated by the Fortun money and power into leaving the house without her child. And she told him about Beau LeBlanc.

"He said he'd get Christien back for me. He was so—nice. So sympathetic. I trusted him. I told him about Stephen's delusions, about how he kept accusing me of being with other men. It wasn't true, any of it. He said he believed me."

And she'd believed him enough to let him go to Sally Fortun on her behalf. A meeting from which he'd returned with two startling options for her to choose from: they could marry and she'd share the Fortun wealth with him, or he would tell the courts that he'd been one of her many lovers and how she'd tried to talk him into killing her husband so she could have his money.

Dodge breathed a soft oath. "But it would just be his word against yours."

"As if that weren't enough, the word of an outsider against two of the biggest families in New Orleans, he had other . . . proof."

"What proof?" he asked, knowing he wasn't going to like it.

"He arranged for several uninvolved and reputable parties to find us together—in a compromising position, in my hotel room. We—we were in my bed, and I was unclothed."

When she paused to gather the strength to go on, Dodge added softly, "And unwilling."

She glanced up at him, grateful for his faith. She looked so damned grateful, he wanted to kill the son of a bitch.

"But that's not what they saw and not what they'd testify to. Tony, if I don't sign over custody of Christien to Stephen's mother, they're going to take me to court for murdering my husband. And even if they don't prove a thing, it won't matter. I won't have Christien. And if you'll still have me, the scandal will ruin your career."

He was silent for a moment. "And that was why you were leaving."

"He brought papers for me to sign. He's waiting over in the hotel. I was going to take Christien far away and start over."

"Without me." When she didn't answer, he looked away, his jaw working fiercely. "God, you must think I'm an awful coward or a bigger fool."

She stared at him, not understanding. She jumped slightly when he turned back toward her, for his dark eyes were filled with an explosive intensity.

"That bastard's not taking your son away from you. And by God, nobody's taking you away from me. We're paying him a visit, the two of us and our lawyer, the Harvard-educated Mr. Banning. He has no idea what he's gotten himself into, now that he's got me riled. He's going to have one helluva fight on his hands—"

"But—"

Dodge broke off his impassioned speech with an impatient "What?" Then his eyes blinked shut while she kissed him long and hard until he was breathless and docile once more.

"I don't deserve you, Hamilton Dodge."

"Well, you've got me and there's not much you can do about getting rid of me."

When she leaned away, it was only a scant inch, so that their hurried breaths mingled.

"Make love to me, Tony. I want us to have a marriage, not an arrangement . . . if that's what you want, too."

She stood, tugging on his hands to bring him up beside her. He crushed her to him, pressing his face into her tumbled hair. "You have no idea how much." Need vibrated through his words.

She melted against him, opening for his plunging kiss, sighing as it gentled into an urgent search for her response. She denied him nothing, answering with equal abandon, only vaguely aware of him opening the back of her gown, of it slipping to the floor, followed quickly by her hoops, corset cover, and the boned undergarment itself, until she wore only her combinations and stockings. Then he kissed the soft skin bared as he peeled back those dainty straps and adored the firm fullness of each white breast. As her fingers clenched in his hair, he lowered that kiss to the black triangle of curls, delving his tongue to explore her with a shocking intimacy. Her legs went weak and watery. Her breath came in short bursts that crested with a sudden explosive jolt of pleasure.

She had no memory of how they got to the bedroom.

With the mattress soft and yielding beneath her

and Dodge all hard masculine angles above, Starla surrendered to the compelling contrast of sensations. She lost herself to her husband's hungry kisses, learning the rock-hewn contours of his arms, back, and shoulders with the eager circling of her palms. No objection arose in either body or mind at the first invasive thrust of his fingers, nor at the deep claiming fullness that followed.

The way Dodge said her name as he buried himself inside her, all low and husky with reverence and awe, fed the emptiness of her soul like nothing before. What followed was all sensual poetry, a sense of completeness and giving of one to the other that brought tears to her eyes and wrung a glorious cry from his lips . . . and afterward, a wonderful contentment found only in entwined arms and legs, and entangled hearts, and peaceful sleep on a bed shared by man and wife.

It was during the cusp between midnight and the new day that Dodge was awakened by the soft snuffling sound. It took a moment for his eyes to adjust to the blackness so he could see his wife huddled on the edge of the bed, shaking with sobs.

What had he done? Had he somehow hurt her, made her feel afraid? The possibility tore his heart asunder. Cautiously he placed his hand upon one quaking shoulder and said her name. She went instantly still.

"Star, what is it? If I've done something—"

She rolled into his arms, burrowing against his chest like a wounded animal, to wail as if it was the most awful thing in the world, "I love you, Tony."

For Dodge the world stood still in a moment of private thanksgiving. Then he went on to address Starla's tears.

"I love you, too. Is that something terrible, sweetheart? It shouldn't be a reason to cry." He began stroking the sleek line of her back and soothing repetitions.

"I've done such shameful things! I'm so afraid you'll come to hate me."

"There's nothing you could ever do that would make me love you any less."

Her head shook violently. "You don't know."

"It doesn't matter, not to me."

"But it will. You don't understand . . . I let it happen. It's my fault. My fault for being weak and foolish."

"Shh. Star, you don't have to tell me any more."

But she continued in a frantic whisper, as if digging in tainted soil to uncover a secret better left buried. Each moment brought that evil closer to the light.

"I was very lonely and I wanted to be loved. That's what I thought it was, the holding and the kisses. I thought it was love."

The bastard! Dodge fought to keep his fury contained. He continued the gentling caresses while in the darkness of his mind he was planning a retribution that would go beyond pain, beyond ruin, to the total destruction of the son of a bitch who'd so abused this woman's fragile trust.

Her voice gave a painful hitch. "He hurt me and he called me a whore and said I'd led him on. And then there was the baby and I didn't know what to do. I couldn't tell him; I couldn't tell anyone. And I must be an awful person, because I prayed so hard that the baby would die, that I would die. How could you love me, Tony? How could you?"

He gave a low, passionate curse, then took her damp face between his palms, lifting her head, holding her so she couldn't evade the sincerity in his stare.

"I love you because you're smart and brave and caring and beautiful, and you have nothing, *nothing*, to apologize for or be ashamed of."

Her tears scalded the backs of his hands as she held his gaze, daring to believe what she was hearing.

"I love you, Starla. I will never, ever stop loving you."

He spent the rest of the night convincing her of it, giving her all he could because she'd already had so much taken from her unfairly. And much later, just as dawn was creeping up on the darkness, she slept in his arms while he rested easy, forgiving her for her imagined sins without another thought, believing that her confessions centered on a selfish son of a bitch in New Orleans who'd used her for his own gain.

But not knowing the confessions weren't about her relationship with a spoiled Southern lawyer.

They were about her relationship with her father.

Chapter 23

Since Starla had anticipated the embarrassment of having to retell her story to Noble Banning, somehow it didn't seem quite so awful in their well-lighted parlor with her husband, solid and supportive, at her side.

Noble was a stoic witness, asking brief questions and making quick notes. When she was finished, she felt drained, not only of energy, but of some of the guilt as well. Especially when Dodge's arm stole about her shoulders for a bracing hug.

"So, what do we do?"

Nothing sounded better to Starla than that all-inclusive "we."

"First, I'll go over to the hotel and introduce myself to that lowlife as your new counsel. Then, with luck, I can reduce him to the cowardly pile of boot scrapings he is with my plan to travel to New Orleans to do extensive interviewing in regard to his character and that of your first husband. Then I plan to gather sworn affadavits in Starla's favor from her banker husband, from her influential distillery owner brother, and from Kentucky's most powerful horse breeder, and I'll even see if I can twist a few good words out of Deacon Sinclair.''

Starla clutched at Dodge's hand, her expression filled with disbelief. ''And they'd do that for me?''

Noble dazzled her with his smile. ''Darlin', we've all known you since you were a baby. How could you think any of us would have a bad word to say? You've got yourself a decent, hard working husband, you're a solid member of a growing community, and you've got ties to some mighty powerful political forces, and I don't think you've got a thing to worry about.''

She sagged into the circle of Dodge's arm, sighing as his kiss brushed her brow.

''Just one more thing,'' Noble added. ''Starla, is there anything else you can add that might weaken their claim on the boy?''

For a long moment, she kept her face buried in the clean starchy scent of her husband's shirt. Then slowly, very slowly, she faced Noble and told him, ''Nothing I can think of, no.''

A lie. A lie because the truth, though it would win her back her son, would also cost her her husband.

Dodge rose up awkwardly along with Noble and extended his hand. ''I appreciate all you're doing. I know you had other plans.''

''Plans I can postpone for a little while. Starla's always been special to me and she deserves a chance to be happy, especially after the good advice she gave me the other night.'' He smiled down at her and she managed to return it.

Dodge saw him to the door, and both of them

stepped outside to meet Tyler, who was just coming up the front steps.

"I heard you was back," was all Tyler had time to get out before Noble lifted him up into a rib-crunching hug that lasted until Tyler was wheezing. Back on his feet, his breath restored, Tyler was all grins. "Didn't think no Yank prison could take the starch outta you, Noble. How the hell are you? Plannin' to stay? Starla get a look at you yet?"

"Fine, for a while, and yes. I've got some things I've got to do. They'll take me about a week. Then I'll be back for some of your daddy's finest."

"I'll be looking forward to it."

Noble nodded to Dodge and went down to collect his horse. Tyler looked after him with a bittersweet smile.

"He used to be a damn good friend."

"He still is." Dodge made no attempt to explain himself.

"Always thought him and Star...." Tyler shrugged. He gave Dodge a long, gauging study. "I want what's best for my sister. That appears to be you, whether it's what *I'd* want for her or not. You make her happy, and for that I'm in your debt."

"You don't owe me for that."

"Maybe not."

"Starla's inside, if you want to see her."

"Not just now. Actually, I came to see you."

He walked to the steps and paused, looking off toward town. Without turning, he mentioned casually, "Yank, were I you, I'd take out fire insurance on that bank of yours. Might come in handy in the next day or two. Tell my sister I said hey.''

Perplexed and alarmed by the nonchalant warning, Dodge stared after him as Tyler made his way down the walk and took the turn toward Pride. He heard Starla come out of the house and sensed her concern in the way she clutched his arm, figuring she'd overheard that last part.

''Think he was serious?''

Starla shivered. ''Does it matter?''

''Can I trust him, you think? Was it a warning, or could he be setting up some kind of trouble of his own?''

''I don't know, Tony,'' she confessed. ''I don't know what kind of man my brother's become.'' And it upset her.

Dodge tucked her up against him. ''I'll trust him . . . with due caution.''

Later that night, while Starla knelt on the mattress, massaging her husband's legs, the matter surfaced again.

''Don't go in to work tomorrow.''

Dodge dragged himself up from his blissful luxury and blinked his eyes open. ''What?''

''Stay home. Stay here with me.'' She continued kneading his muscular calves, refusing to meet his questioning stare.

''Not that I'm not always looking for excuses to stay home, but if your brother's friends have something planned, I need to be there.''

''Why?''

''Why? Because it's my job, Starla. The people of Pride expect me to protect their investment in the bank. I can't do that hiding under the covers at home.'' He made it sound reasonable, but to Starla it was sheer insanity.

''I'd rather have you home under the covers than at the bank risking who knows what. If Tyler was warning you of something that's going to happen, you owe it to yourself, to *me*, to heed his caution.''

''Nothing's going to happen if I'm ready for them.''

''Then I'll come in with you.''

''No.'' His answer brooked no argument.

She frowned in frustration. ''Then ask Reeve to spend the next few days with you. Please. No one would think less of you. There's no civil law in Pride. You have to do what you can to keep yourself safe, and if that means having an extra gun at your side to go up against those cowards, then ask. Tony, please. I'd feel so much better knowing you weren't there alone.''

''I'll ask him.''

Starla leveled herself along him, her body a silken enticement, her soft kiss a velvety reward. ''Thank you, Tony.''

He'd already forgotten the conversation because of something else that had come up, demanding immediate attention. He gripped her slender waist, lifting her to her knees and settling her back and down atop his urgent manhood, taking a moment to absorb the indescribable sensation of her wrapped hot and tight about him. Then he moved her in an increasing rhythm until they both took their pleasure in noisy abandon.

As she curled up against her husband's side, her

fingers playing through the matting of his chest hair, Starla's thoughts grew serious.

"Tony?"

"Hmmmm?"

"Do you mind about Christien coming to live with us? He'll be no trouble. He's a beautiful little boy. I just know you'll love him."

"He's a part of you, Star. That means he's already family."

"I love you, Tony," she cried, pulling him down to smother his face with kisses. Then she hugged him tightly, trying to crush the guilt from her heart.

She was bringing her son home.

Dodge woke early, warmed by the figure of his wife draped over him, and more deeply by his feelings for her. He hadn't thought to ask for more than just her to complete his life, but now she'd given him an unexpected gift, the hope of a family after all. Once he'd gotten over the initial surprise, the notion had settled in, curling contentment about his soul. A son, a boy to nurture and raise, to encourage along the path to manhood to make his own choices and know his own strengths.

Christien. Christian. Chris. Even as he let the name play about his heart, he warned himself not to get excited too soon—not until they knew for sure that Noble could sway LeBlanc and the Louisiana courts. He tried to ignore the quicksilver pang of worry, for already he'd opened his arms to embrace this boy he'd never met.

Too energized to spend another minute abed, he slipped away from Starla, leaving her to a well-deserved slumber, and began to ready himself for work. It was early, but he had things to do if he was to get the jump on those who would jump him.

Placing a light kiss upon his wife's glossy head, Dodge started for the door. He was halfway there before he realized he wasn't using his cane. He'd been so preoccupied, he'd forgotten he needed it.

Perhaps he no longer did.

Grinning in self-congratulation, he snatched up the cane, and with a twirl, tucked it under his arm, proceeding with a bit more care out into the balmy morning. With a fresh cigar clenched between his teeth, he walked toward the bank, enjoying the day and his freedom to move through it on his own.

He was only slightly disturbed by the news that Reeve had gone to Lexington for the day to talk with a prospective horse buyer. Feeling strong enough to hold off the gang of cowards with his bare hands, Dodge went for coffee at Sadie's.

" 'Morning, Delyce. Is that coffee thick enough to float a horseshoe yet?"

"Almost, Mr. Dodge."

"How are your brothers?"

She looked alarmed by the question and stammered, "What do you mean?"

"I mean, what have they been up to lately?"

"They don't discuss their plans with me, Mr. Dodge. Did you want anything else with that coffee?"

"Bring me everything but the hooves and tail, cooked just long enough so it doesn't moo."

She smiled at him shyly, then her eyes went round to see him standing on his own.

Taking advantage of the moment, he asked, "Where are your brothers this morning?"

"What? I think they were going over to Fair Play later on. Mr. Dodge, you're up and walking. That's wonderful!" She gave him a quick hug, then stepped back, embarrassed by her own boldness. It was no secret that her brother Poteet had shot the town's banker in the back. If none of the no-good scoundrels had the decency to feel bad about it, she vowed to make up for it with her own sense of guilt and shame.

Dodge devoured his breakfast, plotting as he chewed. Fair Play. Going to fetch Tyler to participate in their party? Or to lead it? He wished Starla's brother was less of an enigma.

And by the end of the day, he wondered if the sly Southerner had just been fooling with him.

A steady flow of Pride's citizens visited him. Some came for help, some for advice, some to actually make deposits, and a few to express their regrets over Starla's loss of their child. Those few, with their genuine sentiments and shy smiles, were reward enough to offset any difficulties ahead. Slowly, one by one, as Reeve had said, he was making friends in Pride, and acceptance would follow. He was too smart to think it would be an easy road; hearts and minds didn't change overnight. He couldn't work miracles. But for every Deacon Sinclair who slipped beyond the grasp of his assistance, there were a handful of others he could get squared away and moving forward again. Those were the ones he'd concentrate on while he mourned his failure to save the others.

And that's when he got to thinking about the mortgage on Sinclair Manor and something he remembered glimpsing early on, just after he'd arrived in Pride—a grant of ownership to the family deeding them an inalterable right to the house and the land it sat upon.

"Son of a—"

That's what he'd been missing. That old wrinkled land grant, with its florid wording and solid legal claim for as long as a member of the Sinclair family lived. The incontestable right of ownership.

He tore through the haphazardly filed old papers in the bottom desk drawer, the ones he hadn't had the opportunity to send for safekeeping to the state capital. Finding the one that would guarantee Deacon Sinclair a stay from his own foolishness against Tyler's clever scheming. Tyler couldn't refuse the buy-back offer, not under the terms of the original grant.

"Yes," Dodge said with a fierce sense of satisfaction. Such news wouldn't wait until morning. He'd carry it out to the manor himself as soon as business was put away for the night. He'd found his means to settle with Tyler on a less than personal level, in a way that wouldn't trap Starla in the middle or cause her undue pain.

By the time he'd locked up his vault and closed his back doors, the sense of being close to meeting all his ambitions had settled comfortably upon Dodge's shoulders. He had a beautiful wife, was soon to be a father, had a modest home and a successful business, was walking on his own two feet

again, and was on the fringe of community acceptance.

What more could he ask?

As he stepped from the back room of the bank,
smiling at his good fortune, he happened to glance
at his desk and paused in puzzlement. The heavy
leaded glass windmill that Patrice had given to Jonah was missing.

His only warning was a whisper of sound to his
left. Before he could turn toward it, colors exploded
through his head, making everything go black.

The Dermonts and Tad Emmerick arrived at Fair
Play to meet an unusually sober Tyler Fairfax on
the front porch. They all preferred the airy setting
to the stagnant interior of the house.

"We got business to attend to, Tyler," Ray
drawled, already mean drunk and looking to cause
trouble.

Tyler gave him a steady look, seeing the mind-
less anger motivating the man, for the first time
feeling uncomfortable at their association.

"Well now, Ray, I don't rightly know if it's my
business."

"What you talkin' about, Ty?" Poteet demanded, as liquored up and surly as his older
brother. His hand was crudely bandaged, a reminder of his personal interest in this particular
business. "You ain't goin' soft on us, are you?"

Tyler leveled a cold, glassy glare at him that
made him step down from his combative attitude.
"You know me better'n that, Po." He flashed a

lethal smile. "I ain't about to change my spots to a yellow stripe."

"Then what you draggin' your feet for, boy?" Ray patted his back in hardy camaraderie. "We got things to do."

"I'm jus' saying, I think I'll pass on this particular bit of business."

"You got a sudden fondness for Yankee bankers who stick their noses in our way of doing things?"

"No. But I am right fond of my sister, and he's her husband. I never asked questions about what happened here on this porch, and I'll keep it that way, provided you pass me by on this one occasion."

Poteet sputtered in outrage. "You can't back out, Fairfax. We need you—"

"You need my name and my money backing you. You don't need me to light a fire under one stubborn Yank. I'm sitting this one out. When my sister asks if I had anything to do with it, I don't want anything hanging on my conscience when I tell her no."

"You ain't got no conscience." Poteet laughed at the idea.

Tyler smiled with him, a fierce baring of his teeth. "Maybe not, but it makes me feel better to think I do."

"Ty, this is important. You know Judge Banning wants this done, and he's willing to be generous."

"Split the money among yourselves. That ain't why I'm in it, anyway."

"It's 'cause you're a true patriot to the South, right, Ty?" Poteet sneered.

"That's right."

Ray gave him a narrow look, trying to penetrate the wealthy Creole's mask to see what was really behind his reluctance. "I don't like leaving you behind, Tyler."

"Why? You think I'm going to go to the law on you?"

They all laughed at that. Tyler tossed Virg a bottle of Fairfax Bourbon. "That's to get ready. When you boys are finished, stop on by and we'll share another."

"I still don't like it."

Tyler stared through Ray Dermont with a .44-.40 caliber intensity. "An' I don't like anybody making rough with my sister. You want to carry this further, Ray?"

The tip of Tyler's knife suddenly notched in under Dermont's ear, next to the faint welts left by Starla's fingernails, pressing slightly for emphasis. Ray smiled carefully.

"Nossir, Ty. Let's just let it go."

The blade disappeared and Tyler was all charm once more. "I got me some business to tend to myself this afternoon, so if I ain't back when you get here, jus' make yourself to home down at the office."

That meant plenty of free whiskey, and they all were agreeable to that.

After they'd gone, Tyler paced the porch, his mood restless, his mind too clear for his own comfort. The conscience he vowed not to have was stirring up trouble, goading him to do something he'd regret. He'd already warned the obstinate Yank;

what more could he do? If the fool decided to throw caution to the wind, it wasn't his problem.

He wanted a drink—a long, tall tumbler of his daddy's finest. He wiped the back of his hand across his mouth and fought to suppress the need.

He hadn't forgiven Ray Dermont for what had happened to Starla. Someday he'd exact a payment. If Ray was smart, he'd know better than to turn his back ever again. But neither Ray nor his brothers were terribly bright, which was why they were easy to lead. And he liked that about them. They were pack animals, loyal to whomever intimidated them, but what they didn't realize was that Tyler was loyal to only one thing, and that was his sister.

Which was why Tyler found himself loitering by the bank, carefully out of sight and cursing himself for being a fool. His hands were shaking for lack of fortification, and that clarity of thought was beginning to make his head ache.

Maybe Ray and the others had changed their minds. Or gotten too drunk to carry it off.

Then he saw a faint curl of smoke seep out from under the front door to the bank.

He waited.

No alarm sounded. There was no sign of Dodge or any activity in the bank.

Surely the dumb bastards hadn't killed him, or left him inside to burn to death.

He'd lit his share of torches without remorse, but he'd never had a hand in murder. Was that the difference between where he and the Dermonts drew the line? He paced the sidewalk opposite, watching as uneven flickers of light flashed against the bank's leaded panes.

Was everyone else in town blind?

He glanced about anxiously, but no one strolling the walk was paying any mind to what was happening across the street.

Cursing in his mother's native French, he grabbed the arm of one of the area's dirt farmers.

"Hey, what's going on at the bank?"

As the man looked, Tyler slipped away, leaving the fellow to draw his own conclusions. He couldn't get caught up in the matter. But he couldn't keep himself from wondering what would happen to his sister if the scrappy little banker died.

Obviously, the Dermonts had come out through the back, so that was where Tyler headed. Against his better judgment, he slipped inside. And it was there that he found Dodge, sprawled facedown, blinking blood out of his eyes as he tried to crawl toward the smoldering fire. Tyler gripped the back of his coat, hauling him away from the smoke.

"My records," Dodge was groaning.

"Easy, Yank. A little fire ain't gonna touch that big old vault." He dragged the nearly insensible banker out into the back alleyway, where the fresh cut of air got Dodge coughing. He didn't look good, his face all sweat-slicked, his eyes glazed over. "Sit tight. Help's coming."

Tyler started to stand when Dodge's hand cuffed his wrist, pulling him back down.

"My papers . . . in my desk."

Tyler glanced down in dismay at the key Dodge pressed into his palm before swooning dead away.

Tyler looked from the key to the smoke-filled interior.

"He think I'm crazy?" he muttered to himself.

He'd done enough already, first in giving a warning, then in spreading the alarm. Now the damn fool Yank was asking him to risk his life to rescue papers he'd just as soon see destroyed.

"Just because I don't jump to cut your throat don't mean I'm anxious to cut my own. I ain't that crazy."

Chapter 24

He was drowning.

Try as he would, he couldn't make his legs respond to lift himself out of the ever-deepening pool of blood. As it closed over his mouth and nose, his hands flung out wildly. And found solid purchase.

"It's all right, Tony. You're all right," somebody said.

Dodge blinked his eyes open, scattering the last vestiges of his nightmare by clinging to Starla's hands. He focused on her lovely face, bringing the rest into view around her.

She sat on the edge of the bed he was lying in. It wasn't theirs and they weren't at home. It wasn't until he saw Doc Anderson that everything fell into place.

He tried to sit up, a mistake. Agony stabbed through his back, blanking his awareness in a sudden red-hot haze. He fell back, breathing hard to get on top of it while his feet twitched and jumped in their own disassociated rhythm. An equally distressing misery pounded through his head.

"Mr. Dodge, how are you feeling?"

"Like somebody shot me again." Abruptly, his mind was wide awake. "What happened?" He put his fingertips to his temple, feeling a huge contusion there.

"You took a hard hit, Mr. Dodge. But apparently you've got a harder head. As soon as you feel up to it, you can go home. I've given your missus some powders you can take, if the pain gets to bothering you too much. Make him rest, Mrs. Dodge."

Starla looked pale and shaken, but she had a nod for the doctor as he left them and a smile for her husband. It trembled like the damp jewels clinging to the ends of her lashes.

"When they came to get me, I thought— Oh, Tony, I was so scared."

"I'm sorry."

She took a breath. "Someone will be sorry. Who hit you?"

"I don't know . . . I could guess."

"Tyler?" Her eyes begged him to say it wasn't true.

"I don't think so." Blurred images began to come together. He remembered Tyler being there. *Help's coming.* And he remembered the key to his desk. . . . "My papers?"

"They were stacked beside you. How did you ever go back in for them?"

"I didn't. Your brother did. The bank?"

Her somber expression told the worst. He cursed low and passionately, quieting when she stroked the side of his face.

"I want to see for myself."

"Tony, the doctor said—" But at his determined frown, she sighed and went to fetch his crutches.

Wanting to get out of bed and actually accomplishing it were worlds away, Dodge soon discovered. Something was wrong. Something a hell of a lot worse than a headache. Every move he made was accompanied by splinters of pain and numbness shooting down his legs. It scared him, but the alternatives scared him more. Going under the doctor's knife . . . waking up paralyzed, or not at all . . . failing Starla when she depended upon him the most . . . failing Pride just when its citizens had begun to accept him.

Some of them, anyway.

Gritting his teeth, he used his crutches to lever himself to his feet, swaying there as suddenly all went black. He was aware of Starla steadying him, of her cautioning him to go slowly. He focused on the tender concern in her voice to bring him back from the edge of darkness. And he would concentrate on the way she smiled up at him, with confidence, pride, and love, to keep him from crumpling.

He had too much to do to just curl up and die now.

But that was what he felt like doing when he saw what was left of the bank. The brick walls still stood, an empty shell. From out of the steaming ash of roof timbers and woodwork rose the soot-stained vault.

"Every step I've taken, I've had to take one back."

Starla put her arm around him and was gratified when he shifted to let her partially support him. "Not all of them, Tony. Not all of them."

"I want to check inside and hire someone to stand guard until I can get the building enclosed again. Then I want to go home."

He looked terrible, his face sweat dappled and flushed with pain. The brightness in his eyes was part agony, part ambition. She wanted to grab onto him, to beg him to return to the bed, to lie down and be still, and to take no risks with a life that was very precious to her. But she didn't.

"All right."

"I love you, Starla."

"I'm counting on that."

Dodge slept hard, aided by some strong powders the doctor gave him. Beside him Starla lay restless with anxiety, knowing she could lose everything in the space of a minute.

She would never have believed she could come to depend so much on another human being—not just for protection and support, but for the sense of completion she felt when she was with her husband. He made her believe all things were possible . . . that she could put the past behind her . . . that she could be the kind of mother she herself had never known . . . that she could raise a child with love and strength so that child would never know fear or confusion . . . and that a man could love her enough to accept her flaws, even when he wasn't aware of them all.

An unpleasant whisper intruded.

Would he continue loving her if he knew?

Would he accept Christien if he knew the truth? She wanted to think so, but she was a coward, too familiar with broken faith to hold with any conviction. Even for this man who had never failed her.

Dodge woke up hurting too bad to be heroic about it. He pretended it was just his head so as not to worry Starla, but he knew something was different. He sensed that the bullet had shifted in his back and was raising all sorts of hell. Prickles of hot and cold sensation tormented the muscles in his back and thighs, but they were preferable to the absence of any sensation at all, which came and went, then came again for just a bit longer each time.

Starla allowed him to be irritable and petulant, taking his gruff complaints for as long as she could before kissing him close to mindlessness to keep him quiet. He held her tight, then slightly away, so that their gazes met and filled with one another for a long, emotional minute.

"I want your face to be the last one I see and the first one I wake up to."

"It will be."

"I've never been afraid of dying before. I guess that's because I've never had as much to live for as I do now."

"You remember that. You remember what you have waiting for you. And if you scare me like that again, I'll wring your neck myself." She smiled, touching his cheek, touching his heart.

"If anything should happen—"

She put her fingers across his lips. "Nothing will."

He moved her hand with a gentle firmness and repeated, "If anything should happen to me, you and Christien go north to stay with my family. They'll take care of you. I know you're not all that fond of them—"

"I'll go. We'll go. Don't worry about us."

He smiled, and it broke her heart.

While she went to wash and dress, he went over the papers Tyler had rescued from the bank. The grant on Sinclair Manor wasn't among them. He expressed a soft oath. Maybe it had gone up in flames. Or maybe Tyler had seen to that torching himself, upon finding it on his desk. Either way, saving Deacon Sinclair's home was no longer in his power. Perhaps that was the payment for Tyler Fairfax saving his life. When he saw his wife enter their bedroom and experienced a swelling of love so immense he could hardly breathe through it, he knew he'd never mention the deed to another soul. This time, he wouldn't begrudge Tyler the cost.

"Come take a walk with me. Just a short one." While he still could, was what he didn't say.

The morning was cool, a hint of autumn lingering in the air. They walked slowly into town, Dodge depending upon his crutches and momentum to move him along when his legs refused to obey him. He wouldn't complain; he would never complain about any time spent in her company.

He drew up short when they got close enough to see the ruins of the bank. Vaguely he was aware of Starla hugging his arm.

Instead of smoldering beams, the building shell was full of townspeople cleaning out the debris and already pounding up new supports. In the middle of it all was Reeve Garrett, who waved when he saw them.

"Nice of you to show up finally. I thought you kept banker's hours. You gonna supervise this little project, or just stand around and watch?"

Too moved to do more than try to swallow around the huge clog in his throat, Dodge let Starla answer.

"You can have him. But just for a little while." She stretched up to kiss his cheek, her spirit taking a tender turn at the sight of the wordless sentiment shimmering in his eyes. "You take it easy, you hear me? I'll go fetch you some coffee, but promise you won't try climbing any ladders while my back is turned."

He mashed her up against him, murmuring, "I just might."

She pushed at him playfully and let him go, watching with a welling pride and possessiveness as he crossed the street to greet those citizens of Pride who'd accepted him among them. He was building something good in Pride—not just the bank, but the community. And she was honored to be a part of it.

Still smiling, she turned and bumped into the hard chest of Benson, her father's brutish lackey. She gasped and jumped back, but he had her by the arm to jerk her up close. He gestured to his companion.

"Milton here is a crack shot. 'Less you want him

to put that Yankee husband of yours down like a dog where he stands, you'll come along with us real quiet-like.''

Milton parted his duster to let her get a glimpse of his gleaming pistol. She didn't question their willingness to do what they'd promised. So she agreed.

''I won't give you any trouble.''

Though eager to immerse himself in the project at hand, Dodge took a moment to answer an odd prickle of uneasiness. He glanced across the street to where Starla had been standing moments before only to find the boardwalk empty. He frowned, wondering where she could have disappeared to. Sadie's, where she'd been headed to get his coffee, was a straight walk in plain view, yet Starla was nowhere in sight.

''Mr. Dodge, where do you want this?''

His attention was tugged away by the request but returned with a nagging bad feeling. He'd survived too long on intuition to ignore its cautionings.

''Did anyone see where my wife went?''

''I saw her yonder a minute ago talking to two of her daddy's men. She went down thataway with them.''

Absently Dodge nodded his thanks to Harve Bishop as his worried gaze swept the walk and the yawning opening to a back alley Harve had indicated.

The bad feeling just kept getting worse.

*   *   *

Starla stumbled as Benson shoved her roughly into the dimly lit room and closed the door to trap her inside with terror. Though she was quaking inside, she drew herself up to take an independent stance in the face of her father's harsh scrutiny.

"I'm tired of playin' games with you, girl. I asked you nice, and now I'm *tellin'* you how it's gonna be."

Starla couldn't control the shudder of dread sweeping over her like a fatal chill. She recognized the tone of determination and impatience and knew her father was about to draw the final line in their relationship. She was well aware of the penalties for crossing it and him, yet she refused to humble her stand or her attitude.

"And how is that?"

"Don't make me beat that sass outta you. I can, you know. I can do any damn thing I please and no one will stop me."

"My husband will. Tyler will."

Cole Fairfax laughed, a low, gurgling chuckle like something thick and foul going down a drain. "I don't think so, girl. You're as bad as your mama. You jus' don't know how to pick your champions."

"Don't talk to me about my mama."

"Why should you care what I say about her, the useless tramp? Remember, she's the one who left you two younguns here so she could run off with her lover. Yeah, that's right. She favored her pleasures over her responsibility to you. An' you're just like her. Only you ain't gonna get off as easy as she did. Nossir. I know better now. I ain't gonna turn my back on you again. You're here under my roof, and here you're gonna stay."

"You can't keep me a prisoner here." She meant to sound outraged, but an edge of apprehension crept into her tone. Just the possibility that he could make good on what he was saying was enough to set her shivering. "I'd rather be dead."

"That's what your mama said, too. But she didn't mean it, either. Not when it came right down to it." Fairfax smiled to himself as if privy to some vile secret, then downed the contents of his glass. While he did, Starla observed him as dispassionately as she could.

He was old and dying. What could he do? These weren't the old days, when no one dared challenge a man of wealth and power. She had friends in Pride, good friends who wouldn't stand for his ill treatment of her. This time she wasn't a child who would take the abuse in silence, knowing no help would be forthcoming. She was married to a man who was not without a fair amount of influence himself.

"I'm leaving now. I don't want to see you again."

She turned to pull open the doors and found the opening blocked by Cole's burly employees. She tried to push past them, but they wouldn't budge. It was like trying to move a mountain. Her father laughed when she whirled back toward him, spitting fury and beginning to show real fear.

"You can't keep me here!"

"Oh, yes I can. Benson and Milton are going to go everywhere you go. You won't be able to change your drawers without them knowing about it.''

The two behemoths chuckled behind her. Starla felt her skin crawl beneath the nasty speculation in their stares.

''My husband—''

''Will be dead before nightfall.''

He said it as if it were already fact, not just threat. Starla's knees weakened.

''You wouldn't dare!''

''If those fool friends of your brother's had done their job, it would already be accomplished. I'll see to it this time. Your Mr. Dodge has made himself a number of powerful enemies. No one will be surprised and no one will be able to point a finger in my direction.''

''I will!''

''I don't think so, little girl. I found me a real obliging doctor up in Louisville who prescribed just the thing for a high-strung filly like you. I had your mama taking the same tonic for a time, but she tricked me. I won't be fooled again. And you won't even *think* about running to the law. You'll have a hard time remembering more than your name . . . and the fact that you belong to me.''

Fear as raw as the open wounds of past memory tore at her. She remembered what it was like being a possession of her father's. Sickness swelled up over her senses, drowning her in her own helplessness.

''Tyler—''

''Won't do a damn thing. You keep harboring this notion that your brother is some kind of hero or savior. He's nothing but a weak fool, a slave to drink and easy living. He's not gonna jeopardize all he has for a slut like you. He knows better than to threaten me—or he will. You go stirring him up against me, and he's the one who's gonna take the punishment. You remember how that goes, don't you, Starla? You'll be a good little girl and do everything your daddy asks, won't you?''

With a cold certainty, Starla knew her life was over; her father had won. She had nothing to bargain with and everything to lose. Her own future was no longer important to her. It would become a game of pretend. They wouldn't have to force her to take the mind-blanking tonic. She'd swallow it willingly to escape the truth of what her lot would be. But she'd accept her fate on her terms.

''You won't hurt Tyler.''

Cole smiled, feeling generous in his victory. ''Not if you behave and he don't get stupid. You'll see to that, won't you?''

Starla nodded faintly. She understood the rules and the hell that came with breaking them. It wouldn't matter, though, not if her last condition was met.

''And you won't hurt Tony.''

''Tony? The Yankee? Oh, I'm sorry, darlin', I can't promise that. See, he's too dangerous. He's making problems for too many people. The only way he'll let you go is with a very persuasive bullet to the brain. You see, unlike your brother, he is a brave man and he won't be intimidated. That's the way it's got to be.''

Starla fought down the waves of nausea and

fright, resisting the want to curl up and weep in bitter defeat. She had to think. Christien would soon be on his way to Pride. There had to be a way to get her son and her husband to safety no matter *what* she'd have to sacrifice.

"You don't have to kill him," she said with a grim certainty. "I can drive him away. I can get him to hate me so much, he'll leave Pride behind and never want to look back."

"And how would you do that?"

"With the truth. I'll tell him the truth, every disgusting detail, every shameful secret. He won't be able to get away from me fast enough."

Tears streamed down her face as she made that last claim, knowing in her heart it was true, no matter how much she might have wished it not to be. Her husband was no different than any other man. And no man could ever accept the depravity she'd allowed through her weakness and her fear and her pathetic need to be accepted. She'd force the facts into Dodge's face until he squirmed away from them in repugnance. She'd tell him things that would make him sick at the fact that he'd ever touched her. She'd make him despise her . . . and in doing so would spare his life. She met her father's victorious smile with a lift of her chin and a fierce summation.

"You don't have to kill him to get rid of him. I'll do it for you. What man would want any part of a woman like me?"

And from behind them came a soft, sober statement.

"I would."

Chapter 25

$\sim\!\!\infty\!\!\sim$

Starla turned toward the door, not knowing whether to feel relief or dismay. Dodge stood slightly behind Benson and Milton, the big bore of his Navy Colt trained on the two startled men. He sagged on his crutches, his features pinched with pain, but there was no mistaking the bulldog set of his jaw and the all-business directness of the stare he leveled on Cole Fairfax.

"I've come to take my wife home, and this time, by God, you're not getting in my way. Starla, come here."

She hesitated just long enough for Dodge to feel a stab of alarm and for Cole to realize all was not lost.

"Go to him, if you think he'll still want you after he knows what you are," Cole purred with a silky confidence.

Starla looked between her husband and father, indecision warring with logic. She knew her father and what he was capable of. Dodge may have had the upper hand for the moment, but how long would it be before those tables turned? *A bullet to the brain.* Her father would have him killed. She never doubted it.

"I can't go with you, Tony." It was a quiet whisper that echoed through his head like a scream.

"What? Of course you can. He's not going to hurt you."

"You don't understand." She wasn't worried about herself.

"I understand plenty. Come over to me now. Don't be afraid."

Cole chuckled. "I'm afraid you don't understand anything, Mr. Dodge. She's not going anywhere with you, and perhaps that's for the best, considering."

"Considering what?" Dodge was blinking hard, trying to keep the sweat that poured off his brow from blinding him. Struggling to keep the pistol lethal and level.

"Considering the kind of woman you married. Tell him, Starla. Tell him why he's better off without you."

"There's nothing she could tell me to make me believe that."

Starla swallowed down a sob. How sure he sounded. Because he didn't know.

"You tell him, or I will," Fairfax snarled.

"Tell me, Starla," Dodge said with a fierce intensity. "Trust me."

"I can't." How could she look at the man she loved, a man of decency who knew only the goodness of a family's love, and tell him of the horrors embraced by hers?

"I know he hurt you and your brother—"

Starla's laugh was edged in hysteria. God, how naive he was!

"Tell him, Starla. Tell him about that time after your faithless bitch mother ran off with another man, how hard you worked at being Daddy's girl, making sure your daddy never got lonely enough to find himself another wife to replace you in his affections. Tell him how you spent all your time at your daddy's knee, learning to be a teasing little whore to get what you wanted, just like your mama." He paused to emphasize his last claim. "And how to have it all, you took your mama's place."

Starla knew the instant awareness hit Dodge between the eyes like a twenty-pound maul. Shock blanked his stare as he looked to her. And she knew she'd lost him.

And that was when the brown-toothed Milton decided to take advantage of his surprise.

The bulky brawler spun with remarkable speed, knocking the gun aside as he used his foot to sweep Dodge's crutches out from under him. Catching his balance on Benson's shirt collar, the banker managed to make a lunge for the man's holstered pistol just as Milton dealt him a smashing elbow to the kidneys. Dodge dropped with a groan.

Starla took a running step toward him. Her father snagged her up with the tangle of his fist in her hair, jerking her to a standstill at the painful end of that tether.

"Kill the son of a bitch," Fairfax snarled at his men.

Benson looked up in confusion. "In here? We can drag him out back—"

Cole brought Starla to her knees with the wrench of his wrist. "Do it right there. I want her to see it. I want her to know what happens when folks cross me."

Thinking about the mess to the fancy rug and marble floors, Benson shrugged. As long as he didn't have to clean it up. He drew his pistol, eager to repay the surprisingly gutsy little Northerner for nearly crushing his jewels and ruining his love life for better than two weeks. He cocked the pistol, having no trouble closing out the sounds of his boss's daughter's shrieks. The banker's eyes opened, focusing just long enough to register the fact that he was about to die, to challenge his assassin with an "I'll see you in hell!" defiance . . . when Benson staggered back, howling, clutching at the knife hilt protruding from his shoulder.

The sound of a palm gun chambering back froze Milton from intervening as Tyler Fairfax stepped carefully over Dodge to extract his favorite throwing knife.

"Were I you," he murmured, wiping the blade on Benson's shirtfront, "I'd be gone from here quick."

They didn't even look to the elder Fairfax. There was enough menace in the younger man's eyes to convince them that fleeing was the wisest action to follow.

Tyler knelt down over the fallen man, giving him a wry smile when he had his attention. "What did I tell you about watchin' your back?"

"You're getting pretty good at it," Dodge mumbled against the tearing pain.

"Well, it ain't a job I'm lookin' to fill permanent, you understand."

Dodge nodded, his jaw spasming, his eyes closing tight as he tried to ride out the agony. Failing.

"Star, darlin', you c'mere now."

Starla hesitated, looking between brother and father.

Cole smirked at her. "Think he's gonna want you now? Best you just stay where you belong, girl."

Trust me. . . .

Starla jerked free with a cry of, "Yes, yes, he will, because he loves me. That's something you'd never understand." She ran to where her husband now lay insensible and said to Tyler, "Help me get him to the doctor. *Hurry.*"

On Doc Anderson's table, just before the morphine had him completely under, Starla saw to her promise to be the last thing he saw, kneeling by her husband, his slack hand in hers, but she had no idea if he did. Or if he wanted to.

"You'll have to leave now, Mrs. Dodge."

"Just a minute more," she entreated, then leaned over Dodge to whisper close to his ear, "I love you, Tony. Please remember your promise."

She walked into the waiting parlor in a daze, scarcely aware of Reeve and Patrice's presence or of the comfort of her brother's embrace. She was haunted by the look in Dodge's eyes when all of her secrets had been stripped bare before him.

Trust me. . . .

Starla buried her face against Tyler's shoulder, clinging to her faith by the fingernails.

Hours later, a bloody Doc Anderson emerged from the back room. He crossed to Starla and placed a small misshapen bit of lead in her palm.

"He might want to save that as a souvenir."

"Is he going to be all right?" Patrice cried hopefully.

"He made it through the operation. That's all I can say. I can't give any guarantees he'll survive the night, or that if he does, whether he'll be paralyzed. We'll have to wait."

"He's tough," Reeve stated for everyone's benefit. "He'll make it."

Despite his assurances, the waiting was torture. Unable to sit still beneath the sympathetic looks from her friends, Starla excused herself to step out onto the front walk for air, finding little relief in the thick late-day humidity. She sagged against a porch support and let her fears shiver through her unchecked. In her continual prayers for Dodge, she'd forgotten her own troubles. *Let him live, Lord. Just let him live.* She didn't care if he walked. She didn't care if he never wanted to see her again. She just needed to know that his exquisite light didn't expire when its brightness led the way for so many.

"Missy Starla?"

She looked up in surprise to see Matilda clutching at her sleeve. "Tilly, what is it?"

"The mister, how is he?"

"It's too soon to tell. But I've been praying like you taught me."

"Your mama, she be the one who taught you that, not me."

Starla's features hardened and she turned away. Tilly tugged at her determinedly.

"Missy, there be something you need to know, something about your mama. I kept quiet all these years to protect you, but now the truth needs be told."

"What is it, Tilly?"

"Something I should have told you long ago. Something I need to show you."

The earth was rich, cold, and wet where she dug by the riverbank. She was on her knees, unmindful of the black soil staining her gown as shovelful after shovelful of Kentucky topsoil was flung helter-skelter from the ever-deepening hole. A fearfully superstitious Tilly stood at a distance, crossing herself and muttering incantations to prevent disturbing the restless spirits left to roam the unhallowed ground.

Starla sat back, rubbing to ease the low ache in her back, at the same time swiping at the moisture dotting her brow. A dark streak of dirt marred her flushed skin.

"Are you sure this is the place?"

"Yessum." Again the old black woman made an anxious sign of the cross.

Starla sighed in determination and continued to dig until something pale shone through the soil. Faintness threatened her as she scooped the dirt away from the skeletal remains of a once fine hand. Tears wobbled in her eyes as she lifted the fragile bones to remove a ring hanging loosely from one white digit. A big emerald. Like his darlin's eyes, her father had been fond of saying, as he'd admired the jewelry the same greedy way he looked at his wife.

"Oh, Mama," Starla moaned, clutching the ring in her palm as she wept.

After a time, when the dry pinch of anguish grew bearable, she turned to the uneasy Matilda and said, "Help me, Tilly. I want my mama in a proper grave."

Cole Fairfax greeted his daughter with a guarded pleasure that turned sour the minute he saw her expression. For the first time, he saw no fear in her eyes, just a gleam of pure hatred. How like her mother she looked just then.

"You killed them," she spat at him in disgust. "You couldn't stand the thought of her leaving you for another man, and you killed them both and told everyone she'd simply run away. You let everyone pity you for your wife's cruel abandonment when *you* were the one who deprived her children of their mother's love. She was going to take us with her, wasn't she? Is that what drove you to do it?"

Cole's features congealed in a loathing he'd kept too long a secret. "I would have let the bitch go, and good riddance. I would even have let her take you, the brat she bred with her lover. She tried to fool me, but I knew. I couldn't father no more children after Tyler. A sickness, the doctor told me. Then she had you and told me you was mine. I would have let her take you. But she wanted my son as well, and that I couldn't allow.''

Starla's head swam with that unexpected news. ''You're not my father.''

''It was that sneaking Frenchman, the cousin her parents refused to let her marry because he didn't have a bankroll to measure up to mine. She told me when I caught them trying to leave. She told me how you'd been conceived when she was visiting family in New Orleans, and she swore she'd humiliate me before all of Pride County unless I let her take both children with her. She underestimated me, a mistake she made only once.''

''You let me believe I was your daughter. You let me think that I'd allowed my father—'' She couldn't continue, too sick in her soul to express the depths of the mortal anguish she'd suffered. Then she realized the entire consequence of what he'd said. *''You bastard.''*

''No, my dear. I believe that name applies to you. But who will ever believe you, once I have you locked safely away?''

Slowly, with deliberate relish, Starla showed him the ring she wore, waiting for him to pale as he recognized it.

''In this case, the dead *do* tell tales. The bones I've had moved carry the very distinct marks of your dueling pistols, the ones you were arrogant enough to bury with them.''

Cole observed her through narrowed eyes. ''And what do you plan to do with this fantasy you've concocted?''

''I could tell Tyler. Do you think he'll laugh it off as my imagination when he sees the bullet scoring on our mother's ribs? Do you think he'll dutifully return to this house to care for you in your dying days or for the legacy of debauchery you plan to leave him? Or do you think he'll cut out your black heart and set it ablaze in your distillery? Fairfax Bourbon would make a splendid fuel for your pyre, don't you think?''

Cole laughed, a grating, gritty sound. ''You are very much like her, you know, both of you too smart for your own good. What do you want in order to keep your mouth shut? I assume it's something, or you wouldn't be here.''

''I don't want to hurt Tyler with the truth. He deserves to have this grand inheritance from you without the taint of our mother's blood on it. He's earned it. You'll sign it over to him today.''

''And I suppose you want your fair share.''

''I don't want anything from you,'' she hissed, ''except for you to be forever out of my life. You will leave me and my husband alone. There is no kinship between us, and I won't pretend I feel the least bit of remorse about that. If anything happens to Tony or the bank, I'll assume you're behind it, so you'd better be certain your political allies understand that both are off-limits. Is that clear?''

''Is there anything else?'' The bitterness in his tone at one time would have gratified her, giving him a taste of how it felt to be helpless. But now she just wanted to escape him and his foul reach forever.

''No. I just want the pleasure of pretending you never existed.''

A vicious smile. ''Do you think your precious

little Yankee will ever let that happen? Truth won't excuse fact, Starla. You did what you did, and he's not going to ever forget that—or forgive you.''

Those words echoed in her heart and mind as she laid her mother and her unfortunately unnamed lover to rest at Glendower Glade in a service presided over by the county's discreet pastor. He never asked to know the identity of the souls he sent to the blessed beyond.

At long last, sharing the terrible events of the past with a horrified and consoling Patrice, Starla spent a few hours of restless slumber at the peaceful Glade before heading back into Pride to wait at her husband's side for him to awake and decide their future in a way she hadn't imagined twenty-four hours earlier.

''He's awake,'' the doctor told her, then cautioned, ''but he's not very aware of what's going on around him. He's heavily dosed with laudanum and may not even know you. Don't be alarmed if he doesn't make much sense.''

She was terrified that he'd make complete sense. With her breath suspended, she slipped into the back bedroom, where Dodge was lying under the drape of a clean white sheet.

''Tony?''

His eyes flickered faintly, dark lashes appearing as bruises against the pallor of his cheeks. Starla put her free hand on his brow, stroking it lightly. He looked up and seemed to focus for an instant, then the grogginess stole him away. She was about to leave him to his rest when he moistened his lips to murmur, "You weren't here."

It took a second for her to realize he meant when he woke up. "I'm sorry, Tony. I'm here now and I'll be staying, if you want me to."

His head rolled restlessly from side to side, then his attention fixed upon her. She could see him adding up his memories to arrive at some very damning facts. For the first time she cursed the fact that her husband was such a smart man. Slowly he closed his eyes and turned his head away. Whether it was a pointed rejection or merely a meaningless gesture prompted by the numbing drugs in his system, she didn't know.

But she continued to hope as she waited for Dodge to recover his faculties. Then she would have her answer.

Chapter 26

The roar of cannonfire sent him staggering out of his tent and into the slicing rain. The heavens flashed as if an angry God was casting down His censure on brothers who would seek each other's lives.

Covering his ears against the splitting din, he looked about him in panic, seeing his men on the rain-puddled ground, lying facedown in the reddening water. He waded through the mud, breath chugging in anxious gasps as he approached the first dead man. His fault. He'd killed them. They'd been his responsibility and he'd failed them all. Slowly he bent down, reaching for that first man's shoulder, readying to turn him face up so he could see the man's identity. Not wanting to know.

"Tony." She stretched out a slender hand to him. He looked up in confusion, rain skewing his vision. He thought at first that she was an angel; then recognition shocked through him. "I've come to take you home with me."

"But my men . . . I can't leave my men. They depended on me and I let them die. I killed them."

She smiled with the beauty of a sudden ray of sunlight penetrating the gloom of the battlefield. ''No. War killed them. They don't need you any more. Come. You've a promise to keep.''

He took her hand hesitantly. For all her fragile looks, he'd never realized how strong she was. She lifted him out of the mud and blood.

''Come home with me, Tony. You don't need to come back here again.''

Dodge woke with a jerk, blinking his way to complete lucidity after days of hazy shadow. And the first thing he did was look beside him for the one face he needed to see there.

Starla was curled up in a chair at his bedside, her features lovely in repose, yet lined with the strain of her vigil. From her rumpled state, he guessed she'd been there for some time. He started to reach out to her, but something stopped him, some half-realized doubt nagging at the back of his mind.

Christien. Something about Christien, the boy who was going to be his son. His and Starla's.

Starla's and . . . and her father's. . . .

Remembrance hit him with wind-sapping strength, a truth that, no matter how hard he tried to deny it, became more obvious to him. This boy that his wife brought to him was her son, conceived of the most unholy union imaginable. His soul recoiled, its very pain mocking Dodge for his bold words to his wife, words spoken with the incredible arrogance of one who had no idea—no idea what he was promising to forgive.

There's nothing you've done or could ever do that would make me love you any less.

How quick he'd been to absolve her for sins he couldn't have imagined, how quick to refute the feelings that even now overwhelmed him. Feelings that shamed him and scared him and made him wonder if he could ever look at her without suffering from images he couldn't shut out of his mind, made him wonder if he could touch her without thinking . . .

"Tony?"

The sound of her voice acted upon him like an unexpected breeze, chilling him into a rash of gooseflesh while warming his anguished heart. There was such vulnerability in the way she said his name, calling upon him to remember his promises. *Trust me.* Now she was testing that claim, and he wasn't sure he could honor it.

Very slowly he turned his head to look at her. The naked relief in her gaze was quickly shadowed. She gave him a tremulous smile and blinked to scatter the welling anguish pooling in her eyes. "How do you feel?"

"What?" He had no clue as to why she was asking until she placed a pistol ball in his hand. He looked at it for a long moment, trying to equate the piece of lead with the hell he'd carried. Then he reached a hand down to rub the top of his thigh. Feeling nothing. Starla's hand covered his, squeezing gently.

"Doc Anderson said they'd be swelling, that you shouldn't worry."

Yet. Dodge closed his eyes, consumed by grief

and fear and a horrible sense of helplessness. Starla brought his hand up to press her damp cheek into its palm. Her words throbbed with passion.

"It doesn't matter, Tony. It doesn't matter. It won't change anything." Not his worth as a man, not his ability as a husband. Just as knowing her past had changed nothing.

In a leaden tone, he set her straight.

"It changes everything."

With a soft cry, she fled the room.

Not believing he could feel more wretched, Dodge tried to summon the will to call her back, but something stopped him, something he couldn't push aside, something he couldn't get over. Her father. . . .

"What did you say to her?"

Dodge looked up at the soft question, surprised to see Tyler Fairfax glaring down at him through eyes flashing with green fire and fury.

"You sanctimonious son of a bitch." Tyler kept his voice pitched low, but there was no disguising the hatred pulsing behind each syllable. "You and your big talk and smooth lies. Who the hell are you to judge us? You don't know, Mr. Cast-the-First-Stone, what it was like for us, trapped in that house with him. Don't you dare sneer down at her for what she had to do to survive. And don't you think for one minute that she asked for any of what she got. It was him, that monster, that—"

"Tyler, don't."

He broke off his tirade when Starla placed a gentle hand on his arm.

"Are you all right, darlin'?" He backed down

quickly to slip his arm around her. She looked so pale, so fragile.

She smiled at his concern. "Fine. Just a little dizzy is all. From the worrying, I guess."

"I'll take you home." He glared at Dodge, daring him to protest, growing even more furious when he didn't.

"No, Tyler. My place is here."

"But—"

"I'll be all right. You go on home. I'll be fine."

He balked but finally gave before her quiet strength. Placing a tender kiss on her brow, he whispered, "If you need me, you let me know."

She touched his cheek and managed a frail smile before resuming her chair next to the bed. Sitting there with the husband who stared at her as if she were a stranger to him, acting as if the coward deserved the faith she placed in him. Tyler smiled back grimly, making plans to see the banker dead if he didn't carry through on his vows to his sister.

When they were alone, Starla gave Dodge a wan smile.

"I warned you, didn't I?"

Dodge couldn't respond with a smile of his own. He was too numb inside to give her the assurance she desperately needed from him. All his feelings were as numbed as his legs, as the fact kept pounding at him, a barrage of terrible truth battering him down.

"Yes, you did," he answered quietly. But he hadn't listened to the gravity of her claims. And he hadn't believed that anything she could tell him could shake the foundations of his soul.

He'd been wrong.

He was shaken beyond the power of clear thought.

"I don't know what to say," he confessed at last.

Starla laughed softly. "I'm sure you don't. Tyler was right. There's no way you could understand."

Dodge wet his lips, forcing the words. "I want to."

Starla shook her head slightly, her cynical gaze rimmed with diamond-bright anguish. "No, you don't." He was already reeling under the shock of what he'd discovered. Why compound the trauma?

"I need to, Star, if I'm going to get over this. Right now, I don't know if I can."

He was honest. But then, he'd always been honest with her, almost always, and if she'd been the same, things wouldn't have gone so far, and the impact of the truth wouldn't be so devastating.

So with head bent, with gaze fixed upon the hands she'd folded demurely in her lap, she told him how it had been for two lost and frightened children, their mother suddenly abandoning them, taking with her the only love they'd known, their father continually steeped in drink and given to roaring rages. They'd both pretended nothing was wrong inside their home of wealth and privilege, because while they wore those masks of frivolousness, they could push the horror away for a time. But it was always waiting for them, just on the other side of the front door.

Fair Play. Tyler drank to escape it. Starla detached herself from the emotions that screamed inside her. Because they had roles to play and no one could suspect that their lives were anything less than golden. Though many did. At first, they didn't know how to ask for help from those who might have given it. Then pride wouldn't allow them to. A Southern family kept its unpleasant secrets at home, where they belonged, while presenting a smiling face to a society that didn't want the burden of knowing.

It started with verbal abuse heaped upon their mother. Cole Fairfax roamed the halls all day and night, ranting about his faithless wife, about the whore he'd married who'd shamed him in front of his peers within his home. When those angry slurs against an absent victim would no longer serve his boiling rage, he turned it upon the two children who had the misfortune to resemble the object of his ire. With words, then with his hand, he battered them incessantly while they struggled to find ways to please him in order to lessen the punishment. But as Starla grew into the image of her mother, there seemed no way to circumvent his displeasure.

''I think he began to confuse us, to think I was her. He'd come to my room smelling of whiskey and call me by her name. He'd sit at the foot of my bed for hours, weeping, raving about things I couldn't understand. He told me I was his curse, that I was to blame for his unhappiness because I was his reminder of his foolishness and his shame. He'd say it was my duty to fulfill the promises my mother had made him, that I was his reward for what he'd endured, that no one could love children whose own mother didn't want them. We believed him, Tony. He was our father.''

Dodge closed his eyes briefly, unable to say anything for a long minute, then asking hoarsely,''Did Tyler know what he was doing?''

''No. Not until just before he put me on the train. And even then, I-I couldn't tell him everything. It was the night after Father decided that it was time we—you know.''

She said it so emotionlessly, her features a doll-like blank. Dodge's gut clenched in fury and outrage. He wanted to reach out to her then but was afraid to startle her out of her trancelike reflections until all the poison of her past was purged.

''He hit me. A lot. I don't remember much else. Tyler heard me crying later, and he must have guessed what had happened. He packed my clothes and helped me get out of the house. And I left him to deal with that monster all alone. I'm to blame for what he's become.''

''Good Lord! Neither of you is to blame for anything.''

She looked up then, surprised by his fierce outburst and by the emotions working his tense features. She didn't believe him.

Dodge took a deep breath to get control of his inner turmoil. He pitched his voice low and even. ''Did Tyler know about Christien?''

''No. I was so afraid that he would hate me, hate both of us.'' Her smile was small, a fragile bloom of faith restored. ''I was wrong.''

''Your brother's stronger than he looks, stronger than I've been.''

Starla drew a sharp breath as he placed his hands over hers. She didn't move. "I never told anyone. When I found out I was pregnant, I prayed for the father to be Stephen, but every time I looked at Christien, I wondered. It wasn't his fault. So you see, I know how you're feeling."

"I'm sorry, Star, for what happened to you, for what can't be changed. I'm sorry for all you had to go through alone. You won't have to again, not ever again."

She stared at him, a flicker of hope sparking in her teary gaze as his hand pressed tightly over hers.

"And that little boy won't ever have to wonder if he's loved, because we're going to spoil him so shamelessly."

"We?"

"I keep my promises, Starla. I won't fail you. I'm sorry I was a little shaky there for a minute. I tend to give myself more credit than I deserve sometimes. I thought I could handle anything."

She smiled wryly. "It's a lot to handle."

He smiled back. "That's for damn sure. But I'll handle it because I love you and I want you and that little boy more than anything I've ever dreamed of."

She closed her eyes for a brief prayer of thanks. When she opened them, her gaze shone with unconditional belief in everything he said.

"Tony, there are two more things you need to know."

He opened his arm wide. "Tell me from over here."

She went gratefully into his arms, finding no

heaven on earth as perfect as his surrounding embrace. Carefully snuggling close.

"Cole Fairfax isn't my father."

"W-what?"

"The man my mother ran away with, they'd been lovers. Cole Fairfax was punishing her through me. He threatened to harm me if Tilly told me the truth, which she finally did. But he suffered from a terrible fever after Tyler was born. He couldn't have fathered me any more than he could have fathered Christien. Yet he let me think—all these years—"

"He can't hurt you anymore, Starla. He'll never hurt you again. And neither will I."

He tipped up her face, letting her see the sincerity in his eyes before kissing her, slowly, deeply, sealing that vow in exquisite detail . . . until a sudden twinge in his thigh made him wince away. He frowned for a moment, mystified, then began to concentrate.

"Star?"

"Yes, Tony?" She followed his nod to the foot of the bed where his toes were moving under the drape of the sheet. With a joyful cry, she hugged him again, kissing him firmly, whispering how very much she loved him.

He glanced up, remembering suddenly. "What else did you want to tell me?"

Smiling a small, secretive smile, Starla burrowed against him. If what she suspected over the last few mornings was fact, their family number would soon be expanding. But because this moment was just for the two of them, she said, "I'll tell you later, once we're home."

Family, home, the woman he loved, and soon, the boy who would be his son. Dodge was content enough to accept her answer, for in his arms he held the future.

Look for Rosalyn West's next
Men of Pride County book—
Noble Banning's story—
Coming in November 1998
from Avon Books!

Dear Reader,

One of the reasons I love to read romances is that they reaffirm by belief that wishes really can come true. And in next month's Avon Romantic Treasure WHEN DREAMS COME TRUE by Cathy Maxwell, a lonely English lord gets his wish for a bride, when a beautiful, mysterious maiden enters his life. Cathy's love stories are a delight, and this one is especially charming. Don't miss it!

I can't resist a strong hero—he might be infuriating, but you always know he's a man who'll love and protect you. In Alina Adams' contemporary romance, ANNIE'S WILD RIDE, you'll meet Paul, an unforgettable, exasperating man whose love for Annie is so strong he'll do anything for her—even risk his own life.

Of course, I want heroines who know their own mind…just like Aleene in Malia Martin's HER NORMAN CONQUEROR. Aleene must marry to save her beloved castle, but she's reluctant to wed at all…until she meets a virile stranger she is powerless to resist.

And there's nothing more satisfying than a man and woman, destined to be together, just like Raimond LeVeq and Sable Fontaine in Beverly Jenkins' THROUGH THE STORM. Raimond believes that Sable has betrayed him, but then fate reunites this pair in an unforgettable romance.

Enjoy!

Lucia Macro

Lucia Macro
Senior Editor

AEL 0798

Avon Romances—
the best in exceptional authors and unforgettable novels!

TOPAZ   **by Beverly Jenkins**
78660-5/ $5.99 US/ $7.99 Can

STOLEN KISSES   **by Suzanne Enoch**
78813-6/ $5.99 US/ $7.99 Can

CAPTAIN JACK'S WOMAN   **by Stephanie Laurens**
79455-1/ $5.99 US/ $7.99 Can

MOUNTAIN BRIDE   **by Susan Sawyer**
78479-3/ $5.99 US/ $7.99 Can

A TOUGH MAN'S WOMAN   **by Deborah Camp**
78252-9/ $5.99 US/ $7.99 Can

A PRINCE AMONG MEN   **by Kate Moore**
78458-0/ $5.99 US/ $7.99 Can

THE WILD ONE   **by Danelle Harmon**
79262-1/ $5.99 US/ $7.99 Can

HIGHLAND BRIDES: THE LADY   **by Lois Greiman**
AND THE KNIGHT   79433-0/ $5.99 US/ $7.99 Can

A ROSE IN SCOTLAND   **by Joan Overfield**
78007-0/ $5.99 US/ $7.99 Can

A DIME NOVEL HERO   **by Maureen McKade**
79504-3/ $5.99 US/ $7.99 Can